Meet me in Venice

A former English teacher, Barbara Hannay is a city-bred girl with a yen for country life. Many of her forty-plus books are set in rural and outback Australia and have been enjoyed by readers around the world. She has won the RITA, awarded by Romance Writers of America, and has twice won the Romantic Book of the Year award in Australia. In her own version of life imitating art, Barbara and her husband currently live on a misty hillside in beautiful Far North Queensland where they keep heritage pigs and chickens and an untidy but productive garden.

barbarahannay.com

PRAISE FOR BARBARA HANNAY'S BESTSELLERS

'It's a pleasure to follow an author who gets better with every book. Barbara Hannay delights with this cross-generational love story, which is terrifically romantic and full of surprises.'

APPLE iBOOKS, 'BEST BOOKS OF THE MONTH'

'Hannay has once again created a romance rich with the flavour of North Queensland.'

THE CHRONICLE

'Barbara Hannay has delivered another wonderful book . . . For me no one does emotional punch quite like Barbara Hannay.'

HELENE YOUNG

'Gripping tale of outback romance . . . Her most epic novel to date.'

QUEENSLAND COUNTRY LIFE

'Lovers of romance will enjoy this feel-good read. Hannay captures the romantic spirit of the outback perfectly.'

TOWNSVILLE BULLETIN

'Get your hands on a copy of this book and you will not be disappointed.'

WEEKLY TIMES

'An engaging story of joy, tragedy, romance and heartache set within the dusty landscape of the Australian outback.'
BOOK'D OUT

'In beautiful, fluid prose, Hannay once again puts together all the ingredients for a real page-turner.'
THE CHRONICLE

'Everything a romantic reader could want . . . A brilliant piece of work.'
NEWCASTLE HERALD

'Bound to become a new favourite.'
THE AGE

'A breathtaking read. Once again, Barbara Hannay manages to knock this reader over with a feather.'
TALKING BOOKS

'Barbara Hannay writes beautiful visuals of rural and remote Australia . . . This is a remarkable book.'
READING, WRITING AND RIESLING

ALSO AVAILABLE FROM PENGUIN RANDOM HOUSE

Zoe's Muster
Home Before Sundown
Moonlight Plains
The Secret Years
The Grazier's Wife
The Country Wedding
The Summer of Secrets

BARBARA HANNAY

Meet me in Venice

MICHAEL JOSEPH
an imprint of
PENGUIN BOOKS

MICHAEL JOSEPH

UK | USA | Canada | Ireland | Australia
India | New Zealand | South Africa | China

Michael Joseph is part of the Penguin Random House group of companies
whose addresses can be found at global.penguinrandomhouse.com.

First published by Michael Joseph, 2019

Text copyright © Barbara Hannay 2019

The moral right of the author has been asserted.

All rights reserved. No part of this publication may be reproduced, published, performed
in public or communicated to the public in any form or by any means without prior written
permission from Penguin Random House Australia Pty Ltd or its authorised licensees.

Cover design by Louisa Maggio © Penguin Random House Australia Pty Ltd
Cover photographs: Woman and balcony by Ilina Simeonova/Trevillion Images;
scene of Venice by Stefano Cavoretto/Arcangel
Typeset in Sabon by Midland Typesetters, Australia
Printed and bound in Australia by Griffin Press, part of Ovato, an accredited
ISO AS/NZS 14001 Environmental Management Systems printer.

 A catalogue record for this book is available from the National Library of Australia

ISBN 978 0 14379 423 3

penguin.com.au

For Ali Watts.
Thanks for the nudge . . .

CHAPTER ONE

Daisy Benetto blurted out her big idea before it was quite ready.

For days, the plan had circled harmlessly in the privacy of her own thoughts, safe yet cheering, a useful distraction as she'd bravely, *finally*, begun to sort through Leo's things. Such a difficult process that had been, deciding what should go to Vinnies, or into a box in the garage, and what needed to be binned.

Each sweater, shirt or jacket had been laden with memories. Daisy could picture Leo at a party, sending her a covert smile, his eyes bright with secret amusement over some crass remark a slightly sozzled friend had made. She saw him dressing for a night at the theatre, lifting his jaw, just so, as he adjusted the knot on his tie. Leo, coming through the front door, sunburnt but satisfied after coaching their son's soccer team.

The images of her husband, so alive and well, had been too painful, and Daisy had been forced to drag her thoughts elsewhere. Anywhere. Cautiously, she'd toyed with her bright, shiny idea, allowing herself to imagine how each of her children would react. The proposal was still in its infancy, of course. Daisy hadn't made any proper plans.

She was confident, though, that Marc in America, in Silicon Valley, would welcome the chance to visit his father's birthplace. Marc's only problem might be taking time off from his very important IT work. His wife, Bronte, wasn't too enamoured of life in Palo Alto, though, so she would no doubt embrace a European getaway.

Daisy's middle child, Anna, was bound to love the idea too, but she would also have to juggle time off between her acting gigs in London.

At least, taking time off shouldn't be a problem for Ellie. Daisy's youngest was pretty much at a loose end, enjoying a gap year before starting uni, working in cafés at night and surfing or sleeping most days.

As for Daisy herself, after long months of feeling as if she'd fallen through the cracks in life with no one to catch her, this lovely new scheme helped her to feel ever so slightly more normal. In time she hoped to be one of those very capable widows she admired in books. Perhaps planning this holiday could be the first step. And it would bring her family together again.

For a few precious weeks, the Benetto kids would be under one roof, laughing, joking, teasing . . . like the old days.

Just the same, Daisy had no intention of mentioning this plan when she went to lunch with her two best friends. She had tried to argue that turning fifty-seven wasn't a milestone worthy of fuss, but they wouldn't listen to her protests.

Just a small lunch, Daisy. Just the three of us. You know we never miss each other's birthdays.

This was true. Daisy, Freya and Jo had been celebrating each other's birthdays now for more than twenty years, ever since they'd first met in a beachside yoga class and, of course, Daisy appreciated that her friends truly cared about her happiness. In the end, the day turned out to be spectacularly beautiful.

The trio dined on a sunny terrace overlooking the Noosa River where, after a long, hot and gruelling summer, the first hint of autumn had arrived overnight, creeping into Queensland from the south. Despite the pleasantly warm sunshine, Daisy could sense the nip of a cool change in the crisp, dry air. And when she looked out at the blue and cloudless sky, at the familiar, sleepy river, dotted with small boats and lined with stately, white-trunked gumtrees, she felt her shoulders relax.

She took a sip of sparkling wine and, without warning, the words she hadn't planned to utter just tumbled out. 'I'm thinking about shouting my kids a trip to Italy.'

Freya and Jo stared at her, clearly too surprised, or possibly even too stunned, to speak.

Panic flared in Daisy's chest. Why on earth had she spluttered her crazy scheme out loud? She looked at her friends. Both, like her, in their late fifties, middle-class, stylishly dressed – Freya in dark green with a multi-coloured scarf thrown just so, and Jo in smart, smoky grey, with a touch of gold at her ears and throat.

These well-meaning, sensible women would almost certainly try to talk her out of her plan, telling her it was too expensive, or too soon, or even too dangerous to try to hang on to her adult children after they'd flown the nest.

The problem was that even Daisy's closest friends could not really understand how lonely and scared she'd been these past months. They couldn't imagine the terror of having the future she and Leo had so carefully planned – or rather, the future that Leo had planned and Daisy had happily agreed to – suddenly disappear.

Neither Freya nor Jo could be expected to know what it was like to wake in the middle of the night and to reach out, expecting to touch a warm shoulder, or to rub your foot against your husband's ankle, and to find a cold, empty space beside you. They couldn't imagine the sickening slam of anguish that came every time you remembered that space would always be empty.

Daisy had lost her husband and her dreams. She couldn't bear to lose her children as well.

Marc and Anna had come home for the funeral, of course, but they'd been as dazed and shocked as Daisy was. And in no time they'd left again, flying back to their important jobs, to their new and exciting lives on the other side of the world. Meanwhile Ellie, to Daisy's huge surprise, had hunkered down to study especially hard for her final Year 12 exams.

The intense loneliness that followed had nearly consumed Daisy. On a scale of one to ten, she would have put her happiness quotient at sub-zero. But just lately, this new holiday plan had given her such a lift, a glimmer of hope.

That was hardly an excuse for giving voice to her half-baked idea now, though, on her birthday, before it was anywhere near properly planned. If she'd learned anything from her dear Leo, it was the importance of looking at a decision from every angle and carefully calculating the pros and cons before taking any kind of first step. Leo had always been so clever and steady and reliable. Possibly, the only careless, unplanned act the poor man had ever committed was to drop dead of a heart attack six weeks before he was due to retire.

Daisy stamped down on that gut-wrenching reminder before it set her crying again. The last thing she needed today was another bout of tears. She'd wept so much in the past twelve months she'd probably caused permanent damage to her tear ducts.

Now, here she was instead, all smiles and drinking champagne. And spilling the beans on this crazy scheme, when she hadn't even spoken to her accountant to make sure she could cash in those spare shares of Leo's.

'It's just a crazy, silly thought,' she hastily amended, absorbing her friends' surprised expressions and charging straight into damage control. 'I seem to be having all sorts of weird ideas lately.'

Freya, however, was shaking her head, making her hairdresser-enhanced auburn curls bounce. 'No, Daisy, I think it's a fabulous idea.' After a beat, Freya added, '*If* you can afford to be so generous.' But then, almost immediately, she gave a cheeky grin. 'Actually, no, I take that back. It's still a fabulous idea even if you can't afford it.'

'And it's probably just what you need,' added Jo, although she spoke more carefully. Then again, Jo was always careful, just as Leo had been.

Daisy looked from one friend to the other. 'I was sure you'd both tell me I was being ridiculous.'

'Oh, darling,' laughed Freya. 'Even if your scheme was totally harebrained, it's put a sparkle back in your lovely blue eyes and that has to be a good thing.'

'Oh.' Daisy couldn't help smiling at Freya's warmth and enthusiasm, even though *harebrained* wasn't exactly reassuring.

'So, how would your plan work?' asked the ever practical Jo. 'Would you find a hotel or perhaps an apartment that would take all of you?'

'Yes, I suppose so,' said Daisy, wishing that she'd already thought through these finer details.

Planning had never been her strong point. She'd relied heavily on Leo for that, and for so many other things, really. Caution and precision had been Leo's watchwords, whether he'd been planning a family camping trip or balancing their budget. It was why he'd been such a good structural engineer, ensuring the safety of major building projects.

Daisy, on the other hand, had always preferred to follow instructions, rather than taking on too much responsibility. She'd had a range of jobs – as a teacher's aide, an assistant in a garden nursery, and as part of a landscape design company – and she'd prided herself on being a team player, both at home and at work.

She'd seen her role as the family's troubleshooter and nurturer, and she'd never really taken charge of planning anything more serious than their Christmas dinners, birthday parties for the kids, or which annuals to plant in their garden. If she went ahead with this mad idea, she would definitely need to find a nice, friendly and, most of all, *reliable* travel agent.

'Would you go somewhere in Tuscany?' asked Jo. 'That always seems to be popular. I think you can get villas there, can't you?'

Freya gave a knowing nod. 'Like *Under the Tuscan Sun*.'

'Well, yes, I know Tuscany's very popular,' Daisy agreed, and she could easily picture her family on a Tuscan hillside, gathered at a long table draped with white linen and laden with fresh bread or pasta and bottles of rich red wine. The setting would be a cobblestone terrace in front of an ancient stone farmhouse, with views of green hills and valleys dotted with olive groves and striped by rows of grapes. 'But,' she added, 'I was actually thinking of Venice.'

'Venice?' Freya frowned as she digested this, and Daisy immediately began to worry. Perhaps she really should consider Tuscany.

But her friend's frown was quickly replaced her by another warm smile. 'Well, why not Venice? It's beautiful. So romantic.'

'And Leo was born there, wasn't he?' added Jo.

Daisy nodded. This was, of course, her sole reason for choosing Venice. Jo was probably remembering the funeral and the slide show of Leo's life that Marc had quickly collated. There'd been a photo of a fat baby Leo, propped on his mother's knee as she sat on a bench beside the Grand Canal. His mother had looked surprisingly young and rather serious, even sad, almost as if she'd known, way back then, that her son would pass away within just twelve months of her own death.

'Leo's cousin Gina still lives in Venice,' she said. 'I – I thought it might be good for the kids to meet her and learn more about their Italian heritage.'

'Yes, of course, it would be fabulous,' agreed Freya. 'Just lovely.'

Encouraged, Daisy nevertheless felt compelled to justify her decision. 'I mean, these days grandparents Skype with their grandkids all the time.' She was certainly planning to do this when Marc and Bronte started a family. 'But our kids never really knew Leo's parents.'

And Leo was always promising to take me to Venice, she added silently.

A small part of her was angry with him for deserting her like that. Just when they were getting to the best years, free of kids, financially secure, ready to enjoy that most beautiful of words – retirement. And it bothered her, actually, that in all the years of their marriage, Leo had only gone home to Italy once, for a quick visit on his own, when his father died. His parents had, however, come out to Australia twice to visit them.

Unfortunately, these visits hadn't been hugely successful, at least not from Daisy's perspective. The first time had been just after Marc was born and the next, when Ellie was a toddler. Neither of Leo's parents had spoken much English, and Daisy, busy and a tad flustered with caring for her young family, hadn't found time to learn Italian.

Daisy had been tense and the children had somehow picked up on this and had become extra naughty and demanding.

Leo's mother had, however, taught her how to make a perfect pea risotto, which was still a family favourite. In fact, Daisy's freezer was chock-a-block with containers of pea risotto, as she had manically cooked up massive amounts in recent months and then had but Ellie to feed it to.

Venice had, nevertheless, always been at the top of Leo's list for their retirement travel plans.

'It will be so good to have all your chicks together,' Jo said now. 'They're all so clever and they've done so well. You'll have heaps of things to talk about.'

'Yes, you must be so proud of them,' added Freya, who had never been able to have children.

Daisy nodded again as she took another sip of her wine. She was certainly proud of her children, who had exceeded her humble expectations in every respect. Marc had always topped his year level at school and had done brilliantly at university, and now he was doing something even more amazing and incomprehensible in Silicon Valley.

And Anna had dazzled everyone from the moment she'd first skipped onto the stage as a flower fairy in a Christmas panto at the age of four and a half. In the local community, there'd never been any doubt that Anna Benetto would go on to become Australia's next Nicole Kidman or Rose Byrne. And already, after blitzing drama school in Sydney, Anna was making waves in London's West End.

Even Ellie, who for years had been happy to be the sweet, petted baby of the family and who'd never bothered to try too hard at anything, had suddenly pulled up her socks at the very last minute and scored a commendable Year 12 result. Although she hadn't yet decided what she wanted to do next.

'Venice would be wasted on my kids,' Jo said next. 'They're not into the arts. They're all too sporty and their idea of gourmet food is a hamburger with mustard and pickles at Grill'd. But your lot will soak up all that amazing art and history and they'll appreciate that divine Italian food.'

This was Daisy's dream, of course – her family bonding once more over delicious Italian meals and vino, visiting the famous art galleries, exploring the canals and winding streets of Venice, growing closer again, maybe closer than ever, despite living in separate hemispheres.

'The family that plays together stays together,' she suggested hopefully, but even as she said this, she felt nervous again. She was jumping way too far ahead, when she hadn't spoken to any of her children or taken even a tiny peek at the costings. And lurking in the background was the uncomfortable fear that she was somehow trying to buy her children's love.

CHAPTER TWO

At 8.30 p.m. Marc Benetto was dog-tired after a twelve-hour day followed by an hour-long commute back to Palo Alto on a train so crowded he'd had to stand all the way.

When the phone call came from his mother, he was trudging from the Caltrain station to his home on Redwood Circle, contemplating dinner, tossing up between a hasty takeaway from the Chinese on the corner, or another supermarket pasta from the freezer at home.

He almost let the call go through to voicemail. His mother didn't know that Bronte had left him ten days ago and he wasn't sure he had the emotional bandwidth to deal with her call right now.

Then the guilt kicked in.

This was his mother, after all – his widowed mother who'd had one hell of a year – and she didn't phone him very often. Mostly she communicated by email, which suited them both, given his hectic schedule and the difference in their time zones.

Needless to say, these past months hadn't been hard only for her, they'd also been pretty crap for Marc. The shock of his father's sudden death had been bad enough. As the eldest and only son, he'd enjoyed a close relationship with his old man and he'd been hit hard by grief.

The heart attack had been so unexpected. His dad had always been healthy and fit. He'd enjoyed a few drinks, sure, but he'd never smoked, and he was only sixty. Way too young.

It was the kind of random jolt that could stop an ambitious young man in his tracks, and it had forced Marc to contemplate the things he'd always taken for granted. Life. Had anyone really discovered its meaning? Mortality. Fate.

Worse had followed, though. After the funeral, he'd had a mad scramble to make up for the lost time away from work. In the months that followed, he'd used his work as a shield against his grief – until Bronte had forced him to face the hard truth that his marriage was wrecked and sinking faster than the *Titanic*.

The last thing he wanted now, as he let his thumb hover over the answer button, was to find himself entangled in awkward, painful explanations. The phone was almost due to stop ringing when he relented and swiped.

'Hi, Mum.' He injected brightness into his voice and hoped it didn't sound too false.

'Marc, how are you?' His mother sounded upbeat, too, much brighter than she had in ages and Marc sensed that she wasn't just 'putting it on'. He was pleased for her. She deserved a break.

'Not bad, thanks,' he said. 'How are you?'

'Oh, I'm really well.'

'That's great.' Deciding against Chinese, Marc crossed the road while the traffic was clear, leaving behind the shops and offices, and reaching instead a tree-lined pavement where golden light spilled from picture-perfect Californian houses onto manicured green lawns. Through an uncurtained window he could see a family gathered around their dining table, the father at one end, busy on his laptop, while his wife and two school-aged children ate their evening meal.

Busy parents, late dinners. It was typical of life in Palo Alto. *At least they're still together...*

'Are you at home?' his mother asked.

Marc was just two blocks away from his outrageously expensive two-storey home with its formal front garden and spacious backyard. All ready for his own family, the family he would probably never have now.

The house would be sitting in darkness. Empty. His chest tightened. 'Not quite home,' he said. 'Nearly there.'

'Oh, Marc, is this a bad time to ring? I'm sorry. Should I call later after you and Bronte have had dinner?'

'No, no, this is fine.' Since Bronte had moved to a spare bedroom in their friends' condo, meal times for Marc were mere refuelling stops. 'So what's news, Mum?'

He waited. His mother obviously had something important to tell him and he hoped it wasn't bad.

The pause on the other end of the line was longish and it did little to ease Marc's tension. Now he wondered if that bright note in her voice had been as false as his and he found himself imagining the worst – that she'd received a scary medical diagnosis, or maybe Ellie was in trouble, perhaps with drugs, or had got herself pregnant.

Marc grimaced at this, shocked he could instantly leap to such negative conclusions. It showed what a poor sorry bastard he was these days. But surely that was to be expected after his wife had confessed to a one-night stand with a guy she'd met online and then promptly walked out.

At last, his mother spoke. 'I've been thinking how nice it would be if we could all get together. The whole family.'

Marc tried to ignore the sinking sensation in his stomach. 'Well, yes...' he said carefully.

'A family holiday.' His mother sounded nervous now, as if she knew her proposal might not be well received. 'All of us together,

Marc. Somewhere really wonderful. It would be my shout – a sort of belated birthday present to myself – but a present for all of us, really.'

In the middle of the sidewalk, Marc came to a standstill. This was a huge gesture and incredibly generous, given his own astronomical salary, although living in Silicon Valley ate up almost everything he earned. But despite his mother's generosity, there was no way he was ready to face his family. Not now, or in the foreseeable future.

He wasn't sure he'd ever get over the shock of Bronte's bombshell and he was still wrestling with his wish that she would come to her senses, even though her refusal to answer his calls, texts or emails gave him next to no hope.

He totally baulked at the thought of trying to explain his marriage breakdown to his mother and sisters. A strangled sort of 'Arrgh' broke from him.

'I was hoping for two weeks, but I know you might find it difficult to get time off,' his mother said.

This was the understatement of the century. His mum was clueless about life in Silicon Valley. He'd tried to explain that it was like no other place on earth, but no one really 'got' it unless they lived here.

For Marc, landing a job with a company headquartered in the Valley had been the ultimate professional achievement, but that victory came at a high cost. When Marc had arrived from Australia with his PhD, he'd soon learned that he couldn't rest on his laurels.

Suddenly surrounded by a host of freakishly smart, highly ambitious nerds, he'd had to hit the ground running and the pace had never slackened. The concept of a normal work-life balance was anathema here. There was no question – your job had to be the most important thing in your life. It was a reality that neither he nor Bronte had been properly prepared for.

'We'd all have to work around you, of course,' his mother was saying. 'But we're totally prepared to do that, Marc, and if you try, you never know, there might be a window of opportunity for a little time off. It would be so wonderful if you could join us.'

'Look, I really don't think I —'

'It would mean so much to me, darling.'

Darling? His mother hadn't called him darling since his teens. She'd stopped after he'd bawled her out for being too soppy.

Hearing the endearment now, Marc closed his eyes, blocking out his view of the idyllic streetscape, so typical of suburban California, and saw instead a scene tinged with nostalgia for him. The family home at Castaways Beach, the grevillea-filled garden and the yellow front door, then his mother in the kitchen, possibly stirring something in a large pot on the stove.

The bi-fold doors behind her would be open to the backyard and the stretch of lawn where he'd enjoyed so many magical afternoons throughout his childhood. He saw the tree shading the barbecue area, the afternoon sun hitting the garage wall where five surfboards had once lined up – one for each member of the family.

It was all so far away. Unreal. Like a dream.

Reality was here. His job, his wife, soon to be his ex-wife.

'Oh, and I haven't even told you where I've been planning for us to stay,' his mother hurried on, before he could construct a proper objection. 'It's the perfect travel destination for our family, Marc. And I know Bronte will love it, too. You'll never guess.'

Marc didn't want to guess. To do so would imply tacit consent to this dotty plan and he had no intention of joining his mother or his sisters in any kind of family vacation charade. His only goals right now were to finish his current project on time and within budget, and to try to save his marriage.

His mother's words echoed. *And I know Bronte will love it, too.*

'Mum, I'm sorry. I really don't —'

'Venice!' she cried, jumping in quickly.

For a moment Marc couldn't respond. Then – 'Venice?' He knew he sounded shocked.

'Yes. Your father was planning to take me there for our very first trip after he retired and that's where I want to take *us*. Wouldn't it be wonderful?' She sounded triumphant, so pleased with herself, and Marc couldn't deny that in spite of everything that was wrong with taking a family holiday now, Venice, his father's birthplace and the home of his Italian heritage, was the one place on the globe that could possibly tempt him.

Deep down, although he was reluctant to acknowledge it, Marc also knew how important this would be for his mother. Already, after just ten days, he'd learned what it was like to be suddenly, unexpectedly alone in the world. And he'd experienced the very real fear that this new, gut-wrenching solitude might be permanent.

Remembering this, he was awash with sympathy for his gentle, slightly dreamy mum, who hadn't just loved her husband, but had looked up to him as her hero, her champion.

'Look, I'll see what I can do,' he said, but even as the words left his mouth, he was cringing. He was a weak fool, giving his mother false hope.

'Oh, thank you!' she gushed. 'If you and Bronte can join us, it'll be just perfect, Marc.' Her voice squeaked with excitement and Marc had to hold the phone away from his ear.

'I can't promise anything.'

'I know, but I'll keep everything crossed for you.'

'Thanks.' He tried not to sound too despondent.

'I like to believe it's just a matter of putting an idea out there to the universe and everything comes together,' she said next, in a tone reminiscent of her hippie and yoga phase that Marc remembered from his teens. 'As soon as you know the dates when you can be free, I'll make the bookings.'

'Right,' Marc said faintly. 'Okay.'

They said their goodbyes, and he disconnected and walked on in a gloomy, worried daze. Hell, what kind of idiot was he? Even if he got the time off, he would wreck his mother's happy family holiday plans if he turned up alone. No amount of Italian history and romantic architecture or gourmet food could make up for Bronte's absence. His mother would spend the whole time worrying about him – about *them*, as she loved Bronte, too.

The weeks of planning and making bookings for this holiday would be clouded with worry and sympathy for him. The joyous gathering that his mother longed for would be overshadowed by his marital issues. He would probably wreck the whole show.

But how the hell could he persuade Bronte to join him and her in-laws for a fortnight's holiday when she wouldn't even give him five minutes on the phone?

CHAPTER THREE

'And now for the *shavasana* pose,' announced the yoga instructor.

At last! Anna Benetto breathed a massive sigh of relief. *Shavasana* was her favourite part of yoga. After an hour of twisting into tortuous poses, the class was finally invited to recline on the mats and relax. Phew.

The only challenge now for Anna was the relaxing part. She was supposed to truly let go and keep her mind free, without mentally running through her audition lines for the new play in London's West End.

She'd been hoping that the yoga class might help her to calm down and focus her mind. Today was a really big deal. Huge.

Late on the previous afternoon, after tedious weeks of silence from her agent, an audition call had come through. A small but not insignificant part in a brand-new play was up for grabs. The play, *Blitz*, was set in London during World War II and Anna was to audition for the role of Cherry, a brave and spirited young nurse.

She'd sat up late, reading the entire script through, so she understood exactly how Cherry's part fitted into the bigger picture. Then she'd practised the speeches she would have to deliver, and afterwards she'd spent a sleepless night, tossing and turning while Cherry's lines tracked endlessly in her head.

Result? She'd totally needed a yoga class this morning. *Relax, Anna. Meditate. You can do this. Just let go.*

Admittedly, Anna hadn't been to yoga for a while – quite a while, if she was honest – and she'd struggled to hold still without wobbling in bridge and the dreaded camel pose. Wisely, she'd set her mat at the back of the room, not wanting to catch the attention of the super slim and enviably lithe instructor in sky-blue lycra.

Sad truth: Anna had let things slip since she'd first come to London, flush with glowing references and impressive accolades from her Sydney drama school. In those early months, her ambition had burned bright and she'd been ready for any challenge. She'd been conscientious about keeping up her fitness with daily yoga sessions and jogging. She certainly hadn't been totally naïve, though, expecting to walk straight into a leading role.

Just the same, she hadn't dreamed that her wonderful career choice would be quite so demoralising. London was often referred to as the City of Opportunity, but for young actors it could more correctly be called the City of Disappointment. The place was teeming with aspiring actors and a fair swag of them had undeniable talent. Most of them also had useful connections, either from former drama teachers or directors in the UK, or even family links.

Undaunted by these sobering realities, Anna had networked her butt off and forked out for expensive headshots. Following the best advice, she'd made sure she was listed on Spotlight and had kept herself updated with magazines like *Equity* and *Casting Call Pro*. She'd also taken extra acting lessons and voice training, polishing away the last traces of her Aussie accent.

The jobs, however, were depressingly few and far between.

Every time she'd been called to an audition, hundreds of actors had been there, all as hungry as she was for even the smallest one-line part, and with just five minutes for the casting director to make a decision.

Anna had learned to be grateful that she had at least scored a handful of minuscule parts, as well as being an extra in a few television commercials. Of course, she'd exaggerated these achievements a tad, whenever she'd called home, and it had been very gratifying to hear her mum's OTT excitement.

Poor old Mum, Anna's biggest fan, had obviously forgiven her daughter for those teenage years when she'd been a total wanker, swanning about the house as if she was already a star. It would be too sad if her mum knew the brutal truth now.

Of course, everyone in the London theatrical scene had advice, and the general view seemed to be that you just had to be patient, and to keep trying and not give up. There were oodles of stories circulating about famous stars who'd spent their early years invisible and in poverty while waiting for their big break.

Clearly, acting hadn't yet paid well enough to feed Anna or to pay the rent for the poky flat she shared with Florrie, another acting wannabe from Glasgow. To help make ends meet, Anna had worked in box offices and as an usher. Her darling dad had also sent her nice little chunks of money from time to time, no doubt guessing that her life in London wasn't quite as brilliant or successful as she'd made out.

Anna hadn't liked to mention this supplementary income to her mum when she'd flown home, heartbroken, for her dad's funeral. Her mother hadn't mentioned it either. Perhaps she'd been too shocked and sad to think of anything so practical, or perhaps she simply hadn't known about it. In any case, on arriving back in London, Anna's bank balance had dwindled rapidly and she'd taken on extra work as a waitress.

Fortunately, waiting tables turned out to be the perfect backup job for an actor. Most waiters in the good restaurants were also pursuing careers in the entertainment industry, and covering shifts for each other was pretty much an unwritten law. There was always someone who'd step in if you were called for an audition and had to drop everything.

Anna had covered for a Brazilian waiter, Pedro, when he'd auditioned and landed a fabulous part in the dance chorus for a musical, and she'd covered twice now for Florrie. In return, Florrie would be making a huge sacrifice, cancelling a date with her latest crush, to take over Anna's shift this evening.

This evening. Oh, God.

Anna let out her breath in a noisy huff that brought a sharp scowl from the girl on the mat next to her. Anna shut her eyes. *Relax. Breathe. Sink into serenity.*

Sadly, there was no way she could keep her mind blank. Instead, she lay perfectly still on the yoga mat and tried to plan her day. She wouldn't buy a coffee on the way home. Instead, she would get one of those outrageously expensive super-green smoothies with kale and spinach and all manner of mood-boosting, energy-giving goodness. Yeah, she felt virtuous just thinking about it.

She would also rehearse again, of course, until she knew Cherry's part inside out, experimenting with the mood and tone of her delivery. She would wash her hair, too, do her nails, check her wardrobe, and maybe try out a few different combos of tops and bottoms.

Then, a final run-through. If Florrie was home in time, she would use her flatmate as her audience.

Oh, God. Anna bit back another loud sigh. She wished she wasn't so nervous, but she really, really, *really* wanted this role. Her personal life was a dog's breakfast, thanks to a certain prick of a director who'd dated her for weeks before he remembered he was married. Now, she really needed to get her career up and running.

She could make Nurse Cherry come alive. She just knew it. All she needed was a decent role in a stage play and she was sure she could wow the audiences and critics here in London, just as she had back home. She just needed that one chance to shine and she was hoping desperately that tonight would be her turning point.

Anna arrived early for the audition, having conscientiously allowed plenty of time for travel delays. A woman with a clipboard and a large, matronly bosom was fussing at the door like a cross mother hen.

'Name?' she asked as Anna presented herself.

'Anna Benetto.'

The woman frowned at her clipboard, scanning the obviously long list, and several months seemed to crawl by before she located Anna's name and ticked her sheet of paper. 'Right,' she said without a hint of a smile. 'Sit over there until your name is called.'

'Will —' Anna began nervously and then swallowed. 'Will there be a chance to warm up?'

The woman nodded impatiently. 'Of course, but not until your name is called. Over there, please.'

Over there was a wooden seat like a church pew where a row of young women sat. They all looked to be about Anna's age and height. All potential Nurse Cherries.

A few of them smiled nervously at Anna as she took her seat. Others paid no attention to her, which was probably sensible. They were no doubt trying to maintain their focus, concentrating on the task ahead of them, staying 'in the zone'.

Anna tried to cheer herself up by remembering Florrie's enthusiasm this afternoon when she'd listened to Anna deliver her lines.

'You'll kill them. You're purr-fect for this role,' Florrie had assured her in her broadest Glaswegian accent.

After what felt like an hour, but was probably only ten minutes, a cute, ginger-bearded guy dressed in jeans and a black jumper appeared in another doorway. He called out the names of about half a dozen girls and they disappeared with him, presumably to the warm-up space. The rest, Anna included, shuffled their bums up the pew and more audition candidates arrived to take their places.

Don't worry about everyone else, Anna told herself, remembering all the advice she'd heard and shared over the years. This audition wasn't about looks. This was about personality, about getting into Cherry's character and projecting her emotions.

And try not to care too much. It shows.

Yeah, right. As if.

After another ten minutes, Anna was finally called into the warm-up room. She found a corner where she could avoid looking at the others while she did her breathing exercises and shook out her arms and legs, trying to relax. She rolled her neck and shoulders, and said the famous tongue twister several times. 'I thought a thought, but the thought I thought wasn't the thought I thought I thought.'

In her mind, she ran through Cherry's speech, where the nurse tried to persuade an air-raid warden that there was a little boy trapped under the rubble. This afternoon, Anna had managed to produce real tears and Florrie had been effusive in her praise. She hoped she could do it again tonight.

She wondered how long she would have to wait.

'Anna Benetto!' called the ginger-bearded guy.

Oh, help. She was the first of this group to be called into the casting room. She hadn't been expecting that. Anna gulped and told herself this was a good thing. She wouldn't have to stew while she waited. She mustn't panic.

She threw back her shoulders. *You know you can do this. You really can. This part is made for you.*

Babe, you'll ace this audition.

Leaving her small backpack just outside the door, and with her skin tingling all over, she entered.

A handful of people sat behind a long timber desk. Owen Wetherby, the casting director, was in his mid fifties, round bellied, balding, with soft greying whiskers, and glasses that seemed to keep slipping down his nose. Anna remembered him from a previous audition. He pushed his glasses up again as he looked at her.

'Good evening,' he said pleasantly and the people sitting with him, strangers – one of whom might easily have been the producer – all looked tired and bored.

But Anna felt unexpectedly calm now, as she handed over her headshot and résumé. At a nod from Owen Wetherby, she introduced herself, remembering to keep the info brief and to the point. She felt good. Great. She loved being in front of an audience. This was where she belonged. A couple of the bored strangers were actually paying attention now, she noticed. *Fanbloodytastic.* She'd show them.

Owen Wetherby smiled, almost as if he remembered Anna, which she took to be another encouraging sign.

'Right,' he said and pointed to a black cross on the floor. 'If you could stand there, please.'

Anna did so.

Owen Wetherby nodded. 'Whenever you're ready.'

This was it.

Anna remembered to take a moment, to breathe and to collect her thoughts, to get into the character. She recalled her opening lines, felt Cherry's terror.

The bored faces receded. Anna was now on a war-ravaged London street in the middle of the Blitz, shocked, distraught.

The lines she'd rehearsed flowed, confident and clear, with perfect timing, brimming with emotion.

It was going well. Anna could feel it. She had every one of the bored folk's attention now. This was why she'd come to London, for a moment just like —

Quack, quack.

The sound came from the doorway.

Quack, quack. Quack, quack.

Oh, crap. It was a phone.

Anna would have ignored it, would have continued with her lines, but she was ninety-nine point nine percent certain the quacking was coming from her phone. No one else she knew had that silly ring tone.

Quack, quack, quack.

Fuckety-fuck-fuck How could she have forgotten to turn off her bloody phone?

The quacking continued and she wondered if she should run to her backpack to turn the thing off.

'Keep going,' commanded Owen Wetherby and the coolness in his tone sent Anna into a panic.

Her mind was a jumble. Where was she up to? She stammered a few words, hoping to pick up the thread. The quacking stopped, thank heavens.

After a beat or two, the lines came back to her. She continued, trying to recapture the rhythm and emotion of her earlier brilliant delivery.

'Thank you,' Owen Wetherby said when she finished, but he looked almost as bored as the others now and Anna knew she'd blown it.

In that moment, she wanted to die. If only she could apologise, beg for another chance, but she'd made a serious error by allowing an off-stage event to distract her. The casting director wasn't merely looking for talent, he wanted someone who was good to work with. A professional. Being able to concentrate despite distractions was a vital quality for any actor and she'd behaved like a stupid, raw amateur.

Anna couldn't look at the other girls as she took the walk of shame, out through the waiting area, eyes downcast, hugging her wretched backpack with its now silent contents to her chest. As she neared the woman at the door, though, she remembered the golden rule about being polite to everyone. She straightened her shoulders and lifted her chin.

'Thank you.' Anna addressed the stony-faced woman in her sweetest tones and she even managed to smile. She was an actor, after all.

It was chilly outside as she crossed Leicester Square, shivering and miserable. She dragged a jumper from her backpack and pulled it over her head, thrust her arms into the sleeves.

This was so not how she'd wanted to feel this evening. She'd been hoping to feel confident, even triumphant, to know that at least she'd done her damn best. She'd pictured herself ducking past the restaurant and flashing Florrie a hopeful thumbs-up signal.

She was about to tighten the drawstrings on the pack again, when she glimpsed her traitorous phone and winced. In that moment, she would have happily chucked it in the Thames. Unfortunately, she couldn't afford to be so impetuous.

She supposed she might as well check for the missed call. The damage was done and it wasn't the caller's fault.

The screen was blurry at first and Anna realised that her eyes were filled with stupid tears, the tears she'd planned to manufacture for Cherry.

She blinked, swiped at her eyes with the back of her hand, and looked again. The call was from Australia. From her mum.

CHAPTER FOUR

When Ellie Benetto heard about her family's plans for a holiday in Venice, the first person she wanted to tell was Zach.

Which wasn't by any means unusual. Ellie and Zach Cassidy had been best friends since their playdough and finger-painting days, and they had shared most of their triumphs and disasters.

Ellie and Zach had attended the same primary and high schools. When they were six, they'd both joined the local lifesavers Nippers group, and they'd even played in the same soccer team till they were ten.

During their early high-school years, when most girls became awkward around boys, Ellie and Zach had remained good mates. They'd hung out at weekends, helping each other with assignments and strumming guitars, wishing they had enough talent to become famous, and they'd shared their first cigarette, coughing and spluttering.

Now, with twelve years of schooling finally behind them, Zach was working full time at his father's garage. And that was where Ellie found him, on his back under a dusty ute that had its front wheels propped on a ramp.

All Ellie could see of him were his grey overalls and boots sticking out from beneath the ute, but she would recognise those solid thighs and long legs anywhere.

'Hey, grease monkey,' she called. 'What you doing?'

'Brain surgery,' came the muffled reply.

Ellie was smiling as she plonked down on an oil drum and made herself comfortable, crossing her legs, now well tanned, thanks to weeks of surfing, plus the olive complexion she'd inherited from her father.

She didn't expect Zach to drop everything just to speak to her and she was happy to sit for a bit. She rather liked hanging out in the garage. She found the familiar smell of engine oil and the sight of vehicles waiting patiently for a mechanic's attention weirdly comforting. Especially today, when she was still getting her head around her mum's amazing news about Italy.

Like . . . *wow*.

Ellie's only venture overseas so far had been a trip to Japan with the school band. That trip had been an eye-opener and fun, but rather brief and totally regimented. Nothing like her mum's plans for a family holiday in Venice.

Ellie was excited, of course. Who wouldn't be excited about an all-expenses-paid trip to Italy? But she also felt a tad sideswiped. This holiday plan was so random. So totally out of the blue. Ellie was having trouble taking it in.

The thing was, she'd thought she had this gap year sorted. Taking a gap was about allowing yourself space, right? It was about not having to make any hard decisions, not giving in to the pressure to get ahead, to rush off to uni and be 'amazing'. It was about not having to leap onto the conveyor belt, which carried you, as far as Ellie could tell, by the smoothest but undoubtedly most boring route from the cradle to the grave.

Ellie was perfectly content to spend an entire twelve months right here, wallowing in freedom from assignments and exams and other people's expectations, living by a beautiful beach – a stunning beach that her dad had loved, but would never get to enjoy in his retirement.

Her father's death had been a tragedy on so many levels and it was in tribute to him, really, that Ellie now rose early every morning and headed off with her surfboard. She'd adored her father who had taught her to surf almost as soon as she could swim. And she now relished post-school life, meeting Zach on the beach at dawn and riding the waves while the sun climbed out of the sea, painting the sky with oranges and lemons and all-over rosy gorgeousness.

But this morning, over a latish breakfast, her mum had revealed her 'exciting news' that she wanted her to race off to Italy for a 'lovely family get-together'. And Ellie was nervous. She just knew the pressure to plan her future would be on again in full force.

She could already hear the conversations around some flash dinner table in Venice. Her older siblings, Marc and Anna, were so super successful – Overachievers 'R' Us – and the very thought of their earnest, well-meant pep talks made Ellie tense.

Of course you must know what you want to do, Ellie. You surely have to know what you're good at.

Didn't your teachers advise you?

Yeah, it would either be lectures, or Marc and Anna would be so far up their own bums they wouldn't even give Ellie the time of day.

It was all very well for them. They'd always known exactly what they wanted to do when they left school. Zach had been certain, too, for that matter. For as long as Ellie had known him, he'd wanted to be a mechanic and work in his family's business.

You need to set goals, too, she would no doubt be told. *You'll find yourself left behind.*

Ellie had heard it all before, from her teachers and her mother, and again when her surprisingly good final results had come through. Sadly, no one else knew that she'd only worked so bloody hard in those last months of school because she'd been shocked to the core by her father's death. On that fateful day, she'd suddenly known that she mustn't allow herself to flunk her final year. She had to succeed for her dad's sake.

But afterwards?

Why was being left behind such a bad place to be? What was so terribly wrong with living here on the coast, working in cafés and surfing? Surely hordes of people on this planet would sell a kidney for the chance to enjoy such a life?

Ellie was so deeply sunk in her muddled and gloomy thoughts, she almost missed the movement on the garage floor that signalled Zach easing out from under the ute.

Jumping to his feet, he smiled at her. 'Hey there.'

'Hey,' she said.

Zach was a typical beach guy, tanned, lean and athletic, with streaky brown hair bleached on the ends by too much sun and salt water. Nice looking in an understated kind of way, he had high cheekbones and sparkly green eyes.

'What's news?' he asked Ellie now.

'How'd you know I had news?'

He shot her a grin that made his eyes flash as he wiped his hands on a grease-stained rag that he'd pulled from a back pocket. 'You've got that look.'

'I have a look?'

'Yeah. Kinda prune-faced.'

'Prune?'

'Tight,' he said, still smiling. 'Like you're holding something in.'

At this, Ellie smiled too. 'Well, you're dead right, I am holding in news. My mum's planning a holiday.' She paused for added emphasis. 'For all of us. The whole family.'

'That sounds —' Zach looked at her with a puzzled frown and shrugged. 'That sounds great to me.' There'd been an Easter, when they were in Year 9, when he'd joined Ellie's family for a camping holiday out west. They'd had an awesome time, all six of them, hiking in the bush, fishing and canoeing, grilling sausages and toasting hot cross buns over an open fire. Now his eyes narrowed as he studied her. 'It *is* great news, isn't it?'

'I guess,' Ellie said uncertainly.

'Why wouldn't you be happy? Where does your mum want to go?'

'Venice.'

'Venice? As in Italy?'

'Yeah.'

'Wow.' Zach looked impressed. Suitably impressed, Ellie supposed. 'Lucky you,' he said next.

'Yeah, I know.'

He stood still, watching her closely. Then he gave a slow shake of his head. 'Am I missing something here?'

Ellie sighed. 'No, not really. I'm just being a total idiot. A spoiled one, I suppose.'

'What's the problem?' Zach's brow was wrinkled with concern. Or perhaps puzzlement. 'Your mum's great and I thought you got on pretty well with Marc and his wife, and with Anna.'

'Yeah, yeah, they're okay. They're fine. Of course they are. It's just me.'

Now that she was actually trying to explain it, Ellie realised that she didn't truly understand what her problem was. She knew perfectly well that she was lucky, that Venice was one of the most beautiful cities in the world and a little sibling rivalry within a family was perfectly normal. Nothing to get in a stew about.

She glanced again at Zach, standing there in overalls, with studs undone at the neck to reveal a deep V of tanned chest. And she wondered, with a guilty start, if she'd been hoping he would show a sign or two of envy. Or had she even hoped he might be disappointed that she was going away?

Bloody hell. How lame was that? Did she really expect Zach Cassidy to confess that he would miss her, that he minded, just because she wouldn't be available to go surfing in the mornings? Or to hang out with him when she'd finished her shift at the café? It wasn't as if she'd be gone for long, probably a few weeks at the most.

Or was her problem that *she* would miss *him*?

Unfortunately, Ellie knew this was a distinct possibility, but she wouldn't miss him too much, surely? It wasn't as if there was any kind of romantic attraction between them.

Occasionally, she'd been out to the movies with Zach, or for a casual hamburger meal, but they'd never dated as such. They hadn't even partnered each other for the Year 12 formal. Zach had chosen Bridget Hickey and Ellie had gone with Adam Brooker.

Of course, they'd never really discussed how they felt about each other. In fact, they'd agreed on never dating each other back in Year 11, and they didn't want to ruin their perfect friendship by trying to analyse it too deeply. Instead, they'd gently teased each other about the people they'd gone out with, cautiously quizzing, fishing for details. Revealing very little.

Ellie had no idea how many girls Zach had kissed, or how far he'd gone with them. To be honest, she tried not to think about it. And she certainly hadn't shared details with him about that night with Adam after the formal.

'So —' she said now. 'You're still planning to travel overseas at some stage, aren't you?'

Zach nodded. 'When I've saved enough.'

This was reassuring. 'Yeah, me too.' It was one of the things they *had* discussed in detail – heading off overseas, possibly together or as part of a group, and backpacking around the world, exploring, having adventures. 'I guess I can check out Italy and report back,' she said.

This brought another smile from him. 'Send me plenty of photos, won't you?'

'Sure. You'll probably be inundated. Every day.' *Yikes*. Ellie realised how obsessive that sounded and she felt her cheeks grow hot. 'Well, no, not *every* day, obviously.'

'You can send me pics of the hot Italian chicks.'

'Okay, but I think it's the Italian men who are supposed to be hot.' She tried for an extra cheeky smile, as she said this, but it came out a bit weird and wobbly. 'Well, I guess I'll soon find out.'

'No doubt.' Zach's response was smooth, showing clearly that he didn't give a damn if she fell head over heels in love with half a dozen sexy Italian guys. Then he got busy gathering up the tools he'd been using and wiping them down with the rag.

'Okay,' Ellie said as she rose from her seat on the oil drum, because clearly this conversation was over. 'I – ah – just wanted to let you know.' Except she was no longer sure why she'd been in such a rush to share this news. She was supposed to be fretting about interrupting her gap year. She was supposed to be upset about new pressure from her family, especially from Marc and Anna.

But it hadn't come out that way at all.

'Zach, why don't you come, too?'

Ellie gasped, unable to believe those words had actually spilled from her mouth. What on earth had come over her? This wasn't a simple camping trip. Zach would think she was crazy.

She could feel the sudden tension in him, as obvious as her own. He seemed to freeze as he stood there, still holding a spanner and the rag, and for ages, he didn't speak. 'You're shitting me,' he said finally.

What could she say? *Yeah, tricked you? I just wanted to see your reaction?*

She shrugged. 'It's not a totally dumb idea.'

The silence that fell was embarrassing. Ellie felt so stupid she wanted to scream. She knew her face was bright red, but at least Zach wasn't looking at her. He was staring hard at the spanner.

She wished she could think more clearly. One part of her brain was hanging out for Zach's answer, while another part was wondering if she could retract the invitation. But then another thought popped in. Perhaps her mum wouldn't mind if Zach joined them. Her mum liked him and she knew what great mates they were.

Zach used the rag to wipe a final smear of grease from the spanner's jagged jaw. 'Ah, thanks,' he said, without looking up. 'But I couldn't. I wouldn't . . .' He hesitated, obviously struggling to find the right words.

'Sorry, I put you on the spot.' Ellie was shocked to realise how disappointed she was. Zach hadn't shown the slightest spark of interest.

'Yeah, well.' He flicked a wary glance her way. 'I'm just settling into this job and everything.'

'Of course you are. That's okay. It was just a thought that —' She flapped her hands, trying to fill in the rest of the sentence with something better than *popped into my head*.

Zach looked directly at her now and she saw a sheen in his eyes that made her heart flip in her chest.

He said, 'You're full of bright ideas, Benetto.'

'But you gotta admit they're usually pretty good ones.'

His sad smile caused fluttery shivers all over her skin.

Hopelessly flustered, and maybe a tad terrified, Ellie spoke quickly, trying to cover the mess she'd created. 'Okay, yeah, well, anyway – I know your dad might not appreciate it if you asked for time off when you've only just started. My boss will probably crack it, too. I guess I'll have to find a new job when I get back.' She raised her hand to wave as she backed towards the door. 'See you. Bye.'

Before Zach could respond, Ellie scarpered.

CHAPTER FIVE

Daisy smiled at her accountant, Reg Augustine, across his gleaming timber desk. She felt totally comfortable about this meeting. Reg was an old friend of Leo's, a fellow Rotarian. Solid and reliable. 'So I've decided I'd like to cash in Leo's shares, rather than dipping into his super money.' She pushed a bulging cardboard folder, carefully labelled in Leo's neat script, towards Reg. 'All the paperwork's in here.'

'I see, shares – hmm —' Uncertainty flickered in the accountant's eyes as he lifted a corner of the folder without actually opening it. 'Which shares are these again?'

'I don't think we have a lot of choice, do we?' Daisy said, somewhat surprised. 'As far as I know, there's just the one bundle. Is that what you call it? I know Leo was putting as much money as he could spare into his super fund. But there's —'

She paused, smiled shyly. 'Excuse me, a moment.'

Reg lifted his hand as Daisy leaned forward and opened the folder, tapping a thick envelope sitting on top of the financial reports. 'I was hoping we could cash in these.'

Reg's brow wrinkled as he picked up the envelope. Slowly and in silence, he opened it and his frown deepened as he took out the contents. With eyes narrowed behind dark-framed glasses, he scanned the first page. 'Hmm,' he said, without looking up.

Daisy repressed an impatient sigh. She'd expected this to be perfectly straightforward. She had total confidence in Leo and she knew he'd left his affairs in order. Their executor, a lawyer friend of the family, hadn't mentioned any hassles regarding the will.

Now, however, the accountant looked unhappy, and she couldn't help feeling anxious.

'This is just as I thought,' he said.

Daisy waited, holding her breath. What? she wanted to demand. Surely there couldn't be a problem?

Reg looked up again, and his gaze was rather more solemn than Daisy would have liked, but perhaps it was an impression caused by his bushy grey brows. Folding his hands together and resting them on the papers, he said, with unexpected gentleness, 'I'm afraid you can't access these shares, Daisy.'

A small noise escaped her, a rush of exhaled breath.

'You see,' Reg continued. 'They're held in trust.'

Daisy didn't really see, but she nodded. Leo must have set the shares aside for the children. Such generous foresight was typical of her husband, but she was surprised he'd never mentioned it. Or perhaps he had mentioned it, ages ago, and she hadn't been paying close enough attention. She could be a bit of a scatterbrain.

She offered an apologetic smile. 'I suppose I should have known about that. Sorry. I wouldn't want to get in the way of my children's inheritance.'

Reg frowned again and shifted in his chair.

Why was he uncomfortable about this? Now Daisy found that she was frowning too. It was hard to miss the awkward vibes emanating from the accountant.

She said, just to clarify the situation, 'I'm assuming the shares must be held in trust for our children?'

'Actually, no,' Reg said.

'Oh.' Ever so slightly perturbed, Daisy waited. When Reg remained silent, she inched forward on her chair. 'So what's the story?' she asked and, to her dismay, a nervous little titter escaped her lips.

'Leo never told you anything about these shares?'

Daisy shook her head. 'I don't think we actually discussed them.' She would have remembered, surely? She might not be a financial genius, and she hadn't always paid attention, especially if Leo was rattling on about work or politics. But surely she wouldn't have missed something as important as this? She wasn't a total airhead.

'These shares are held in trust and annual dividends are paid to a group in Italy,' Reg said.

'A *group*? In *Italy*?' Daisy's voice cracked as she repeated this astonishing information. She was totally shocked. And now, she was absolutely certain that Leo had never mentioned this to her.

'What kind of group?' she managed to ask.

'I'm not completely sure, but I suspect it's a – family.'

Daisy accepted this news a little more calmly. She supposed it was possible that her husband had been sending money home to his family all this time. It was the sort of thing Italian migrants did, wasn't it? But why had he kept it secret from her? He must have known that she wouldn't have minded.

She couldn't help feeling hurt. She thought there'd been no secrets between them.

'So, this family,' she said. 'I assume it's Leo's family, the Benettos?'

Reg gave another slow shake of his head. 'The name is Vincini.'

This was a fresh shock. The name Vincini meant nothing to Daisy. 'I'm pretty sure Leo's mother's maiden name was —' She had to stop and think for a moment. 'Sacchi. Yes, that's right. His mother was Anna Sacchi before she was married.'

Again, Reg shook his head. 'The only name here is Vincini.'

Dizziness threatened. Daisy took a deep breath, trying to calm down. *Vincini.* As far as she knew, there was no one in Leo's family by that name, and she couldn't remember him ever mentioning it. Why on earth would he set up a trust fund for a strange family in Italy? Was this a charity of some sort? Were these people distant relatives? In dire straits? She had no idea.

Tears threatened and, for a terrible moment, Daisy feared she might give in to them. She felt so lonely sitting there, faced by all these questions. So at a loss. If only she could contact Leo, just for a moment. If only she could glimpse his dear face, topped by curling grey hair and lit by warm brown eyes. If only she could ask him to explain.

Leo would reassure her – Daisy knew that for certain – and then she would laugh with relief.

Alas, that wasn't going to happen. Leo had left her on her own and now she just had to manage the best she could. Not wanting Reg Augustine to see how upset she was, Daisy widened her eyes to hold back the tears.

'I must admit this is a surprise,' she said, pleased that she managed to sound quite calm, even brave. 'But I – I trust Leo, of course.'

'Would you like me to make further investigations?' Reg asked. 'I think we should track down more details from Italy, but it might take a while.'

Daisy considered this. She was torn. On the one hand, she would very much like to know what this Vincini business was all about, but she didn't want anything to threaten the lovely Italian holiday she had planned for her family. Her patience was already strained to the max while she waited for confirmation from Marc and Bronte.

She shook her head and offered the accountant a smile that she hoped was convincing. 'I don't think so, thank you, Reg. I certainly won't worry about it for the time being. I'll just have to dip into that super money after all.'

Fortunately, one thing Daisy was good at was sticking to a decision once it was made. Now, after the long, dark and miserable months of mourning, she wanted this holiday to be as happy and upbeat as possible. The last thing any of her children needed was the shadow of a dark secret from their father's past.

CHAPTER SIX

Are you free? Can we meet? Something's come up. Need to talk.

Bronte's heart sank when she saw the latest text message from Marc. It was only twelve days since she'd left her husband. Twelve days since she'd walked out of their home in Palo Alto, trying to ignore the shock and pain in his eyes.

Now she was living in a spare room in her friends' condo. Jaya and Sandeep Gupta had been wonderfully understanding, refraining from grilling her about what had gone wrong, and they'd even avoided offering unsolicited advice, for which Bronte was especially grateful. But despite the Guptas' gentle consideration, she hadn't had an easy time.

After all, she'd initiated the end of a marriage that most outsiders believed to be about as close to perfect as a marriage could be. Which just showed how easy it was to put on a good front. Or perhaps it showed that the truth is complicated. Always.

Now, Bronte's first impulse was to ignore Marc's text and pretend she was too busy. It wasn't a total twisting of the truth. She was busy – busy with all manner of emotional distractions. Mostly she was busy justifying to herself that she'd done the right thing.

By moving out, she had taken the first necessary step, which was also the hardest step, according to the self-help articles she'd found online. And while she might not feel any happier yet, she would be happy, just as soon as she took the next really big step and flew home to Australia.

Before then, she would have to speak to Marc, of course. Practical considerations like joint bank accounts and health insurance couldn't be ignored, but there was no point in attempting to talk in any depth about their personal problems. Bronte knew from wearying years of trying that it was impossible for Marc to understand her deep disappointment. Their efforts to talk to a counsellor had been equally unsuccessful.

She looked again at the phone's screen.

Something's come up.

Bronte had no idea what this something might be. Why did Marc have to be so cryptic? He could at least have given her a clue.

No doubt he was super busy, firing off this text to her in between a dozen business emails. After all, Marc's busyness and the breakneck pace of his work that never let up were the main reasons Bronte had decided to leave. Her husband wasn't going to change. She'd given him enough chances.

But now —

Something's come up. Need to talk.

Bronte could only assume that this something wasn't suitable for discussion over the phone. Marc wanted to meet her.

She indulged in a heavy sigh and wished she didn't still feel so vulnerable and confused and, yeah, guilty. But she knew she couldn't refuse to see him forever. Deep down, she suspected that she would actually feel better if she and Marc really talked, even fought and argued and got things out in the open, including that date with Henry. It had to happen sometime and if she knocked back this meeting now, she was only delaying the inevitable.

She texted back. *When and where?*

Marc's reply was immediate. *Why don't I pick you up? In 30 mins?*

Bronte imagined her husband pulling up outside the Guptas' condo, saw herself getting into his car and sitting beside him. No way. It would be too normal. Too familiar. She was trying to distance herself from Marc.

She tapped a quick response. *Meet me at the Blue Parrot in an hour.*

At least a café was neutral ground and using Uber was preferable to travelling in her husband's car.

Marc's answering text was a little slower this time. Almost certainly, he was shooting off another email or three before replying. Miffed, Bronte sifted through her clothes, trying to decide which jeans and sweater to wear. Not the green top, it was Marc's favourite. Her phone pinged.

OK. Thanks. M

She took a deep breath. Right. She would do this, but she had to be careful. Face to face with Marc, she had to be strong, keeping the reasons for their separation at the forefront of her mind. She mustn't forget all the times he'd fobbed her off when she'd tried to tell him how unhappy she was here in Silicon Valley.

Heading for the shower, however, Bronte couldn't shrug aside a treacherous pang of regret as she remembered how excited she and Marc had been when they'd first arrived in California, straight after their honeymoon.

Marc had worked so hard at Queensland Uni, where he'd been studying when they'd met, and after handing in his brilliant PhD, he'd scored his dream job. He'd been ecstatic and Bronte was so proud of her tech-savvy, talented man, she'd happily surrendered her own modest dreams.

At first she hadn't minded about the visa restrictions that prohibited the partners of immigrant software engineers from working, despite the high cost of living in Silicon Valley. Marc's salary package was really generous, providing more than enough for both of them, and with a Fine Arts degree and a keen interest in painting, Bronte was confident she could keep herself occupied.

Two years had passed before the stark realities of Valley life had begun to wear her down. Throughout that time Marc continued to work crazy-long hours, ridiculous by any normal standards, living and breathing his job, while Bronte grew lonelier and sadder.

Sure, she'd tried to make friends, but it was damned difficult when everyone around her was totally obsessed with trying to be more successful than everyone else. She'd soon had a gutful of the patronising smirks she received whenever she admitted she wasn't a tech guru, but filled her days with painting and Pilates.

How cute.

Most of Bronte's girlfriends were the wives of other immigrants, like Jaya Gupta. Which was fine, but it was hard to feel at home with so few American 'buddies'.

As for any thoughts of starting a family, Bronte wouldn't contemplate raising kids in the Valley's fiercely competitive environment. Even quite young children recited their knowledge of the hierarchy in the Ivy League colleges that their parents had attended. Meanwhile, the parents programmed their children's play dates into iPhones, as if they were meetings with high-level clients. Family time had to be negotiated.

The people here lived in a bubble, Bronte had decided. They were hardly conscious of a wider world. It wasn't at all like the family life she'd wanted for her kids.

Admittedly, Bronte's idea of family life was based on fanciful hopes and dreams rather than any personal experience. As the only child of academic parents who'd divorced when she was ten, the fun factor in her childhood and been pretty damn low. But even when she'd tried to be brutally realistic, she'd become more and more conscious of the painful fact that she would never fit in here.

It was hard, though, not to feel guilty. Only a miserable moaning cow would resent a lifestyle that afforded so much luxury. Bronte had given herself any number of pep talks, reminding herself about the millions of refugees in the world who would never have such a fine roof over their heads.

She'd even lectured herself about the wives of the early settlers who'd accompanied their husbands into the Australian bush, or to Alaska, or to other wilderness landscapes. Everyone knew those women had coped heroically with untold hardships. Then again, those women had worked alongside their husbands, making clothes, baking bread, planting crops and bottling preserves. Their lives might have been hard, but they'd had meaning.

In Silicon Valley, on the other hand, the luxury might be dazzling, but it couldn't fill a personal sense of emptiness. For Bronte, it couldn't erase the feeling that she had no purpose in the US. And it couldn't blot out an impossible yearning for Australia.

Bronte missed home. Missed hearing Aussie accents in the street and seeing the cricket on TV, even though she wasn't an actual fan. She missed the friendliness of Aussies, the way they could happily strike up a conversation with a stranger. And she missed the larrikin sense of humour. She even missed the habitual swearing, but most of all she missed the glorious laid-back, no-worries attitude.

Any time she'd tried to talk to Marc about the future, however, he'd told her he couldn't contemplate moving anywhere for at least another six months.

And then there would be another six months. And another.

Marc loved it here, of course. He adored his work. That was the problem.

*

Now, showered and dressed in a plain grey T-shirt and skinny jeans, with a fine gold chain at her throat, Bronte eyed her reflection in the mirror. She'd pulled her auburn hair back into a severe knot, rather than leaving it free the way Marc liked, and she'd used just the merest hint of tinted moisturiser. No point in trying to look attractive when she was initiating a breakup.

She needed earrings, though. Plain gold hoops would do. Unfortunately, when she tried to thread these into place her hands were shaking. The first little hoop still wasn't fixed when a beep outside announced the Uber's arrival. Abandoning the earrings, Bronte snatched up her shoulder bag and hurried out into the golden glow of a Californian sunset.

Just remember, don't weaken, she reminded herself as she climbed into the Uber's back seat.

Marc was waiting at the Blue Parrot, sitting at a table towards the back of the airy space, with an apparently untouched glass of beer in front of him. Bronte's breathing faltered when she saw him. With his father's dark hair and his mother's blue eyes, her husband had always been eye-catching.

Now, everything about Marc was so totally familiar – the longish shape of his face, his thick black hair cut super short, his broad shoulders and stubble-lined jaw – even his black T-shirt that advertised his favourite running shoes.

But after a break of just twelve days, Bronte was also aware of a new sense of distance from her husband. And with that realisation came sadness, tugging down the corners of her mouth, tightening her throat.

Don't weaken. She had to remember this split was about regaining her life. She mustn't forget that Marc was quite happy to spend sixteen to eighteen hours a day hunched over a laptop or spreadsheet, apparently unaware that he treated her like another item in his diary, to connect or disconnect with, work permitting.

By staying with Marc she was in danger of disappearing in a puddle of misery. The only reason she'd come to this meeting was to hear this *something* he needed to tell her.

Of course, he was texting on his phone as she approached his table, but he must have sensed her presence and looked up. His smile was warm, but it couldn't quite hide the tension in his eyes.

Bronte's heart gave a guilty thud as she remembered their last brutal conversation, the night before she'd walked out, when she'd told Marc, in total desperation, about Henry, the guy that she'd met online. The pain in Marc's face had been more than she'd bargained for and she'd almost given in then and confessed the whole sorry truth about that date.

But embarrassing honesty hadn't been necessary. Marc must have realised how very serious she was and he'd let her go without a horrendous fight. Bronte told herself she'd been lucky.

Now, ever the gentleman, her husband rose from his seat. 'Hi.'

She drew a quick breath, hoping it would calm her. 'Hi.'

He nodded towards the bar. 'Can I get you a drink?'

Given the state of her nerves, Bronte was tempted to ask for a hefty cocktail or even a rum and Coke, but this wasn't a night for relaxing. 'Just a chai latte, please.'

'Right. Take a seat. I won't be a moment.'

The bar wasn't busy and Marc returned quickly with Bronte's latte. His smile was careful as he sat opposite her and, now that she was over the first greeting, she could see that he looked paler and possibly thinner. Shadows lay under his eyes.

The past twelve days had been hard for him too.

Don't weaken.

'So,' she said, needing to get straight down to business. 'What's this all about, Marc? You said something's come up?'

'Yeah.' His mouth tilted in a crooked half-smile that hinted at embarrassment. 'I've had a call from Australia. From my mother.'

Bronte had always liked her mother-in-law and now her stomach gave a sickening lurch. Any way she looked at it, breaking their news to Daisy and Marc's sisters was going to be hard and hurtful. She'd figured it would be her responsibility, but perhaps Marc had spared her that difficult task. 'Have you told Daisy? About us?'

Marc shook his head. 'No, not yet. I have quite the opposite problem, actually.'

Bronte frowned. This didn't make sense. If their meeting wasn't about their breakup, why the urgency? An unpleasant thought struck. 'Daisy's not sick?'

'No, no,' Marc said. 'Nothing like that. Mum's fine, but she's had this bright idea and she's got herself all worked up.'

'Oh?'

'She wants to shout us a trip to Venice.'

Bronte knew that she must have been gaping as she stared at him. She couldn't speak. She was truly astonished.

'I know,' he said. 'It's insane.'

'But why?' Bronte finally managed to ask. 'I mean, why would Daisy want to send us on a holiday?' Had his mother concluded via some kind of sixth sense that their marriage was in deep trouble?

'Well, that's the thing,' Marc went on. 'It's not just us. She wants the whole family to be there, to have a holiday together.'

'In Venice?'

'Yeah. And she's paying.'

A shocked, nervous laugh spilled from Bronte.

'I know.' Marc stared unhappily at his beer. 'Of all the curve balls —'

'Are you sure she's quite well?' Bronte couldn't help asking.

He nodded. 'Don't worry, I double-checked. And apparently Anna did too. She was worried this might have been some kind of dying wish, but Mum's perfectly healthy, apparently. Just grieving for Dad and . . .' He shrugged. 'And feeling nostalgic, I guess.'

Which was perfectly understandable. Bronte picked up a spoon and stirred her latte, making the spices on its surface swirl. 'What did you tell her?'

'That I can't get away, of course.'

'Of course.' She allowed herself a small sigh of relief.

'But I felt pretty bad,' Marc said next. 'This plan seems to mean so much to her.'

'She understands it's impossible, though?' Surely, Daisy Benetto must know that her son was highly allergic to taking time off. Even though quite a few of the bigger tech companies in the Valley had generously lifted annual vacation restrictions, many of their employees, Marc included, had actually used the freedom to take even shorter breaks.

Now Marc shrugged and looked uncomfortable.

Bronte stiffened. 'Marc, what have you told her?'

'The thing is,' he said, 'Mum's had such a rotten year.'

This was undeniably true. When they'd gone back for the funeral, the whole family had been in a daze, but Bronte had been especially upset to see Daisy so flattened by her loss.

Bronte genuinely liked the Benettos. Given her own family background, she'd valued the way Marc's family had welcomed her into their noisy midst. She had wonderful memories of rowdy gatherings at Christmas, of barbecues in the backyard at Castaways Beach, the air filled with laughter and the scent of onions and sausages.

Once she and Marc finalised their breakup, Bronte knew she would miss the warm sense of belonging that his family had given her.

'What are you trying to tell me, Marc? You want to go on this trip to Venice?'

'I think I should.'

'Well, that's okay, I guess.' Bronte tried not to sound too surprised and hurt that he could find the time for a vacation with his family when he'd had so little time for her. 'When does Daisy want to go?'

'Pretty soon. A couple of weeks in April or May, if possible, before the summer season when Venice gets really crowded.'

'That makes sense, but I'm not sure why you'd need to consult me.'

He hesitated, twisting the beer glass in front of him without lifting it to his lips, before he said, 'I'd really like you to come, too.'

Bronte gasped. Was Marc for real? Did he honestly expect her to front up to his family as if they were still together? As if she hadn't walked out on their marriage? As if she'd never confessed about that night with Henry?

Apparently, the answer was yes. Marc did expect all of the above. He sat very still, watching Bronte with a worried intensity, ignoring his smartphone, instead of pouncing on it as he usually did whenever it pinged with a message.

Alarmed, she tried to think straight, to get her head around this impossible scenario. 'Marc, you know I can't go on a holiday with you.'

'I know it would be hard, but —'

Hard? It was impossible. 'There aren't any buts.' Bronte was firm. *Don't weaken now.* 'I'm sorry, but you'll have to tell them I won't be there.'

His face twisted in a grimace. 'It would wreck the whole plan.'

'Too bad,' she snapped, her anger welling as she remembered all the reasons she'd walked out on this man. 'You can't do this to me now. It's always the same. Every time I've tried to talk to you about things I want, you've fobbed me off. Just six more months, you say, but nothing changes. You're so bloody selfish.' Bronte's voice had risen during this tirade and she was aware of people at nearby tables turning.

Let them stare, she thought. This was one battle she couldn't afford to lose. She picked up her latte, as yet untasted, and took a sip, annoyed to discover it had already cooled.

'You're right,' Marc said with unexpected humility. 'I've been a selfish prick and I know you're – I know *we're* . . .' Pain shimmered again in his blue eyes. His jaw tightened as if he was struggling to hold himself together.

Bronte looked away. She couldn't bear this.

'Bronte,' Marc said more calmly.

Super-cautiously, she dragged her gaze back to meet his.

'Look,' he said. 'I'm not at all comfortable about asking you to do this. But it isn't for me.'

Stay strong. If she caved on this, it would be like taking a leap into freedom only to find a rope still tied around her waist.

Marc continued. 'I'm only asking this for my mother's sake. She's so excited about this holiday plan. On the phone she sounded so happy, almost like her old self, and if I told her the truth – about us – it would ruin everything.'

Gulp.

Bronte sagged in her chair, horrified to realise that Marc was right. She could totally picture Daisy's blue eyes, lit with excitement over her grand scheme to have her family together in her husband's beautiful, famous home city. Bronte could also imagine how gutted Daisy would be by the news of her breakup with Marc. The whole Venice idea would be —

Oh, God. A memory stirred. Venice. The city Leo Benetto had left behind when he'd migrated to Australia, alone, as a young man. The strange message on Facebook.

It came back to Bronte now in a rush. Despite Marc's job in IT, she was the only member of the Benetto family who regularly used

Facebook. It had been her way of keeping in touch with her friends back in Australia and, of course, she'd posted a message about Leo's death, a nice tribute to her father-in-law, along with a lovely photo of him when he was young.

A day or two later a private message had come through from a woman in Venice, Italy. She had written about what a wonderful man Leo had been, a true hero, who would live in her heart forever.

Bronte struggled now to remember the woman's name. Sofia someone. She couldn't remember the surname. Vincini, perhaps? Something like that. At the time of the funeral, when Bronte had mentioned the woman's name to the Benetto siblings, none of them had heard of her. The Facebook message had remained a weird mystery, and she hadn't liked to pester Daisy, who'd barely been coping as it was.

Bronte had simply written back to this Sofia, politely thanking her, and the exchange had ended. She'd forgotten about it till now.

Back then, however, Bronte had found the message unsettling. And now, as she thought about Daisy blithely and generously gathering her family from far-flung corners of the globe and whisking them on a sentimental journey to her husband's birthplace, Bronte's memory of this mysterious Sofia caused a fresh pang of disquiet.

More importantly, she knew that Marc's mother would be distressed by their breakup, deeply distressed. It would absolutely spoil her lovely holiday plans.

Overwhelmed by the spinning of her thoughts, Bronte groaned softly, dropped her head into her hands. It was crazy to think that her presence in Venice could help her mother-in-law, that she could bolster Daisy in any way, but out of nowhere the knowledge arrived. It was the right thing to do.

'Bronte,' Marc said softly, sounding worried.

When she looked up, she saw his hand, hovering close to hers, as if he'd wanted to touch her, but feared she would hate it.

She was grateful for his caution. His touch was dangerous. When he withdrew his hand, however, her resolve crumpled.

'Look, all right,' she said, hardly believing her own ears. 'I'll do this. I'll go to Venice, Marc.' Oh, God, had she really said that? 'But I'll be doing it for Daisy. Okay?'

'Yeah. Sure.' Relief shone in his eyes. 'That's fantastic. Thank you.'

Bronte's heartbeat was racing now. She'd thoroughly scared herself. 'But it doesn't change our situation,' she stressed.

'Yeah, I get that.'

'We'll put on a show for your family. Nothing more. It doesn't mean we're getting back together.'

Marc nodded.

Bronte added, nervously, just to be totally clear, 'I suppose we might have to make some kind of announcement at the end of the holiday.'

After staring hard at his beer, Marc seemed to remember he was supposed to drink it. Muscles in his throat worked as he swallowed.

Bronte looked away. 'That's fair,' she said. 'We'll tell them at the end. Okay?'

It felt like an age before he spoke. 'I guess we'll work out the best way to do that when the time comes.'

'I guess.'

They sat in strained silence. Bronte took another sip of her cold latte. Marc finished off his beer and grimaced. It was probably too warm.

'You do realise you'll be the only male, surrounded by a host of bossy women,' she said.

'Thanks for the sympathy.'

She countered this with an offhand shrug. 'Forewarned is forearmed.'

Setting the glass down, he said, 'I imagine the accommodation arrangements will be out of our hands. Mum will want us all together.'

Oh, no. The accommodation. Of course. If the family was in a shared space and she and Marc were supposed to be still happily married, they would be expected to sleep in a double room. Bloody hell. And there'd probably be an ensuite bathroom that would involve all kinds of awkward ducking and dodging behind towels.

A groan broke from Bronte. Why hadn't she thought this through more carefully before she opened her big mouth? She'd been swayed by sympathy for her mother-in-law, but she was also traversing the quicksands of a breakup and she should have been looking after her own interests.

She squared her shoulders. 'I don't want to regret this, Marc. We'll have to lay down some ground rules.'

He regarded her with narrowed eyes and an expression she couldn't quite read. 'Rules?'

'About the accommodation. About sharing a room.' She couldn't quite bring herself to say the word *bed*.

'So you're going to write our own Ten Commandments?'

'Why not? That's a great idea.' She certainly couldn't afford to lose an inch of this battleground. Somehow, she was going to get through two whole weeks in Italy by her husband's side, without weakening her resolve to regain her life. 'I'll be making my expectations very clear,' she said tightly.

'Fine.'

Marc's phone pinged again and this time Bronte held her breath. No doubt it was foolish to treat the moment as a kind of litmus test, but she sensed deep in her bones that the next few seconds were crucial to her future.

If Marc picked up the phone and frowned at the screen, giving it his complete attention, she would know for sure that her husband wasn't going to change, and her perennial annoyance with him was justified. She should keep her plans for the breakup in place.

A second ping sounded and Bronte found herself sitting on a knife edge.

Marc picked up the phone and, without offering any attempt to excuse himself, clicked on the message.

Phew. Bronte let out the breath she'd been holding. *Result.* Two weeks – even two weeks in romantic Italy – weren't going to sabotage her plans for freedom.

CHAPTER SEVEN

'Yoo-hoo, Daisy? Hello, are you there?' Freya's musical voice floated through the open front door.

'Yes, come on in,' Daisy called to her. 'I'm in the bedroom.' Daisy was indeed standing in the middle of her bedroom, surrounded by chaos, with clothing scattered in haphazard piles all over the bed, belts and scarves flung over the back of a chair, and a half-packed suitcase on the floor.

Arriving at the bedroom doorway, Freya saw this mess and offered Daisy a sympathetic smile. 'Packing's always the worst part of any holiday.'

Daisy nodded, smiling ruefully as she eyed the jeans and slacks, the T-shirts and blouses. 'I have so much trouble choosing. I know I'll end up taking far too much stuff. I always do, even if I'm just going for a weekend in Brisbane.'

'Well, they say the golden rule for travelling light is to stick to a basic colour like navy or black.' Freya was speaking from experience, having made quite a few overseas trips with her husband.

'I couldn't possibly stick to one colour,' Daisy said. 'I'd be bored.'

Freya gave an easy shrug. 'Well, you'll work it out. You always look lovely. My only other tip is to roll your clothes rather than laying them flat. My niece Ivy told me that. Remember her? The ballet dancer based in London? We tried to tee up a meeting between her and Anna, but they were both always so busy I don't think it ever happened.'

'Oh, yes. I remember.' Daisy smiled. 'It's quite dizzying how busy those young people are.' She was still pinching herself over the lucky coincidence that both Marc and Anna had been able to prise themselves away from their work commitments for this spontaneous Italian holiday.

In the end, her plans had come together with surprising ease, with everything happening much faster than she'd expected. It was a sign, she'd decided, that this holiday was meant to happen.

'It's a pity Jo couldn't make it today,' she said.

'I know. But Toby has soccer or something.'

'I'll make sure I ring her to say goodbye.'

With a nod, Freya held out a smart beige trench coat. 'Anyway, this is the coat I promised you could borrow.'

'Oh, isn't it perfect?' Daisy had discovered it would still be quite cool in Venice in late April and Freya's kind offer was so much more practical than her own heavy wool coat. 'Thanks so much. I suppose it'll fit me?' Daisy was quite a bit rounder than her tall, slim friend.

'I'm sure it will,' Freya reassured her. 'I bought it for Europe in the middle of winter, so I got a bigger size that would fit over layers.'

Daisy slipped the trench coat on and turned to inspect her reflection in the mirrored wardrobe door. Goodness, how different she looked. The coat was in the classic style, double breasted, with rows of brown buttons and straps on the sleeves. And when she did up the buttons and buckled the belt, it fitted her perfectly. For a moment, she felt quite transformed. Glamorous. Throw on a pair of sunglasses and she might have been an anyone – an American First Lady or a Russian spy.

She suppressed an urge to giggle. 'I love it,' she said, turning to Freya with a beaming grin.

'You look great.'

Impulsively, Daisy gave her friend a hug and a kiss. 'Thank you.'

'My pleasure. I hope you have a fabulous time.'

Excited now, Daisy swung back to once again admire her reflection. 'I'll be able to wear it with pretty much anything, won't I?'

'Absolutely. I lived in that coat on our trip. It went with everything from T-shirts and jeans to a little black dress.'

Daisy could already picture herself, decked in this smart gaberdine, strolling along an ancient cobblestone street or wandering beside a canal.

'And you can always pretty it up with a scarf,' Freya added.

'Yes.' Daisy cast a glance at the jumble of scarves hanging on the back of the chair. She'd been struggling to decide which ones to take.

'This animal print one would be perfect,' Freya suggested, picking it up and draping it over Daisy's shoulder. 'But you should probably wait till you get to Venice and buy yourself a gorgeous scarf there.'

'Yes.' At the thought of looping a genuine Italian silk scarf around her neck, a ripple of pleasure shimmied over Daisy's skin. Almost immediately she felt guilty, though. After months of grieving, such bubbling happiness still felt wrong. Selfish.

And now doubts rushed in. In two days, she would actually be there, walking the streets of Venice, soaking up the famous sights, dining in some fascinating little restaurant overlooking a canal, exploring the galleries.

Without Leo.

Was she making a terrible mistake? Could she bear to be there, in Leo's home city without him? It was hard not to feel guilty that this holiday had grown out of her own need to be happy again.

She was uncomfortably conscious of the disruption she was causing her family, and the sneaking suspicion that her children were doing this to please her rather than experiencing genuine excitement. But it was too late to back out now.

And she certainly couldn't admit to Freya the doubts that had flared in her accountant's office – the niggling fear that there was more to Leo's Italian background than she'd bargained for.

The whole idea of going to Venice had been triggered by a need to somehow feel closer to Leo. But if Daisy was truly, painfully honest with herself, she should admit that she'd always sensed her husband might be hiding something from his past. Why else had he never taken the step of returning to Venice for more than a flying visit?

Contemplating this, Daisy shuddered.

'Daisy? Are you okay?'

'Yes, of course.' Hastily, Daisy squeezed her face muscles, forcing a smile and reminding herself that this trip was all about sharing the wonders of a beautiful city with her family, with the offspring her husband had adored.

Her motives were fine and it was time to remind herself that she wasn't going to allow anything, including the revelation about the Vincini trust fund, to cloud their enjoyment of this nostalgic journey.

'So Ellie's not home?' Freya asked next, tactfully moving their conversation along.

'No,' Daisy said. 'Ellie's working tonight. At the café.' Slipping out of the coat, she found a hanger for it. 'This is her last night. And then after work, she's going to some party with Zach Cassidy. A bit of a farewell, I gather.'

'A farewell?' Freya looked amused. 'She's not leaving for six months in the Antarctic.'

'No.' Daisy clamped her lips together before she said more, but she was still rather annoyed with Ellie.

Admittedly, Ellie's boss hadn't been thrilled about her sudden request for leave and Ellie was going to have to hunt for a new job when she got back, but of the three children, Daisy's youngest had been the least enthusiastic about this holiday, which Daisy found irritating. After all, Ellie was on a gap year and, unlike her mega-busy siblings, had no serious commitments.

No point in dwelling on this minor concern, though. Daisy flashed a smile to Freya. 'You'll have a drink with me, won't you?'

'To toast your holiday?'

'Why not?'

'What a great idea.'

Abandoning the packing, which Daisy knew would take hardly any time once she really set her mind to it, the women went through to the kitchen that she'd always liked to think of as the heart of her home.

This house that she and Leo had built in Castaways Beach wasn't a two-storey McMansion on the seafront with amazing views, but a low-set sprawling bungalow in a quiet back street. Four slender stone columns graced the front patio – the only concession to Leo's Italian heritage – and the shady front garden was filled with Daisy's favourite Australian natives, mostly grevilleas that tolerated the sandy soil.

Daisy had always loved this house. It had begun as a simple two-bedder and, in time, when they could afford it, extensions had been planned, carefully, by Leo. Now there were four bedrooms, two and a half bathrooms and a family room for watching television that opened onto a generously sized paved entertaining area. In the backyard there was also a massive barbecue, complete with wood box and pizza oven that Leo had built, meticulously laying the bricks himself.

The house was probably a bit big for her these days, but with luck there'd be grandchildren before too long. Besides, downsizing wasn't an option. Daisy couldn't bear to leave.

And now, Freya perched on a stool at the island bench, crossing her elegant long legs.

'Check out the place where we're staying.' Daisy handed her phone to her friend and clicked to the specially saved site. 'I ended up booking through Airbnb.'

'Good for you.'

'It was Marc's idea. I was a bit doubtful at first. I was sure I should go through a travel agent, but Marc knows the fellows who started Airbnb in San Francisco and he says everyone's using it, so why not us? Anyway, I gave it a try and it was surprisingly easy in the end, and I found us a lovely three-bedroom apartment. Or, at least, I really like it. Take a squiz.'

She stood beside Freya, watching as her friend flicked through the photos on the screen. 'It's only a three-minute walk from the vaporetto stop,' she said. 'That's the water bus.'

Freya grinned at her. 'And you've already got the lingo.'

'Hardly.' Daisy laughed. 'I have two words in Italian now: vaporetto and vino.'

'Oh, that's all you need, really, but I'm sure you know more.'

'Oh, yeah, cappuccino.'

They both laughed and Freya turned her attention to the photos again. And even though Daisy had pored over them endlessly, she couldn't resist taking another peek at the beautiful shots. The apartment must have been old, as its walls were built from stone, but there were renovated bathrooms, sumptuously upholstered white sofas, chandeliers and candles in the living room, elegant bedrooms with pale rugs on the floors and exposed ceiling beams, and doors that opened onto tiny balconies.

'Ooh, this room looks very romantic.' Freya had come to the

shot of the all-white bedroom with a king-size bed scattered with heart-shaped pillows.

Daisy smiled. 'I've decided Marc and Bronte should have that room.'

'Lovely. They'll adore it. It'll be almost like a second honeymoon for them.'

'Yes.' Daisy felt especially good about this decision. Another smaller bedroom on the apartment's lower floor would be fine for herself. She didn't need a view of the canal. She would be perfectly happy looking out into the pine trees in the back garden. After all, she loved gardens.

Freya flicked to the next room with two single beds. 'And will Anna and Ellie share this?'

'Yes.' This had been another small bone of contention, as Ellie hadn't been thrilled at the prospect of sharing a room with her sister. She hadn't complained, exactly. She was smart enough to know that she couldn't look a gift horse in the mouth, but she'd been noticeably low-key in her response to the apartment, which was disappointing.

Then again, Ellie was still a teenager and they were notoriously difficult, weren't they?

As Freya continued to ooh and aah over the lovely photos, Daisy went to the fridge to fetch the bottle of bubbly she'd been keeping for just such an occasion, as well as the last of the cheese and olives. From an overhead cupboard she collected glasses, a little brown and white dish for the olives and a matching plate for the cheese.

The cork eased out of the bottle with a pleasing pop and the pale wine fizzed deliciously as she poured it. 'I bought prosecco, of course,' she said, grinning, as she handed Freya a glass.

'Of course. And now that you mention it, prosecco's another important Italian word that you already know.'

Daisy laughed. 'Along with arrivederci.'

'And ciao.'

'That's not a bad start.'

'It's brilliant. You've got the basics covered.' They were both laughing as they clinked their glasses. 'Here's to a wonderful trip.'

CHAPTER EIGHT

Anna was the first of the Benettos to arrive in Venice. The flight from London to Marco Polo airport only took three hours, and thanks to advice from her mate Renzo, who'd been living in Venice for the past six months, Anna's chosen seat offered her a perfect view as they came in to land.

The late afternoon sky was washed with pink as the plane swooped low, and the waters of the Venetian Lagoon were a deepening blue. Against this backdrop, the famous islands appeared to be floating and Anna leaned closer to the glass.

Now she could see rooftops and more rooftops, all glistening reddish brown in the afternoon light and crowded shoulder to shoulder with glamorous Renaissance palaces and ancient bell towers. Goosebumps prickled her skin. This was so incredibly exciting.

Anna had been on a high since she'd first heard about her mum's plans. How did she feel about a chance to escape from London? Could she manage a couple of weeks to explore the famous Italian city dripping with art and history and culture? Yes, please. For Anna it had arrived like a gift from the gods.

Just in time, she'd remembered to play down her excitement. The last thing she needed was for her family to guess the pitiful state of her dismal career. Her mother, especially, was ridiculously contented believing that her daughter was a rising star.

Anna did feel guilty about letting the others assume she was squeezing this holiday in between important gigs, but there was little to be gained by spoiling her mum's illusions. Not till the end of this trip, at any rate.

And now, as the plane touched down, Anna was more than ready for a change of scenery, especially for the incomparable beauty of Venice. Bonus, her friend Renzo was at the busy airport to meet her with a smile as wide as his open arms.

'Ciao, bella! It's so good to see you.'

'G'day, mate.' Anna couldn't resist answering in her best Aussie accent.

Renzo kissed her European style on both cheeks, then hugged her hard and Anna returned his hug, happily matching his enthusiasm. For the foreseeable future she was a relationship-free zone, thanks to a certain arsehole director. And Renzo Del Rosso was tall, dark and handsome as sin. And gay. *Perfetto*.

Hailing from country Victoria, Renzo was also an Aussie of Italian descent who had hoped for an acting career in London. Six months ago he'd given up the fight, and Anna was eager to hear about his new life in Venice. Apparently, he was renting a tiny apartment and working as a tour guide and, by all reports, as happy as a pig in the proverbial.

'Seriously, you're looking as beautiful as ever,' Renzo told Anna.

'You, too.' She really meant it. Renzo had always been attractive, with dark curly hair and classic Italian features, but now there was a new air of confidence about him, a fresh vitality. 'Venice must really agree with you.'

'I love it here.' He said this simply, but with such convincing sincerity that Anna was stabbed by a pang of envy. How long had it been since she'd loved anything about her life?

'I thought we'd take the water bus – the Alilaguna – and then a vaporetto to your apartment,' he said, as soon as she'd collected her luggage. 'I hope that's okay. I've already jumped in and bought the tickets.'

'Wow, of course it's okay. Thanks. Fantastic.'

'And once you're settled, we can find a nice place for dinner, if you like.'

'Sounds perfect to me. I want to hear all about your new life here. But dinner will be my shout.' After all, Renzo had bought tickets and given up a whole afternoon for her. 'Can you take me somewhere the tourists don't know?'

'*Certamente*,' Renzo responded with a good-natured grin. 'I'll take you to one of Venice's best kept secrets.'

Anna grinned back at him. 'Awesome. Then I can show off my local knowledge to the rest of the family when they arrive.' One-upmanship still ruled in the Benetto mob, surely?

Thirty minutes later, on the crowded vaporetto, with her suitcase wedged between them and her shoulder bag tucked under her arm, safe from the pickpockets Renzo had warned her about, Anna watched in awe as the city of water opened up to them.

Venice was so famous, she'd seen countless scenes on TV or in movies and had almost felt as if she already knew the place. But now, the reality was so much more than a collection of iconic images.

The Grand Canal was bustling with life. Gondolas carrying tourists criss-crossed the water, dodging the bigger boats that were busily making deliveries of mail and parcels, wine and vegetables, even dry-cleaning. So many boats made sense, considering there were no cars in Venice. And watching over all this busyness were the palaces rising majestically from the water.

'You know, Venice is a group of islands built on millions of tree stumps pounded into the mud and topped with stone,' Renzo told her.

'Really?' Anna looked around her in disbelief. The buildings lining the canal were quite splendid, most of them several stories high and made of solid brick and stone. She couldn't believe the whole place was standing on what amounted to stilts. 'But how can all that wood last in water?' she asked. 'Doesn't it rot?'

Renzo shook his head. 'The stumps are encased in mud, away from oxygen, and apparently that protects them.'

'Amazing.' She smiled. 'And how lucky am I to have a friend who knows all this random stuff?'

Another grin. 'If you like random stuff about art and culture and music, I'm your man.'

The apartment was, just as her mum had assured them, only a few streets from the vaporetto stop. Better still, it was situated, so Renzo informed Anna, in an area away from the main tourist trails, where the regular Venetians lived.

Through the gathering dusk, Anna trundled her suitcase across an ancient stone courtyard, more correctly called a *campo*, she was told. Here, boys kicked a soccer ball against a church wall, and two dogs lapped at a crumbling fountain, while old men sat on benches watching everyone go by. Already, it felt like a different world.

Leaving the campo and turning into a narrow street, Anna was enchanted anew. An open door in a pale stone wall showed a glimpse of a secret garden, a trellis covered with white wisteria, terracotta pots brimming with violets. Around another bend, a tortoiseshell cat sat on a doorstep licking its dappled coat in the last of the sunlight. An old woman watered herbs on her windowsill.

Anna had to pinch herself. After two years in London, she should have been a seasoned traveller, but she'd never had enough spare cash for trips to Europe. Now, here she was, in a famously romantic and ancient city. The Serene City it had been dubbed, and so very different from bustling, self-important London, and light years away from her suburban home on the Sunshine Coast in Queensland.

And yet, she had roots here. Somewhere on these islands, her grandparents had lived, and so had her father for his first twenty or so years. Anna's dark hair and eyes and her olive complexion were testament to her Italian heritage. And now, as the little street took yet another turn, she caught the scent of simmering tomatoes and herbs and a hint of garlic coming from a kitchen, and she had the strangest sense of belonging. Of coming home.

The reaction was so unexpected, her throat felt choked and her eyes welled with sudden tears. She lifted her face to the three-quarters moon in a darkening sky, willing the tears to dry, hoping that Renzo hadn't noticed.

'And here you are,' he said, pointing ahead to an iron gate set in a stone wall.

Wow. She was still feeling strangely emotional as they pushed the gate open and entered a small courtyard covered with old and worn pavers with tufts of grass growing between them. Directly ahead, a brilliant blue door was set in a pale yellow wall and on either side of the door, clusters of terracotta pots of all sizes overflowed with bright geraniums and herbs. In a corner of the courtyard, a tree, possibly a peach, was an umbrella of pretty pink blossoms. A rustic clothesline swung from a metal hook on one wall to a similar hook on another.

It was all so simple, so picture-postcard charming. And for Anna, it was love at first sight.

'Isn't it gorgeous?' she almost whispered to Renzo. 'Wasn't my mum clever to find this place?'

'Yeah, she's done well. Do you have to collect a key?'

Oh, yes, the key. Apparently, Simonetta, the owner, worked most evenings, but there was supposed to be a key in a metal box. 'It should be near the door somewhere,' Anna said.

They found the box, after only a little searching, tucked behind a pot of basil and an old metal watering can. The box was rusty and Anna needed Renzo's help to open it.

'Simonetta certainly didn't want to make this easy,' he said, grimacing as he finally prised the lid free.

Anna shrugged. 'It's a novel security system, but I guess it works.'

At least the key fitted easily into the lock and the door swung smoothly open to reveal a small foyer and a set of concrete stairs leading upwards.

'The apartment must be up there, I guess,' Anna said, peering into the darkness above.

Renzo nodded. 'No sensible Venetian lives on the ground floor.'

'Really?'

'*Acqua alta* – the high tides,' he said. 'You could wake up and find the canal all around you.'

'Goodness.' Anna had heard about Venice's problem tides, but she'd never considered the practical realities.

'You should be fine upstairs,' Renzo added. 'Anyway, November is the worst month.'

Relieved, Anna climbed the stairs and another door opened to an interior that was a complete contrast to the rustic courtyard below. Modern and spacious and decorated in neutral tones, the apartment was obviously designed for space and practical comfort rather than atmosphere. After an initial pang of disappointment, Anna realised this was probably a sensible choice for five adults who were no longer used to living together.

'It certainly looks comfortable,' she said after a quick scrutiny of the gleaming kitchen benches and the dining area complete with chandelier.

'It's great,' said Renzo. 'My place is a shoebox by comparison.'

'Yeah, but you're not living with your entire family. I have to share a room with my sister. Speaking of which —' Anna headed across the living area to what she assumed was a bedroom doorway. 'Oh, God, talking of shoeboxes —' Anna's high spirits sank a little.

Cramped would best describe this room with two single beds that she and Ellie were expected to share. She hadn't shared a bedroom since she was ten, apart from six weeks when she was out of work and stony-broke and had slept on the floor in a friend's studio flat. She wasn't looking forward to having to divvy up this space now with her baby sister.

She had memories of being in her teens and finding Ellie such a nuisance, even though they were no longer sharing a room. Their dad had built an extension, providing Marc with his own bedroom and very own bathroom, which meant the girls got a room each. Even so, when Anna had been in her first school play and their mum had bought her special makeup, Ellie, who'd been about six or seven, had snuck into Anna's room, found the makeup and played with it, mixing the eye shadows into a muddy sludge and snapping off the lipstick. Her very first lipstick!

Sharing with Ellie after all this time was the one aspect of this holiday Anna had been disappointed about. Unfortunately, beggars couldn't be choosers.

She set her suitcase at the foot of the bed nearest the window and made sure she was smiling as she turned to Renzo. 'Now, I owe you a scrumptious Italian dinner.' In London she was mostly busy serving at tables, rather than dining, so she was ready to splurge this evening, especially when Renzo had been so helpful and generous with his time.

'Do you like seafood?' he asked.

'Does the pope wear a funny hat?'

The restaurant Renzo chose was hidden so far along a quiet canal that Anna could understand why tourists were unlikely to find it.

'It's one of the oldest *osteria* in Venice,' he told her. 'The seafood's excellent – everything from spaghetti cooked with black squid ink to mussels and grilled sea bass.'

It was indeed perfect, with tables covered with white cloths and candles in glass holders set beneath a pergola covered in vines and twinkling lights.

'If you think you'll be cold we can go inside.' Renzo gallantly pointed through a doorway to a cosy wood-panelled dining room.

'No, no, I'm fine, let's eat out here,' Anna insisted. 'It's a beautiful night.' She'd brought a jumper and Renzo had a jacket, and from here they could see the moon sailing high over the rooftops, while the water lapped gently against the canal wall.

All was quiet. The only sounds were the muted voices of diners, the clink of cutlery or the occasional gondola that passed, playing music from old romantic movies.

Anna, in heaven, was more than happy to let Renzo order the wine. It arrived, delivered by a jaw-droppingly handsome, dark-eyed waiter, and was rich, fruity and red and served in a carafe along with a small plate of bread and a dish of olive oil.

'*Ecco la bellissima Venezia.*' Renzo raised his glass to touch Anna's.

'To *bellissima Venezia*,' she repeated, carefully copying his pronunciation.

Taking a sip of delicious wine, she looked about her at the vines, at the twinkling lights, at the quiet canal and the rooftops limned in moonlight, and it was all so romantic, she almost wished her companion wasn't gay.

Renzo translated the menu and Anna paid close attention, trying to memorise as many Italian words as she could. It would be cool if she, in turn, could help her family, none of whom knew the language. She chose the pasta of the day, tagliatelle tossed with sea scallops and a bright green fresh herb pesto. The pesto was just light enough to let the scallops be the star and Anna couldn't remember the last time she'd eaten food so good.

'How clever of you to come to live and work here, instead of just heading back home,' she said and, again, she saw a look of quiet confidence shining in her friend's eyes. 'And I'm very impressed with your Italian,' Anna added as she twisted her fork to catch tasty strips of pasta. 'You've learned it so fast.'

'I'm still learning,' Renzo corrected. 'I've done a couple of beginner courses and I'm picking up new stuff all the time, but I still have a long way to go before I'm fluent. I've mostly been studying as much as I can about the art and music and history of the place. That's what I need as a tour guide. On the tours, I actually speak English most of the time.'

'And you love it.' It was a statement, not a question.

'I do, yeah.'

Nearby, on the canal, a young Venetian cruised past with rap music blaring. Anna smiled as she watched the white wake of his boat, but then a sigh broke from her. She hated to feel sorry for herself, but everything about this floating city seemed so much more exciting and fun than her own life.

She'd left Australia so brimming full of hope. But now . . .

'Dare I ask how things are going for you in London?' Renzo asked gently.

She pulled a face. 'Oh, just the same old, same old.'

His smile was sympathetic as he topped up their glasses.

After another sip or two, Anna set her glass down before she gave in to the temptation to swill the wine in one miserable gulp. 'Do you miss the acting?' The question felt suddenly, terribly important.

Renzo shrugged. 'To be honest, I think I'm still acting. At the very least, I reckon an acting background has helped my job here.'

This was a surprise. Anna had expected him to tell her that he didn't miss acting in the least. 'I suppose,' she said, thinking aloud, 'tour guides are still performing, aren't they?'

'I think so, yes. Each group of tourists is like a mini audience, and I guess I know how to put the right energy into my delivery. And I know how to read their faces, to judge —'

'Whether they're bored or totally engaged?' She couldn't help jumping in. 'Or when it's time to move on?'

'Yeah, all of that.'

'Of course. That makes so much sense. I imagine you'd be fabulous.' She could picture it so clearly – Renzo living in this amazing city and telling stories about it every day to a captive audience. Making the stories as amusing and interesting as possible. Working the crowd.

She'd be good at those things, too. She knew it.

'If you wanted to give it a go here, I could put in a good word for you,' Renzo said next.

Anna's heart thumped.

He'd obviously guessed the direction of her thoughts and, in that moment, all her doubts and insecurities about her life in London rushed back, a river in full flood. She was sorely tempted.

Any way she looked at her current career, it was down a very dark tube. The prospect of making a new life in Italy in a totally different field that still used her talents – not to mention her heritage – had instant, *massive* appeal. Renzo's offer was like a lifeline thrown to save her from drowning.

For all of five seconds, Anna's heart continued to race with excitement and hope. Then her head checked in, bringing a chilling dose of reality. In the morning her family were due to arrive and once they were here in Venice, her chances of surreptitiously investigating a job as a tour guide were zilch. Already she could hear their questions and comments.

Why would you want to do something as risky as that when you're such a hotshot actress?

Don't be so impetuous, Anna. Now's not the time, surely? Isn't your career taking off?

What do you know about the art or history of Venice? You can't even speak Italian.

'It was just a throwaway suggestion, sweetie.' Renzo spoke gently, as if he'd sensed her dilemma.

'Yes, I realise that.' Anna fiddled with the stem of her wine glass. 'But thanks, anyway. I've got to admit, I'm tempted.'

They sat for a minute, their gazes locked in mutual sympathy, like returned soldiers remembering the battles they'd fought and lost.

'Speaking of temptation,' Renzo said with a smile. 'Were you planning on having sweets?'

Out of habit, Anna almost said no. She was so used to having to think about her waistline. But now she remembered she was also hosting this dinner. 'Yes, of course, we must have sweets. What do you recommend?'

The handsome waiter was beckoned, and given the eye contact Anna observed, she suspected that Renzo had a crush on him. Then the menu under the enticing heading *Dolce* was examined. *Oh, my God.* Anna was sure she couldn't possibly choose between a hazelnut and fig gelato and a creamy, alcoholic tiramisu.

In the end she and Renzo ordered one of each and shared.

And after indulging in their sinful desserts, they drank *limoncello*, which was Anna's brainwave, and then they had another. By which time, Anna was so relaxed – okay, perhaps a little pissed – she told her amused companion about the quacking phone audition. Of course she acted out the pitiful scene with all the appropriate gestures and facial expressions and sound effects. And Renzo laughed so hard he could scarcely breathe.

Eventually, they finished with coffee, thick and black. And necessary. Anna paid with her credit card and slipped her arm through Renzo's as they walked back through the quiet streets.

'This has been amazing,' she said. 'How do you say "a perfect night" in Italian?'

'*Una notte perfetta.*'

'Yep. That's the one. *Una notte perfetta*. Even if the rest of this holiday goes pear shaped, I've had the best night, so *mucho apreciado*.'

'Now you're speaking Spanish.'

'You're lucky it isn't Double Dutch. I'm slightly drunk and kinda sad and just a bit nervous about the fam arriving.'

As Anna made this confession, something fell, almost hitting her before it crashed into the street.

'Shit.' She jumped back. 'What was that?'

White chunks of plaster lay shattered at her feet.

Renzo looked up at the ancient wall of the building beside them. 'It's fallen from up there,' he said, pointing.

Warily, Anna eyed a crumbling cornice.

'Happens here a lot, I'm afraid,' he said. 'The buildings are in a pretty bad state, so old and surrounded by so much water.'

He gave her arm an encouraging pat. 'You'll get used to it. And don't worry about your family. You'll feel differently in the morning.'

'You reckon?'

CHAPTER NINE

Bronte and Marc were the last to arrive at the apartment. The door was open, but there was no sign of anyone inside. A note, however, had been left on the kitchen bench, held in place by a vase of pink and orange poppies. Marc picked it up, read it in silence and handed it to Bronte.

Ciao, Bronte and Marc!

Mum and Ellie are jet-lagged and have hit the hay. I'm out buying a few groceries, but should be back soon. Make yourselves at home. Vino in the fridge and your room is upstairs. Enjoy the view.

Anna xxx

'We may as well take our things up,' Marc said. 'Give me your bag.' He spoke quietly, presumably to avoid disturbing the sleepers in nearby rooms.

'It's okay. I can manage.' Bronte's response was, perhaps, a little too sharp, but she was as tense as a bowstring.

During the fourteen-hour journey from San Francisco she and

Marc had spoken as little as possible, an undertaking that had been made easier by booking aisle seats one behind the other. Marc had spent most of the trip on his laptop, of course, while Bronte had read or watched movies.

'Bronte,' he said now, and she saw the flash of a challenge in his eyes, followed by an air of impatience as he held out his hand.

'Oh, all right.' She gave him the suitcase, rather ungraciously, but she was annoyed that he'd decided to play the helpful husband at this point, when he'd left her to manage her own luggage at the airports and on the vaporetto. Now, somewhat wearily, Bronte followed Marc up the winding stairs, wondering what they would find at the top.

They reached a small landing with an arched window that offered a view of a weeping willow leaning over a canal, no doubt a tributary of the main canal. Ahead of them a doorway presumably led to the bedroom. Marc stopped, standing with a suitcase in each hand, blocking Bronte's way.

'What's the matter?' She tried to peer around him and caught a glimpse of white ceilings striped by ancient timber beams. White walls. Even the timber floor seemed to be white.

'Nothing's the matter,' he said smoothly. 'It's great. Five-star.' He continued into the room and Bronte followed.

Straight away she saw the problem. The all-white room was dominated by a gigantic bed and, if there was a size bigger than king, this bed would qualify. Worse, it was covered by a mountain of heart-shaped cushions – cotton, satin, frilled, plain and embroidered.

The cushion in the middle bore the words *ti amo* in thick red satin stitch and although Bronte had limited Italian, she'd seen enough chick flicks to know what the words meant. *I love you.*

'Seems we scored the bridal suite,' Marc said dryly as he came to a halt at the end of the bed. 'Lucky us.'

Bronte let out an exaggerated, heavy sigh. She felt seriously depressed as she unwound the long scarf that had provided an extra layer of warmth during the flight. 'Yeah, lucky us.'

Setting the luggage down, Marc bent to lift the bedcover. 'Looks like there's two king singles pushed together. I guess we could separate them.'

'Why?'

He frowned his annoyance, lifted his hands in a gesture of helplessness. 'I assumed that's what you'd want.'

'Well, stop making assumptions without thinking things through, Marc. How long do you imagine we could sleep in separate beds without anyone in your family noticing?'

He glared at her.

'And don't give me that look.' With an angry huff, Bronte tossed her scarf onto a chair and folded her arms across her chest as she glared back at him. 'You're the one who wants to pretend everything's hunky dory between us. So what's the point of splitting the beds?'

'Okay, okay. You tell me how you want to do this.'

'The damn thing is so big, it makes it easier, doesn't it?'

'So you'll take one side and I'll have the other?'

'Of course. And we can pile all those pillows down the middle.'

'Like the Berlin Wall?'

'Exactly,' Bronte snapped, freshly annoyed by the spark of amusement that now lurked in his blue eyes.

She looked away and checked out the rest of their room. Huge mirrors covered one wall and a doorway in another wall led to an ensuite bathroom. Facing the bed were green shuttered doors, and on opening them she discovered a small, quaint balcony yielding yet another view of the willow and the quiet canal. The water was so still she could also see a perfect reflection of the willow's trailing branches against a background of faded terracotta walls and windowsills crowded with pot plants, a curved stone bridge complete with cupids.

The scene was truly beautiful.

Marc came a few paces behind Bronte. 'A room with a view,' he remarked with an unmissable note of sarcasm.

'Yes.' Daisy had been incredibly generous to give them this room. In fact, his mother had been incredibly generous to invite them to this remarkable city and Bronte wished she felt more grateful. Instead she felt guilty and decidedly uncomfortable about the charade that she'd agreed to.

'Do you want to change your mind about taking a rest now?' Marc asked.

'No, thank you.' After a fourteen-hour flight via Frankfurt, Bronte couldn't deny she was feeling pretty darn jet-lagged, but she was also sure she should try to stay awake till the evening. Most travel advice suggested this, and in their case, it made especially good sense for the two of them to be dog-tired when they hit the sack together for the first time in well over a month.

'Mum and Ellie are out to it,' he said, with another glance to the bed, as if he was ready to crash.

'They've come a lot further than we have. Their flight was something like twenty-two hours and God knows how many time zones they've crossed. I reckon we should hold off for as long as we can.'

From downstairs came the sound of a door opening and footsteps on tiles. Probably Anna, back from her shopping.

'We should go down and say hello,' said Marc.

'You go.' Bronte was fighting a flash of panic. 'I'll be down in a minute or two. I need to freshen up.'

'You're okay, aren't you?' Marc's concern, which seemed genuine, was almost her undoing.

'Yes, of course.'

He stood watching her for longer than was necessary before turning to leave. Unexpectedly shaken, Bronte went through to the ensuite bathroom, washed her face, brushed her hair and cleaned her teeth. Redid her makeup.

Marc had left the door open and voices drifted up from below. Marc and Anna greeted each other warmly. Then Daisy.

'Marc, darling, you're safely here. How wonderful. How's Bronte?'

Marc's voice, explaining. 'She's fine. She'll be down in a minute.'

'Poor thing.' Daisy was full of sympathy. 'She's probably exhausted. Perhaps she should rest?'

'No, she's fine.'

'If she's having a shower, you'd better warn her,' Anna called out. 'The water takes ages to heat up.'

'Thanks, but she'll be down in a sec.'

'Do you like your room?'

'Mum, it's amazing. Perfect. Thank you.'

Then Ellie's voice coming from further away, from another room perhaps. Her words were indistinct, but she sounded grouchy, as if she'd been woken before she was ready. Whatever she said, however, was greeted by laughter, so clearly she'd managed to amuse them.

Bronte turned to her reflection in the mirror. Freshly made up, she certainly looked better. She only wished she felt better too. She needed more time and head space to improve her mood. Minutes earlier, fighting with her husband had felt all too easy. Almost natural.

If she was going to spend the next fortnight pretending that she and Marc were problem-free and still blissfully in love, she was going to have to be as good an actor as Anna. Bronte only hoped her nerves were up to the challenge.

In the meantime, she was on borrowed time. When this holiday was over, the Benetto family would once again go their separate ways. She would return to Silicon Valley to pack her bags for Australia and there was a good chance that by then they would hate her.

CHAPTER TEN

With nightfall, the world beyond the apartment's windows receded. Clouds hid the moon and rain fell, streaking the smooth surface of the canal and making street lights fuzzy. Daisy, ensconced in a comfortable armchair inside the cosy, brightly lit apartment, a glass of red wine in hand, looked around her with deep satisfaction.

Her children had insisted that she mustn't do a thing this evening and now Anna and Bronte were at the island kitchen bench, Anna diligently peeling prawns in the sink, while Bronte chopped fresh herbs to add to the pasta sauce that was already simmering on the stove. A large pot of water was close to the boil.

Marc had offered to help, but had been shooed away. Thus dismissed, he'd found glasses and poured wine, which he handed around along with a plate of olives and cheese. Meanwhile, Ellie, cross-legged on the sofa, was hunting through a pile of CDs, searching for music she deemed suitable.

Daisy smiled. This was exactly what she'd hoped for . . .

Here we are, Leo. All of us in Venice at last. Wish you were here, too, my darling man . . .

She wondered if he knew.

Could he sense her presence here in the city where he'd lived for twenty-three years?

It was useless to wish for the impossible, but she couldn't help imagining an alternative scenario with her husband at her side. If only his heart attack had been less severe, something that could be overcome with surgery perhaps, or medication, nursing and physiotherapy.

Daisy knew that under such circumstances she would have looked after Leo beautifully and he would have been extremely disciplined about any exercise or diet regime the medicos advised. It was so unfair that he'd been denied even a little time to enjoy his retirement, to sit in the backyard and admire the beauty of the white tabebuia he'd planted right at the start of their marriage.

How differently they might have spent those final days, if only they'd known . . .

A backyard barbecue with friends, a walk at dusk along the seashore, a night of wine and lovemaking . . .

Oh, Leo . . .

Grief speared Daisy's chest, arriving so fiercely she doubled in two.

Gasping, she felt her eyes and throat fill with tears. She blinked hard, blinked again and hoped that no one had heard her or noticed.

A deep breath helped. Fighting for calm, she gathered her dignity, told herself that she mustn't let any cracks show. She took a fortifying sip of wine, settled deeper into her comfy chair and willed herself to stay strong.

At least none of the others seemed to have noticed her 'moment'. Ellie was still absorbed in shuffling through CDs. Anna and Bronte were busy in the kitchen and if Marc, who appeared to be distracted by his phone, had noticed anything, he wasn't letting on.

With her peace restored, Daisy smiled indulgently at her tribe. All three of her children had Leo's dark hair and olive complexion, but their differences were also quite distinct. Marc's face was narrower than Leo's had been and his eyes were the same blue as Daisy's, a striking contrast against his tanned skin. Anna's eyes were dark, but she was surprisingly petite, no doubt taking after Leo's mother.

Anna wore her hair in an artistic bob, cropped short on one side, while curls hung to her jawline on the other, while Ellie, tall and loose limbed, reminding Daisy of her own dad's lanky build, had let her hair grow long and a little wild, curling past her shoulders.

In complete contrast to this trio was Bronte, with beautiful coppery hair, straight as a pin, the pale skin of a true redhead, and the most bewitching deep dimple in one cheek. Daisy was impatient for Marc and Bronte to start a family. How fascinating it would be to see which of their parents' very different features the children inherited.

'This music's all so ancient.' Ellie's voice cut into Daisy's musings. Her daughter gave a helpless shake of her head. 'Dean Martin, for f—'

Ellie held back from swearing, much to Daisy's relief, but she let out a noisy sigh. 'There's only Barry Manilow, Pavarotti and a whole host of classical.'

Anna looked up from her pile of shelled prawns. 'Shouldn't we play Vivaldi, seeing we're in Venice?'

'He was certainly Venetian,' Bronte agreed. 'But please, not *The Four Seasons*. It's been done to death.'

Ellie pulled a face. 'There's a ton of his other violin concertos.'

'Give them a go,' chipped in Marc.

Ellie clearly hadn't lost her respect for her big brother. With a small shrug of resignation, she slipped a CD into the player and within moments the apartment was filled with lively strings at their jauntiest. 'Well, at least it's upbeat,' Ellie said, holding her wine glass out for a refill.

'I think Vivaldi's perfect for tonight.' Daisy, now sunk in deep cushions and munching on cheese, let the cheerful music flow around her and was relieved to feel the grief retreating.

Content once more, she tapped a foot to the beat and watched Bronte at the stove, adding herbs to sautéed tomatoes, onions and garlic.

The decision to eat in tonight had been unanimous, assisted by the fact that Anna, bless her, had assumed the travellers might have little energy for exploring or eating out, and had, judiciously, procured provisions.

She'd discovered a shop that apparently sold pasta of every shape and size and colour and had gleefully bought three varieties. At another place that specialised in cheese, she'd bought parmesan and pecorino, while the fresh prawns had come from a *pescivendolo* and the sauce ingredients from local markets.

She had wanted to cook the whole meal, but Bronte had insisted on helping and Marc had ducked out for the wine, which he'd found at a little bar just around the corner.

And now, as Ellie set the table and Marc refilled glasses, Daisy told herself that everything was wonderful, with – just as she'd hoped – the family relaxed and happy to be together at last. Tomorrow, refreshed, they would be ready for adventures. They would spend the day exploring churches, galleries, markets and squares and would lunch sumptuously at a beautiful café beside a canal.

Daisy told herself that if anything seemed a trifle offbeat this evening, if there was any small vibe of tension, it could be put down to jet lag. Okay, so maybe there hadn't been much light-hearted chatter, with everyone falling over each other to share their news, but she was silly to imagine anything truly amiss. It wasn't so surprising that her children were trying hard, concentrating on pleasing her. They were simply falling into old patterns as families often did when they came back together.

Daisy could remember when her three were still in primary school, all competing to present her with the most glittering and creative handmade card for her birthday or Mother's Day. Tonight was simply the grown-up equivalent.

She mustn't spoil this first special evening by worrying.

Anna and Bronte were getting on beautifully as they prepared dinner together and Marc seemed perfectly content circling with the wine and his platter of snacks.

As for Ellie – who'd been quiet and almost subdued on the long flight and had spent her arrival in Venice madly snapping photos with her phone that she instantly sent whizzing elsewhere – Daisy had expected from the outset that her youngest might be a tad difficult.

Ellie was still a teenager after all, although Daisy had to admit she was a little disappointed that her daughter didn't seem to truly appreciate how very fortunate she was to be travelling overseas at such a young age.

What was it with young people these days? They seemed so . . . old. What had happened to youthful curiosity and excited wonder?

She supposed the internet was to blame. It seemed to be the cause of most problems for Millennials. Perhaps young people felt they already knew everything anyway, or could find it out with a few flicks of their thumbs on their phones.

Daisy could never work out how they typed like that with their thumbs flying. She could only manage texting with one finger and even then she was slow and clumsy.

Then again, perhaps 'lurve' was Ellie's problem? Daisy had next to no idea about her daughter's social life. Ellie had never chatted to her in the confiding way that Anna had in high school. It was always possible that Ellie might be missing a secret boyfriend.

Daisy wondered if Anna might be able to help. She was only five years older than Ellie, although so far, the girls were behaving more like polite acquaintances than close sisters. And that room they had to share was disappointingly poky. It hadn't looked so small on the internet. Simonetta's photographer had clearly used a wide-angle lens. She hoped the girls didn't mind.

Stop it. Stop worrying. Everything's fine.

Leo would be mad at her for fretting. He would no doubt tell her that Ellie simply needed to work out what she wanted to do with her life.

Daisy had been similarly at sea in her youth, of course, until she'd discovered her green thumb's earning capacity. Her own parents had urged her to do something meaningful like teaching or nursing, but she'd floated through several casual positions until she'd landed her first job with a landscape gardener.

In the end, she'd found huge satisfaction in helping others to create lovely gardens and it had boosted her confidence no end to realise how little some people knew about keeping plants alive.

'Grub's up!' Anna announced cheerfully, cutting into her mother's thoughts.

It was only then, as she heaved herself out of the chair, that Daisy realised how desperately tired she was. They were all tired, of course. But there were sensational smells, red wine, and the Benettos all under one roof. In Venice. Life was good.

CHAPTER ELEVEN

Ellie couldn't sleep. She'd stopped checking the time on her phone, and she'd given up counting the boats passing on the canal outside, but she knew she'd been tossing and turning for hours.

In the next bed, mere inches away, Anna groaned.

'Sorry,' Ellie said. 'I can't sleep.'

'No kidding,' Anna muttered.

Ellie sat up. 'I probably should have had more wine with dinner.'

'You're only eighteen.' Now Anna sounded wide awake too, and straight into bossy big sister mode. 'Grog's not the answer. Your problem is jet lag. You spent half the afternoon sleeping and now your body clock's out of whack.'

Thanks for the lecture, sis. 'I'll go and lie on the sofa,' Ellie said. 'So I don't disturb you.'

When Anna didn't respond, Ellie threw off her bedclothes and swung her legs over the edge.

'No, don't go,' Anna said quickly. 'Mum will only start worrying that we're not getting on or something.'

Which was more than likely the truth. Ellie was all too aware that their mum was desperate for this holiday to be a roaring success. 'I feel bad about keeping you awake.'

'I don't mind if you want to read,' Anna said.

'Thanks, but I don't think it'll work.' Ellie had tried reading on the plane. It had made her tired and irritable, but hadn't helped her to nod off. She'd been better off listening to music with earbuds, but she wasn't in the mood for that now. She needed sleep!

She tried to settle down again, rearranged the sheet and the doona over her, banged the pillow into shape.

Anna's voice came through the darkness. 'So Mum seems pretty okay. But how's she been coping since Dad died, really? I could never quite tell when she talked on the phone.'

Surprised, Ellie wasn't sure how to answer this. She and Anna had never been especially close, the way sisters were supposed to be. The age gap was partly to blame, and Anna's teenage years when she'd still lived at home had been crazily busy. Even back then, her life had been filled with constant rehearsals, always preparing for high-school productions, or for plays with the local drama club. And after she'd left home, she'd mostly communicated with their parents.

Now, Ellie found the unfamiliarity of being alone with her sister for the first time in years rather awkward. Actually, the whole family seemed a bit strained. Even at dinner this evening, the conversation had been stilted.

Apart from Anna telling them about her friend Renzo, who was working here in Venice as a tour guide and had all sorts of great sightseeing tips, talk over dinner had mostly entailed their mum asking questions of the others and getting only the vaguest of answers, and then her filling them in with lame gossip about family friends and neighbours back home.

The Benetto siblings now knew who in Castaways Beach was getting divorced, who'd been in hospital and who was moving interstate, but there'd been very little news about London or Silicon Valley.

And now, out of the blue, or rather, out of the darkness, Anna was asking about their mother and Ellie was remembering the horror weeks after the funeral when their mother had barely functioned.

'It's been tough for her,' she said. 'She was a mess for ages, but she's so much better now than she used to be. It was pretty bad at first.'

'Was it?' Anna sounded worried. 'What kind of bad?'

Ellie thought about the especially scary afternoon, not long after the funeral, when she'd come home from school and found her mum still in her dressing gown, sitting in the kitchen with breakfast bowls and coffee mugs on the bench unwashed, as if she hadn't moved all day, but had simply sat there, staring out into the backyard.

She hadn't even responded at first when Ellie had spoken to her. In a panic, Ellie had rung her mother's friend Freya, who'd rushed straight over and then organised an appointment with their GP. Dr Miller had prescribed anti-depressants and it hadn't been too long after that when her mother had reached a kind of turning point. Luckily, those days were behind them now.

'She was in a kind of daze for a while there,' Ellie said now, not wanting to get bogged down in too many details. 'She's still taking anti-depressants.'

'The poor thing,' Anna said softly. 'Ellie, why didn't you ring me? I could have come home and helped.'

'There wasn't much you could have done, really. And Mum didn't want me to bother you.'

'But I'm her daughter, too.'

There was no mistaking the hurt in Anna's voice. Ellie didn't like to remind her sister that she could have picked up the phone at any time to ask these questions.

'You know what Mum's like,' she said instead. 'So proud of you and your achievements and everything.'

Silence followed this.

Aware that her sister might still feel hurt, Ellie felt compelled to add, 'Mum didn't tell Marc either. She didn't want to worry either of you. And her besties, Freya and Jo, were fantastic. They cooked casseroles and brought wine around and stayed with her for nice long chats, or they took her out for walks on the beach, lunch at Noosa or movies. Stuff like that.'

'Still. I really had no idea.'

'Yeah, well . . .' Ellie wasn't totally guilt-free either. She'd probably spent more time shut away in her room studying than had been strictly necessary.

Actually, before her father's sudden and untimely death, Ellie had been on track to become a full-on rebellious teenager, fighting with her parents over everything – clothes, food, the colour of her bedroom walls, where she went and how she got there. Losing her dad had forcibly yanked her off her self-absorbed planet. And watching her mum fall apart and then be helped by her friends had been both awesome and eye-opening. A true wake-up call.

Her dad's death had also taught Ellie about the importance of making the most of her life, of making the right choices and not just drifting into a career path because others, namely teachers and parents, thought it might suit her.

'Anyway, Mum's pretty good now,' she told Anna. 'And she's so excited about this holiday. Having us all together.'

'We'd better make sure it works then, hadn't we?'

'Yeah.' Ellie was wide awake now, but it still felt weird to be having a conversation in pitch darkness. Since the rain, there wasn't a trace of moonlight creeping around the shuttered windows.

'You haven't told us much about your work,' she said to Anna, deciding she might as well dive in with a question or two of her own.

But Anna didn't answer straight away and when she did, she sounded cautious. 'To be honest, there's not a whole lot to tell about endless rehearsals.'

Really? Did this mean that her sister had stopped enjoying the acting life? Or was this Anna's code for 'don't pry'?

Before Ellie could think of a suitable response, Anna said, 'You've been pretty quiet, too. You haven't told us about your plans for the future.'

Here we go. Even though Ellie had been braced for this exact question, she couldn't hold back a heavy sigh. 'I was hoping you wouldn't start on that subject the minute I got here.'

'No need to get salty. I was only trying to show an interest.'

'Mmm,' was all Ellie could manage.

'I care, you know, sis.' Anna might have been acting, but she managed to sound genuine.

And it *was* a fair enough question, Ellie supposed. She just wished she had a satisfactory answer. 'I'm on a gap year,' she said defensively. 'I'm taking a complete break and I'll make the big decisions when I'm good and ready.'

'Okay. Message received.'

From Anna's bed came the sound of movements as if she was getting more comfortable. Conversation over.

'So, how's your love life?' Anna asked.

Ellie's face flamed. She was glad of the darkness now, totally sideswiped by this new query and shocked by the sudden turmoil inside her. 'I don't have a love life.'

'Go on. I don't believe that.'

'I'm serious.' Ellie was glad her mother's bedroom was safely on the far side of the apartment, separated from theirs by the living area and almost certainly out of hearing range.

She didn't want Anna to think she was a total loser, though, so she said, 'I'm on the lookout for a cute Italian guy.'

It was more or less the truth. Ellie had already stolen a sneaky snapshot on her phone of a super-cute Italian chap with coal black hair and dark eyes to match, designer stubble and ripped Giorgio Armani jeans. He'd been reading a paperback novel at San Marco airport and she'd sent the pic to Zach.

The local scenery, she'd texted as an accompaniment.

Zach had texted back. *Beard, glasses and reading a book. Adorkable?*

Her friend was such a smart-arse.

'Italian men are certainly hot,' Anna agreed. 'A good proportion of them, at any rate.' A smile warmed her voice now. 'So yeah, that's an ambition worth working on.'

'What about you?' Ellie felt emboldened to ask.

'What do you mean?'

Another avoidance tactic? Ellie persisted. 'How's *your* love life?'

This was met by more annoying silence. From outside came the sound of rainwater dripping from leaky guttering. Ellie wasn't going to let her sister off the hook.

'Anna?'

'By a strange coincidence, I'm fancy-free too.'

Something about this sounded off to Ellie. If her intuition was correct, her glamorous sister was either pulling her leg, or someone had broken her heart. Anna was truly beautiful with lustrous, dark, naturally wavy hair and a vivacious face that always turned heads. On her last trip home, she'd hinted at an awesome social life, rubbing shoulders with famous actors and showbiz celebs.

'But you've had plenty of boyfriends?' Ellie asked.

'None worth keeping.'

Anna's tone was almost offhand, careless even, but Ellie, listening carefully, was sure she caught an underlying note of desolation. Again, she wasn't sure how to respond.

Anna sighed. 'A word of warning from the older and now wiser, Ellie Belly. Remember to check whether the guys you date are married.'

'Sounds like you're speaking from experience.'

Anna let out another sigh, heavier and sadder.

'How long were you going out with him before he told you?'

'He didn't tell me. I found out the hard way – friends and the internet.'

'That's messed up.'

'Yeah, it was royally messed up.' Anna didn't try to hide the pain in her voice now. 'But let's leave it at that. I'd rather not go into details, if you don't mind.'

'Yeah, sure.' But Ellie was wider awake than ever now, and while she was sympathetic to Anna's plight, she was also bursting with curiosity. 'Can I ask about all that "me too" stuff? Have you had any problems with that? With directors or whatever trying to seduce you?'

'Jeez, Ellie, you're coming on heavy with the questions.'

'Sorry.' Ellie supposed she'd gone a step too far, especially for the first night. She was tempted, though, to say, *Cos I care, you know, sis*, using the same concerned tone Anna had used to kickstart this conversation. But she didn't want to piss her sister off.

She waited. Maybe, if she shut up, Anna might volunteer something. But when the silence continued, she couldn't contain her curiosity a moment longer. 'Did some bastard try it on with you?' she whispered.

'Only the one,' Anna responded quietly.

A shocked gasp broke from Ellie. She turned towards the other bed and wished she could see her sister. 'What was he like?' she whispered. 'Was he ugly? Did you tell him to get knotted?'

Anna let out a grunt of annoyance. 'This was a very bad idea, starting a conversation with you in the middle of the night.'

'But you can't tell me something like that and leave me hanging.'

'Course I can.'

'I'll never get to sleep.'

Another sigh followed. 'If you really must know, he was actually drop-dead gorgeous and we had a raging affair.'

'You're joking.'

'I wish I was.'

'Bloody hell.'

'He was hot as hell, clever and charming, and I fell for the whole package. Oh, and of course, I was dead-set certain I was going to land the lead role in the brand-new West End play he was directing. For a little while there, I was in heaven. We met for three separate dates before I discovered he was married. But by then I was . . .'

'In love?' Ellie supplied when Anna left the sentence dangling.

'More deeply than you could possibly believe.'

Ellie shivered as she heard the depth of emotion in her sister's voice. 'And you kept seeing him?'

'For a couple of months, even though I knew it was —' Anna let out yet another, even heavier sigh. 'You get the picture. He tried to tell me how unhappy he was with her – his wife. The whole thing was such a cliché.'

Ellie knew it was probably time to discreetly shut up. If she was braver, she would reach over and touch Anna. Give her a consoling pat on the arm, even a sisterly hug, but she felt too shy and awkward. They'd lost that kind of closeness.

But, of course, she couldn't hold back on a final question. 'Dare I ask if you still got the part?'

'What do you think?'

'Anna, that's awful. I'm so sorry.'

'Yeah, well, you live and learn, et cetera. It's all in the past and, if nothing else, I'm older and wiser.'

'I don't suppose Mum knows.'

'God no, and don't you dare tell her.'

'I wouldn't. Of course I wouldn't. You can trust me, honestly.'

'Yes, I know,' Anna said more gently. 'But that's officially enough for one night. Go to sleep.'

Ellie wasn't confident about her chances of nodding off, but she rolled over and closed her eyes. It was kinda comforting to know that her big sister wasn't quite as perfect and bulletproof as Ellie had always believed. And somehow she didn't feel quite so immature and foolish about sending that pic to Zach. Maybe she'd relax now and catch some *zzzs* after all.

CHAPTER TWELVE

When Bronte woke, she was snuggled close to her husband's warm, broad back and she lay that way for quite a few moments, enjoying the drowsy interlude between sleep and total awareness.

Half asleep, she paid no attention to the strange surroundings, the enormous bed, the cushions scattered hither and yon. She was simply snug and peacefully conscious that she'd indulged in long hours of refreshing sleep.

Her left leg was hooked over Marc's bare legs in a loose, casual coupling and she was about to cuddle closer, to slip her arm around his waist, when church bells, loud and summoning, pealed outside. Opening her eyes, she took in the creamy light of morning, the strange bed and the floor-to-ceiling mirrors, the shuttered doors, where brighter light glittered around the edges.

Venice. *Oh, God.*

Bronte's heart leapt and then hammered stronger than the bells as she whipped away from Marc. How could she have forgotten she was in Italy? That their marriage was, for all intents and purposes, over?

And what had happened to their Berlin Wall?

Warm under the doona, Marc was clad in nothing more than boxer shorts, while she, thank goodness, was still wearing the totally respectable, long-legged, long-sleeved, button-down pyjamas that she'd changed into last night behind the closed ensuite door. She'd stayed in the bathroom so long that Marc had been asleep, or at least making a good pretence of sleeping, by the time she'd come to bed.

It had all seemed perfectly safe. How on earth had she ended up wrapped around him? Had he noticed?

Dismayed, Bronte jumped out of bed and hurried around its foot, dodging the cushions now scattered on the floor, as she made her way to the safety of the ensuite.

'What time is it?' Marc's sleepy voice reached her from the bed.

'I've no idea. I haven't checked.' Bronte glanced at the light forcing its way around the edges of the shutters. 'But it's probably quite late.' As if to confirm this, the church bells rang again. She went to the French doors, pushed them open and bright sunshine flooded the room, bringing with it the scent of verbena that climbed a trellis attached to the wall below.

She saw the willow tree and the canal, the ancient church steeple with its chiming bell, the bridge and, above it, a flock of pigeons fluttering against a sky washed pale and clean by the rain. Across the canal, construction workers yelled and banged as they erected scaffolding around an old stone building.

Marc, still in bed, reached for his phone.

Of course. Back to reality.

'It's half past eight,' he said.

Not too late then. To Bronte's surprise, he put the phone back on the night stand without checking his emails.

'How'd you sleep?' he asked.

'Fine, thanks.' Was there a hint of a smile in his eyes? Had he been aware that she'd snuggled so close? She hoped he wouldn't mention the disintegrated Berlin Wall.

To her relief, he said, 'I can smell coffee.'

'Yes.' Bronte could smell it, too, drifting from below.

'I'll go down and fetch us some if you like.' His eyes glowed with disturbing warmth and friendliness.

Bronte hesitated. Under normal circumstances, coffee in bed on the first day of their holiday would be blissful. Actually, there'd been a time in the early years when they wouldn't have even bothered with coffee. They would have been too busy rolling in the sack, passion-crazed and madly in love. But that was before the realities of their new life had worn her down.

Now . . . Bronte shook her head, rejecting the coffee suggestion. 'I need to get dressed. I'll use the bathroom first if that's okay.'

'Sure.' Marc's voice was tight, his gaze hardened.

She had almost reached the sanctuary of the bathroom when a gentle knock sounded on the bedroom door.

'Who is it?' Marc called.

'Me, Anna. Are you guys decent?'

'Sure.' Shooting Bronte a sharp, challenging glance, he called, 'Hang on, Anna. I'm coming.'

He opened the door to reveal his sister, bright and smiling, dressed in jeans and a crimson sweater and carrying a tray with a coffee pot, mugs and a small platter.

'I thought I'd spoil you two with breakfast in bed on your first morning.'

'Wow, that's very thoughtful of you. Thanks.' Marc sounded genuinely delighted as he accepted the tray.

'It's just coffee and little offerings from the *pasticceria* around the corner,' Anna said.

'Sounds perfect,' Marc assured her. 'Really good of you to bother.'

Anna's gaze flashed from her brother clad in nothing but his boxers to Bronte in her safe, striped, neck-to-ankle pyjamas. She must have found the contrast in their attire interesting, but she was too polite to comment.

Nevertheless, Bronte was rattled and she wished she'd had the good sense to duck into the bathroom before Marc let his sister in. Actually, the most sensible thing she could have done was to refuse to come on this holiday. She could now foresee endless difficulties piling on top of each other over the next two weeks.

At least Anna departed quickly. Marc nudged the door shut with his elbow and set the tray on a small side table.

'The coffee smells good,' he commented.

'Shouldn't you put some clothes on?'

He turned to Bronte, eyebrows raised. As their gazes connected, his smile faded and his expression soured, and without another word, he went to the chair in the corner where he'd left his jeans and hauled them on, wrenching the zip in the fly upwards and snapping the press stud at the waist. Then he rummaged through his as yet unpacked suitcase and found a long-sleeved grey T-shirt.

Throughout this procedure, Bronte remained motionless, riveted to the spot by a strange, inexplicable misery.

In silence, Marc returned to the tray, picked up the coffee pot and began to pour. He handed her a mug.

'Thanks.' The coffee smelled rich and tempting and yet she knew it would curdle in her churning stomach.

'Just one question,' he said, watching her with a cool, steady gaze. 'While we were separated – did it help? Did you feel any better?'

Bronte opened her mouth to answer, but she couldn't confess the truth, that she'd spent the whole time feeling empty and lost and uselessly longing for the impossible – that her husband would miraculously change.

Clutching her mug in two hands, she gave a helpless, frustrated shrug. 'It wasn't long enough. I didn't really get a chance to – to adjust —'

Marc didn't seem too impressed by her answer. Without another word, he selected an S-shaped almond cookie from the plate and took it, with his coffee, onto the little balcony. There, with his back to her, he stared out at the view.

Didn't he have a gazillion emails to check?

Bronte almost called out to him. Perhaps an argument would help, bring things out in the open, clear the air. Except that everyone downstairs would hear. Instead, she selected a small brioche with a dab of melted chocolate in its centre. It looked delicious, but she'd lost her appetite.

Setting it down again beside her untouched coffee, she went through to the bathroom to shower and wash her hair, and beneath the streaming water, she let hopeless tears flow.

The family had agreed that they should have complete freedom to explore and enjoy Venice however they wished, but they would spend this first morning together. They would start by checking out the most obvious tourist attractions such as St Mark's Square at the mouth of the Grand Canal, as well as its famous basilica, the Doge's Palace and the Bridge of Sighs.

Bronte, walking sedately beside Marc, was determined to shake off the morning's unsettling start. *Stay strong.*

She concentrated on soaking up the beauty of their amazing surroundings. With so much time-worn grandeur and the intriguing, beautiful waterways, it wasn't too hard to set aside her personal worries and to drink in the enchanting atmosphere. The gondolas, the interesting bridges and the romantic architecture of Venice were all completely charming, but she found the people fascinating, too.

Tourists wandered everywhere, of course, queueing for the vaporetto, poring over maps, taking a multitude of photographs.

Their noisy excitement or quiet enchantment were equally perceptible, but Bronte was even more intrigued by the residents of Venice. With no wide roads or vehicles of any description, their lifestyles were different from anything she'd ever experienced.

Instead of loading a week's shopping into the backs of their cars, even elderly people trundled two-wheeled carts, large enough to carry the day's groceries and small enough to pull over the steps on the many pedestrian bridges. Others leaned from windows to hang washing on an intricate network of clotheslines, or to lower bags with their day's rubbish, which they left dangling to await the collection boat.

Bronte also enjoyed seeing the men and women gathered in cafés, drinking coffee and conversing volubly and with an energetic waving of hands, no doubt discussing politics or other matters of local importance. And then there were the market stall vendors enthusiastically yet patiently selling their fruit and vegetables and fish.

Venice was another world, unique, almost dreamlike, enveloping her in its beauty and more than a thousand years of history. For Bronte, it was the perfect antidote to the twenty-first-century, tech-crazy, permanent adolescence of Silicon Valley that she was so desperate to escape.

Daisy and her offspring were similarly awestruck and the family was so busy taking everything in that conversation was limited. Daisy, smiling, almost floating, seemed perfectly happy to go with the flow, as if just being here with her family was all that mattered.

Ellie was the keenest photographer, using her phone to snap away constantly, especially when they reached the San Marco Basin with gondolas in rows along the shoreline and the island of San Giorgio Maggiore in the background. Anna, meanwhile, paid commendable attention to a guide book, passing on historical details she thought might be of interest.

Anna was particularly taken with the Bridge of Sighs which had been built to join the amazing Doge's Palace to the Prigioni or prison. The sighs were supposedly made by the prisoners as they passed the tiny latticed windows in the bridge and caught their last glimpse of Venice before their incarceration, although Anna admitted there seemed to be some doubt about the authenticity of this claim.

'But listen to this,' she said, dramatically beckoning to her family to come closer, as if she was on stage in a pantomime. 'If a couple in a gondola kiss when they pass under this bridge at sunset and while the bells of St Mark's are tolling, their love will last forever.' Of course, she made a point of winking at Marc and Bronte.

And naturally, Bronte's face burst into flames. She didn't dare catch Marc's eye.

'Is that all they have to do?' piped up Ellie's cheeky voice. 'Surely it can't be as easy as that? Are you sure they don't have to be dressed in green and have two white doves land on the gondolier's head?'

Everyone laughed and Bronte, grateful for the distraction, could have kissed Ellie.

Mid-morning they stopped at a gelateria.

'Oh, I've got to try one of these,' Ellie exclaimed, eyeing the range of brightly coloured ices.

They had fun choosing flavours – apple, pear, blueberry watermelon. Bronte selected ginger, which was called *zenzero*, coloured white, and totally delicious.

Marc's choice was pistachio, despite its unattractive grey-green colour.

'It tastes great,' he assured Bronte, when she pulled a face. And then he held the gelato out to her. 'Try it and see for yourself.'

He had already taken a bite. The shape of his mouth on the pistachio ice was clear and Bronte almost shot him a dirty look for putting her in such an awkwardly intimate situation in front of his family. Just in time, she curbed the urge.

'No thanks,' she said instead. 'I'm happy with my *zenzero*.' But then she caught the expression on Anna's face – a kind of wary vigilance. If she wasn't careful, Anna would see through their charade on this very first day of the holiday and Daisy's happy plans would be completely ruined.

For Daisy's sake . . .

Bronte submitted. 'Oh, all right,' she responded as graciously as she could manage. 'I'll try it.' Fixing a smile, she stepped closer and lifted her chin, opening her lips to accept Marc's offering.

For a heartbeat her gaze met her husband's and the emotion shimmering in Marc's eyes almost made her gasp.

Don't do this, she pleaded silently. *Play fair* . . .

She looked down and, of necessity, concentrated her attention on the khaki-coloured ice. Marc obliged by turning the cone to offer her the untouched side and she leaned in to take a dainty bite.

The pistachio was probably as tasty as he'd claimed, but Bronte was too disconcerted to notice. Too aware of his proximity. Almost touching now, chest to chest, she caught the still familiar scent of his aftershave, and her cheeks were burning with embarrassment and the stress of their guilty secret.

As the cool ice slid down her throat, she glanced up again and found that Marc was still watching her. His blue eyes were too shiny and his mouth was tilted crookedly in a sad little smile. To Bronte's horror, her knees gave way.

Luckily, he caught her when she stumbled, holding her in a one-armed hug, close against his chest. Embarrassed, she buried her face in the grey knit of his sweater and heard his heart pounding.

Oh, God. This was too hard. How was she ever going to get through a whole fortnight?

'Look at you two love birds,' cooed Ellie.

Marc lowered his mouth to whisper in Bronte's ear. 'You're doing great,' he murmured. 'Thank you.'

CHAPTER THIRTEEN

Daisy had her heart set on lunch at an outdoor café beside a quiet canal. She had no particular café in mind, just so long as there was the right amount of ambience and a canal-side setting, preferably with gondolas passing by.

'I've been picturing all of us dining somewhere lovely and atmospheric ever since I first came up with the idea for this holiday,' she told the others. 'Let's do it today, while the weather's so lovely.'

And while we're getting on so well, she added silently. Not that she had any real fears about family squabbles, but you never knew...

Fortunately, everyone was happy with the plan and Marc, using the internet on his phone, was the first to find a suitable place. No surprises there. He showed Daisy photos of a café, which looked absolutely ideal, and then guided them there using his Maps app.

The only downside of this venture was that it involved quite a lot of walking to reach the restaurant and Daisy was aware of a nagging twinge in her left knee that threatened to become worse. She hoped it wasn't the beginnings of arthritis. Her feet were sore, too.

She knew all the walking required in Venice had to be good for her, but she was afraid she would have to wear more sensible shoes if she was to keep up with the young ones. She'd never been fond of the sneakers look with smart clothes, but perhaps it was time to let comfort win out over vanity.

At least, when they eventually found the restaurant, it was everything Daisy had hoped for. Filling a long narrow space beside a quiet canal and separated from the water by wrought-iron railings, the café's setting was picture perfect.

The surrounding buildings were of different colours – bright yellow, terracotta, pale green – and these were invariably decorated with painted shutters and window boxes overflowing with bright flowers. To add to the perfection, gondolas were moored close by and tied to green and white candy-striped poles.

'Oh, isn't it lovely? Well done, Marc,' Daisy declared. 'I don't remember ever seeing pink tablecloths in a restaurant before. Isn't it interesting how little touches make such a difference?'

The rest of the family were clearly not quite as taken by the pink tablecloths. They merely shrugged and smiled, as if their mother was a dotty but sweet relative, who needed to be indulged.

Oh, dear, Daisy thought. *I suppose that's exactly what I am.*

It had already occurred to her that if she travelled overseas again, she might ask Freya and Jo if they were interested in joining her. It was bound to be easier with companions of her own generation. Not that she didn't love being with the family, of course.

A dark-eyed young man, strikingly handsome and reminding her a little of how Leo had looked many years ago, asked them to wait – *un momento por favor* – while he rearranged a table setting to accommodate the five of them. Then they were seated, poring over menus, chatting, laughing, enjoying the scenery and the gentle sunshine.

Perfect.

A young woman who spoke English came to serve them and she suggested they might like to try Bellinis, an Italian drink combining prosecco with peach juice.

'That sounds just the thing for lunchtime,' Daisy decided. 'I'm afraid I can't handle a heavy red in the middle of the day.'

Luckily, Bronte, Anna and Ellie were happy to go with her choice and Marc ordered a Peroni, which was, apparently, his favourite beer. The menu was relaxed and tourist-friendly. Nothing too posh or complicated, mostly a selection of pizzas and pastas, salads and sandwiches.

'These touristy places can rip you off,' warned Anna, who considered herself something of an expert on Venice now that she'd had input from her tour guide friend.

Daisy waved this aside. 'Oh, it won't hurt this once. We are tourists, after all. We can enjoy authentic meals another time.' The girls happily ordered pizzas with individually selected toppings and Marc chose an amazing-sounding sandwich, which proved to be white bread filled with tuna, olives, hard-boiled eggs, prosciutto and cheese.

'*Fantastico!*' he declared when the plate was set before him and everyone, including the waitress, grinned.

Daisy, meanwhile, had ordered gnocchi, which she rarely ate at home, and when it arrived, it was so melt-in-the-mouth divine, she let out a groan of pleasure. Then she laughed at herself. 'I sound like I'm on one of those TV cooking shows.'

'Like Maeve O'Meara on *Food Safari*, when she makes all those mmms and ahhhs?' asked Anna.

'Yes,' laughed Daisy. 'But I don't have the right T-shirt or the figure to fill it.'

Anna closed her eyes. 'Mmm,' she murmured in a very stagey purring imitation of an onscreen foodie.

'You sound like you're having sex,' teased Ellie.

Daisy gasped. *Good grief.* She still liked to think of Ellie as her baby.

Anna's eyes flashed open and she stared at her sister. 'I thought you said you didn't have a boyfriend.'

Poor Ellie turned bright red. 'I don't,' she said. 'But everyone knows —' She stopped and her mouth pulled out of shape with embarrassment.

It was one of those awkward moments when no one knew what to say. Marc and Bronte looked distinctly uneasy and Daisy wasn't sure if she should scold Anna or soothe Ellie, or simply pretend she hadn't heard.

Before she could decide on a course of action, however, Anna slipped her arm around Ellie's shoulders. 'I was only teasing,' she said. 'And of course, you're right. We only have to watch PG movies to learn all about noisy sex.'

Ellie accepted this olive branch with a shy, gratified half-smile. After a discreet pause, Marc, ever the diplomat, tactfully changed the subject by directing a question to Daisy.

'So, I imagine we'll be visiting Dad's cousin Gina while we're here?'

'Oh, yes,' Daisy said quickly. 'I meant to mention that last night.' Over the years they'd had limited contact with Gina Pesano as her English was minimal, and she'd missed Leo's funeral because she'd been recovering from a hip replacement at the time. 'I wrote to Gina to let her know we were coming,' Daisy said now. 'And I told her I'd telephone once we were settled in.'

'She's the only person left here in Dad's family, isn't she?' asked Anna.

'Yes, I'm afraid she is. There's her daughter, Chiara, but she's married and lives somewhere down in the south. Sicily, I think.' Daisy speared a piece of gnocchi with her fork. 'It won't be easy, trying to have a conversation without a translator. I guess there'll be a lot of smiling and hand gestures.'

'Did you bring photos?' asked Bronte. 'They can be useful. You know what they say about pictures and a thousand words.'

'I brought a few photos. But I always send snaps with Christmas cards, too, so Gina already has quite a lot.'

'I must admit I'd forgotten we had a relative who lives here,' said Ellie. She smiled. 'How awesome is that?'

'Maybe our hostess, Simonetta, would help with translating the phone call,' Anna suggested.

'That's an idea. I'll try to catch her before she leaves for work. It's a pity we chose a host who does night shift.'

'Where does Simonetta work?' asked Anna.

'At the hospital, apparently.'

'Oh, well, that could be handy.'

'I certainly hope not.' Daisy snorted. The very thought of hospitals caused a shudder. Anna's brand of humour could be rather insensitive at times.

'If Simonetta's not available, I could always ask my mate Renzo,' Anna said next, instantly redeeming herself in her mother's eyes. 'His Italian's pretty good.'

'Thanks, darling. That might be the perfect solution, actually.'

'I wonder why Dad left Venice,' mused Marc.

The others nodded, their expressions more thoughtful as they looked around them again, taking in their surroundings, the beautiful canal, the grand old buildings, and the blue sky perfectly reflected in the still water. On a day like this, it was hard to imagine why anyone would want to leave this place.

'Did Dad ever say much about why he left Italy?' asked Anna.

As so often happened when Daisy was faced with questions about Leo, she found herself threatened by a wave of despair. *Deep breath.*

'All Leo ever really told me,' she said carefully and calmly, 'was that he came out for a new start. He had a friend who was also heading off for Australia and I think it just seemed like a great adventure.'

'That friend was the fellow who came up from Melbourne for the funeral, wasn't it?' Marc asked next. 'Gino someone? Gino Moretti? I remember chatting to him. He said he was a builder?'

'Yes, that's right.' Daisy's memory of the time around the funeral was hazy at best. Those days had been a nightmare blur of shock and grief, but she remembered Gino Moretti. She'd also met him a few times in the past. 'Actually, I think Gino's more than a mere builder. He's a big-time developer now. Worth a fortune.'

'A pity Dad didn't go into business with him then,' suggested Anna. 'A structural engineer and a builder based in Melbourne. Sounds like a match made in heaven.'

Marc was grinning. 'Well, we know why that didn't happen. Dad came up from Melbourne for a holiday at Noosa and he fell in love with the Sunshine Coast.'

'Or rather, he fell in love with Mum,' corrected Ellie.

'I'm sure it was a bit of both,' said Daisy and, even though talk of meeting Leo brought a raft of unbearably sweet memories, she managed to smile. Perhaps she was even blushing. At the same time, however, she caught a look of unmistakable tension flashing between Marc and Bronte.

Oh, dear. Not again.

Daisy was sure she'd sensed a similar tension between her son and his wife last evening, but she'd told herself it was merely their tiredness from the journey. Now she wasn't so sure.

There couldn't be too much wrong, surely? Marc and Bronte were here in Venice, after all, and they would never have agreed to this family holiday if they'd had any real problems. As Daisy scooped up her final mouthful of the gorgeous gnocchi, she was determined to remain positive. And, almost as if she was being rewarded for her faith in her son and his lovely wife, Bronte turned to her with a smile.

'I was wondering, Daisy?'

'Yes, love?'

'Have you heard from a woman called Sofia Vincini?'

Daisy spluttered, almost choking.

Of course she remembered the name *Vincini*. Daisy still felt stressed whenever she thought about that mysterious recipient of dividends from Leo's shares, and she'd tried to blank the name out.

How very strange and unfortunate that Marc's wife should mention it now.

'Did you say Vincini?' Daisy asked fearfully, hoping she'd misheard.

'Yes,' said Bronte. 'Sofia Vincini. I think she lives right here in Venice.'

Daisy's pulse raced. 'How – how do you know her?'

'I don't know her at all really. It's only a Facebook thing. A woman called Sofia Vincini sent me a personal message. I guess she must have searched for the name Benetto after Leo died and she must have found my post. I mentioned that we were going back to Australia for the funeral. And she contacted me.'

'Really?' Daisy couldn't help sounding scared.

'I'm sorry,' said Bronte. 'I didn't mean to upset you. I didn't mention it at the time, because I thought you had enough to deal with.'

Daisy really didn't want to deal with this now either, but she forced herself to ask, 'What did this woman say?'

'Do we need to worry about her now?' Ellie was watching this conversation with a worried frown. 'Over a lovely lunch on a beautiful day?'

'No, of course not,' Bronte said quickly. 'Sorry I mentioned it.'

'No need to apologise.' Daisy couldn't help herself. The genie was out of the bottle and she would drive herself crazy with worry if she didn't know more. 'Tell me, Bronte. What did this Sofia Vincini say?'

'It was just a message of condolence, really.' Poor Bronte looked as if she totally regretted raising this subject. 'She wrote saying how wonderful Leo was. If I remember correctly, I think she might have called him a hero. I – I suppose she must have known him when she was young.'

'Yes,' said Daisy faintly. 'I suppose she must have.'

Sofia Vincini must have known Leo extremely well for him to have made a secret financial arrangement with her.

Oh, Leo . . . why?

You were always so careful, so straight down the line. How could you leave me with a mystery concerning another woman?

The table setting with its pretty pink cloth seemed to swim before Daisy's eyes.

Anna's voice sounded. 'Mum, what's the matter?'

Then Marc was beside Daisy, reaching for her hand. 'Mum, are you all right? Would you like some water?'

Someone was pouring water from a jug into a green glass tumbler and handing it to her. Daisy's hand was shaking.

Taking the glass between two hands she obediently sipped, and told herself to get over this, to think rationally. Leo was a wonderful husband and father. They'd had a perfectly happy marriage and no matter what his involvement with this Vincini woman had entailed, it was an arrangement made years ago. It had never bothered her in the past and she shouldn't let it bother her now.

I'm all right. I won't let this spoil the holiday . . .

'I'm okay,' she told the family. 'That water's done the trick.'

'Are you sure?' asked Marc.

Daisy almost faltered. She couldn't help worrying that she'd been foolish to bring her family here, wrenching them away from their own lives and expecting some kind of magical fantasy reunion. 'Yes, darling, I'm fine.'

'At least we can take a vaporetto for the trip home,' he said.

'Wonderful.' Daisy smiled at everyone to prove that she really was fine. 'I must see to the bill,' she said.

As she rose from her seat, Marc stopped her with his hand on her arm. 'No, Mum, this lunch is my shout. You can't pay for everything.'

His smile was so much like Leo's. She kissed his cheek. 'Thank you, Marc.'

Now the others were rising from their chairs. It was time to leave. Looking about her again, Daisy realised that the sun had moved, leaving the café in shadow, and a breeze whistled up the canal, bringing a chill.

CHAPTER FOURTEEN

Mid-afternoon, Anna caught up with Renzo at a small, out-of-the-way osteria. It was great to have a little free time with her old friend, especially as the rest of the family were quite happily occupied. As Anna left the apartment, her mum had been heading for her bedroom to put her feet up, Marc was busy checking work emails and Bronte was reading a novel, while Ellie had taken off to investigate nearby streets with her camera.

'How's it all going?' Renzo asked as soon as they were settled with their glasses of prosecco.

'Great,' Anna said. 'So far.'

'So far?' His gaze was quizzical. 'Sounds like you're worried it won't last.'

'No, we're good. It's been great to catch up with the family. But you know how it can be, especially when you've been living literally hemispheres apart.'

'Yeah, whenever I go home, my lot seem to fall straight back into the old patterns from childhood.' Renzo smiled. 'One kid's the favourite, another's the clown, another starts the fights.'

'I hadn't thought about it like that, but I guess you're right. Marc was always the firstborn son, the Golden Child.' Anna gave a dramatic eye-roll. 'I suppose I probably fit the middle-child mould. In my case, the clown, showing off every chance I get.'

'Get away. That doesn't sound like you.'

Anna gave his arm a playful punch. 'Cheeky. What about you? How do you fit into your family?'

'Well, I'm the youngest of four boys. The baby. Sweet as apple pie. Can't put a foot wrong.'

'That'd be right.' Anna thought about the way their mother was perfectly happy for Ellie to spend a gap year after high school doing virtually nothing, while she and Marc had been expected to go – no, *coerced* – straight into tertiary education and slaving their guts out. 'The youngest kids sure have it easy when it comes to pleasing their parents.'

'Except the poor little buggers hardly get a word in edgeways. The older kids are always making too much noise, trying to grab all the attention.'

'You reckon?' This was something Anna had never considered. 'I suppose Ellie is pretty quiet,' she admitted. 'Anyway, speaking of families. I was wondering if I could ask a favour.'

'A free tour?'

'No, nothing like that. Thanks all the same, but any tours we take, we'll pay our way. But it would be great if you could help out with a little translation. Dad's cousin, Gina, lives here in Venice and Mum wants to visit her. But Gina can't speak much English and our Italian is *zilchioso*.'

Renzo nodded. 'Sure.'

'Maybe if you could even help with an initial phone call to set up a meeting?'

'Yeah, of course.'

'We haven't had a lot of contact with my dad's family,' she added. 'It's sad, really. There's only Gina these days, and her daughter, but the daughter's moved away. It's the opposite on Mum's side. She has two sisters who both live on the Sunshine Coast and they have big families, so we've been surrounded by oodles of cousins.'

Renzo nodded. 'Sounds like our lot. Family coming out your ears.'

'Yeah. As kids, we used to see the cousins practically every week. It was nearly always someone's birthday, or anniversary, and then there was Christmas and Easter. Any excuse, really.'

'Well, I'd be happy to help you get in touch with your Venetian family,' Renzo confirmed. 'Any time.'

'Thanks, mate.'

'*Prego.*'

Anna smiled. She loved the way he slipped in the odd Italian word. To her he sounded completely authentic. 'Actually, if you're free after we've finished here, maybe we could pop back to the apartment and get things rolling?'

'Yep. I'm heading out later, but that should be fine.'

'You have a hot date?'

To Anna's delight, her friend actually blushed. 'Early days, but he's pretty special.'

'An Italian?'

'Yeah.'

'That's great.' She was really happy that at least someone she knew had a promising love life. These days she wasn't even sure about Marc and Bronte.

'So, I've been giving this tour guide business some serious thought,' she said, not wanting to dwell on the worrying possibility that her brother's marriage might be shaky. 'I've started reading about Venice's history. It's so cool. So many amazing stories.'

'I know. The place is just dripping with history and it sucks you right in.'

'Yeah, it's all so romantic. Not just the history, but the architecture, the culture, the canals.'

'*Sì, certo*. That's why the tourists flock here.'

'So there's plenty of work for tour guides?'

'Seems to be, but are you seriously planning to give up acting?'

Anna pulled a face. She'd been told many times that she was too impetuous. 'I don't know for sure, but tour guiding here has to be an improvement on waiting tables in London, which is pretty much all I've done for the past six months. I'm certainly thinking about throwing in the towel.'

'Well, if you're prepared to do the training, I could put in a good word for you.'

'Thanks, mate. That's really sweet of you. But don't say anything yet. I'm still chewing it over.'

Renzo nodded. 'I reckon you have the right personality. You've certainly got great energy and you know how to entertain, and you're used to delivering the same old lines day after day without sounding tired and jaded.'

'That's important, I guess.'

'Absolutely.' Renzo drained his glass. 'Another one?'

'Sure, but I'll get it.'

'And after that we should check out about making this phone call.'

'That'd be great.' Anna downed her drink, too. 'Oh, and by the way, when you're talking to my mum, don't act surprised if she waxes lyrical about my brilliant London career.'

'Okay,' Renzo said, but he was frowning now. 'So —' He paused, as if he was working out how to pose a delicate question.

Anna's mouth twisted in an awkward grimace. 'So my family aren't exactly up to date with my true status in the London drama scene.'

'Right.'

From the doubtful note in her friend's voice, Anna could read what he was thinking. 'It's pathetic of me, I know,' she said. 'You must think I'm a coward.'

'I know you're not that. Not on stage at least.'

To Anna's dismay, her eyes filled with tears. She blinked. 'It's just so hard – with my family and everything. I mean – when I was a kid, I was the ultimate Drama Queen. In every school production. Usually the star. Mum was convinced and *I* was convinced that I was going to hit the big time. No question.'

'It can still happen. You have a formidable talent.'

She gave a helpless little laugh. 'Kind of you to say so.' She hadn't brought tissues, so she swiped at her eyes with her fingers. 'Just as well I'm not wearing mascara.'

Abruptly, she jumped to her feet. 'Don't move while I get those drinks.'

Luckily, she was feeling calmer by the time she returned. For a moment or two she and Renzo sat in silence, sipping their drinks and soaking up the last of the day, watching passers-by tread the smooth, ancient cobblestones – school kids with satchels, shoppers with little trolleys, a woman with a pram holding twins.

'Anna,' Renzo said gently. 'For what it's worth, I reckon you should stick it out in London. You've really got what it takes. But you shouldn't be ashamed about admitting the truth either. Your family should probably know that London's a really, really tough gig and most aspiring actors fall by the wayside.'

'Yeah.' She sighed. 'I guess.'

'And anyway, I bet any woman who's mothered you would be strong enough to handle the truth.'

'You're right. I probably don't give them enough credit. Thanks, Renzo.' Anna couldn't help smiling as she reached for his hand and gave his fingers a grateful squeeze. 'It's just that Mum's been through a really tough time. Losing Dad and everything was so hard for her. And we're here for a fun holiday, so she doesn't need too much heavy reality.'

Her friend smiled. 'I get it. And I promise I won't say a thing out of line. You can trust me.'

***

'You've finished already?' Bronte couldn't help commenting when Marc set aside his phone. He'd probably spent less than half an hour on emails, which had to be a record.

His answer was an unpleasant scowl. 'I'm limiting the work contact as much as possible. I thought you'd be pleased.'

'Well, yes. I'm pleased. Just surprised, I suppose.'

They'd chosen to spend this time in the apartment's living room, rather than retreating upstairs where there was only the one big bed. Marc was on the sofa and Bronte in an armchair.

'If you're pleased, you're not very good at showing it,' he said now. 'And the whole time I've been working, you've been sitting there, so tense, you were practically breathing fire.'

'That's rubbish, Marc.'

'Keep your voice down.' He shot a sharp glance towards the doorway to his mother's room. Then he glared at Bronte. 'You've caused enough trouble already.'

'What are you talking about?'

This brought an exasperated eye-roll. 'As if you don't know.'

'I have no idea.' Bronte bristled. If they were going to have a conversation of whispered insults, they might as well retire upstairs.

'Did you have to bring up that Vincini woman today at lunch?' Marc asked next, still scowling. 'On the very first day? When we were having such a great time?' His voice was low, so he didn't disturb his mother, but it reached Bronte with cutting clarity.

'I'm sorry,' she whispered. 'I had no idea it would upset Daisy.'

'You know she's still fragile. Still grieving. Not all women are as tough as you, Bronte.'

This was definitely a hit below the belt. Bronte felt anything but tough. After just one day with Marc's family, the strain of keeping up appearances was really getting to her.

Agreeing to come on this holiday had been a terrible mistake. It wasn't just the pretence, which was hard enough, but it hurt Bronte deeply to see Marc trying so hard to please his mother, when he'd made next to no effort to meet her own needs during these past couple of years.

'Marc?'

Daisy's voice sounded from the bedroom. A moment later she appeared in the doorway, barefoot, her hair still tousled from lying down. Her eyes were round with concern. 'Is everything all right?'

'Yes, of course.' Marc looked embarrassed. 'Sorry if we disturbed you.'

'I wasn't asleep. Just resting my feet. But I couldn't help wondering.' She looked from her son to Bronte, who struggled to smile. 'I just – wondered if —' Daisy gave a helpless shake of her head. 'I just had this sense that something was – oh, I don't know.' She was obviously being careful, trying not to make matters worse by saying the wrong thing.

'Please, don't worry, Mum.' Marc had jumped to his feet. 'Can I get you something? Would you like a cuppa?'

'Oh, I'd adore a cup of tea, but I think we only have coffee.'

'I have teabags,' said Bronte, also jumping to her feet. 'I guessed Italy might be all about coffee and so I brought a selection. English breakfast, earl grey and peppermint.'

'Oh, Bronte, how clever of you. You're an angel.'

It was a relief to have something positive to offer. Even so, Bronte could sense Marc's lingering hostility and she cautiously avoided his gaze. 'They're still in my bag,' she told Daisy. 'I'll just pop upstairs.'

*

In the safety of the bedroom, Bronte let out a long and heavy sigh.

Just do your best, she told herself. *If the Benettos have to find out sooner rather than later, it will be a pity, but it can't be helped. All you can do is your best.*

This 'doing her best' message was one that Bronte's own mother had instilled in her regularly throughout her childhood – before exams or sporting carnivals or art shows.

'Just do your best, Bronte. That's all anyone can ask of you. It's all you can ask of yourself.'

It was one of the few messages from her somewhat emotionally distanced mother that Bronte had found truly comforting.

Now, in the bathroom, she washed her face and brushed her hair, then retrieved the box of teabags from her suitcase.

When she came downstairs Anna was there, introducing a young man, Renzo, an Australian of obvious Italian descent.

'Renzo's going to ring cousin Gina for us,' Anna said.

Everyone was smiling and it seemed that, for now, peace had been restored.

CHAPTER FIFTEEN

Everything was arranged. Cousin Gina had invited the Benettos to dinner on Thursday and no, *grazie*, they didn't need to bring anything. It would be her pleasure. She was very excited about seeing all of Leo's family here in Venice.

To help with the conversation, Anna had turned on her phone's speaker and there'd been a three-way dialogue between Gina's halting English and Daisy's non-existent Italian, with Renzo working hard as go-between and translator.

'And you, nice boy, Renzo. You come too,' Gina had said. '*Di giovedì*. You speak Italiano.'

'Yes,' Daisy had insisted. 'Please come with us, Renzo. You're such a wonderful help. That's if you're free, of course.'

Renzo had confirmed that he would be free and so it was settled.

'Great. And now Marc will have male company for once,' said Anna, who'd been feeling a bit sorry for her brother, surrounded by so many women.

'Absolutely,' said Marc. 'You have my deepest gratitude, Renzo.' The two guys were grinning as they shook hands.

Of course, the Benetto family wanted to take Renzo out to

dinner now, this evening, but he politely declined. There was, necessarily, a fuss and Daisy tried to insist.

'Hey, let the poor fellow go,' Anna intervened. 'He has a hot date.'

At which, Daisy immediately backed off and Renzo, with a shy smile and a wave, was gone.

To Anna's surprise, her mother came and gave her a hug. 'Thank you, darling. Renzo's a sweetheart and so good at Italian. He was absolutely perfect and having him with us on Thursday will make everything so much easier for Gina.'

'Yes, it's a lucky coincidence that I happen to have a good mate who's chosen to work here.'

'Yes, but such a pity, too. The poor boy must be so disappointed that things didn't work out in London.'

Anna frowned rather deliberately, hoping to make it clear that Renzo's choice wasn't a disaster. 'He loves it here.'

'Yes, that's understandable. But still – to give up acting —'

'Renzo's cool about it, Mum.'

With Marc, Bronte and Ellie all right there in the apartment, listening attentively, the last thing Anna wanted was for her mother to make a big deal about Renzo's decision. It would almost certainly lead to her asking searching questions about Anna's own acting prospects in London.

Fortunately, Bronte spoke up at that moment. 'I was wondering about dinner.'

Anna sent her sister-in-law a smile of gratitude. First cups of tea, now dinner . . . Bronte was like a reliable anchor, pulling them back from dangerous rocks.

'Do we want to bother with going out?' Bronte asked. 'I must admit I don't need much. I'm still quite full from lunch.'

'I definitely need more to eat,' Ellie called from her comfy spot, curled at one end of the sofa.

'You have hollow legs,' Marc told her.

Ellie pouted. 'Maybe I'm still growing.'

'And maybe you are,' her mother agreed fondly. 'But I must admit I've done enough walking for one day. I vote we stay here and have something simple like scrambled eggs.'

'Sure. I can make that if you like,' volunteered Anna. Scrambled eggs with a few tasty additions and plenty of toast had become a staple in London, perfect on a low budget for feeding a horde of hungry, diet-conscious actors, and she considered herself an expert.

'No, Anna,' her mother protested. 'You and Bronte cooked dinner last night. It must be my turn.'

'Or Ellie's,' suggested Anna slyly.

Ellie grinned and threw up her hand like a kid in school. 'I'll volunteer to look after the toast.'

'And perhaps Marc can take care of the eggs.' This suggestion came from Bronte, and Anna saw a distinct look of challenge exchanged between her brother and his wife.

'Sure,' Marc said tightly.

Bronte's jaw dropped. 'You mean you actually remember how food is cooked?'

Yikes. Anna had the sudden impression they were watching the outbreak of war. 'Relax, you guys,' she said quickly. 'Scrambled eggs just happens to be my area of culinary expertise, so I'm going to cook them. Marc, you can be butler and take care of the drinks.'

'Butler?' Her brother looked mildly horrified. 'You've been living in England too long.'

Anna sent him her snootiest smile before she busied herself in the kitchen collecting eggs, butter, milk, along with the goat cheese, spinach and sundried tomatoes she'd bought at the markets yesterday. As she cracked the eggs into a bowl, she found herself recalling her earlier conversation with Renzo and his observation about family patterns of behaviour.

Weirdly, the dynamics here were already starting to feel like the old days at Castaways Beach. She and Marc had always been competitive, getting into squabbles and annoying their parents, while Ellie, the sweet baby, kept out of trouble.

Anna was pouring the egg mix into the skillet of wilted spinach when her brother came up beside her.

'What can I offer you to drink, signorina?' Marc was smiling. A truce, perhaps?

'I'm good for now, thanks. I had prosecco with Renzo.'

'Mineral water?'

'Actually, yes, that'd be great. Thanks.'

After he'd filled a glass for her, Marc stood beside her for a bit, watching as she gently stirred the contents of the pan.

'Just observing an expert at work.' There was no missing the tease in his voice.

'Eff off,' Anna muttered, but then she sent him a wily smile. 'So *do* you know how to cook stuff like scrambled eggs?'

'Doesn't everyone?'

'Everyone, including you?'

He shrugged.

'Marc doesn't have time for cooking any more.' This comment came from Bronte who had moved from the lounge to a stool at the kitchen counter. 'There was a time in the dim, distant past when we actually did cooking classes together, but now he's too busy working twenty-four hours a day.'

'Don't exaggerate,' Marc shot at her.

'Okay. Maybe it's only eighteen or twenty hours.'

'Every day?' asked Anna.

'Not quite every —' Marc began.

'Yes,' Bronte intervened. 'Every day.'

'You must really need this holiday then,' Anna said, hoping to dissipate some of the awful tension zinging between them. Then she turned to concentrate on the eggs, stirring before they set too quickly. But she didn't miss another blistering look that passed between Marc and Bronte.

CHAPTER SIXTEEN

Bronte knew she'd gone a step too far by needling Marc in front of Anna, but it annoyed the hell out of her that he was carrying on as if such a relaxed attitude to meals was the norm in their own household. In reality, Marc paid next to no attention to the food Bronte put in front of him. Meals were usually shared with his laptop or phone.

Just the same, Bronte knew she had to make amends and she took more care during dinner. The conversation was safe, which helped, mostly about which places people wanted to explore the next day. It was as they were finishing their light supper that Daisy sprang her surprise.

'Guess what I brought with me,' she challenged her family, as she sent a beaming smile around the table.

This was met by blank faces from her daughters and son. It was clear to Bronte, observing this moment from her seat at one end of the table, that, like her, none of the others had a clue.

'The DVD of our family movies,' Daisy announced with an abracadabra-like flourish.

'Oh,' said Anna and Marc together.

Probably not the reception Daisy had been hoping for.

'I thought it would be nice to watch.' A defensive note had crept into Daisy's voice. 'A nice way to remember your father. All of us together.'

Ellie looked worried. 'Won't it make you too sad?'

Daisy's smile faltered. 'Maybe. I can't promise I won't cry, but I just thought —' She gave a helpless little shrug. 'I just thought – it would be *nice*,' she said yet again.

'Of course, Mum.' Ellie spoke gently and sounded surprisingly grown up. 'It's a lovely idea.'

'Thanks, love. I've already checked and an Australian DVD should work here.'

'Then what's stopping us?' Ellie gave a cheeky grin. 'I'm only on the DVD for about five minutes, anyway. It's mostly all about Marc and Anna. And you guys want to see it, don't you?' Ellie looked from one sibling to the other.

Marc gave a careful nod, but Bronte could tell he wasn't entirely keen.

Anna rolled her eyes. 'I don't know, Mum. Do we really have to watch all those scenes of me showing off. Again?'

Daisy shrugged, but Ellie sent her sister a withering smile. 'You know you love it. What about you, Bronte? Have you ever seen our family movies?'

'No, I don't believe I have.'

'Then you must see them. Dad had all the old bits and pieces spliced together onto one DVD.'

'Are you sure you want to sit through this?' Marc asked Bronte quickly.

Bronte had never seen a family video. Her own early years had been spent in carefully selected childcare centres and private schools, and her parents would have died rather than be caught taking home movies, so she couldn't imagine what one might entail. She was curious.

'I'd love to see it,' she said, but she avoided direct eye contact with Marc.

'Great. Bronte has the casting vote. It's settled. We'll watch it now then.' Ellie jumped from her seat. 'I'll do the dishes later, Mum.' Already she'd found the remote and, with a click, the DVD player slid open. 'Make sure you all have drinks.'

'We should have popcorn too.' This came from Anna.

'You'll have to make do with nuts.'

A little fussing followed while people got themselves settled on sofas, rearranging cushions and finding somewhere to stow glasses. Marc set an opened bottle of wine on the coffee table. Anna discovered a packet of nuts in the pantry and found a bowl for them.

Bronte sat next to Marc, as was expected, but she was careful to make sure they weren't touching. Then a dreadful soundtrack of honky-tonk piano music filled the room.

'Oh, God,' groaned Ellie. 'I can't believe I used to love that music.'

The movie started rolling.

A young Daisy with very blonde, fluffy hair in a high, nineties-style ponytail and a huge sappy smile was dressed in shorts and a tank top and sitting cross-legged on the living room floor in the house at Castaways Beach. Beside her on an obviously handmade patchwork quilt, a chubby baby boy sat, propped by pillows.

The baby had dark hair and bright blue eyes.

Marc. Unrecognisable, except for those sparkling, beautiful eyes that still looked the same all these years later.

Pain bubbled and swelled in Bronte's throat and she felt her mouth twisting out of shape.

Too late, she knew this was a bad idea. A really bad idea.

On the screen, baby Marc was trying to grab a tower of brightly coloured stackable plastic rings, reaching with his fat little fingers and determined to have them. Again and again he tried, patting at the air, hitting and missing, and rocking his hips as he tried to propel himself forward.

With Daisy cheering at his side, he finally clutched at the top ring, closed his hand around it and then pulled it straight into his mouth.

'Go, Marc,' cried Anna and the family cheered, as if they'd never seen this heroic achievement before.

'See what you're in for,' Marc commented out of the side of his mouth.

Unable to speak, Bronte nodded and kept her eyes extra wide in an attempt to hold threatening tears at bay. *Why do I care? I'm over him.*

The movie rolled on with more shots of Marc progressing through babyhood. His father, Leo, was there from time to time, looking young and fit, crawling on his hands and knees as toddler Marc rode on his back. In another scene, Leo, tall and tanned and wearing budgie smugglers – yellow ones, for heaven's sake – was taking Marc for a dip in the shallows at the beach.

Bronte shot a quick glance to Daisy, but although her expression was wistful, she didn't look too desperately overcome.

In due course, baby Anna arrived and there was a scene of her lying in a baby capsule, with a young Marc leaning in to kiss her forehead. This was followed by Daisy hugging her little son and obviously telling him what a good boy he was.

Somehow, Bronte sat through this. Another well-filled glass of wine helped, although she was aware she'd probably passed her usual limit. Plenty of beach scenes ensued, with castle building and Benetto children in togs, sunscreen and floppy hats, learning to swim or to ride surfboards. These were followed by a family Christmas scene, again in the house at Castaways Beach. Midsummer, with sunlight streaming into a crowded living-dining room, filled with aunts, uncles and hordes of cousins, much laughter and pulling of bonbons and people donning unbecoming paper hats.

Then an obviously favourite moment arrived. Bronte was aware of the Benettos, as one, suddenly edging forward on their seats, grinning at the screen, eagerly watching as Daisy processed from the kitchen carrying a platter with a massive roast turkey and all its trimmings.

'Here it comes!' cried Ellie with a delighted, almost childish giggle.

On the screen the camera zoomed in to focus on the impressive turkey platter in Daisy's hands. At that same moment the platter wobbled. Terror crossed Daisy's face and a shriek emerged from the viewers as, a second later, the turkey slid with a noisy splat and skidded across the floor tiles.

The watching Benettos roared and bellowed with laughter as the camera wobbled, but continued recording the turkey's journey till it crashed into the dining room's skirting board, leaving a streak of grease in its wake.

Even Daisy was laughing. 'Worst Christmas ever,' she groaned.

'No, it was the best,' insisted Ellie.

'It was a disaster. I slaved over that darned turkey.' But she seemed perfectly happy to recall it now.

'And it was delicious,' Marc assured her.

'So you still ate it?' Bronte knew that her own mother would have been so humiliated she'd have turfed the lot in the bin and insisted they decamp to the nearest available restaurant. Not that her mother had ever roasted a turkey.

'Of course we ate it,' said Marc. 'Dad quickly dumped the camera, dived in to rescue the turkey and Uncle Dick, who's a chef, explained to everyone about the ten-second rule.'

'What's that?'

'If food's only been on the floor for ten seconds or less, it's perfectly okay to eat.'

'Especially when it's been roasting in a hot oven for several hours,' said his mother.

'And especially when Mum had spent most of Christmas Eve mopping the floors,' added Anna.

Bronte grinned. 'Well, that's a relief.' And she couldn't help thinking how wonderful it would have been to be there, part of that big rowdy mob. Her own childhood Christmases had mostly been spent in hotel dining rooms, just her and her parents and a whole lot of strangers. Her mother hadn't got on with their extended families and, anyhow, she could never be fussed with all that domesticated cooking nonsense.

Meanwhile, on screen, the movie rolled to a scene of the family barbecue beneath the big shady tree in the Benettos' backyard, with Anna standing on a seat and singing 'Over the Rainbow'. Singing it bloody well, too, for a ten-year-old.

Watching this, Anna groaned. 'Somebody, please, throw a rotten tomato and shut me up.'

'We thought you were marvellous,' protested Daisy. 'The next Judy Garland.'

But Anna had stuck her fingers in her ears and she looked pained, shaking her head. 'At least I wasn't singing into my bloody hairbrush.'

Other shots followed, mostly of Anna on stage in various costumes and poor Anna scowled and glared through all of that footage, while Daisy beamed with maternal pride.

'We always knew you'd make it,' she told her daughter.

Had Anna made it? Bronte wondered. There'd been very little talk of the shows she'd been in lately, but Bronte hadn't liked to ask.

Then the screen switched to a camping trip with a backdrop of gumtrees and tents beside a creek. Ellie and a young boy, a family friend called Zach, Daisy quickly explained, were grilling sausages over an open fire and looking ridiculously happy.

Nearly always in the background, either Daisy or Leo was there as well, giving a child a hug, or a pat on the back. Daisy with Marc, who smiled proudly as he held up an impressive swimming trophy, and then she was with Anna showing off a cup she'd won at an eisteddfod. Later, Leo was there, his arms full of water bottles for Ellie's mixed soccer team – again with her good mate Zach – after they'd won a local carnival event.

One scene, probably a wedding anniversary, showed Daisy and Leo alone together in the front garden that Daisy had so lovingly tended. Marc's voice was calling, 'Come on, Dad, kiss your bride.'

Marc must have been filming, and the happy couple hugged and kissed while Anna and Ellie danced on the lawn around them.

Watching this obviously romantic moment, a terrible pain burned Bronte's throat and her vision blurred. She couldn't help it. She was heartbroken. For Daisy, who had lost her lovely Leo way too soon. But for herself, too.

These images of happy family life were exactly what Bronte had dreamed of and hoped for, what she'd expected when she and Marc had married. Kids and a husband who was there for them, coaching soccer or teaching them to surf, cooking sausages on a barbecue. *Not* glued to a computer.

A carefree, unpretentious, *ordinary* Aussie family.

Tears arrived, dripping remorselessly. Bronte couldn't stop them, but the Benettos were also a bit weepy, remembering Leo, so nobody, except perhaps Marc, seemed to find her reaction strange.

He was watching her carefully, his mouth bracketed by lines of pain. But she couldn't tell if he was sad too, or merely panicking that someone in the family might guess the true cause of her distress.

On the screen, the movie finished with brief footage of Marc's high-school graduation and Anna, shouting directions as she filmed him, tall and handsome in his school uniform, with a proud parent on either side.

Bronte sighed. *And I met him when I started university just a few years later...*

Ellie finally flicked the remote and the screen went blank. Tissues were handed round.

'Well, that was a blast from the past,' remarked Anna.

'Yes.' Daisy was smiling as she blotted her eyes with a tissue.

Ellie sniffed. 'It was weirder than I expected – watching all those scenes from home while we're here in Venice where Dad grew up.'

'Weird, but okay.' Anna blinked to clear the glistening sheen in her eyes. 'I reckon Dad would have loved to know that we're doing this.'

Rising to her feet, Daisy tucked a balled tissue into a pocket. 'Thanks, everyone, for letting me be so blatantly sentimental. Who'd like a cuppa now?'

'Not for me, thanks,' said Bronte quickly. 'If it's okay, I'll hit the hay.'

'Yes, of course.' Daisy came and gave her a gentle motherly kiss on her cheek. 'Sleep tight.'

Sleep tight.

Talk about being sentimental. Bronte hadn't heard those words since her childhood. They took her straight back to her grandparents' farm – on holidays and being tucked into bed by Pop after he'd read her *Blinky Bill*. She could still picture the back bedroom with its blue painted walls and the faded rose chenille bedspread. The moon peeping through the blinds.

Tears welled again. This evening she'd been overwhelmed by memories. And regrets. She bit her lip to hold back an embarrassing sob, before she turned abruptly and hurried up the stairs.

*

By the time Marc appeared, she had showered and changed into her pyjamas, but she knew her eyes were still red and her cheeks blotchy from crying, despite her best efforts with a warm facecloth.

'Everyone's worried about you,' Marc said when he saw her.

'Everyone except you?' She knew it was a cheap shot, but snapping at him had become an easy habit.

'No. Including me. Come on, Bronte, give me a break.'

She sat very stiffly on the edge of the bed, jaw clenched, hands tightly fisted.

'What's got into you?' Marc demanded.

'You know very well.'

'I wouldn't ask if I did.'

'Then you must be dumber than you pretend.' Bronte inwardly cringed to hear herself sounding so waspish and pathetic. To Marc's credit, he didn't snipe back.

'Was it seeing the family?' he asked. 'You always wanted to have kids.'

It was the worst possible question to ask her now. She was sure she couldn't answer and retain her composure, and she would never forgive herself if she broke down. Humiliation aside, the others would hear her, their happy holiday would be ruined and it would all be her fault.

'Is that the problem?' Marc persisted. 'You wanted a family?'

'Not in Silicon Valley.'

'And not with me.'

Oh, Marc. He must know her reasons. She'd complained often enough about his obsessive work habits. On top of all of that, she'd also told Marc about the online date with Henry and he'd taken that news far too calmly, which had to mean that he no longer cared.

And yet now, standing in the all-white bridal suite in Venice on the far side of their enormous bed, her husband looked distraught.

Lost. And Bronte was sure she was falling. Splintering. But if she allowed herself to cry again now, she might never stop.

She heard Marc's sigh and couldn't help looking up. He stood very still, his face a bleak mask, tapping his fist against the palm of his other hand.

She watched his big, long-fingered, elegant hands that had once caressed her so intimately. So lovingly and expertly.

Don't think about that now.

The problem was, she could see all too clearly that Marc was hurting too. She supposed it was possible that he felt as fractured and miserable as she did. But what could she possibly say that would make any difference? And what might Marc say in response when they both knew he was never going to change?

Like that baby struggling to grab at a coloured plastic ring, Marc Benetto was one hundred percent committed, not just to his work, but to being the best in his field.

'Now's not the time to have this discussion,' she said.

'No,' replied her husband coldly. 'It never is.'

'Exactly, because you're always too busy.'

'I'm here now.'

'And your family's downstairs, trying to relax and enjoy a special time.'

'I'm glad you've remembered that.'

Her response was a disgusted grunt. It was easier to feel angry than heartbroken.

She climbed into bed and at least she wasn't crying any more as she pulled up the covers and lay listening to the sounds of Marc in the bathroom. When he came to bed, she would pretend to be asleep.

CHAPTER SEVENTEEN

Marc stood in the dark bedroom, staring down at the outline of his wife beneath the white duvet. Tonight the Berlin Wall of cushions was back in place, even though it hadn't worked last night. He'd woken to the warmth of Bronte's body pressed close and, despite her super-safe pyjamas, he'd been excruciatingly aware of her proximity, of her breasts against his back, the intimacy of her leg hooked over his.

That slice of heaven hadn't lasted, of course. As soon as Bronte realised her mistake she'd whipped out of bed as if a fire alarm had gone off.

And now . . . Marc faced another night of keeping strictly to one side of the bed, while Bronte lay within arm's reach. Another night with her hair spilled across the pillow beside him, scented with her favourite rosemary and mint shampoo. Another night of trying not to care that she no longer wanted him in her life. Of trying not to remember the happier times.

That damn movie tonight had been torture. He might have vetoed the viewing if Ellie hadn't jumped in to support their mother with so much enthusiasm. But it was no problem for Ellie to dredge up all that nostalgia. At almost nineteen, his baby sister still hadn't been burdened by baggage. As far as Marc could tell, Ellie wasn't in any way worried about her future, but still carelessly living day to day. Lucky little brat.

Marc was also quite sure that both his sisters, particularly Ellie, had escaped the extra level of fatherly pressure that Leo Benetto had reserved for his eldest child, his only son. This evening, there'd been no evidence in the movie of their dad's nightly inspections of Marc's homework. No hint that if Leo had ever found his son slacking off, he'd delivered stern lectures about laziness being a disease. No scenes of Leo hauling Marc out of bed every morning before dawn for the swimming training sessions that had gained him those trophies.

Now, silently, barefoot, Marc went to the French windows. Bronte had been so keen to beat him into bed that she hadn't even bothered to close the shutters. Stepping onto the balcony, he looked out at the view where moonlight shimmered on rooftops and the campanile was silhouetted against a night sky studded with silver stars. Below, a row of moored gondolas had been covered with blue canvas for the night. A man and a woman strolled beside the canal, their heads pressed close, their arms around each other.

By anyone's terms, the scene was romantic and beautiful. Marc knew this was the kind of place Bronte's artistic spirit yearned for, the kind of place he should have brought her to long before this. Just the two of them.

Instead, he'd been focused on getting ahead, building a rock-solid career and gaining financial security.

Would a shrink also suggest that he'd still been hoping to gain his father's praise?

Whatever. In doing so he'd ignored his wife's needs and the bottom line was he'd stuffed up. Spectacularly. And now, before too long, Bronte would leave him again and all he would have left would be memories.

Releasing his breath in a huffing sigh, Marc leaned on the railing, staring out into the night. The calmness of the city at this hour seemed to mock him as he wrestled with the mounting evidence of his magnificent failings.

He'd let Bronte down in every way. And as if that knowledge wasn't awful enough, he found himself now, relentlessly, tracking back to the happy times before everything went wrong, then back further still, to the very beginning of their relationship, to the day he and Bronte had first met.

Stop it. Don't torture yourself.

But no matter how hard Marc tried to resist, he kept seeing himself there in the house in Brisbane that he'd shared with uni mates. Kept reliving that moment when the doorbell rang . . .

It was a Tuesday afternoon and he'd had no lectures scheduled, so he'd been delegated to interview the new applicant for their student share house. He'd been in his room working on his laptop, deep in an assignment about embedded system design, and the doorbell had rung several times before he'd remembered he was supposed to answer it. Hastily saving his work, he'd slid off the bed and hurried in shabby jeans and bare feet through the living area to the front door.

The porch was empty, and a girl was heading back down the path to the gate.

'Hi,' Marc called after her.

Later, he never liked to think of that moment as one of those cheesy Hollywood scenes. But when that girl turned around, her amazing copper hair rippled silkily in the sunlight, and she had the loveliest face, smart looking but pretty, with one deep dimple that went even deeper when she smiled.

From that first glimpse of her, Marc had the whole breathless thing happening.

'Oh, hi!' she called, hurrying back up the path to him. 'I thought no one was home and I must have the wrong day.'

'No, sorry, my fault. I was kinda distracted.'

They'd stood for a moment, Marc on the porch and the girl on the top step. Up close, her skin was incredible, the really pale, petal-soft complexion that goes with red hair, but with a healthy glow.

'I'm Bronte Harrison,' she said as she took the final step onto the porch. She held out her hand and that first touch gave the sweetest kick to his heart.

'I applied for a room in your share house?' she explained.

'Oh, yeah,' he managed. *Great start, genius.* At least he remembered to shake her hand. 'Come on inside. I'll – uh – show you the room.'

She followed him into the lounge room and luckily Rachael had been rostered for cleaning that week, so it was relatively tidy. Marc yanked the door shut on the mess in his own room as he steered Bronte down the hallway.

'The room's at the back of the house, on the corner, so it has plenty of windows and gets good light. You might find that handy. I think your application said you're studying art?'

'Yes,' she said. 'I'm only in first year, though, so it's mostly art theory for now.' They had arrived at the doorway to the room. It was very plain, with an old wardrobe painted an unattractive olive shade and marks on the wall where the previous owner's posters had hung, while the bed was stripped bare exposing a somewhat tattered mattress.

'Oh, it's great,' Bronte said with surprising enthusiasm and she turned to Marc with another delighted smile.

Marc was probably grinning too. Certainly, his thoughts had

raced deliriously ahead, imagining this girl living here in the same house with him. Yes, please.

As he took her back through the rest of the house, he forced his thoughts to the practical info he'd been delegated to impart.

'So, there are five other people in the house – which makes three to each bathroom. The bathroom you'd use is back down the hall. Here,' he said a moment later, pushing the door open, and again Rach had done a great job of tidying the towels on the rack and wiping toothpaste off the mirror. 'You'd share this with Rachael and – ah – moi.'

Marc hoped to hell he hadn't gone red. 'And the kitchen's this way,' he added, beckoning. 'It's pretty big and there are two fridges and a freezer, so there's plenty of space for storing your own food. And out the back, there's also a laundry with a washing machine and a clothesline.'

'It's perfect,' Bronte said and her eyes were quite wide with what appeared to be genuine excitement. Checking out the kitchen, she asked, 'Do you have some kind of whiteboard where you keep a roster or whatever?'

This was where Marc hit his stride. 'We use a Google calendar. It works well.' Pulling his phone from his pocket he flipped to the app and offered it to her. 'This way, we know each other's schedules, and when the rent's due, who's on holiday, who's got chores and when. All that stuff.'

'That's impressive.' She didn't take the phone, but leaned closer and stared at it politely. 'I'm a pen and paper kind of girl, but I guess I'd get the hang of it.'

'Of course you would. I can show you on your phone. It's a cinch.'

Her eyes – by now Marc knew they were greenish-grey – narrowed shrewdly. 'Are you a geek?'

'I guess.' He held up his hands in an admission of guilt. 'I'm studying computer engineering. Third year.'

Bronte laughed as if she found this highly amusing. And then, after a bit, 'So what do you want to know about me?'

A flurry of impossible questions flashed through Marc's hormone-flooded brain. He quickly deleted them, but no sensible substitutes came to mind. 'Ah – you filled in the application form, so I think you've covered the basics.' He knew he must sound like an idiot. An idiot geek. *Great effort, Benetto.*

'But maybe you'd like a cup of coffee?' he suggested, grateful for the sudden brainwave. 'And then we could discuss —'

He wasn't quite sure what he and Bronte Harrison might discuss, but to his delight, she loved the idea of coffee. Happily, the coffee maker had been his contribution to the kitchen, so he was quite proud of his skills in this area.

Bronte perched on a kitchen stool. She was wearing a green sundress with thin shoulder straps and buttons down the front. The dress's skirt fell open when she crossed her legs, which she did while she watched with keen interest as he made the coffee.

He was so distracted by her shapely, pale legs he nearly burned himself, but when he presented her with a mug, she expressed her admiration and declared the result delicious.

Then they did find things to talk about. Marc filled her in about his housemates, painting the rosiest picture possible. And they talked a bit about themselves and discovered they liked the same music – Radiohead, Arcade Fire and Animal Collective – and they both enjoyed Star Wars and foreign films with subtitles and curried lentil burgers, even though neither of them was strictly vegetarian.

They didn't talk about their dreams or the future – they were too absorbed by the here and now. And, yeah, by the time Bronte left, Marc was head-over-heels smitten.

*

Even from the first, winning Bronte hadn't been smooth sailing, though, Marc remembered. A problem had come a few days later, when his housemates had reviewed the applications for the room. They'd narrowed down the choice to two girls – Bronte and another chick, who was studying archaeology.

'I'm not so sure we want someone who's studying art,' Josh said. He liked to think of himself as the head of their household, and as he made this pronouncement, he leaned back in an armchair with his feet up on the coffee table and a plate of tinned spaghetti and meatballs balanced precariously on his thighs. 'Artists can be pretty temperamental.'

'How many artists do you know?' Marc challenged.

Josh shrugged. 'It's common knowledge, isn't it? Look at van Gogh slicing off his ear.'

Marc couldn't believe that a guy with two-thirds of a degree in biochemistry could throw up such a random example and present it as a universally proven theory. To make matters worse, the others were nodding.

As he saw the most attractive girl on the planet disappearing out of his life, Marc grabbed at first thing he could think of. 'But Bronte's a great cook.'

Josh frowned and held out his hand to Rachael, who passed him the application forms like an obedient secretary.

With the air of a CEO of a huge corporation, Josh squinted as he scanned Bronte's application. 'Doesn't say anything here about cooking.'

'No,' said Marc. 'There's no question about cooking and Bronte's pretty modest about it, but she told me when she came for the inspection, she's done courses.'

'Wow,' said Rachael. 'And she actually likes cooking? For others, not just for herself?'

'Loves it.' Marc couldn't quite believe he'd told such a

spectacular fib, but he'd also never felt quite so hopelessly desperate.

Josh forked a rather dubious meatball, eyed it before popping it into his gob and then gave another shrug. 'I guess it wouldn't hurt to have a cook in the house.'

Binh, who was Vietnamese and currently their best cook, which wasn't saying a lot, gave a nod. 'Bronte gets my vote.'

'And mine,' said Davo, who only seemed to know how to make cup noodles.

'And mine,' added Rach.

Josh held up his hands in surrender. It was settled. 'Okay, then, I'll call her and give her the good news.'

Which was cause for another moment of panic on Marc's part. 'You shouldn't have to make the call, Josh. I'll do it.'

'So that's what this is all about,' Josh said with a knowing smile. 'You've got the hots for this chick, you sneaky prick. You want to wreck the dynamics of this place.'

Marc refrained from reacting with a one-fingered salute. 'No way.' To his annoyance, he sounded a shade too self-righteous. As calmly and reasonably as he could, he added, 'It's just that I was the one who interviewed her, so it makes sense that I call her back.'

'Whatever.' Josh was still grinning. 'She's all yours.'

Marc hadn't wanted to appear too anxious, so he'd waited a tedious hour and fifteen minutes before he'd walked to the end of the street to make the call to Bronte.

'I have good news about the room, but are you free?' he asked. 'Can we meet?' He wasn't keen to explain his claims about her cooking prowess over the phone. Such dishonesty required a face-to-face confession and an apology.

She was understandably puzzled. 'You want to meet now? Tonight?'

'Yeah. It's cool, Bronte. The room's yours. There's just a minor matter I'd like to clear up.'

'Um —'

'It's no big deal.'

'Okay. I guess I'm free, but can we – ah – meet somewhere public, like a café?'

'Sure,' Marc said, but he cursed himself. The poor girl must be worried he was some kind of deviant. He couldn't believe he'd handled this so badly. He'd had girlfriends before – quite a few, actually – and he'd never stuffed them around like this. Usually, he was Mr Cool.

They settled on a café in Paddington. Marc showered and shaved and changed into clean jeans and T-shirt and arrived ten minutes early. Bronte was ten minutes late. She was also dressed in jeans and a T-shirt, all black, and her hair glowed in a beautiful coppery contrast.

When she slid into the opposite seat in Marc's booth, she looked even lovelier than before. She also looked a tad worried.

'So what can I get you?' Marc asked. 'Coffee? Glass of wine? Dessert?'

'Peppermint tea?' she asked demurely.

'Good choice.' Marc had never drunk peppermint tea, but he ordered one now for himself as well.

Bronte got straight down to business. 'So what's the problem? Is it me or the room?'

Marc swallowed and tried not to stare at her lovely face, at her soft pink lips. 'There's no problem with either,' he said. 'I just wanted to clarify one matter – about your cooking credentials.'

Her eyes popped with worried surprise. 'Cooking credentials? There was nothing about cooking on the application form.'

'No.' Marc hurried to appease her. 'That's right. Don't worry. Cooking skills aren't essential and the room's yours. I just – wondered.' He grimaced, swallowed and tried again. 'I may have – ah – exaggerated your talents in the kitchen.'

'Really?' Bronte slumped in her seat, looking both puzzled and disappointed, which was totally understandable. 'I didn't know cooking mattered. I thought everyone in share houses looked after their own food.'

'Yes, we do usually – and you're right, the cooking doesn't matter. It's just, well, Josh was pushing for this other girl – and . . .' Marc offered an apologetic smile. 'I might as well be honest. I didn't want you to miss out and I may have bumped up your application's chances by mentioning that you'd done a few classes.'

'Cooking classes?'

'Yeah.'

She sat for a moment, as if taking this in.

Marc tried again. 'I knew you'd suit the dynamics of the house.'

'The dynamics?' Now she looked mildly amused and Marc suspected she was totally clued to the sad and sorry truth of this scenario.

Their tea arrived in silver pots. The scent of peppermint was strong but surprisingly soothing, and a tiny square of chocolate brownie sat on each of their saucers. Their conversation lapsed as they thanked the waiter.

When they were alone again, Bronte said, 'I hate to be the bearer of bad news, Marc, but I'm afraid I'm not much of a cook at all. I can do a basic spag bol and a simple chicken casserole. Nothing fancy.'

'It's okay,' he assured her again. 'I just wanted to apologise in advance – and to warn you – in case anyone in the house says anything. But I'll explain to them that I made up the cooking story, and the others will be cool.'

Josh would give him hell, of course, but he'd cop it sweet.

Bronte was smiling shrewdly now as she popped her tiny brownie into her mouth. And she continued to look surprisingly relaxed as she chewed and then swallowed the morsel, a process Marc found fascinating. Then she actually laughed.

What was so funny? Marc couldn't blame her if she told him she'd changed her mind and wanted out, but he wasn't sure he'd get over the disappointment.

'You know,' she said, after a bit. 'There is a solution.'

'What's that?'

'I *could* take a couple of cooking classes. Maybe a little Italian or Thai.'

His relief was so intense he almost punched the air. 'Well, yeah, sure,' he said eagerly. 'I'd pay.'

'Okay, thanks, but actually, I think you should come too.'

He needed a moment to compute this. 'You and me? Doing cooking classes together?'

'Yes.' There was a challenge in Bronte's eyes now, and Marc sensed she was flirting.

No, he didn't just sense it. She was definitely flirting and now he was laughing too – with surprise, with delight. Their first cooking class could be their first date. 'That's a great idea,' he said. 'I'm game if you're game.'

'Sounds like a plan.' Bronte lifted her hand for a high five.

The girl was one in a million.

And Marc, alone on a balcony in Venice, was left with a burning question. When had he stopped paying attention?

CHAPTER EIGHTEEN

Ellie deleted the *wish you were here* message before she sent another pic of Venice zapping across the world to Zach. If she was honest, she wasn't actually sure if her mate would like it here. Venice wasn't the best place for young people. It was mostly about history and Renaissance art and classical concerts, and there were only so many churches and museums a person needed to see.

Even so, Ellie had become intrigued by what she liked to call 'Private Venice'. She couldn't have imagined a place more different from her beloved Sunshine Coast, and yet she was totally bewitched by the world just two or three streets back from the main tourist drag, where the real Venetians lived.

Here lay an enchanting maze of tiny streets connected by the cutest footbridges imaginable. It was like roaming in a storybook land.

Some of the streets were only as wide as Ellie's outstretched hands and, always, there were surprises around every bend. A secret garden, a tiny church with a choir practising inside, a candle in a glass holder set on a stone windowsill, an alley dead-ending at a dark canal.

So many great photo opportunities. Ellie was going crazy with her camera. While walking these back streets – calli, the Venetians called them – she'd discovered people relaxing in courtyards or chatting in tiny bars, or strolling in beautiful parks where dogs could run free.

She didn't take photos of the private scenes, obviously, but she was surprised by how much she still enjoyed stealing glimpses into other people's lives. In many ways these folk were just the same as people back home, going to work, cooking meals, shopping and gardening. But in just as many ways – in their looks, their language, in the colourful laundry they strung between buildings, the pot plants they grew and the amazing smells that came from their kitchens – they were completely different. From another world. Venice was almost like one huge film set, where real life had to fit in with the setting. Ellie felt as if she was seeing everyday things through a new pair of eyes.

Of course, she sent a fair swag of her photos back to Zach and he was very good about replying, either expressing appreciation or offering a witty observation.

Seems like you've been bitten by the travel bug, he had texted yesterday after he'd been inundated with countless snaps of tiny streets and flower boxes and cats on doorsteps.

Zach was right, of course. Until now, Ellie had always believed that the Sunshine Coast was the very best place in the world to live and possibly, on balance, it still was. But already, by travelling to this one new place, she realised how truly limited her experiences had been and her appetite for exploring the rest of this amazing planet was well and truly whetted.

In the past, whenever Zach had talked of taking off and backpacking around the world, Ellie had simply agreed it was a good idea in theory, mainly because she didn't have a better plan. But now she was inspired. When this holiday was over, she would sign up for a hospitality course, so she'd be fully qualified to work in cafés and bars all over the world. Zach, no doubt, would always find work as a mechanic.

Fingers crossed he would still be keen to travel with her.

Of course, every so often, just to tease her friend, Ellie sent him a photo of a hot Italian guy and made out she was scoring left, right and centre. And then, so she didn't totally piss Zach off, she'd slip in a few shots of young Italian women. But she made sure they weren't too gorgeous. She didn't like to question herself too deeply as to why that caution seemed important.

It was during Ellie's second solo sortie into Venice's back streets that she met Tyler Davenport. He was standing in the doorway of a café, leaning an impressive shoulder against the door frame, and he made no attempt to hide the fact that he'd been watching Ellie as she came down the paved alley towards him.

He was youngish, at a guess no more than nineteen or twenty, and dressed in a deep blue button-down shirt that he'd teamed with beige chinos and tan leather loafers. With a navy sweater hooked over two fingers and draped casually over his shoulder, plus carefully groomed blond hair and a clean-cut vibe, he'd nailed the all-American college look.

So it was no surprise that the smile he sent Ellie was warmer and way more confident than any of the covert but appreciative glances she'd received from Italian guys. And with that smile came the flash of super white, perfectly straight teeth.

Snap. He *had* to be an American.

As Ellie drew near, he edged away from the door frame and came forward to greet her.

'Hi, there.' He was smiling as if they were already friends. 'I was hoping you'd come by this way again.'

Ellie was a little thrown by this directness. Wiping any possibility of an answering smile, she took a careful step back.

He gave a courteous dip of his head, and despite his confidence, his blue eyes conveyed the barest hint of an apology. 'I've seen you around,' he said. 'I'm Tyler, by the way. Tyler Davenport.' And he kept his hands in his pockets, as if he might actually be shy.

Finding herself now more intrigued than intimidated, Ellie said, 'Hi. My name's Ellie. Ellie Benetto. I'm from Australia.'

Tyler nodded. 'I guessed. I heard your accent the other day when you were with your family.'

'Have you been stalking me?'

'Not exactly.' Again, his smile was more charming than predatory. 'Our apartment is just around the corner from yours. I've seen you about.'

'I see. And are you travelling with your family?'

'Officially, I'm here with my father, but he's keener on the museums than I am, so . . .' Tyler gave a shrug.

Clearly, he was at a loose end, just as she was. Ellie was just wondering if his parents were divorced when he said, 'My mother died about a year ago.'

She swallowed to ease the sudden lump in her throat. 'I'm sorry.' After a beat, 'We lost our dad about a year ago, too.'

'I'm so sorry. I wondered.'

It seemed weird that two strangers should have something so personal and sad in common, but Ellie decided it was also okay. They stood together in the gentle Italian sunshine outside the café, smiling carefully at each other.

'Have you been in Venice long?' Ellie asked.

'About a week. We're here for a month.'

'Wow.'

'So, I was wondering if you're free, if you'd like to hang out for a bit?'

'Now?'

'Why not?'

She didn't feel at all nervous in his company, but she was sure she should be careful. 'What did you have in mind?'

'We could go somewhere for a drink.'

It was a golden opportunity, surely? Ellie wasn't expected back at the apartment for a good couple of hours. She had her phone in her pocket if she needed to call Anna or Marc to be rescued, but she sensed Tyler Davenport was simply keen for younger company, just as she was. She didn't hesitate. 'Why not? That sounds cool.'

He let out a breath and his shoulders relaxed.

So he had been tense after all.

'I like the Campo Santa Margherita,' he said. 'It's near the college – the University of Venice – in the Dorsoduro district. It's where the locals, especially the young ones, tend to hang out.'

Ellie nodded. 'Sounds perfect. Show me the way.'

It wasn't too far to walk and as they followed a street beside a canal, she and Tyler chatted comfortably. He told her that he was starting college in the northern hemisphere autumn – or fall – and he was planning to study architecture, following in his father's footsteps. Tyler had his future sorted, half his luck, but he was gratifyingly sympathetic when Ellie confessed to her own confusion re planning her next step.

'I guess you're still in that phase where you're weighing up possibilities, sorting through the pros and cons.'

Ellie liked the idea that her year of dithering might actually be a phase, a necessary interval. And then Tyler told her that he lived in New York City, which impressed the hell out of her.

'Wow,' she said. 'I'm in Venice in the company of a fair dinkum New Yorker.'

'I don't know about fair dinkum, but I'm certainly a New Yorker.'

She tried to picture what it might be like to actually live in that famous city, the setting of so many of the TV shows she'd grown up with. *Seinfeld, Friends, Sex and the City, Girls.* It blew her mind to think of Tyler living there for his whole life, as a little kid and then going to school, in NYC, forever surrounded by those celebrated skyscrapers and yellow taxi cabs, not to mention the restaurants and theatres and Central Park.

'What about you?' he asked.

'Oh – I live at the beach. It's part of a long stretch of beaches, actually, called the Sunshine Coast. In Queensland. It's pretty gorgeous. Great surf. I guess it's probably a bit like California.'

A certain smugness in Tyler's smile seemed to suggest that Ellie might be deluded if she believed any beach in Australia could be comparable to California's.

For a moment she was miffed and she almost snarled back a smart retort. But then she remembered that travel was supposed to be about discovering other points of view, broadening her mind, getting things in perspective.

No doubt she and Tyler both had a lot to learn.

'Okay, so I'll ask the obvious clueless question about living in New York,' she said instead. 'Do you see celebrities on a regular basis?'

'On just about every street corner.'

'No way.'

'Way.' Her companion grinned.

And she frowned back at him. 'You're joking.'

Now he laughed. 'Okay, maybe we don't run into George Clooney on every street corner. But it wouldn't be unusual to see Beyoncé or Kate Hudson in our local Italian.'

'How awesome. What do you do?'

He gave another shrug. 'Just act totally cool. It's, like, one of the rules for New Yorkers – Do Not Stare at the Celebrities.'

'I'd be hopeless.' Ellie had once seen the Aussie actor David Wenham in a café at Noosa and she'd stared and gaped like a total idiot.

'You get used to it,' Tyler said.

'I guess.' She tried to picture arriving in New York with Zach, both of them with their bulging backpacks, soaking up the view of the famous Manhattan skyline, walking the streets and avenues that, after so many small-screen viewings, were almost as familiar as her own suburb.

How cool would it be to trek over the Brooklyn Bridge with a good friend like Zach? Or to stop with him at a hot-dog stand and have someone ask if they wanted chilli or mustard?

Just the two of them. Together. Alone. In an exciting new world.

Butterflies danced in Ellie's stomach. Yeah, she most definitely wanted to travel.

'So here's the campo,' Tyler said and, indeed, they had reached a long courtyard surrounded by centuries-old houses, and fronted by restaurants. Scattered around the perimeter were bars and news stands and stalls under green umbrellas where vendors sold fruit and vegetables to the locals.

With a gentlemanly hand at her elbow, Tyler steered her to an osteria.

'I checked this out earlier,' he told her with a shy smile and then he ordered glasses of wine for them both, plus *cicchetti*, which proved to be a plate of savoury Venetian snacks. Ellie felt wonderfully grown up.

Here she was dining out with a handsome American in Venice. It was like something out of a movie.

'So,' she said as she selected a dainty pork rissole on a toothpick. 'Have you travelled anywhere else in Europe besides Venice?'

Tyler nodded. 'Dad and I started this trip in London, and then we took the Channel Tunnel to Paris, then on to Madrid, Barcelona, Rome and Florence —'

'Wow.' Ellie was conscious that she might have overused this word during their conversation, but she was seriously impressed. 'It sounds like you're doing the Grand Tour.'

He smiled, but then his expression sobered. 'This trip was Dad's idea. I'm sure he thought it would help.'

'After losing your mum?'

'Yeah.' Momentary sadness darkened Tyler's blue eyes, a cloud passing over the sun.

'It's a bit like that for us, too,' Ellie said. 'Although we're only seeing Venice. But it was Mum's idea. Dad was born here, you see.'

'That's neat. I guess you should try to learn as much about the place as you can. Have you been on any of the tours?'

'Not yet. Not proper ones with guides, although my sister spends most of her time with her nose stuck in a guide book and she's carrying on like she's already an expert.'

'It's worth taking a walking tour. You can learn the coolest stuff. See that church over there?' Tyler nodded towards an old building that fronted one side of the campo.

Ellie frowned. 'That tall stone building?'

'Yeah.'

'Is it a church?' There were none of the usual crosses on show.

'It's the original Santa Margherita church,' Tyler said. 'But it's been de-consecrated, so it's no longer used for masses.'

'Okay.' *But why does that make it interesting?* Ellie almost asked.

Tyler was clearly keen to tell her. 'In modern times, it's been used as a tobacco factory, a sculptor's studio and a cinema. I think the university uses it as a lecture hall these days, but the really cool thing —' He was quite animated now. He'd taken a sardine-wrapped olive from the plate, but he set it on a paper napkin, so he could point. 'You can't see it very clearly from here, but there's a little dragon on a plaque on the campanile —'

'On the what?'

'The bell tower.'

'Oh, yeah, that's right. I should have remembered from Anna's spiel. And there's a dragon?'

'A-huh. And the story goes, the dragon swallowed poor Saint Margherita, but she made a sign of the cross while she was in its stomach and of course the dragon exploded, leaving her perfectly unharmed.'

Ellie laughed. 'I love it.' Then, more seriously, 'Can you imagine what it must have been like to be living here in medieval times and believing that stuff?'

'You can't help but think about the past.'

She sat for a bit, her thoughts drifting back into the distant, dreamlike possibilities of ancient times. 'And some of those people were probably my relatives.'

'Maybe you could research your family history.'

Ellie pulled a face. 'Dunno if I'm *that* keen. I'd probably have to learn Italian first.' And history wasn't really her thing. 'I wish we'd asked Dad more questions about Italy, though. I wish he'd told us stuff. He hardly ever talked about it.'

This brought a sympathetic nod from Tyler.

'Maybe there were things he wanted to forget,' Ellie said, but she didn't like to think of her fun-loving dad having anything sad in his past.

'Was your father sick for very long?'

She shook her head. 'It was a sudden heart attack. One day he was perfectly fine and then it was all over in a blink.' She drew a quick, sharp breath. It still hurt to remember that dreadful day. 'What about your mum?'

'It was slow for her.' Tyler's mouth pulled tight and he looked away. 'Leukaemia.'

'That must have been hard. For all of you.'

'I guess it's always hard, however it happens.'

'No question.'

Ellie swallowed and looked around her at the paved campo with its raised well in the centre where people had once come to draw drinking water, at the old buildings hiding centuries of history. Then she looked at the bars with modern students in jeans and bright sweaters, gathered around tables, drinking, talking and laughing, their eyes on the future. 'Is it a thing, do you think? Coming to Venice after someone dies?'

'If you're lucky, I guess it might be.' Perhaps their mood might have become totally maudlin, but Tyler deftly changed the subject. 'Anyway, I was wondering if you'd like to maybe go see a movie sometime.'

Ellie blinked at this change of tack. 'Um . . . I guess, but wouldn't the movies be in Italian?'

'Probably, but there's a theatre showing the latest *Mission: Impossible*. I thought it could still be fun to watch all those chases and explosions and Tom Cruise tearing about and yelling in another language.'

'Well, yes, I guess it could be pretty cool.' Now that Ellie thought about it, she really liked the idea. And she couldn't help feeling flattered to be invited on a proper date by a handsome American. In Venice. 'Why not?'

'Great.' Tyler grinned and flashed those perfect white teeth again. 'And how about another glass of vino?'

'Yes, please. Oh, and then I must remember to take a selfie of us here. If that's okay.'

'Sure.' He gave an offhand shrug. 'Is it for Facebook or Instagram?'

'Oh, I don't bother much with social media.' Moving to crouch beside Tyler and leaning in against his shoulder, Ellie held up her phone and smiled at their framed images, set against a backdrop of the busy bar. 'I'll probably just send it to a friend back home.'

CHAPTER NINETEEN

Daisy hated the way her stomach knotted at the thought of visiting Leo's cousin. From all reports, Gina was a sweetheart and it seemed wrong that Daisy's anticipation of a perfectly pleasant family reunion could be spoiled by the spectre of Leo's trust fund and Sofia bloody Vincini.

Unhappily, Daisy knew she would have to find an opportunity during the visit to ask Gina about the Vincini woman. It was a daunting prospect that she longed to put off, but to do so would be as foolish as delaying a medical test for fear of bad news. Some things just had to be faced and avoiding them only caused more stress in the end.

At least the days leading up to visiting Gina were very pleasant. Away from the main tourist bottlenecks, Venice was quiet and relaxing. With no roads or cars, everyone from firemen to fruit sellers had to get about on foot or by boat and there were very strict fines for speeding on the water, apparently, so the pace everywhere was slow and easy.

This morning, Daisy was enjoying the chance to potter and to do a little shopping on her own. The day was beautiful and sunny, the perfect temperature for walking, and she couldn't possibly feel lonely when everyone in Venice was out walking too, apart from the occasional nuisance tourists who blocked narrow bridges or pathways while they took photos using those annoying selfie sticks.

Anyway, it was important to give her offspring space to 'do their own thing' and Daisy was pleased, really, that Ellie had found a pleasant young American to keep her entertained. Daisy had met Tyler's father, Charles Davenport, who was extremely courteous and charming, as only Americans could be, so she was quite relaxed and rather relieved that Ellie was in good hands.

Actually, Charles Davenport had met Daisy crossing the campo near their apartment and, after he'd introduced himself, he'd invited her to join him for coffee. She'd decided she might as well. After all, holidays in foreign places were all about meeting people. She'd found him very pleasant and interesting, not at all pushy or boring. Before they'd parted he'd invited her to attend a Vivaldi concert with him in San Marco.

'Vivaldi doesn't really float my son's boat,' he'd said. 'But I thought you might enjoy it one evening?'

At first, Daisy wasn't sure what to say. In thirty years, she hadn't been out with any man except Leo, but she couldn't deny it would be rather sad to attend a Vivaldi concert in Venice on your own. And she would be foolish to think that Leo might mind. Besides, this invitation wasn't a date.

'Thank you, Charles,' she'd said politely, perhaps a little too politely, because she was so cautious. Secretly, she was chuffed to have her own little outing to look forward to.

In the meantime, this morning, Anna had been very keen to take a tour with her mate Renzo, which was also rather nice, although Daisy was a little concerned about Anna's zealous interest in tour guiding. Surely Anna couldn't be planning to follow Renzo and turn her back on acting? She had far too much talent and had spent too many years, not to mention far too much money, in training. The only career Anna had ever wanted was to be on the stage or screen.

Daisy planned to have a quiet word with her daughter about this, but she would have to be careful to choose the right moment. She couldn't bear to spoil this precious holiday with a row, so perhaps it was a conversation best left till near the end of their time here. Fingers crossed, Anna wouldn't still be totally fixated on Venice by then.

As for Marc and Bronte, Daisy was especially pleased that they were having time alone this morning. It was becoming more and more apparent that the pressures of Silicon Valley had taken a toll. Daisy could only hope that this holiday was exactly the break the young couple needed. Perhaps Venice with its quiet sense of mystery and romance would weave a special soothing magic? She certainly hoped so.

Meanwhile, the shopping was genuine retail therapy. Daisy was searching for gifts to take home, things that were light to pack. Beautiful silk scarves for Freya and Jo. An elegant tie for her kind neighbour, Jim Nicholson, who was not only watering her garden while she was away, but also feeding Madonna, her cat, and letting her sleep on a cushion on his back porch.

Unfortunately for Daisy's budget, the jewellery in Venice was also very eye-catching. *Oh, my goodness, yes.* The necklaces of multi-coloured glass beads were divine.

Awestruck by a quaint little shop's window display, Daisy stayed safely outside on the footpath, but she couldn't help looking and wondering if she might buy herself a bracelet, a little keepsake, the sort of thing Leo might have bought for her if he'd been here.

It did occur to her that she might be allocating qualities to Leo that he hadn't actually demonstrated in real life. He'd always been very careful with his money. *Except when it came to Sofia Vincini.*

A dismayed grunt broke from Daisy as that undesirable name re-surfaced. Damn it – she would buy herself a bracelet no matter what. A consolation, perhaps. Which bracelet, though? The colours and combinations were all so lovely.

Perhaps —

A reflection in the window glass interrupted Daisy's eager search. A scene on the opposite side of the street, a little way down. People sitting at a cluster of tables outside a café, enjoying coffee and sunshine.

Bronte and Marc.

They were seated at one of the tables. Bronte's bright copper hair glinted in the sunlight, a happy contrast to her pretty blue floral shirt-dress.

A sharp chill zipped through Daisy, as she recognised something far less welcome. Bronte and Marc were as tense as boxers facing off. Their hostility was obvious in their stiff backs, in the way Marc stared religiously at his phone, while Bronte lifted her hands in gestures of unmistakable anger.

Please . . . no . . .

This morning should have offered a chance for these two to settle whatever had been bothering them. Clearly, this wasn't the case.

Daisy found herself unable to move as she continued to watch their reflection. Bronte's angry gestures went on, while Marc stubbornly kept his gaze glued to his damned phone.

Daisy wanted to shake her son, and she supposed that was what Bronte would have liked to do too. Even as she watched, Bronte stood abruptly, snatched up her handbag, and marched away from the table.

At last, too late, Marc looked up. He was frowning and was clearly unhappy as he watched his wife storm off, but he didn't make a move from his seat.

Frozen by despair and frustration, Daisy remained stock-still. She had no idea what was troubling her son's marriage, but Marc's stonewalling couldn't possibly be helping. She was so upset, she didn't realise that Bronte was heading her way until she was almost level.

'Daisy?'

At the sound of Bronte's voice, Daisy turned. Her daughter-in-law's eyes were shiny with tears, her face a tight, miserable mask. Daisy suspected that her own face was equally bleak.

'Oh, Bronte, hello.' She tried to sound surprised. 'I – I've been looking at this gorgeous jewellery.' She waved to the window display.

Politely, Bronte stepped closer to look in the shop's window. 'They're lovely, aren't they?'

'Quite amazing, really.' Daisy wondered if they were mad to be having this conversation. Ignoring the obvious . . .

Bronte's mouth tilted in the faintest of smiles. 'They make those glass beads here, you know. On the island of Murano.'

'Well, yes. I'm sure you're right. Venetian glass is famous, isn't it?'

'I'd love to see how they do it.'

'Oh?'

'I think they have workshops.'

Daisy, who'd been expecting to console or counsel her daughter-in-law, was somewhat rattled by this, until she realised it might actually be a perfect solution to a tricky situation. Bronte had always been very artistic and crafty, so it made sense that she would be interested in the glass-bead making. And perhaps this chance meeting in the street wasn't the right time or place to try to quiz her about her marriage.

'What a great idea,' Daisy said brightly. 'I'd love to see how they make glass. I'd go there with you, Bronte, if you like. Would we have time this morning? If you're free, of course?'

'I – ah – think I have brochures.' Bronte had already unclipped her shoulder bag and as she fished around in its depths for the brochures, Daisy shot a quick look back to the café. Marc was no longer there.

Her dismay quickly morphed into determination. Damn her son. She was suddenly, totally certain she would like nothing better than to spend the rest of the morning on the island of Murano with his wife.

CHAPTER TWENTY

Anna arrived back at the apartment with an armful of white calla lilies she'd bought from a flower stall in Rialto and with her thoughts buzzing about the amazing places she'd visited on her walking tour of 'hidden Venice'. Renzo had taken her to the former artisan quarters and to an old prison in San Polo for tax evaders, as well as the old red light district of Carampane, where Casanova used to hang out, the dirty devil.

Now, however, Anna was planning to arrange these lilies in a vase and then put her feet up. With luck, Ellie would be out for some time and Anna could have their room to herself to read, or even to nap for a bit.

As she let herself into the apartment, the last person she expected to find was her brother, alone and stretched out on the couch.

'Oh, hello,' she said as Marc heaved himself upright and scowled at her. 'Don't get up. It's only me.'

With a muffled grunt, Marc slumped back on the couch. He looked pale, Anna thought, and pretty damn miserable.

'Bronte home?' she asked.

'Nup,' Marc said without looking up.

Anna set the lilies in the sink and then hunted for a vase or a jar to hold them. This evening she would take them to Gina's, a contribution she deemed important given that her mum was footing the rest of the bill for this holiday.

'Where've you been?' Marc asked, glancing up from his phone.

'On an amazing tour with Renzo. I reckon you'd love it, Marc.'

'You think?'

'Sure. It's so other-worldly. There's this old red light district and a famous bridge called the Ponte delle Tette. That's Italian for "Bridge of Tits". The prostitutes used to hang out of the windows above the bridge, showing off their breasts to try to drum up trade.'

Marc frowned at her like she had a screw loose. 'And I need to see this because —?'

Anna decided to ignore him as she filled a jug with water and added the lilies. Her brother could be such a pain. With the flowers attended to, she was about to grab a mineral water and flounce off to her room, but despite her annoyance, there was a lingering melancholy hanging over Marc that bothered her.

Instead of leaving him, she took two small bottles from the fridge and carried one to the couch. 'Fancy a mineral water?'

He looked up again without smiling. 'Yeah, sure. Thanks.'

There was every chance he wouldn't welcome Anna's company, but she sat down anyway, taking an armchair and casually crossing her legs as she unscrewed the cap on the bottle.

'So how are things?' she asked, after taking a sip.

Marc frowned. 'What do you mean?'

For Anna, his evasiveness proved her point. 'I'm just hoping everything's okay for you, bro. For you and Bronte.'

'We're fine,' he said tightly.

Anna sighed. There'd been a time in their teens when she and Marc had confided in each other quite regularly – about problems at school, problems with the olds, even on occasions about problems in their love lives – but perhaps it was too much to expect that same closeness now.

Still, her brother looked unhappy and she felt compelled to try. 'I can't help feeling you and Bronte are putting on a show for us.'

Marc shook his head. 'That imagination of yours is getting carried away.'

'Okay. I'd be happy if you can assure me I'm wrong.'

'You're totally wrong.' Marc set aside his phone and swung upright again. 'You wouldn't have a clue, Anna. Wait till you're married. There's always something on the go.' He took a swig from his drink, gave a small shrug. 'So maybe we have a few issues, but we're fine.'

'Or at least that's what you want Mum to believe.'

He stared at her, his gaze hard, almost resentful.

'Listen,' she said gently. 'Don't think you're alone in this, mate. I know what you're going through.'

'How could you?'

At last, a chink. 'I'm under pressure too, to keep stuff from Mum.'

'Boyfriend trouble?' Marc sent her a dismissive, pitying smile. 'Not quite the same.'

'Try this then.' Anna sucked in a deep breath and hurried on before she lost her nerve. 'My career's a sham. It started off okay, but I haven't had a decent acting job in twelve months, just a couple of TV commercials. And I've shagged a guy who was already married. Admittedly, I didn't know he was married, not at first at any rate, but he was a director and I was an idiot eager to please.'

'And he was an arse,' Marc interrupted.

'Well, yes, that, too.' Anna tried for a smile and missed. 'But now I'm not only an emotional wreck, I also reckon I've next to no choices. It's either invent a new career, or go home to Oz with my tail between my legs.'

Anna found it hard to get this out without blubbing. She was trembling by the time she finished. Closing her eyes, she took a deep swig of her drink and willed herself to hold it together.

'Wow, sis, I'm sorry.'

'Thanks.' Keeping her gaze averted, she took several deep breaths, hoping they would calm her.

'You wouldn't give up acting, though,' said Marc.

'I might as well if I can't earn a living from it.'

'But you love it.'

Yeah, thought Anna, *there's the rub.* She truly did love acting. She, along with all the other talented and intelligent actors who endured a mostly impoverished life of making coffees and waiting on tables. She loved that feeling of being in a role, of losing her ego as she stepped onto a stage and fully diving into a character, of connecting deeply at an almost transcendental level with the other actors.

She sighed. 'I guess I've reached a point where I need to be realistic.'

Marc seemed to brood on this. After a bit, he said, 'If things are that bad, why didn't you just find an excuse to stay away, instead of putting yourself through all the extra stress of coming here with the family?'

'Good question.' She shot him a sharp glance. 'Why didn't you?'

Marc didn't answer for what felt like ages. They were sitting opposite each other, eyeing each other cautiously, sharing hesitant, sad micro-smiles.

Eventually, Marc said, 'The thing is you're right, damn it. Bronte and I do have problems. Big problems. Chances are we'll split.'

'Oh, God, Marc.'

He held up a hand. 'I don't want to talk about it, okay? I just can't.'

Anna felt terrible. Gutted. She hadn't guessed things were this bad. She wondered how Marc would react if she gave him a hug.

Marc sighed heavily. 'But I guess I do know why I came here.'
'For Mum?'
'Yeah, because – well, because she's worth it, isn't she?'

Anna could have kissed him then, as well as hugging him. She might have done so if she wasn't afraid they'd both end up in messy tears. But Marc couldn't have found a better way to sum up how they all felt about their sweet, uncomplaining mum.

She's worth it, isn't she?

Perhaps Marc was remembering the way their mum had intervened when their dad's temper had blown, like those times Marc's exam results slipped, or the wrist-slitting embarrassment of their dad publicly arguing with an eisteddfod judge who'd given Anna a low score.

'You couldn't have put it better,' Anna said softly now. 'Mum deserves to be happy. She doesn't need our rubbish and, for her sake, we need to make this holiday as close to perfect as we can.' She drained her drink before she added, 'But I can't help thinking Mum's putting on a brave face, too.'

'You don't think she and Dad —'

'God, no,' Anna hurried to assure him. 'I'm sure Mum and Dad were fine. Dad was always soft on her and, anyway, Ellie was living at home with them. She would have known if there was a problem and she's never hinted at anything like that. No, it's something else. I can't put my finger on it. I just sense that Mum's worried too. Mind you, I think most mums have a built-in worry detector.'

'Still, we should try harder, I guess, so she's not worrying about us.'

'That's a deal.' Anna's smile warmed to a grin now and she saluted as if Marc had issued an order. 'And we need to make sure that tonight's visit to cousin Gina's is really special.'

CHAPTER TWENTY-ONE

Strolling with Tyler on another photo-snapping expedition, Ellie checked her phone for the umpteenth time. Still nothing from Zach. Which meant she hadn't heard from him since she'd sent him the photo of her and Tyler together at Campo Santa Margherita.

She'd sent Zach a dozen messages since then. More photos, simple hellos, a quick question about the weather on the Sunny Coast, the condition of the surf. Another text telling him about the *Mission: Impossible* movie in Italian. He'd never once responded.

Ellie wasn't sure what to think. Zach had never gone silent on her before. Until recently, he'd patiently responded to every text or photo, often with a clever remark that made her laugh. Now she had no way of knowing whether he was bored with her deluge of photos, or just busy and having too good a time to be bothered answering.

More recently, she'd worried that something bad might have happened. Zach might be sick, or even injured. In hospital.

Ellie knew this last was just her active imagination going overboard, but it was hard not to worry. Zach was her best friend.

At least Tyler was a pleasant enough distraction. Ellie had spent quite a deal of time with him these past few days. She'd taken to rising early as she did at home and Tyler had joined her for explorations of the city while it was quiet and devoid of tourists.

Venice was at its most photogenic just after dawn and Ellie had taken some awesome shots. At this early hour, it was almost like going backstage before one of Anna's plays and watching the actors warm up. She saw stallholders pushing their carts laden with souvenirs down narrow alleys, a young boy diligently polishing a jewellery shop window. A gondolier, with his striped shirt folded on the seat beside him, reclining in his boat with his legs outstretched while he read a newspaper and smoked a cigarette.

Apart from Ellie, none of these folk had a camera or took up space in the middle of a bridge.

'I love seeing the real Venetians,' Ellie commented.

'Yeah, but unfortunately they're an endangered species.' Tyler had been on yet another guided tour with his father. 'It's sad – only sixty thousand people still live here these days. The flooding has forced a lot of them out, as well as all the tourism and the rising cost of real estate.'

This reality was indeed sobering. Ellie was glad that she wasn't a day tripper from a cruise ship merely skimming through the obvious attractions, and she wasn't sure how to react when Tyler insisted on taking her on a gondola ride.

At first, she tried to talk him out of it. Gondolas were too expensive, too touristy. She avoided saying they were too romantic, but that was also a concern. She didn't want Tyler to get the wrong idea.

But expense wasn't an issue for him, apparently, and he waved aside any talk of 'tourist traps'.

'It just seems like a cool and fun thing to do,' he said. 'When in Venice . . . et cetera. But it wouldn't be much fun on my own.'

Ellie couldn't really argue with this and, in the end, the gondola ride was pretty damn cool. She felt like a princess when the stripe-shirted gondolier held her hand as she stepped into his elegant and slim black boat. And it was quite a luxury to sit back in comfy, cushioned seats as their gondola glided silently across serene water with a backdrop of palaces – baroque palaces, to be accurate. Ellie even knew a little about Venetian architecture now, thanks to Tyler.

And while their previous explorations of back streets had been fun, their gondolier took them to places that couldn't be reached on foot, beneath the most amazing bridges and down wonderfully secluded canals, home to all kinds of hidden gems. A sweet little church, a tiny pet cemetery, a children's playground, a courtyard crammed with potted flowers being watered by an old lady with a walking frame.

Remembering Anna's legend about the Bridge of Sighs and everlasting love, Ellie was a bit nervous when they headed for this famous landmark, but it was a long way off sunset and Tyler didn't try to kiss her. So that was okay.

It was different on the way home, though. After they'd disembarked and were in the privacy of a narrow alley, Tyler did draw Ellie in close for a kiss.

She was quite flattered, actually, and if Tyler hadn't tried to kiss her by this stage, she might have wondered if he was gay, or whether she needed breath freshener.

Of course, she tried to throw herself into the moment. Really, she did. After all, Tyler was good looking and charming company and they were together, alone, in what might possibly be the world's most romantic city.

He did everything right, Ellie was sure, holding her close but not too tightly and applying just the right amount of pressure as his lips met hers, and his lips weren't cold or wet. Problem was, she wasn't supposed to be analysing what was happening, as if she was an outside observer, was she? She knew she should be carried away and breathless with excitement. Swooning.

Unfortunately, she couldn't relax and she couldn't *feel* anything, apart from the hard bulge in Tyler's trousers. Not even a tiny tingle of delight. As Ellie returned his kiss, she closed her eyes and leaned in and hoped he couldn't tell how much of an effort this was for her.

Sadly, she'd had a similar reaction to Adam Brooker's kisses and groping after the school formal and she'd wondered then if there was something wrong with her. A gene missing? Maybe she was the one who was gay? Although she was pretty sure she'd never fancied girls in that way.

Perhaps she was doomed to remain a virgin forever.

'Want to come back to my place?' Tyler murmured close to her ear.

Whoops. Ellie knew she should have been ready for this next step. Surely now was the appropriate moment to explain that she only wanted to be friends with Tyler? But if that was the case, he might justifiably ask why she'd let him kiss her so enthusiastically.

Thank heavens she had the perfect excuse. 'I'm sorry,' she said gently. 'But I need to get back to the apartment. We're going to a family dinner tonight at my father's cousin's place.'

Phew.

She knew she'd disappointed Tyler, but he was awfully good about it. He dropped a gentlemanly kiss on her brow. 'Bad timing and bad luck for me,' he said.

He really was the nicest guy. Ellie hoped he couldn't guess how guiltily grateful she was that she had a plausible reason to escape.

CHAPTER TWENTY-TWO

Changed and ready for the dinner at Gina's, Daisy took a deep breath as she studied her reflection in the mirror. She'd chosen a simple dress of deep blue wool that brought out the colour in her eyes. It was her 'safe' dress, not too casual or too fussy. In the past it had often given her a little confidence boost and tonight a silk scarf, carefully arranged and tied, along with her new multi-coloured glass bead bracelet from Murano, added just the right touch of pizzazz.

'You'll do,' she told her reflection.

In return, Daisy saw her mouth quiver in a tremulous attempt at a smile.

Oh, come on, you'll have to try harder than that.

From beyond the bedroom door she could hear her children and Bronte gathered in the lounge. Laughter tinkled. Such a wonderful sound.

The young ones all seemed to be much more relaxed this evening. Bronte, who'd thoroughly enjoyed her session at the glass factory, showed every sign of having thrown off her former unhappiness.

During their trip to Murano, Daisy hadn't liked to pry into

the cause of the argument with Marc. Perhaps it was her natural reluctance to stir trouble, or perhaps she was a coward, but Bronte had been so engaged and inspired by the amazing demonstrations of glass blowing and the possibility of signing up for a course in making glass beads that Daisy had abandoned her plan to pose searching questions.

Now, the laughter was a good omen, she decided as she fingered a final wispy blonde curl into place.

But I have to be brave this evening, she reminded herself. *I really must raise the matter of Sofia Vincini.* With luck, there would be a quiet moment to speak to Gina alone, in the kitchen perhaps, although the language problem was a huge hurdle. But with a little extra luck, the mystery would be cleared up quite happily and the small cloud that had threatened Daisy's enjoyment of her husband's birthplace would be banished.

'Just do it,' she told her reflection. 'And whatever happens, I'll be proud of you.'

As she came into the lounge room she was greeted by smiles from everyone. 'Oh, don't you all look lovely,' she said and it was true.

Anna was wearing black velvet trousers with a white pirate-style blouse with ruffles and loose sleeves, and she carried a beautiful red and silver pashmina for warmth. Ellie, meanwhile, had teamed a thick brown cardigan and boots with a long floral dress and somehow had made the combination look stylish.

Bronte was the most glamorous of all, however, in a lovely figure-skimming black sheath, while Marc was handsome in a navy sports coat, blue shirt and tan trousers.

If only Leo could see them . . .

But she mustn't think like that. This evening she had to be stronger than ever.

'We have the wine, chocolates and flowers,' Anna announced. 'So all we need now is Renzo and your sweet self, Mamsy.'

Daisy smiled, as did the others, at hearing Anna call her by this nickname. Back in her teens, Anna had invented names for the entire family, first dubbing Leo as Pappy or The Papster. Then Marc had become Marco or Polo, and Ellie, Ellie Belly, while she, Daisy, was Mamsy.

Remembering this now, Daisy felt a little rush of delight shimmy over her skin, an echo of happier times.

Definitely a good sign.

Renzo arrived exactly on the dot of eight, as Venetians ate quite late, apparently. They all took the vaporetto to the stop nearest to Gina's apartment and then walked a short distance down an ancient cobbled street.

The building that housed Gina's apartment was old, which was to be expected in Venice, but it was also quite modest, with cracks showing in the walls and without a fancy roof line or visible balconies. The plain, boxlike walls were relieved, however, by green shutters and window boxes spilling bright red geraniums.

A woman in an elegant black dress, with silver streaked hair arranged in a stylish chignon, was waiting at the open front door. Three cats lounged nearby, a lazy guard of honour. A tabby rose and stretched sleepily as they approached.

'Gina?' Daisy asked, trying to reconcile this woman's older, lined face with the photos in their family album.

'Sì, sì.' Gina Pesano nodded vigorously. 'Ciao, Daisy. *Buonasera. Benvenuto*!' Her beaming smile made her brown face fall into deeper creases as she opened her arms wide. For a moment, Daisy saw a flicker of likeness to Leo, but then it was gone.

There were hugs all round, especially for Renzo who said something obviously sweet to Gina in Italian, and then the family managed their introductions by pointing at their chests and speaking their names extra clearly. This achieved, Gina gestured to the stairs, and said something in Italian that seemed to mean 'come on up'.

They followed her up a faintly cat-smelling staircase, past closed doors, until they reached her apartment near the top. Daisy, conscious of her stiff knee, couldn't help wondering how the senior citizens in Venice managed with so many stairs and no lifts. Even the bridges were mostly stepped with no sign of ramps for wheelie walkers.

'*Entra*,' said Gina, pushing her door open to reveal a very welcoming room with pale terracotta floors softened by Turkish rugs, whitewashed walls and ceilings striped by centuries-old exposed beams.

'How lovely!' Daisy exclaimed, pausing for a moment to take in the carefully polished antique furniture, the paintings, the nick-nacks and vases set on crocheted doilies, the cabinets filled with books.

'*Bellissimo*!' she announced, using one of the few Italian words she knew and extending her arms to indicate the lovely space.

Clearly delighted, Gina launched into enthusiastic Italian which Renzo promptly translated.

'This apartment belonged to Gina's grandparents. They were your husband Leo's grandparents, too. Their daughter, Anna, was Leo's mother and Leo was born here.'

Daisy gasped. 'Actually born here? In this apartment?'

Gina nodded energetically and continued her story.

'He was born in the back bedroom,' Renzo translated.

With this, Gina beckoned everyone to follow her across the living area to a bedroom painted pale blue with a four-poster bed and a white crocheted spread and a window with a view of a church steeple.

'My goodness,' Daisy whispered, trying to picture poor Leo's mother in this bed, in labour, giving birth. And then the tiny baby. Little Leo with a cap of thick dark hair taking his very first breath. Right here. 'I hadn't expected —'

It was impossible to hold back a rush of sentimental tears. But it didn't seem to matter, for Gina was crying too, and a moment later they were hugging again.

Gina spoke gently in Italian as she patted Daisy's shoulder and again Renzo translated. 'Tears are good. They come from the soul.'

Nodding, Daisy was able to smile as she found a tissue and mopped at her face. The crying had helped to break the tension. She now felt surprisingly calmer.

With a perfect sense of timing, Anna then handed over the chocolates and flowers, which Gina graciously received. Marc offered the bottle of red wine and soon the tears were forgotten as they were ushered into the kitchen where a huge old table was set with red placemats and white crockery. The wine was opened and poured and glasses were handed around.

'*Siediti*,' Gina insisted, motioning for them to sit down as she produced a platter of beautiful, shiny green olives, which Renzo quickly explained were fresh and locally grown.

And so the meal began. Gina had gone to a great deal of trouble and everything was already prepared and being kept warm. After the olives, she served an entrée of mini asparagus quiches with a fresh, herbed cucumber salad. This was delicious and the praise was effusive.

Poor Renzo worked hard, fielding questions and supplying answers.

The family learned that in earlier times, the Benettos had owned a farm on the mainland. Since then, however, four generations of the family had lived here in Venice. The men had mostly been builders and Leo had been the first in their family to go to university.

By the time Leo left Venice, many people were leaving the city, mostly because of problems with the flooding – the acqua alta.

Marc suggested that as an engineer, perhaps his father should have stayed to help plan ways to protect Venice.

Bronte frowned at him for this, although Daisy thought Marc had a point. But Gina merely smiled and shook her head. 'Leo was young and he had his sights set on a new life in a new world. That's how it should be.'

It was gratifying to watch the way Anna and Ellie jumped up to help with clearing the table and carrying the next course, which proved to be delicious anchovies and shrimp fried in a light batter and served with a pea risotto.

'Oh, wow!' exclaimed Ellie as she set a deep dish of risotto on the table. 'This looks exactly like your risotto, Mum.'

It did too, and when Daisy sampled it, she was amazed by the familiar taste and texture. Her pea risotto had become a firm family favourite. 'Leo's mother gave me the recipe,' she said.

Gina was nodding and beaming.

'Pea risotto is traditional Venetian food,' Renzo translated. 'Made with fresh spring peas.'

'And a broth made with the pea pods,' added Daisy.

'It's delicious,' avowed Bronte, who probably hadn't experienced it before and had been quiet for most of the evening, although she seemed to be enjoying herself and taking everything in.

Next, Gina made coffee and she divided the chocolates Anna had brought into glass dishes and placed them at either end of the table within easy reach. By now, she had also produced photo albums that were passed around. Pages were turned and photographs examined, accompanied by smiles and nods and a certain amount of pointing, while announcing names.

Leo, Anna, Mario, Nonna, Nonno . . .

Too many names, really. Daisy couldn't take them all in. And then, unexpectedly —

Sofia.

This name, spoken by Gina, zapped through Daisy as if she'd touched a live wire. Startled, and without stopping to self-censor, she quickly asked, 'Not Sofia Vincini?'

'Sì.' Gina nodded. 'Sofia Vincini.' She tapped a bony finger to a photo of a young woman, slim and very attractive with dark, curling shoulder-length hair.

And just like that, the topic Daisy had been dreading was out in the open.

Gina's smile had vanished, though, as she pushed the album a little closer to Daisy so she could see it more clearly. Anxious knots pulled tight in Daisy's stomach. She knew there were young men in the photo with Sofia and she almost didn't want to look for fear of finding Leo.

But even as her mind cringed from the task, her eyes locked onto the snapshot of a young trio. Sofia was leaning against a waist-high stone wall beside a canal with a young man on either side of her. Sofia's dress was purple and very short, revealing long, shapely brown legs. She and the men had their arms looped around each other's shoulders and they all looked exceptionally happy. Quite possibly they were laughing.

And yes, of course, one of the young men was Leo. Daisy couldn't tell if it was a trick of the camera, but he appeared to be gazing adoringly at Sofia.

For Daisy, it was like taking a step off a cliff into thin air.

No, please, no.

Her stomach was churning now, making the evening's dinner rise in her throat in a hot, nauseating wave. She pressed a hand to her mouth, another to her stomach. After a moment or two, the unpleasant sensation passed, thank heavens, but she was left with a cold sense of dread.

She was also aware that Anna and Bronte were both watching her closely, cautiously. Expectantly?

Just do it.

Every cell in Daisy's body urged her to remain silent, but she forced herself to speak to Renzo. 'Could – could you please ask Gina to explain about this woman? Sofia Vincini? Is she part of the family? Did Leo know her well?'

Renzo turned to Gina and the woman's face darkened as he broached the questions. Frowning, he turned back to Daisy. 'Gina is surprised you don't know about Sofia.'

Oh, help. This was certainly not the answer Daisy wanted to hear. If only she could just abandon this conversation right now, thank Gina profusely for a beautiful evening and walk away. With their lives intact, with her faith in her husband unaltered.

But that way cowardice lay, and Daisy had vowed to be strong. She mustn't back down now.

'I don't know anything about Sofia,' she said bravely. 'Leo never mentioned her.'

When this was conveyed to Gina, the woman snorted, gave a shake of her head and made a stopping gesture with her hands. Clearly, she also wanted this conversation to end.

Daisy cast a desperate glance around the table, saw her children's concerned expressions. Normally, in such an obviously uncomfortable situation, she would discreetly withdraw and accept that perhaps, after all, this topic was better left unexplored. But her husband had been sending money to Sofia Vincini, spending his children's inheritance on a woman he'd kept secret.

The possible reasons for this were appalling and Daisy's imagination had been driving her crazy.

'I'm sorry,' she said, addressing both Renzo and Gina. 'I would really like to know everything you can tell me about this woman. It's – it's important.'

Gina continued to shake her head. 'No, no,' she was insisting. But then, with a doleful sigh, she finally leaned closer to Renzo and spoke quietly.

CHAPTER TWENTY-THREE

Bronte, listening as Gina reluctantly answered Renzo's questions, was seized by a childish impulse to stick her fingers in her ears. She felt distinctly uncomfortable, like an eavesdropper listening in to an intensely private moment. She didn't want to hear whatever Gina had to say about Sofia Vincini.

It was obvious from the woman's body language that Gina feared her answers might not be welcomed by the Benettos and the atmosphere in the kitchen was super tense. If the news was bad, everyone would be affected and Bronte couldn't help feeling a tad resentful. Almost certainly, she was about to lose the hard-won serenity she'd found today while exploring Murano.

Such a wonderful time she'd had, watching those craftsmen on Murano working patiently, heating and cooling the molten glass, tapping and twirling it to create art of extraordinary beauty. Bronte had been rapt. Transported. Completely inspired.

Her expectations of Venice had been rather low, which probably proved how jaded she'd become. But already, after just a few days in this delightful city of more than a hundred tiny islands, she'd discovered that art and craftsmanship and beauty were not just revered here, but a way of life.

This simple revelation had given her new hope, a window into the artistic lifestyle she longed to embrace and to make her own. For most of the day and into this evening, she'd been floating on hope. She had a new vision of how her life could be.

Now, though, she could sense that a storm cloud was about to burst. Everyone in the room was tense, too, she realised, not least cousin Gina. A muscle was jerking in Marc's jaw, a sure sign that he was uptight. Even Ellie had stopped looking at her phone – lately the girl had been even more addicted to her phone than Marc was, which was saying something. And, surely, no messenger could look less happy than poor Renzo, as he carefully, almost unwillingly, began to translate Gina's story.

The gist of it was that Leo Benetto, as a young man, had been quite hopelessly in love with Sofia Vincini.

All eyes flashed to Daisy as soon as they heard this. Poor Daisy sat very still and Bronte suspected she was holding her breath as the story continued.

Gina was sorry – she didn't know all the details. After their school days, she and Leo hadn't been close, so she only knew what she'd been told via family gossip. Leo had wanted to marry Sofia, but she had refused him. After that, broken-hearted, Leo had left for Australia.

A worried silence fell over the group. Bronte, like the others, waited for Gina to say something more.

When she didn't, Daisy spoke carefully. 'I see,' she said. 'So – so I'm assuming Sofia married another man?'

Once again Renzo passed on the question and received a reply. 'No,' he told Daisy. 'Sofia never married.'

It was hard to tell if Daisy was disappointed or relieved. 'Oh,' she said simply. 'That seems a pity.'

Bronte thought her mother-in-law's dignity was admirable, considering the circumstances.

'So,' Daisy asked next, 'Sofia has no family?'

When this question was relayed, Gina didn't answer at first and Bronte was aware of Marc beside her, as silent and tense as a tripwire.

Looking pained, Renzo translated. A few months after Leo left for Australia, Sofia had given birth to a son.

'Gabriele,' Gina said, grave-faced. 'Gabriele Vincini.'

Bronte's mind was spinning now. The baby, this Gabriele Vincini, would be a man now, older than Marc.

'But —' Daisy's face was white, her eyes agonised, her lips trembling. She seemed to be trying to speak, but no words emerged.

It was Marc who voiced the next terrible question. 'Are you telling us that this baby was my father's son?'

Again, poor Renzo translated.

Gina had seen very little of the Vincinis in recent years and she'd never been a personal friend of Sofia's, but yes, Gina had always believed that Gabriele Vincini was Leo Benetto's son.

At the far end of the table, Anna swore.

'But that's crazy,' protested Marc.

'I don't believe it,' cried Ellie, who looked ready to cry, while poor Daisy sagged in her chair, completely flattened.

'*Mi dispiace*,' Gina said now, softly, over and over and she seemed close to tears too.

'Gina is so sorry,' Renzo unhappily translated.

It was too late to be sorry, Bronte wanted to tell him. The cat was out of the bag, snarling and spitting and clawing. Breaking hearts.

But this wasn't Renzo's fault, of course. He and Gina had been pressured to share this regrettable news.

Guiltily, Bronte couldn't help wondering if this ghastly situation might never have arisen if she'd kept quiet about that Facebook message from Sofia.

Leo was a wonderful man, the woman had written. *A true hero, and he will live in my heart forever.*

Even at the time, the words had made Bronte uncomfortable. Surely, Sofia was a little too effusive? And it hadn't really made sense that Sofia would send such a message to Bronte, the Benettos' daughter-in-law, without trying to contact anyone from Leo's immediate family. What had Sofia hoped to achieve?

Now, Bronte couldn't help feeling partly to blame for this shocking bombshell. By raising the subject of Sofia Vincini, she had probably made Daisy anxious, pushed her to ask questions best left unvoiced.

She looked to Marc again and he glared back at her, but for once, she didn't feel anger so much as sympathy for her husband. Right now, the poor guy would be battling with the very real possibility that he wasn't his father's firstborn son after all.

The prince had been dethroned.

And this evening couldn't really be resurrected.

Bronte tried, along with Anna, to help Gina attend to the dirty dishes, but their hostess waved their offers aside and pointed to the dishwasher.

They thanked her profusely, of course, and there were hugs and an invitation for her to join them for another meal before they left Venice, but despite everyone's best efforts, the mood was subdued. One by one, the Benettos went back down the narrow staircase and Gina didn't come with them.

As they stepped out into the cool Venetian night, donning jackets and pashminas against the chill, Bronte heard Marc's hoarse, stunned voice.

'It can't be true.'

'No, it can't,' chimed in Ellie. 'Dad would have said something.'

'I agree,' declared Anna. 'There's no way Dad would have abandoned a pregnant woman, or left his child with no support.'

Out of the corner of her eye, Bronte saw Daisy come to an abrupt halt. Her mother-in-law stood with her eyes closed, as if she longed to escape, her mouth drawn down in lines of deepest distress.

CHAPTER TWENTY-FOUR

Marc was reeling as they made their way back to the canal to catch the vaporetto. He was dimly aware that Anna had given Renzo a quick hug and an apology for dragging him into such an awkward situation, but he was more concerned about his mother. She would be as sideswiped by Gina's news as he was. He might have put a comforting arm around her, but Ellie beat him to it.

Nobody else spoke as they walked down the narrow street. This part of Venice was eerily quiet and the only sounds were their footsteps on the cobbled stones. Marc supposed the others were as afraid as he was of saying something that would upset their mother, or just generally make matters worse.

He still couldn't quite take in the news that his dad had not only fathered another son, but had then taken off to the far side of the world. It didn't make sense. It certainly didn't line up with the way Marc had always viewed his father.

There could be no doubt. Leo Benetto had raised Marc as his prized, firstborn and only son.

Now, beneath a cold Venetian sky where crisp stars showed between ancient rooftops, Marc's thoughts were flooded by intimate memories of his father. So many little moments – his dad teaching him to swim and how to tie his shoelaces, how to wax his first surfboard, making sure he created a good bump pattern that would give his feet something to grip on.

He remembered the shed in the backyard, his father's man cave, and Marc's pride in being allowed to hang out there. The tins of paint neatly stacked, the gardening rakes and spades hanging from hooks on the wall in an orderly row, the little drawers of nails, tacks and screws, carefully separated. Quite different from their mum's little potting shed that was always messy and disorganised.

Marc had downed his first beer in that shed with his dad. He'd probably been fifteen when his father had extracted the tins from the little fridge beneath his workbench.

'It's always good to have your first beer at home,' Leo had told him. 'Then, hopefully, you won't be quite so stupid when you start drinking with your mates.'

'Is that what you did?' Marc had asked. 'You drank beer at home with your dad?'

'With your nonno it was vino.' Leo had grinned then, making creases in the skin at the corners of his dark eyes as he raised his glass. 'Vino, beer, pot. Some blokes go a little crazy, but you don't want to be one of them.'

Even now, Marc could remember how his dad's Italian accent had made the word 'blokes' sound a little strange. But Leo had been trying to talk 'strine', to help his son to relax.

Hell. Thinking back to that time, Marc felt his eyes water. He'd been desperate to live up to his father's expectations. Even when the bar had kept rising.

Marc had always known that he'd held a privileged position within the family, as Leo's only son. He'd assumed it was partly because his dad was Italian – a 'new Australian' was the term most people had used back when they were kids.

Leo had talked with a different accent, of course, but he also hadn't been quite as easygoing or laid-back as the other kids' dads. Leo had never been one to spend weekends fishing or golfing with his mates. He'd spent most weekends at home, tinkering about their house or their garden, fixing a window hinge, repainting the guttering, mowing the lawn and neatly trimming the hedges, building the best paved and bricked barbecue area in the entire district.

The only weekend time spent away from these tasks had been when he'd taken Marc to soccer training – soccer, not rugby league, the code so beloved by so many Queensland dads – or to the surf club's Nippers, where he would watch from the sidelines and roar advice to Marc.

Later, Leo hadn't shown nearly as much interest in the girls' sporting activities. Anna hadn't wanted to play soccer, of course. She'd been all about singing and dancing from a very early age, but when Ellie had joined a soccer team, along with her good mate Zach, their mum had mostly been the one who'd gone to the matches.

Daisy might not have known much about the game, but she'd cut up the oranges and brought the teams' jerseys home to be washed. By then, their father had been too busy coaching Marc's team, pushing them to win a regional premiership, as well as stepping in as treasurer for Marc's school's P and C.

In his high-school years, Marc had expressed an interest in engineering and Leo had been over the moon. Even when Marc's interest had veered towards computer engineering, Leo had still cheered his son on. He'd also been the first to raise the subject of Silicon Valley.

'If you want to work in IT and you want to succeed, why wouldn't you strive to be in the one place where the finest and brightest in your field are gathered?'

With Leo's wholehearted backing, leaving Australia and heading for the Valley had made perfect sense. Marc had put everything into achieving that goal and from the moment he'd arrived in California, he'd been driven and ambitious. Quite possibly, after his father had died, he'd worked even harder still.

Next thing he'd known, his wife had walked out.

And now . . .

Shit.

The question had to be asked. During those hundreds of intimate, meaningful moments with his dad while Marc was growing up, had Leo also been thinking about another son, the Italian boy he'd left behind?

The possibility was unbearable. Impossible. And yet, Gina had shown no sign of doubt.

And the hardest thing for Marc to grasp now, the thing that made absolutely no sense, was the fact that his father had walked away from this other kid.

Was Leo Benetto a coward?

Marc had always believed that his dad had come to Australia to start a new life, to put his university degree and his engineering skills to good use in a new world. He'd left home to build a better life for his future family than he could have achieved in Italy.

But now? As the vaporetto chugged back down the canal, it sure as hell looked as if Leo Benetto had been little more than a chicken-hearted runaway. He'd run from rejection, from failure to win the woman he loved and he'd turned his back on his first son.

And where did that leave their mum?

A groan burst from Marc, making the others turn to stare at him. They looked as strained as he felt and Bronte —

Thud. The sympathy and worry in his wife's eyes made him want to weep. But her sympathy was momentary, he was sure. This wouldn't change her plans to leave him. Now, not just his marriage, but everything about his life was totally screwed.

But how much worse must it be for their mother? He and his sisters had always believed that their dad adored Daisy, but had she been some kind of consolation prize?

The possibility was too sickening to contemplate.

As the vaporetto slowed on approaching their dock, the immensity of Gina's revelations weighed on Marc, like a gloomy, suffocating cloud. But if he was totally gutted, he couldn't imagine how bad his mother must feel.

CHAPTER TWENTY-FIVE

It was time to move, to rise from her seat and leave the vaporetto, but Daisy was stricken by a strange immobility. Anna was still beside her, as she'd been throughout the short trip, silently holding her hand, while Ellie sat opposite them, texting madly. Daisy chose not to speculate about the news her daughter might be sharing, or whom she was sending it to. She could only hope that folk back home at Castaways Beach weren't already agog with Benetto gossip.

Marc and Bronte were seated behind her, out of sight, but Renzo had spent the journey in the bow of the vaporetto, standing at the railing, the wind lifting his dark hair as he stared ahead at the silky water. God knew what the poor fellow was thinking.

In the meantime, Daisy's own thoughts had been tracking endlessly back and forth, scouring almost forensically through the decades of her marriage, trying to recall a time, even a single moment, when Leo had given her an inkling that his past held a secret.

She'd found nothing. From the first summer night when she'd met her handsome Italian at a Mooloolaba Surf Club Christmas party till the day he'd come home from work unexpectedly early, complaining of tiredness, only to collapse on their bed never to rise again, her husband had been steady, reliable, rock solid. Daisy had never doubted Leo's love or his loyalty.

Leo might have been unimaginative at times, especially when it came to garden design, and he could be annoying, with an engineer's zeal for nit-picky precision, but he'd been a surprisingly passionate lover. A devoted family man and always utterly trustworthy. He'd never once given Daisy a single reason to doubt or to question him.

Until that day in the accountant's office.

Until this evening in his cousin Gina's kitchen.

'Mum, are you okay?' Anna was gently urging Daisy to her feet. 'Let me help you.'

With a hand at Daisy's elbow, Anna supported her as she rose stiffly. The vaporetto rocked a little at its mooring and Daisy felt a tad light-headed, so she was glad of her daughter's arm, even though she was embarrassed to be behaving like a ninety-year-old, allowing herself to be carefully steered across the deck and down the small ramp to the wharf.

On solid ground once more at their regular stop, Daisy felt steadier. She looked around at the familiar surroundings, at the café, now closed and shuttered, at the campo, emptied of children and old folk, but its fountain still trickling. The drops of water sparkled in the light of the street lamps and she felt as if she was waking from a dream. Or rather a nightmare. The last time she'd seen this place, she and her family had been dressed in their finery and were looking forward to a pleasant evening out.

Now, everything felt different.

Daisy wondered if this was what it had been like for Londoners during the Blitz, returning to their suburbs to find their homes and all their possessions destroyed. Only this evening, the buildings were still intact and it was she who'd been wiped out.

Leo . . . how could you live such an ordinary, respectable life and then leave me with such a mystery?

Renzo was saying farewell, Daisy realised. The poor fellow still looked shaken. She kissed him on both cheeks. It was becoming a habit. 'I can't thank you enough, Renzo, but I'm so sorry we landed you in such an awkward situation.'

He offered a sympathetic smile. 'I hope you enjoy the rest of your stay in Venice.' He spoke politely and Anna jumped in and gave him an extra warm hug as she wished him goodnight.

'*Buona notte*,' he called to the others and then with a wave, he was off, disappearing into darkness and no doubt relieved to escape.

The family walked on. The night was clear and cool and from a nearby garden the scent of verbena hung in the air. For Daisy, no sight would be more welcome than the door in the wall that opened onto the little courtyard and their apartment. Their home away from home.

She no longer needed assistance, but although her legs were steadier, her thoughts kept whirling in a thousand directions.

Why, oh, why had Leo never told her about Sofia Vincini? His silence just didn't make sense. It wasn't a crime for a man to have had previous relationships. It was normal, surely?

Daisy had told him about a couple of her old boyfriends. She'd even kept their photographs in an album and looked at them very occasionally, just for old times' sake. But she'd never regretted breaking up with those boys and they hadn't fathered her child. And they certainly hadn't been sending her money for the past several decades.

At this thought, Daisy stumbled.

'Mum.' Anna was beside her again with a helping hand. 'Take it easy,' she said gently.

'I'm fine, thanks, love. Just misjudged a cobblestone.'

'Yes, they can be tricky.'

Bronte and Marc were a few paces ahead of Daisy, walking in silence and not touching, which was unfortunate. Once, they would have been arm in arm, protected by the bubble of their love.

She wondered if this evening had made things worse for them. Poor Marc would be in shock. He'd adored his father.

Anna and Ellie were on either side of her, but they were quiet, too, no doubt studiously avoiding any mention of the evening's disturbing revelations.

Daisy knew she should say something to ease their anxiety. She should reassure her family that Gina must be mistaken, that there had to be another explanation, another father for Gabriele Vincini.

Unfortunately, the only way to clarify this now was to bravely arrange a face-to-face meeting with his mother, Sofia. She mentally winced at the thought. *Lordy.* How could one brief holiday require so much courage?

Just broaching those questions to Gina tonight had required enormous bravery on Daisy's part, and look how that had ended. She couldn't help wondering if she shouldn't have left the whole matter of the Vincinis in the past, dead and buried along with her husband.

Now it was too late to undo the evening's damage. The questions had been asked and the answers had left them with heartache and serious gaps in their understanding.

As they rounded the final corner, Daisy saw Charles Davenport coming down the *calle* from the opposite direction. He looked very elegant in a dark suit and white crisp collared shirt, with the trailing ends of a silver silk scarf flipped over his shoulder, echoing his silvery grey hair.

Tomorrow evening he was going to escort her to a Vivaldi concert, an event she was very much looking forward to. It would be a welcome change from this evening's circus. Lifting a hand, Daisy waved to him.

Crack.

She only had a split second to register the sound of something overhead, possibly breaking from a rooftop, before a whooshing sound followed. Then —

Whack!

A heavy object smashed hard into Daisy's forehead. She saw stars, literally, as pain shot through her skull. Staggering, she held out her arms to her daughters, hoping they might catch her.

'*Mum!*'

Daisy heard the girls scream as they reached out, arms flailing, but they were too late. The cobblestones came up to meet her and everything went black.

CHAPTER TWENTY-SIX

'Mum!' Anna screamed as she dropped to her knees in terror. 'Oh, God, *Mum*!'

Daisy didn't move. She lay on the cobblestones surrounded by shattered chunks of dirty white plaster. Her eyes were closed and there was a horrible bloody gash on her forehead.

'Mum!' Anna yelled again and she reached for her mother's hand, but there was no response. Daisy's fingers were as limp as a rag doll's.

Ellie, kneeling on the other side, was sobbing, and by now Marc and Bronte were there too, as well as the American. They all looked as shocked and terrified as Anna felt.

'What happened?' Ellie cried.

'A piece of plaster fell from up there.' Anna pointed up to a crumbling corner of roof line. 'Mum!' she said again, gently patting her mother's cheek.

Still, there was no response.

'Is she breathing?' asked the American.

'I'm not sure.' Anna had never felt quite so helpless or more scared.

'We need to call an ambulance.' Marc had already extracted his phone from his pocket, but as he looked at the screen he groaned. 'Hell. I should have thought to save the number.'

'Google it,' snapped Ellie.

'Yeah, yeah. I'm on it.' Already he was scrolling madly.

Charles Davenport leaned over Daisy now and pressed two fingers to the side of her neck. Fearfully, Anna watched, hoping he knew what he was doing. The skirt of her mother's blue wool dress had ridden up, exposing her pale, plumpish thighs and Anna tugged the fabric back down to a demure knee length. One of Daisy's shoes had come off as well and was lying on its side, its kitten heel snapped. The knee of her stocking showed a hole.

'Can you feel a pulse?' Anna asked.

Charles Davenport looked worried, but he nodded. 'I think so – yes. And I can see that she's breathing.'

Thank God.

Marc was still fiddling for his phone, while Bronte looked on, chewing her lip anxiously.

'It would help if I knew the Italian for ambulance,' Marc muttered.

Anna wanted to scream at him. He was supposed to be a computer genius with all the knowledge in the world at his fingertips.

'I think it's *ambulanza*,' said Charles Davenport.

'Actually, I think there's a central emergency number for Europe,' Anna added as she suddenly recalled something she'd read in one of Renzo's guide books. 'You know – for fire, police, ambulance. Like triple zero. It's 11 something, I think.'

'Oh, yeah, got it. 112.' Marc keyed in the number, held the phone to his ear and gave her a thumbs up. A second later, he grimaced. 'Everything's in bloody Italian.'

'Well, of course it is, idiot.' Ellie had clearly lost all patience.

Ignoring her, Marc turned his back on them as he spoke into the phone. 'English, please. I only speak English.'

Watching in horror as Charles Davenport continued to kneel beside their unresponsive mother, Anna wondered if she should ring Renzo and drag the poor guy back to help them with yet another round of translations and Benetto drama.

She was fumbling for her phone in her handbag when she was struck by a better idea. 'Simonetta! I'll see if she's home.'

Simonetta, their Airbnb hostess, spoke Italian, obviously. Not only that, she was a nurse and tonight she could be a lifesaver.

As Marc dealt with the person on the other end of his phone, Anna took off.

'Isn't Simonetta on night shift?' Bronte called after her.

'Not every night,' Anna yelled back.

She wasn't in the habit of praying, but she prayed now as she rushed across the little courtyard and up the stairs to knock on Simonetta's door. *Please, God, let her be home.*

The knock was rather louder than Anna had intended, but it had the desired effect. Simonetta appeared quickly, having obviously come from the bathroom with a towel wrapped, turban style, around her head. She was knotting the sash of a pink towelling bathrobe and her feet were covered in fluffy lime-green slippers. Behind her in her small kitchen, steam rose from a pot on the stove.

'Mum's had an accident,' Anna explained without ceremony. 'Can you come? We need your help.'

'*Certamente.*'

To Anna's relief, Simonetta stepped outside quickly, remembering first to turn down the heat on the stove and to grab her keys from the kitchen counter. 'What's happened?' she asked as she slipped the keys into a pocket in her robe and followed Anna down the stairs.

'A piece of plaster fell from a building and hit Mum on the head. It's knocked her out cold.'

Simonetta's response was in Italian and might well have involved swearing. 'So Daisy's not at home?' she asked as Anna hurried past the closed door to their apartment.

'No, she's still out in the street.' A sob rose in Anna's throat as she called this information over her shoulder while hurrying back across the courtyard.

They emerged through the little doorway in the wall to see her poor mother still lying on the cobblestones with Marc, Bronte, Ellie and Charles Davenport all huddled around her.

'Thank God,' Marc said when he saw them. 'I did my best with the ambulance and they're on their way, but it was bloody hard trying to explain exactly where we are.'

'The ambulance comes by water,' Simonetta told him.

'Of course it does,' said Bronte softly and she sighed, possibly thinking, as Anna was, that Venice's canals could easily lose their romance in an emergency.

'I can phone them and give the address,' Simonetta offered. 'But first. A little room, please.'

The others made way for her and she knelt in her short towelling robe, bare knees on the cold stones as she examined Daisy, checking her pulse, her breathing, and then trying, gently, to rouse her.

'Mrs Benetto, Daisy, wake up. Can you hear me?'

The horror of watching her mother lie there, unresponsive, almost as if she was dead, was beyond anything Anna had ever experienced.

'Should we turn her onto her side?' Bronte was asking.

Simonetta shook her head. 'No. Best not to move her. Her airways and circulation are clear.'

'Don't worry about phoning with the address. I'll go down to the canal, so I can show the ambulance people the way,' Anna suggested. She needed to do something more practical than standing around helplessly.

'Good idea,' cried Ellie, jumping to her feet. 'I'll come with you.'

'Perhaps I should come too,' said Marc.

'No,' said Anna and Bronte together. 'You stay here,' Anna added. 'In case Mum wakes up. She'll want to see someone from the family. I'll ring you as soon as I spot the ambulance to let you know they're coming.'

The girls set off, walking swiftly.

'Poor Mum,' said Ellie. 'I can't believe this has happened. It's such a freak accident.'

'You bet it is.' Anna sighed.

'And it's so unfair that something like this happened to *her*,' said Ellie. 'I mean, this holiday was Mum's idea. She's paying for it and she wanted everything to be perfect.' She stopped abruptly, her words ending in a sob.

Anna threw an arm around her sister's shoulders, gave her a hug. 'Try not to stress too much, Ells. I'm sure she'll be okay. The ambulance is coming. They'll take good care of her.'

'They'd bloody better.' Ellie found a tissue and blew her nose. 'But it's just not fair,' she said again as they walked on. 'Everything was going so well here in Venice until tonight. We were having a really great holiday – the *best* time – and then, in just one night everything's been ruined.'

'Yeah,' Anna agreed. 'It's like tonight was cursed, or something. Maybe we should have read our stars. There might have been a warning.'

They reached the canal. All was quiet and the water was still, a perfect mirror for the lights that spilled from street lamps and windows. It was late, close to midnight. No sign of an ambulance speeding towards them.

'It's amazing how quickly Venice shuts down at night, considering how busy it is during the day,' Anna said.

'Tyler reckons most of the tourists come on cruise ships and don't even spend one night here.' Ellie leaned her elbows on a mooring post, staring into the water. 'Maybe they have the right idea. We should have stayed at the apartment tonight, or just gone for a drink somewhere nearby. Then we wouldn't have had to listen to Gina telling us that crazy rubbish about Dad. And that plaster would have just crashed into an empty street and scared a couple of alley cats. Mum would still be perfectly fine.'

'Maybe.'

Ellie rounded on her. 'What do you mean *maybe*? It's obvious. We should never have gone to Gina's.'

'We can't really blame Gina. And anyway,' Anna found herself quoting Lady Macbeth, *'what's done cannot be undone.'*

This earned her a sharp, suspicious look from her sister.

Anna was about to justify her choice of words when her phone rang. It was Marc. 'Yes?' Anna said quickly.

'Mum's awake.'

Anna gasped with relief. 'Mum's awake,' she told Ellie, who immediately let out a whoop of relief. 'How is she?' Anna asked Marc.

'Not too bad. She threw up, poor thing, but Simonetta said that's pretty normal after a hit on the head. And she says it's promising that Mum's conscious again so quickly.'

'That's good to know.'

'Any sign of the ambulance?'

Anna scanned the canal. In the distance, a small speck that was possibly a speedboat seemed to be hurrying towards them. 'Maybe. There's a boat coming. Hang on, I think it's painted yellow and —' She squinted. 'And yes, there's a red stripe, so I reckon it's them.'

'Great. We'll be ready.'

Everything happened rather quickly after that. The boat was indeed an ambulance and as soon as it docked, two paramedics in fluoro jackets, a man and a woman, disembarked with businesslike speed, bringing medical packs and what looked like a collapsible stretcher. The woman spoke English, which was a huge relief, and Anna reported the good news that their mother was conscious.

'We go this way,' she added, probably speaking a little too loudly as they headed off once more across the empty campo.

When they arrived back at the scene of the accident, Daisy was still lying on the ground, but someone had brought her a blanket and a pillow. Simonetta was still in her bathrobe and slippers and, by now, neighbours had emerged from the surrounding buildings. Some of them were in dressing gowns and watching with concern from a discreet distance.

The paramedics were very efficient. In no time they had checked Daisy over and then transferred her to their stretcher. They let Anna and Ellie speak to her briefly.

'You'll be okay now, Mum,' Anna told her. 'You're in safe hands.'

Her mum gave a faint nod.

The paramedics explained that she would need to be taken to Ospedale SS Giovanni e Paolo in Castello. There was a very good chance she would be admitted and would stay overnight, possibly longer.

'I've packed a bag with a few of Daisy's things,' Bronte told Anna. 'A nightie, toiletries. Her purse and phone.'

'Oh, that's genius. Well done, and thanks.' Anna turned back to the paramedics. 'Would I be able to come with you, to the hospital?' It would be scary for her mum to be in a strange hospital in a foreign country, with everybody speaking Italian.

Her question was barely out, however, when she felt a hand on her arm. It was Marc. 'If anyone goes to the hospital, it should be me,' he said.

Anna was about to protest. She needed to be in the centre of things. She always had and she would probably never change. But the serious intensity in Marc's gaze silenced her. She supposed he was the eldest after all, the 'man of the family' and, perhaps, after tonight's shock at Gina's, he needed to make that quite clear – to himself, to all of them.

She nodded and the paramedics agreed that Marc could accompany them.

'You'll ring us to let us know what's happening, won't you?' Anna said.

'Of course.'

Bronte came forward and kissed Marc's cheek. He and his wife shared a sad smile and held hands for a moment, but as far as Anna could tell they didn't speak and the simmering tension between them hadn't abated. She wished she could wave a magic wand and cure whatever their problem was, cure their mum as well. Cure herself. Hell, while she was about it, she might as well also try to cure the past and whatever mistakes their father might have made.

Life sure could get messy.

CHAPTER TWENTY-SEVEN

'Hi, Mrs Cassidy. It's Ellie.'

'Ellie? Where are you ringing from? I thought you were in Italy.'

'Yes, I am. We're still in Venice.' Ellie kept her voice low. It was after midnight and Anna and Bronte were in the living room drinking hot chocolate. Ellie had retired to the bedroom, but there was no way she could sleep. She needed, more than anything, to talk to Zach.

All her life, she'd shared the big moments with Zach, their highs and their lows. He was her best friend, after all. Actually, their history reached back to before she and Zach were born, to when their fathers were in the same surf club.

Zach's parents had built their house just a short block away from the Benettos, and from an early age, Ellie had been allowed to visit them on her own, as long as she went by the quiet back streets. The Cassidys' backyard ran down to a creek and Ellie and Zach had built a cubby house on its bank.

Crawling through the tangled lantana that grew there and playing war games with Zach and his brother Ben were among her favourite childhood memories. One summer, Ellie had been bitten by a tick and it was Zach's mother who'd pulled the pesky insect out with tweezers before dabbing tea-tree oil on the bite. Another time, Zach had ridden his skateboard in the Benettos' cul de sac and had fallen, breaking his collar bone. Daisy had taken him to Emergency.

Their childhoods had been so blended, their mums had joked that they were interchangeable, which had caused their dads to laugh uproariously.

After Ellie's father had died, the first person she'd turned to was Zach. He'd taken her to the beach and they'd sat on a smooth rock on the headland for ages. With his arm around her, she'd wept on his shoulder and just knowing he was there for her had helped. So much.

Now she was on the other side of the world, dealing with a crisis almost as bad as her father's death. If that falling piece of plaster had been a bit heavier or sharper . . .

Ellie's emotions were spinning. The possibility of losing her mother as well as her father was just too huge to take in, but she didn't want to break down in front of the others. They seemed to be handling this way more calmly, and she would feel like a baby. Zach would understand this, but he still wasn't answering her calls. Ellie wasn't sure if he was even bothering to read her texts.

He mustn't be, surely?

In desperation, she'd tried his home phone.

'Is everything okay?' Mrs Cassidy asked.

'Not really. Mum's had an accident.'

'Oh, no. Oh, Ellie, darling. Poor Daisy, I'm so sorry. Is – is she badly hurt?'

'I – we're not sure. We're still waiting to hear from the hospital.' Despite her impatience to reach Zach, Ellie explained about the falling masonry, including her horror at seeing her mother unconscious, and she was grateful for Mrs Cassidy's caring sympathy. And then, before she burst, 'I – I wondered if Zach was home.'

'Well, no, Ellie, he's at work. It's almost ten o'clock in the morning here.'

'Oh, yes. Sorry. With everything that's happened, I forgot about the time zones. So – so, he's all right then?'

'Yes, Ellie, Zach's fine. You know, same as always, up early to the beach and then off to work.'

This was a relief, kind of, although it meant that Zach's silence was even more of a mystery. Unfortunately, Ellie couldn't really ask his mother if her son was distracted by a hot new girlfriend. 'It's just that I haven't heard from him in ages.'

'Oh. I – ah . . .' Mrs Cassidy sounded caught out. 'I suppose Zach might have thought you were too busy enjoying yourself and he didn't want to bother you.'

No, Ellie thought. That wouldn't be the reason, not if Zach had been reading her texts pleading for a word from him.

'Maybe he's lost his phone,' Ellie said, wincing as she realised how pathetic this sounded.

'No, I don't think —' Mrs Cassidy began, but then she seemed to correct herself. 'Well, I suppose it's possible, but he hasn't mentioned it. I'll definitely tell him that you rang about Daisy's accident.'

Ellie suppressed an urge to sigh. 'Good. Thanks.'

'I do hope your mum will be all right, Ellie.'

'Yes, thanks. Fingers crossed.'

'I'm sure the hospitals in Italy are very good.'

'Yes, I hope so.'

'Let me know if there's anything we can do from our end, love. If you need me to contact your travel insurers, or anything like that, please call, won't you?'

'Yes, I will. Thanks, Mrs C.' A little helplessly, Ellie said, 'Bye.'

'Bye bye, Ellie.'

The bedroom door opened as this conversation ended and Anna

appeared. 'I thought I heard you talking. It wasn't a call from the hospital, was it?'

Ellie shook her head. 'I rang Zach's place and got Mrs Cassidy. I told her about Mum.'

'Oh, right.' Anna nodded. 'I tend to forget how close you've always been to the Cassidys.' She smiled. 'Your second family.'

Not so sure about that, Ellie thought sadly.

Anna shoved aside a pile of clothes on the end of her bed and sat. She was still dressed in the things she'd worn out, the black velvet trousers and ruffled shirt, and Ellie thought she looked exhausted but beautiful.

'What's Zach doing these days?' Anna asked.

'Working in his dad's garage.'

Anna's eyebrows rose. 'So he's on a gap year, too?'

'No, he's working full time as a mechanic, doing his apprenticeship and everything.'

'No plans for uni?'

'Nope.'

Anna seemed to consider this for a moment or two and then gave a shrug. 'Sensible guy. The world will always need good mechanics.'

'Mmm.' Ellie was keen to put an end to this line of enquiry. If she wasn't careful, she'd find herself forced to defend her lack of ambition or direction when it came to her own career. But she was tired and couldn't think of a way to silence her sister.

'You still keen on him?' Anna asked.

'Huh?'

'You still keen on Zach?'

Heat exploded in Ellie's face. 'Are you crazy?' Panic tightened her throat, making her voice squeak. She swallowed and tried to ignore the sudden pounding of her heartbeat. 'Give me a break, Anna. You know Zach and I are just friends. That's all we've ever been. Best friends.'

Or at least we were until recently. Before his silent treatment.

Anna made no comment, just sat there with one ankle propped on a knee and an annoyingly shrewd gleam in her eyes. 'Yeah, right,' she said, without the slightest hint of conviction.

Ellie felt as if she was suffocating. This wasn't the first time people had accused her of having a crush on Zach. Her friends at school had rubbished her about it. Why couldn't everyone just accept that two people of the opposite sex could be really good friends without any romantic rubbish?

She glared at her sister. 'We shouldn't be talking about Zach. We should be concentrating all our thoughts on Mum.'

'You're right about that,' said Anna. 'I'm going to ring Marc.'

'Wouldn't you let Bronte do that?'

'She's gone upstairs. If she's sensible she'll be in bed. Anyway, I'm sure she wouldn't have a problem with us calling him.'

Ellie accepted this with a nod that was swiftly overtaken by a huge yawn. 'We should all be in bed,' she said, and promptly yawned again. She began to undress while Anna rang Marc's number.

'Okay,' she heard Anna say. 'Okay, Marc, right, thanks. That's good. Will you be fine to find your way home at this hour? Yes, catch a private taxi, if you can. It's too far to walk.'

Ellie was dragging on her pyjama top as Anna disconnected. 'How's Mum?' she asked as her head emerged through the neck hole.

'She's had a CT scan of her brain and there are no obvious problems. Just the large laceration on her forehead.'

'Thank God for that.'

'Yes, it's great news. But she's still feeling giddy, so they're keeping her in till the giddiness subsides.'

'Right.'

'Marc says he's really impressed with the hospital. They're on the ball and being really nice to Mum.'

'Great.' Ellie yawned again. Now that she knew that her mother was out of danger, she was swamped by a tsunami of weariness. 'Think I'll hit the hay.'

'Good idea. I might wait up for Marc.'

'Really?' Ellie felt guilty, but she was quite sure she couldn't keep her eyes open a minute longer.

'Yeah, I'll be fine,' said Anna. 'I'll wait out on the couch.'

'You're a good sister.'

'I know. I deserve an award,' Anna said dryly before she slipped out of the room, closing the door behind her.

Left in the darkness, Ellie thought again about Zach and his strange, hurtful silence. On top of the scare about her mum, it really was too much. Softly, so Anna couldn't hear, she cried herself to sleep.

CHAPTER TWENTY-EIGHT

Bronte slept late. At some point in the early hours Marc had come home, but as soon as he'd assured her that Daisy had escaped serious injury, she'd fallen quickly back to sleep.

Now, while her husband lay exhausted beside her, she watched sunlight blaze around the edges of the bedroom shutters. From outside on the canal, motorboats zipped past. The day was well and truly underway.

Bronte reached for her phone. It was ten past ten. Wow. She couldn't remember the last time she'd slept so late.

Dressing quickly and quietly so as not to disturb Marc, she headed downstairs to make coffee. The door to Anna and Ellie's room was still closed, so presumably, the girls were both still asleep.

The aroma of brewing coffee might wake them, Bronte decided, so she changed her plans. She would slip out to a café.

As she returned upstairs to fetch her purse, she moved as stealthily as she could. Even so, Marc stirred.

'Would you like me to bring you back a takeaway?' she asked.

He stared at her through narrowed, sleepy eyes, then shook his head and rolled away with his back to her. No smile. No thanks. No 'see you later'.

The slug of disappointment hit Bronte harder than it should have. Hopeless and heartsick, she went back downstairs and out into the street. She told herself she had to get used to this. What else could she expect from Marc? So much had gone wrong for him, he must feel under siege.

Not only was he dealing with the strain of keeping their relationship troubles under wraps, but now he had the double whammy of his mother's accident and the disturbing news about his father and the Vincinis.

There was a limit to how many shocks a man could take and Bronte felt genuine compassion for her husband. She would have liked to tell him this, but she could hardly expect him to believe or accept her sympathy when he knew jolly well that she planned to walk away from him forever.

That was still her plan. She mustn't give it up.

Even though she and Marc still hadn't had the in-depth discussion she felt they needed, and even though *everything* felt so very different here, away from the Valley, she had to stick to her guns. If she allowed this holiday to weaken her resolve, she and Marc would just fall back into the same old patterns. Nothing would change.

I'm tired, Bronte told herself. *That's why I feel so down.*

Unfortunately, her choice to sit at a wrought-iron table in a patch of sunlight didn't cheer her at all. The scenario should have been perfect. A nearby wall was covered with a sweetly scented flowering creeper, her coffee was divine and her croissant dainty and delicious. This morning, however, it seemed that nothing could raise her spirits.

She decided to continue wandering. She knew the Benettos didn't need her. If they decided to head off to the hospital, Anna would almost certainly leave a message on her phone, or a note at the apartment. And, anyway, Daisy wouldn't want a crowd of visitors.

Bronte continued on, dawdling without any particular plan, trying to soak up the atmosphere of this romantic and dreamlike city and not to brood about Marc. She followed streets she'd missed on previous explorations and allowed herself to imagine what it might be like to live here in Venice, for a year perhaps. Making daily purchases from the market stalls, attending classes in glass-bead making and learning Italian, perhaps taking a cooking class or two.

Deep in these fantasies, Bronte almost missed the gondola on the canal decorated with white ribbons and carrying a bride. The cheers from people gathered on the bank caught her attention at first and then she saw the lovely bride with dark hair and dark eyes like Anna's, dressed in a traditional white dress, with elegant lace sleeves and a billowing veil.

Beside the bride sat her father, looking distinguished with thick grey hair that contrasted strikingly with his dark formal suit. Behind them, in a second gondola, four little flower girls were also dressed in white.

The gondolas slowed just ahead of Bronte and pulled into a mooring. Her intrigue deepened when she realised there was a little campo and the most exquisite church positioned right there beside the canal.

A wedding was about to take place almost in front of Bronte.

Fascinated, she watched two older men, possibly the bride's uncles, helping her and her father from the boat. They were quite charming, she thought, taking inordinate care with the bride's veil and bouquet.

The scene plucked at poor Bronte's heartstrings. And for irrational reasons she didn't understand, she suddenly needed, most desperately, to slip into the back of the church and to watch this bride's arrival inside. To catch a glimpse of her happiness, perhaps?

Bronte hoped no one would mind.

Luck was on her side. She was able to follow a group of guests through the church's beautiful stone arches and no one seemed worried that she was a stranger, or that she wasn't dressed as formally as the rest of the congregation. At least she'd worn a cream silk shirt with her black jeans and boots today, so she didn't feel too shabby. She sat in the very back pew, planning to steal away before the ceremony actually started.

Bronte wasn't a very experienced churchgoer. Her parents had been staunch agnostics who never set foot in a church from one year to the next and Bronte's understanding of Christianity was pretty much limited to what she'd gleaned from festivals like Christmas and Easter or from literature and art history.

Leo Benetto had been raised a Catholic, but he hadn't insisted on a church wedding for Marc, so theirs had been a civil ceremony in a garden in the Sunshine Coast hinterland. Now, as Bronte admired this church's interior, she felt a strange calmness descend, not unlike the way she'd always felt when she entered an art gallery or a library.

Despite her upbringing, she'd always been rather curious about churches, especially Catholic churches with their grottos and statues. In Venice, there were so many and whether they were huge and magnificent like St Mark's Basilica or small and exquisite like this one, their beauty was enchanting. More than once Bronte had found herself contemplating the faith that had inspired such amazing efforts in architecture and craftsmanship.

The walls of this building were decorated both inside and out with lovely coloured marble. At the front, above the altar, the coloured glass in two gorgeous rose windows glowed with sunlight.

Huge urns of white roses decorated the nave, as well as the mandatory statue of the Virgin Mary. A chubby baby Jesus looked as if he was trying to wriggle out of Mary's arms and Bronte couldn't help smiling.

Behind the altar was a magnificent painting, all swirling dark clouds with angels and devils, and on either side of the nave old wooden choir stalls stood tall. Today there was no choir, however, just a single harp being played softly, while the groom took his place at the chancel steps to wait nervously for his bride.

The groom looked nice, Bronte decided. He had dark curly hair and was wonderfully ordinary, really. Almost handsome but wearing glasses and looking perhaps like an accountant. She found herself wishing fervently that his marriage would be a happy one. She hoped he looked after his bride.

Don't think about Marc.

A woman, probably in her fifties, arrived and walked down the aisle alone. Plump and dressed in a cerise suit with a corsage pinned to her bosom, she was, almost certainly, the bride's mother. She looked both proud and sentimental. A stupid stone lodged in Bronte's throat.

Oh, God. I'm not going to cry. I can't. Not here, not over strangers.

It was time to make her escape, quickly, before the service got underway. But by the time Bronte felt calm enough to leave with any kind of dignity, it was already too late. The harp had given way to pipe-organ music and the bridal party was assembled at the back of the church, ready to process. There was no way out.

Keeping her eyes wide open in a bid to ward off tears, Bronte stayed.

The flower girls came first. Two were dark and two fair, and they looked ever so sweet in ankle-length white dresses, with circlets of ivy and tiny white flowers in their hair. They carried baskets filled with rose petals, which they conscientiously scattered as they progressed down the aisle.

One of the fairer flower girls, the smaller of the two, who might have only been three or four, looked rather overawed and waved to someone in the congregation. So, so cute. The stone in Bronte's throat grew into a boulder.

Now came the bride, beside her proud father . . .

She looked beautiful, of course, and even the misty veil over her face couldn't hide her radiant smile.

Bronte was shocked by the wave of emotions that flooded her. As the happy procession moved past, she could feel her mouth pulling down at the corners, her lips trembling, her eyes filling with tears. What was wrong with her? How had she ever thought that snooping on a stranger's wedding was a sane idea?

Luckily there was a tissue in the pocket of her jeans. She swiped at her eyes as the bride and groom met at the end of the red carpeted aisle.

Now. She should make her escape now.

Bronte stood and turned to do just that, but the two ushers at the church door both frowned at her. Chastened, she sat again. The bride's father was shaking the groom's hand, and then he kissed his daughter before joining his wife in the front pew.

After this, the bride and groom climbed the stone steps to the splendidly robed priest who waited in front of the altar and the ceremony began.

Of course, everything was in Italian. It was strangely comforting, however, to let that melodious language roll over her. And, with the bride and groom at some distance now, Bronte felt calmer. Until they reached the vows.

Io, Luigi, prendo te, Giulia, come mia sposa e prometto . . .

Bronte could only guess what the groom was saying, but now, at the crucial moment, her head was invaded by memories of her own wedding. Their ceremony hadn't been in a church, but she and Marc had settled on traditional vows.

Will you, Bronte Elizabeth, have Marc Leo to be your husband? Will you love him, comfort and keep him, and forsaking all others remain true to him, as long as you both shall live?

Oh, help.

This was crazy. Her tears ran freely now and the tissue was soaked. She couldn't believe she'd been so stupid as to come here. What on earth had she hoped to achieve by witnessing the beginning of another couple's marriage when she planned to end her own?

She should have known those vows would get to her.

Bronte struggled to recall a counsellor's advice. It was important to remember that she shouldn't punish herself if she needed to break those vows. Divorce was a sensible option when a marriage wasn't working. One in three marriages ended that way.

But how many of those one in three couples felt this kind of pain?

When Bronte's own parents had divorced, she'd never really understood what their problem was, although she'd been aware that they only just tolerated each other's company. Neither her mother nor her father was keen on deep and meaningful chats, but her mother had made a comment that marriage wasn't a sacred contract. That concept was old-fashioned, restrictive nonsense.

What her mother had failed to mention at the time was that she actually preferred women. That had become apparent later, when she'd moved in with Hilary, a senior lecturer in English at the same university. However, Bronte couldn't use sexual preferences as an excuse for her own failures. She most definitely preferred men.

Sad truth, she preferred Marc. She'd always found him attractive and sexy – he'd just become damned impossible to live with. But now, when she imagined telling people in the future how her marriage had ended in Venice, she almost broke down completely.

Meanwhile, this ceremony was coming to an end. The groom kissed the bride and the members of the congregation clapped.

Bronte clapped too and forced herself to smile. And as the organ burst into a triumphant fanfare and the happy couple processed out of the church, she knew she had no choice but to put her problems aside to be dealt with later, when Daisy was stronger. Endless dwelling on them never helped.

Bronte waited till most of the guests had followed the bride and groom before she moved out of her pew. Some of the guests nodded and smiled at her, obviously thinking they should know her. She supposed she should add wedding-guest imposter to her list of sins.

Outside, tourists had stopped to stare while the newlyweds posed for photos on the church steps. Guests gathered in the campo in happy clusters, greeting each other with kisses on both cheeks, laughing as the flower girls blew bubbles.

Backing away to mingle with the crowd, Bronte couldn't resist using her phone to snap one quick photo. When she checked it she gasped. The happy couple had kissed just as she'd clicked and she'd captured a perfect shot of them framed by the beautiful church, with the little flower girls in the foreground sending up a romantic haze of rainbow-tinted bubbles.

The picture was so lovely, so poignant and perfect, Bronte almost deleted it. Why torture herself with another couple's bliss?

Somehow, she couldn't quite let it go.

Slipping the phone into her pocket, she walked on.

CHAPTER TWENTY-NINE

Anna stopped to check the mud map Simonetta had drawn for her. She was looking for an apartment tucked away in a back street of the Rialto district near the Ca' d'Oro palazzo and she was confident she was closing in on it.

Judging by Simonetta's rough sketch and arrows, the apartment should be around the next corner. Anna's pulse quickened as she continued. Today she was focused on her destination rather than the centuries of history and the atmospheric buildings. She needed to find number sixty-one. To her relief, as she rounded the corner, there it was, just as Simonetta had indicated.

The wrought-iron gate in a high brick wall looked daunting, but when Anna checked, there was no security code needed and the gate wasn't locked. It squeaked as she opened it, squeaked again as she closed it behind her.

A narrow path lay ahead and the brick walls continued on either side. At the end of this alley, a huge V-shaped arch supported by impressive stone columns opened into a small courtyard.

Aware that she was entering a very private domain, Anna almost tiptoed as she moved forward. A niche in one wall of the courtyard held an urn filled with flowers. A fountain whispered softly. It was like arriving in another world.

Her nervousness mounted. Beyond the courtyard was a double set of arches fitted with hefty wooden doors. Almost certainly, these doors led to the apartments. Anna was looking for number two, and there it was, on the right.

Here goes . . .

The door was shiny black with a brass knocker in the shape of a fox. Anna lifted it and knocked and her heartbeat seemed to double as she waited.

And waited . . . listening intently for any sound from within.

The place remained silent.

After several minutes and two more attempts with the knocker, it was clear. No one was home.

Anna swore none too softly. She'd carefully timed this visit for the early evening when most people were home from work but had not yet started their dinner.

All day, since she'd first made these plans, she'd been sick and anxious and, now, the disappointment of being foiled was almost more than she could bear. She was of a mind to simply sit and wait.

Turning, she looked for a seat in the courtyard, but as she did so, she heard the squeak of the gate. A man, thirty-ish, tall, and dark, was coming up the path.

'*Buonasera*,' he said politely as he approached.

He was wearing a smart business suit, white shirt and striped tie. His dark hair was thick and slightly shaggy, his jaw covered with a five o'clock shadow and his eyes were as dark as black coffee. He was absurdly good looking.

'*Buonasera*,' said Anna. 'I – I mean, hello.' She might as well make it clear from the start that she didn't speak Italian.

'Can I help you?' he asked in careful English.

'I hope so. I'm looking for Gabriele Vincini.'

The guy smiled and – *oh, my God* – the sparkle in his dark eyes almost robbed Anna of breath.

Behave yourself, Anna. He could be your freaking brother.

'I am Gabriele Vincini,' he said.

His voice was a deep rumble. *Of course it is.*

Anna struggled to rein in her over-the-top reaction. This was her quarry, after all, and it was important to remain circumspect. She had serious questions to ask him, and she hoped that he knew the answers and was willing to share them without animosity.

Rather a lot was at stake. Like her entire family's future happiness.

She hadn't told her siblings she was coming here. During the past twenty-four hours Ellie had sunk into a gloomy sulk and was next to useless, and Anna certainly hadn't wanted Marc muscling in on this meeting. She had visions of her brother and Gabriele in a macho stand-off. Pistols at dawn.

She'd decided it was up to her to approach Gabriele Vincini on behalf of her family, and to ask the difficult questions. Swooning over his good looks was most definitely not an option.

'Hi, Gabriele,' she said. 'My name's Anna Benetto.'

'Benetto?' He frowned and stepped closer.

Anna held her breath.

'Are you from Australia?'

'I am, yes.'

'Are you related to Leo Benetto?'

Gulp. 'That's right.' She nodded. 'I'm Leo's daughter.'

Anna wasn't sure what she'd expected then, but Gabriele's broad grin was a surprise.

'This is wonderful,' he declared. 'I'm very pleased to meet you, Anna.'

'Ah – thanks. You, too.'

She'd anticipated a handshake, but Gabriele Vincini was an Italian, after all. As he stepped closer, she realised he planned to kiss her on both cheeks and, to steady herself, Anna found it necessary to grip his arm. Embarrassing heat suffused her. Almost certainly she'd turned fifty shades of red, even though his lips had barely brushed her skin.

'Are you here on holiday or for work?' Gabriele asked as she released him.

'A holiday.' Anna reminded herself to breathe, and she decided not to mention the rest of her family just yet. 'I didn't have too far to come, though. I work in London.'

Gabriele looked intrigued. 'In what field?'

'I'm an actor.'

'Ah.' This brought a warm smile. 'How wonderful.'

Anna had been hoping that he would invite her in for a proper conversation, but they were still standing in the courtyard.

'What sort of work do you do?' she asked.

'I'm a doctor,' Gabriele said. '*Un pediatra*. Sorry – a paediatrician.'

Another surprise. A huge one, actually. Anna had been half expecting him to tell her that he modelled for Gucci or some other Italian fashion house.

She hoped she didn't look stunned, but when she pictured this drop-dead gorgeous guy in hospital whites with a stethoscope around his neck and a sweet little newborn in his arms, her heart gave a strange little clunk. 'How – how wonderful.'

She knew she was parroting his exact words, but her head was a complete muddle, making it hard to think.

'You'll come inside, won't you,' Gabriele said now, as he unlocked the black door.

'Thank you.' *At last.*

'Will you have a drink with me?'

Anna had anticipated a more formal, businesslike meeting. It might well be dangerous to relax.

'I don't want to interrupt your plans,' she said. After all, she had no idea if Gabriele had a live-in girlfriend, a wife, a family.

'I have no special plans for this evening.'

'You live alone?' Her stupid cheeks flamed again as she asked this.

He smiled. 'Sì.' Then nodded towards his doorway. 'Come.'

'Thank you.'

The door opened to reveal a narrow marble staircase and as Anna followed him up these steps to his apartment, she had the strange sense of ascending to a stage to play a major role in a very important scene. Problem was, she only knew half the script, the questions she'd come here to ask.

Gabriele's answers, on the other hand, were still a mystery and had the potential to break her heart.

The stairs opened into a living area, not large, but very tasteful with parquetry flooring and trendy red sofas loaded with white cushions.

'Excuse me one moment,' Gabriele said as he took off his coat and draped it over the back of a sofa, before removing his tie and loosening the buttons at his throat, an activity Anna found far more fascinating than was appropriate.

He smiled. 'Have you also visited my mother?'

'No, not yet.' When Anna had begun her search earlier in the day, hunting through the phone directory for Sofia Vincini, she'd found a separate entry for Gabriele and had decided to approach the son rather than upset yet another Venetian matron.

She'd also figured that someone from a younger generation might be more likely to speak English and she was pleased she'd been right. Now the first hurdle was behind her.

If only she knew how many hurdles lay ahead.

'I'll get wine glasses.' Already, Gabriele was heading for a small kitchen to one side of the living space. 'Do you like prosecco?' he called over his shoulder.

'Yes, please.' He hadn't invited her to follow him and Anna, feeling a little shy, stayed put. The apartment was compact but stylish, the windows, doors and ceiling mouldings all carrying hints of the old-world charm that was synonymous with Venice. At the far end of the living room, French doors led to a small stone balcony and Anna went to investigate. It looked down into the courtyard and the fountain.

'There's another balcony off the kitchen with a view of a canal,' Gabriele called from the kitchen doorway.

Anna turned.

He had rolled back his sleeves to just below the elbows, revealing muscular forearms. *Sigh*. He'd already looked good in his business suit, but now his casual look was even hotter.

Crikey. Marc was so not going to enjoy meeting this guy.

'You should come and see it,' he said.

'Excuse me?'

'The balcony. It's very nice at this time of day.'

'Oh, yeah. Sure.'

'Sometimes there's a sunset.'

'That sounds lovely.'

She crossed to the kitchen. Gabriele hadn't wasted time, having already assembled glasses, a wine bottle and a small blue dish with olives and cheese.

'Can I carry something?' she asked.

'Thank you.' He handed her the dish of olives while he gathered up everything else.

Access to the kitchen balcony involved climbing through a low window, but with this achieved, the balcony was gorgeous. Tiny but just big enough for a table and two chairs, and incredibly private, it offered the promised view of a narrow canal complete with gondolas, as well as a lovely vista of sky and assorted rooftops.

'Oh, wow!' Anna said. 'How awesome is this? Like an eyrie.'

'Excuse me? An ear— how you say?'

'Sorry – an eyrie is an eagle's nest. And that's what this little balcony feels like.' She waved her hand to indicate the canal below, the sky above.

Gabriele's response was another of his gorgeous grins. 'An eagle's nest. Sì, sì.'

'And we might be in luck with a sunset,' said Anna.

Even as Gabriele released the cork and poured the bubbling wine into their glasses, the sky had begun to turn a shimmering pink, making silhouettes of the rooftops, including a dome and a distant steeple.

'This is just perfect,' she murmured.

Or rather, this setting would have been perfect if she'd come here simply to enjoy the sunset and drink prosecco with a handsome Italian. Unfortunately, she was a woman on a mission.

Gabriele touched his glass to hers. '*Salute.*'

'Salute,' Anna repeated and when she sipped the wine it was deliciously cool and fizzed on her tongue.

Leaning back in his chair, Gabriele certainly looked very relaxed. He took a sip of his wine and sent her another of his super charming smiles. 'This is a wonderful surprise, Anna.'

It was silly to love the sound of her name when he said it. 'Thanks for having me. It's – great to meet you.'

'And you're an actor, you said?'

'Yes.'

'Might I have seen you in a film? On the big screen?'

'Oh, no.' Anna almost wished she hadn't told him about the acting. She probably should have just said that she worked in a restaurant. 'I mainly do stage work,' she said. 'And a little television.'

'I'm sure you're very good at your job. You have such an expressive face.'

'I do?'

'Yes,' Gabriele said. 'So much emotion.'

Could he read her emotions? *Careful, Anna. He can probably see how impressed you are.* She gave a little laugh to cover her confusion and she was working up to an intelligent question about Gabriele's role in paediatrics when his expression sobered.

'I understand that Leo has died.' He said this very gently.

Anna nodded. 'Yes, Dad died last year. It was terrible. So sudden, just before he was due to retire.'

'A heart attack?'

'Yeah.'

'I'm so sorry, Anna. Please accept my condolences.'

'Thank you.' She wondered what else Gabriele knew about her family.

'Your father and my mother were very good friends when they were young.'

'Yes,' she said cautiously. 'So I believe.' She was surprised Gabriele could tell her this so calmly.

He offered her the little blue dish. 'Try an olive and the cheese together,' he said. 'They complement each other very well.'

She did as he suggested and had to agree. The taste combo of the green olive and salty cheese was perfect. She gave a happy little sigh and looked up at the sky where the pink was already deepening to rosy gold. A breeze whispered up the canal. She watched it play with Gabriele's shirt collar and lift his dark hair.

It was incredibly tempting to forget why she'd come here and to simply enjoy his balcony, the view, his pleasant company, the wine . . .

But then Gabriele said, 'I suppose Leo must have told you about my mother and me. I imagine that's why you're here.'

'Sort of.' Anna dragged her attention back to the matter at hand and realised it was time to be honest. She took a deep breath for courage. 'Actually, no, Gabriele. Dad never told us about your mother. And he never mentioned you.'

'Never?'

'I don't believe so, no.'

Frowning, Gabriele set his glass down, sat straighter. 'But Leo's always been such wonderful support for my mother. You must know that.' He gave a puzzled shrug. 'So why are you here?'

So. They were getting to the pointy end of this conversation. Anna sat a little straighter too. She had no idea what Gabriele meant about her father's 'support' for his mother. She wondered why he hadn't mentioned his own relationship to Leo.

'We – or at least I – found out about you through my father's cousin, Gina Pesano. She lives here in Venice, too. Do you know her?'

'I know the name,' said Gabriele. 'I think that perhaps my mother knew her, but it would have been quite a long time ago.'

Anna waited, hoping that he might tell her more without prompting.

Instead, he topped up her wine glass and then his, but he was also watching her carefully. 'What's troubling you, Anna? That expressive face of yours is sending me worrying messages.'

'Sorry. I guess I am pretty tense.' She certainly wasn't doing very well as an actor this evening. 'But it's me, Gabriele, not you. Nothing to do with your wonderful hospitality. This is so lovely here.'

'But something is wrong. Can I help?'

Anna tried to smile. He really was very sweet. It seemed almost too good to be true that a man could be so considerate and so hot all in the one package.

She said, 'There are certain things I'm trying to understand about my father.'

'I'll certainly help if I can.'

'Thanks.' Anna fiddled with the stem of her wine glass, took a deep breath. 'It's been suggested that my father was in love with Sofia – with your mother. He wanted to marry her, but she rejected him and so – so he left for Australia.'

There was no missing the surprise in Gabriele's eyes. 'Is that what Gina Pesano told you?'

'More or less.' Anna grimaced, then hurried on. 'And it seems that you were born just a few months after Dad left here.'

Gabriele gave a careful nod. 'I believe that much is correct.'

'Which kind of suggests, that perhaps my father – Leo – was potentially your father, too?'

Gabriele stared at her now. He sat very still and his gaze was disturbingly serious.

Anna swallowed nervously. 'So what do you think?'

'I think,' he said, 'that there are definite gaps in your knowledge. You need to know the whole story.'

CHAPTER THIRTY

Daisy woke just as daylight filtered into her hospital room, and she knew straight away that she was much better. Her forehead had stopped throbbing and she could move her head from side to side without feeling dizzy.

Carefully, she sat up. Still no dizziness. Wonderful. Perhaps they would release her today.

Daisy couldn't complain about her care in this hospital, and she was grateful to the medical staff, but a two-day stay was quite long enough, thank you very much. Now she was eager to get out.

Hopefully, when she was back in the apartment with only a sticking plaster on her forehead as a reminder of the accident, she and her family could resume their holiday.

More than anything, Daisy wanted to recapture the fun and excitement of those early days in Venice. There were still so many things to see and do here. Anna had told her about a lovely restaurant that Renzo had taken her to, which was apparently a must. And a nurse here at the hospital had mentioned Venice's most popular beach, the Lido, just ten minutes by vaporetto from St Mark's Square. As a beach-loving family, the Benettos couldn't go home without a swim in the Adriatic Sea. And it would probably be worth taking a day trip or two, heading further afield.

Daisy had been checking out options for day trips on her phone and there was a wonderful selection out of Venice – to Croatia, to Austria, the Dolomites, Lake Como. All of them sounded amazing.

More than anything, Daisy wanted – or, rather, needed – to keep busy. If it was humanly possible, she needed to delete that night at Gina Pesano's from her thoughts. She couldn't bear to dig any deeper into Leo's past, so it was best to set Gina's disturbing story aside, to try to forget it and to move on.

The past couldn't be changed and Daisy wanted to continue on now as if she'd never known about Leo and Sofia Vincini. She wasn't sure if it was possible to just wipe such hurtful information from her brain, but she was jolly well going to try. She could only hope that her children could also put that night's disclosure behind them.

Anna seemed to be coping the best, Daisy had decided, but her daughter was so good at acting it was often hard to tell how she really felt. Ellie was a mess, poor kid. Even Tyler Davenport's pleasant company didn't seem to be helping her at the moment.

As for Marc, Daisy had no idea how her son was faring since the shock at Gina's. He'd been wonderful on the night of the accident, staying with Daisy the whole time, both on the ambulance boat and in Emergency, waiting patiently while she was wheeled away through a sprawling labyrinth of hallways, gleaming and waxed like hospitals everywhere, to be examined and given scans.

It wasn't till the early hours of the next morning that Daisy had finally been admitted and brought to this room and Marc had stayed with her throughout the night. As her son had kissed her goodbye, Daisy had tried to tell him she was sorry.

Marc had shushed her. 'Don't,' he'd said. 'You have nothing to apologise for.'

She would have liked to explain that she hadn't been apologising for her own behaviour, but that she was sorry for Marc. Sorry that he'd received such shocking news about his father. But she'd been too dizzy at the time to get her thoughts in order.

She hadn't seen Marc since. The others had all visited at least once – Ellie, Anna, Bronte, even Charles and Tyler Davenport, but Marc had stayed away.

'How is he?' Daisy had asked Bronte.

Bronte had simply shrugged. 'It's hard to say, to be honest. He's really withdrawn. Hardly communicating at all.' Then she'd given a crooked smile and tried to reassure Daisy. 'But I'm trying not to read too much into it. Marc can be like that sometimes.'

Remembering this now, Daisy let out her breath on a worried sigh. *Damn you, Leo.*

Despite her new resolve, the mere thought of her husband brought a deluge of memories and although she tried to resist them, the scenes from the past were unstoppable. She found herself transported back to their home in Castaways Beach, reliving a time just after they'd moved in, when they still had no lawn, no gardens. Leo, however, had already planted the white tabebuia tree in the backyard.

It was no more than a twig, tied to a stake by a piece of stocking, but he'd called Daisy outside to admire it.

'One day this will be tall and beautiful,' he'd told her. 'It will spread its branches and shade our barbecue area.'

Daisy had grinned. 'So we're going to have a barbecue area?'

'Of course we are,' Leo had cried and he'd hugged Daisy hard and then proceeded to outline his plans, pacing out the backyard, showing her where the paving would go and explaining about the wood-fired pizza oven he was going to build and the tiled benches that would go on either side of the barbecue.

'And our family will sit here in the shade of this magnificent tree.'

In that moment, Daisy Benetto had been the happiest woman on earth and quite possibly the luckiest, she was sure. It was only a week or two later that she'd gone to the doctor and come home with the happy news that the first little member of their family was already on its way.

Leo had been ecstatic. 'Oh, Daisy, darling, you clever, clever girl.' He'd been about to dance her around the living room when he realised that perhaps he should be gentle, but he'd been so happy he'd had tears in his eyes.

Two months later a scan had revealed that their baby was a boy. Daisy would have liked to keep the baby's gender a surprise to be discovered at the birth, but Leo had been anxious to know straight away. He practically did handstands when they were told that their firstborn would be a son. So proud, Daisy thought he might burst.

Two packages arrived in the mail a few weeks after this, one from Sydney and another from Milan in Italy. Daisy was itching with curiosity, but the parcels were addressed to Leo, so she waited till he came home from work.

He grinned with delight when he saw them, but he wanted Daisy to open them.

'They're for the baby,' he told her and of course she was excited then, too.

Her curiosity mounted as she wrestled with the packaging. The parcels were too flat to hold teddy bears, but perhaps she would find a lovely crocheted baby blanket or a handmade patchwork quilt.

What she discovered, however, as she peeled the inner wrappings away, were baby-sized soccer jerseys. One in the green and gold of the Australian team, the Socceroos, and the other blue, with a white stripe on the sleeve and an embroidered shield, striped in red, white and green.

'My goodness.' Daisy was so surprised, this was all she could manage to say.

'For our little boy,' Leo announced.

'Yes, so I gathered.' She laughed then. The jerseys were quite ridiculous, but of course, she should have known Leo wouldn't be buying crocheted baby shawls or handmade quilts.

She held up the blue jersey. 'Is this the Italian soccer team?'

'Yes,' he said. '*Gli Azzurri*, the Blues. I want our son to know his heritage.'

Oh, boy.

Looking back now and remembering her husband's incredible joy over Marc's arrival, Daisy found it hard to imagine that Leo had already fathered a son and then abandoned him. But then, she supposed his over-the-top excitement about Marc might have been some kind of compensation.

That possibility made Daisy want to cry, but she was determined not to give in to tears. She helped herself to a glass of water from the jug on the bedside table. Next to the jug was a vase of flowers from Charles Davenport – lovely freesias and lily of the valley – and a note reminding her that Charles was still looking forward to their Vivaldi night, which had been rescheduled after her accident.

It was lovely of him to bother about her, but his note was also a timely reminder that Daisy had plenty to look forward to. And she would most definitely have that night out.

Yes. Damn Leo.

The doctor arrived just as Daisy was finishing her breakfast and after careful questioning and a conscientious examination, he pronounced her fit to go home.

She rang Anna with the good news.

'Oh, that's fabulous,' her daughter declared. 'But can you hang on a bit, Mum?'

Hang on? 'Well, yes, sure.'

'I just want to check – um – the ferry times et cetera, so I can tell you exactly when I'll be there to collect you.'

'Oh, of course. All right.'

More than five minutes passed before Anna rang back, which was rather deflating for Daisy who was on tenterhooks to leave. At last there was a call.

'I'll be there at midday, Mum. Is that too long to wait? They don't want to kick you out before that, do they?'

'No,' said Daisy. 'At least, I don't think so.'

'Great.'

Daisy knew it was silly to be disappointed simply because her daughter wasn't rushing to the hospital to collect her at the very first opportunity. Nevertheless, the delay did seem a little strange, and out of character. 'Is everything all right, Anna?'

'Yes, sure. Why?'

'Oh, no reason, I guess. I just . . .'

'It's okay, Mum. We haven't trashed the apartment while you've been gone.'

'Of course you haven't. That never occurred to me. I just . . .' For the second time, Daisy let her sentence trail away. 'Are Marc and Ellie okay?' she asked instead.

'Sure. At least, I'm pretty sure. I'm not at home right now, but I know they'll be excited to hear your good news. I'll certainly pass it on.'

'Okay.' Daisy was still puzzled. Was it her imagination, or was Anna was being strangely mysterious?

She tried to shrug this concern aside. She checked with a nurse who could speak English and was reassured that a midday departure would be okay, so she showered and changed into street clothes, put on a little makeup and packed the small overnight bag that Bronte had thoughtfully provided on the night of the accident.

Rather than climbing back onto the bed, Daisy sat in a chair to flick through the magazines the girls had brought her. She wasn't as relaxed as she would have liked, though. There'd been a cryptic quality to the conversation with Anna that left her unsettled, which wasn't helpful when she was trying to get herself and her family back on an even emotional keel.

The minutes ticked around slowly. Daisy sent text messages to both Freya and Jo back in Australia. Ellie had let them know about the accident, so now she shared the good news that she was well again.

Freya replied immediately. *Wonderful news. Such a relief. Have been so worried. Make sure you enjoy the rest of your holiday. Can't wait to hear all about it. Lots of love. F xxxx*

She didn't hear from Jo, but that was no surprise, as it would be dinner time in Queensland now and her friend would be busy feeding her family.

It was good to think about her friends, though, to know they would be there, waiting with open arms when she got home. Friends were so much less complicated than family.

Feeling restless still, Daisy went for a walk down the pristine polished hallways, tiptoeing past rooms housing patients who looked extremely ill, grateful that she felt physically fine now. She found a window that looked onto the busy square filled with tourists. They probably never realised that the grand façade of a fifteenth-century monastery now housed a major hospital.

The sun was bright outside, the sky a clear and pretty pastel blue. Daisy was beginning to wish that she'd checked herself out of hospital, found her own way home. But at last it was almost noon, and she went back to her room.

'Mum!' Anna burst through the doorway, her face alight with excitement, immediately banishing her mother's previous annoyance. 'It's so good to see you looking so well.'

'You, too, darling.'

As they kissed and hugged, Daisy couldn't help noticing the new radiance in Anna's smile. What on earth had happened?

Before she could voice this question, her daughter turned back to the doorway.

'I've brought you a visitor,' Anna said, and her eyes were shining, her face glowing.

A man came into the room. A very handsome, youngish man, almost certainly Italian.

'Hello, Mrs Benetto,' the young fellow said politely.

'H-hello.' Daisy's response was uncertain.

'Mum,' said Anna, taking the young man's hand in a surprisingly intimate fashion and drawing him forward. 'Let me introduce Gabriele Vincini.'

Oh, dear heavens. Daisy's dizziness seemed to have returned. *Oh, Anna, no. Please no. Not this.*

'It's okay, don't panic,' Anna said quickly. 'Gabriele's just like the famous archangel. He brings you glad tidings of great joy.'

'Oh, Anna.' Daisy had no idea what her daughter was talking about, but she felt so shaken she had to sit down.

Anna was immediately contrite. 'Mum, sorry. I didn't want to upset you.'

How, Daisy wondered, could she not be upset? Anna was forcing her into a face-to-face meeting with Gabriele Vincini just when she was trying her hardest to forget all about him.

'Gabriele's a doctor,' Anna went on. 'Can you believe it? He works here in this hospital in the paediatric ward.'

'How . . . nice,' Daisy said lamely, while a voice in her head snapped: *So that's where Leo's money went.*

She supposed she should be ashamed of herself. Gabriele Vincini was probably a very admirable young man. But had her husband paid for his education? Was Gabriele his other son?

'Gabriele doesn't have long before he has to be back on the ward,' Anna continued, as if she hadn't noticed her mother's discomfort. 'But he wanted to meet you and to explain everything. About Dad.'

CHAPTER THIRTY-ONE

Ellie smoothed the sheets on her mother's bed, tucked them under the mattress and then settled the doona back into place. She was rather proud that she'd thought to wash the bed linen and remake the bed without being prompted, ready for her mum's return. Clean sheets were only a small luxury, but they helped when your life had turned to shit.

And right now, shitty was the best word Ellie could come up with to describe how her life felt. Their mum was spending her precious holiday in hospital, Marc had a perpetual scowl, as if he was ready to punch someone just for looking at him, and Bronte seemed permanently worried. Meanwhile, Anna had pretty much wandered off, probably to drown her sorrows with her mate Renzo.

As for Ellie, she couldn't remember ever feeling so stressed and sad. Poor Tyler Davenport had tried to cheer her up, but she'd almost bitten his head off over some small thing. She couldn't even remember what had made her angry now, but Tyler had quietly backed away. Sensible bloke.

Ellie knew she'd feel better if Zach would call her, just once, but he was continuing with the silent treatment and she was rather shocked by how mad this made her. Mad and miserable.

His mother was sure to have passed on Ellie's news about the accident, so there was no excuse for Zach's silence. It could only mean one thing – Zach didn't care about Ellie or her family. But this didn't make sense.

How could a friendly, caring, 'always there for you' guy change so quickly and so drastically? Zach's silence was almost as unbelievable as Gina Pesano's story about their dad and Sofia Vincini.

And dealing with all this crap was extra hard for Ellie when she was on the other side of the planet.

She longed to be home at the beach with her friends, surfing every morning, hanging out at the café, seeing Zach on a daily basis, even if it was only for half an hour. All she had here in Venice were her moping family, stupid canals, old crumbling churches and people who spoke Italian. The fact that Ellie had found every one of these things utterly fascinating mere days ago was a mystery now.

Ellie was still sunk in these miserable musings when her phone buzzed in her pocket. When she took it out, her heart almost burst through her chest.

Zach's name showed in the caller ID.

Finally.

She was so surprised, though, she was trembling. She had to swallow before she could speak. 'Hello.'

''Lo, Ellie. How ya doin'?'

Laid-back as always and with the hint of a smile, Zach's voice melted through her like warmed honey. It was so-o-o good to hear him. But – *how was she doing?* Could he really ask that question so casually, when she was practically having a breakdown?

'You've got a nerve,' she responded tightly. 'Asking me how I am when you haven't bothered to answer any of my texts or calls for the last three days.'

'Yeah, well, my phone was flat. Ran outta battery.'

'That's the lamest excuse ever invented, Zach Cassidy.'

'It's the truth.'

'Come on, Zach. You can't live without your phone. Letting it run out of battery just isn't an option.'

'Listen, are you going to give me a lecture, or are you going to come and say hello?'

He was right about the lecture. Ellie knew she shouldn't get stuck into Zach when she was actually all kinds of grateful and happy that he'd finally rung. But she couldn't help also being mad with him. And anyway, he wasn't making sense.

'Have you been hit on the head, mate? You know I'm in Venice.'

'Course I do.'

'Then how can I come and say hello?'

'I guess you might have better things to do with that Tyler dude.'

'But you aren't —' Ellie was suddenly so breathless she could scarcely speak. 'You're not actually here in Venice, are you?'

'Reckon I am.'

'Truly *here*?'

'A-huh.'

'But that's demented.' She let out a scared little disbelieving laugh. Tears spilled. 'Where – where are you?'

'Judging by my map, I'd say I must be right next to the Rialto Bridge. But, Ellie, I just bought a piece of pizza and it's crap.'

Ellie screamed. 'You really are here. Oh, my God!'

'Isn't that what I just told you? You want to meet up?'

'Yes, yes, of course I do. Hang on, I'm coming.' Shaking with shock, still clutching her phone to her ear, Ellie tore through the apartment to her room where she grabbed a hairbrush and dragged it through her hair. There was no time to change her clothes or to bother with makeup, but Zach had seen her in these jeans and T-shirt a gazillion times and —

Holy cow! He's here!

'Zach, please tell me you're not pulling my leg.'

'No, Ells, I've just spent twenty-four hours on a plane and I'm currently keeping an eye on two dodgy-looking blokes on the bridge. I reckon one's a lookout scout and the other's got this card table set up. He's trying to con people into guessing where he's hidden a bean under a walnut shell.'

Oh, my God. Zach couldn't have made this up. He had to be there on the famous Rialto Bridge that spanned the Grand Canal. Ellie almost tripped over her own excitement as she dashed out of the apartment.

'Yeah, those guys are illegal,' she told Zach as she charged down the stairs, across the courtyard and into the street. 'I've actually seen them pack up and run from the cops. That bridge and the railway station are the worst places for dodgy types – pickpockets, purse-grabbers, luggage thieves.'

'Handy to know. I'll keep an eye out.'

'Hey, listen, Zach. I'm on my way. I won't be too long. I could try to catch a vaporetto, but it might be quicker if I come on foot.' Ellie could run most of the way, but she needn't tell him that. She didn't want to sound too ridiculously eager. 'And yeah, the pizza around that bridge is tourist rubbish. I can show you way better places to eat.'

'Glad to hear it.'

'So, I might hang up for now, so I can move faster.'

'Cool. See you soon, Ells. Oh, hang on, one thing. How's your mum?'

'A lot better, thanks. The dizziness seems to have gone and they're letting her out of hospital.'

'That's great. See you when I see you, then.'

'Yeah, won't be too long.' Pocketing her phone, Ellie began to race, ducking and dodging around clumps of tourists.

It was surreal to think that Zach was actually here in Venice. Here. In. Venice.

All these hours when she'd been sulking and wanting to slit her wrists, he'd been on a plane, thirty thousand feet in the air, heading her way. How insane was that?

Now Ellie was grateful for all the mornings she'd spent exploring Venice with her camera. She knew the best routes, including a few shortcuts that avoided the most congested tourist spots.

There was no point in wasting time stopping to ring Anna or Marc. Anna was busy collecting their mum from the hospital, so Ellie would ring them a bit later, and she had no idea where Marc might be, or Bronte for that matter. Those two seemed to be having their own personal crisis.

Right now, Ellie was over crises. She had something to celebrate.

When she reached the Rialto Bridge, the whole area was crowded, so it was hard to pick out one individual. Her phone buzzed again. It was Zach.

'I can see you,' he said when she answered.

'Where? Where are you?' Ellie could hardly hear her own voice over her thundering heartbeat.

'On the bridge. Right at the top, looking down at the canal.'

Lifting her gaze, Ellie saw a familiar sight at the apex where the two ramps of the Rialto joined. Tall and suntanned, with his longish, untidy, sun-bleached hair, and a backpack dangling from one shoulder, Zach was unmissable now. This wasn't the crazy prank she'd half-feared.

She ran up the many steps on the bridge, which was a good excuse for being totally breathless by the time she hurled herself into Zach's arms. Fortunately, she didn't knock him over, although she heard him grunt as they collided. But then his arms came around her, hugging her close, and as she buried her face in his chest, she stupidly burst into tears.

'Why on earth would you let your phone go flat?'

This wasn't the first question Ellie posed after she and Zach left the bridge and made their way to an atmospheric osteria in a quiet backstreet of San Polo. On the way, Zach was gratifyingly appreciative of the very different world that Venice presented, and Ellie waited until he'd sampled the craft beer and a crostini topped with prosciutto, watching him as he grinned and groaned with pleasure.

This was her dream, to share these new discoveries with Zach, and she could feel herself growing calmer and happier, as if her world had been off-kilter and had now settled back on its axis. Zach had been a big part of her life for so long.

She could remember how he'd looked as a skinny, cheeky six-year-old, getting his new front teeth. And when he was ten and his mum had let him get a ridiculous haircut with shaved sides and spikes on top. For six months, until his hair had grown out, Zach had looked like a porcupine, although Ellie had bashed up another kid who'd called him by that name and she'd been sent to the principal's office.

Now, although her friend had changed over the years, growing taller and more broad shouldered, acquiring cheekbones and jaw stubble, his smile had the same stirring warmth and his eyes were still the same sparkly green. Which meant he still had the ability to lift Ellie's feel-good factor from the doldrums to the heights.

'So this is what Italy's all about?' he asked as he raised his beer glass.

'Yep.' Ellie grinned. 'Good food and grog. And then loads of churches and old buildings and history coming out your ears.'

'No cars, though. I wouldn't get a job here.'

'Well, no. I guess not. Maybe you'd have to learn how to fix motorboats, but there are plenty of cars on the mainland.' Ellie frowned. 'Would you want to get a job here?'

'Not sure yet. Just arrived, haven't I?'

True, but the fact that Zach had even toyed with the possibility of finding a job in Italy was a surprise.

'Are you still thinking about travel?' she asked.

'Of course. Aren't you?'

'Um . . . yeah.' If Ellie was honest, she'd gone hot and cold on the whole travel idea. Just lately, she'd been as uncertain about that as she was about anything else in her life. She'd discussed her lack of direction with Tyler, and he'd suggested that with her interests in history and photography, as well as surfing and travel, she was a multi-potentialite.

She suspected he'd made the word up, but she liked it. She totally appreciated the idea of keeping her options wide open, but she was pretty sure it wouldn't wash with her mum if she got to the end of her gap year and still had no firm plans.

Shrugging those concerns aside now, she had to ask Zach, 'So why didn't you tell me you were coming?'

He gave a dismissive shrug. 'Hard to say. It just seemed like a good idea and next thing I was jumping on a plane.'

Ellie knew the decision couldn't have been as simple as that. She frowned at him, sending a silent question he couldn't really miss.

'You were having a great time here,' he said. 'You and that Tyler bloke, and this place, the epicentre of happiness – but then I saw all your texts.'

'You saw them *eventually*,' Ellie corrected. 'After you remembered to recharge your phone.' And she couldn't resist digging deeper. 'I still don't get how you could let your phone go flat. You're always using it.'

Zach shrugged, and stared long and hard at his beer. 'Maybe I needed a break.'

'From your phone?'

'Maybe.'

She knew this wasn't right. 'Or a break from me?' she asked. 'Was I driving you nuts?'

Zach looked up then, allowing the hint of a sheepish smile. 'A bit.'

Ellie thought of the scads of photos she'd sent him – not just the scenes of Venice, the epicentre of happiness he'd referred to, but the cute Italian guys, and the one of her and Tyler in Campo Santa Margherita. It had been rather immature of her, she supposed, and maybe deep down she had been hoping to make Zach a tad envious, but she hadn't really thought he would care.

He couldn't have been jealous, surely?

'I turned my phone back on after you rang Mum,' Zach said as he helped himself to a chunk of salted cod on a toothpick.

'And you found all my angsty messages?'

'Yeah. You were so upset and worried, I felt pretty bad, so I thought maybe I should hop on a plane after all.'

'And it was the very best surprise.'

Ellie wanted to reach out then, to touch his arm perhaps, or even to give his hand a friendly squeeze, but she felt too shy, too over-awed by the hugeness of his gesture in flying across the world just to cheer her up. She'd already made a fool of herself on the bridge, throwing herself at him and weeping.

Not that he'd seemed to mind.

'What about the other stuff you mentioned?' Zach asked now. 'That Gina woman suggesting your dad had some sort of secret son here in Italy?'

Ellie told him the disturbing Vincini story as she understood it and he listened carefully without interrupting.

'Jeez,' he said as she finished. 'That's hardcore.'

'I know. It's awful, especially for poor Mum.'

Zach's brow creased in a puzzled frown. 'It doesn't make sense to me. I can't imagine Leo running away from his own kid and keeping him a secret. It just doesn't sound like him.'

'I know. It's sickening to think he might have been hiding such a secret all that time. And then, when Mum had the accident on the very same night . . .' Ellie could feel herself sinking back into the gloom. With deliberate effort she shook it aside. 'Anyway, Mum's okay again now and it'll cheer her no end to know that you've turned up.'

This time, Ellie did reach out to give Zach's arm a friendly touch. 'You must be jet-lagged,' she said.

'Yeah. A bit.'

'They say you should try to stay awake, to get into the rhythms here, but I don't know. If you have a rest this afternoon, you'd be fresh for tonight.'

He looked directly into her eyes then, trapping her with his smile. 'You got plans for tonight?'

A weird lightning-bolt sensation zapped through her. 'Now you're here? Yeah, sure.'

They both smiled then. Smiled into each other's eyes for the longest time. Ellie didn't realise she'd also been holding her breath, until she suddenly needed air and let out an embarrassing gasp. Then, of course, she blushed.

'Listen,' she said, struggling to concentrate on practical matters. 'I'm not sure if there's room for you at our apartment. I guess you could sleep on the sofa. Or Anna's friend Renzo might be able to put you up – a mattress on the floor or something. Or maybe we could speak to Simonetta —'

'It's okay.' Zach held up a hand. 'I don't want to crash in on your family. I've booked myself into an Airbnb. I organised it before I left.'

Ellie blinked. 'Aren't you clever?'

'It's only a tiny place, cheap as chips, but I'm sure it'll do.'

'Whereabouts?'

Zach reached into a pocket and pulled out his phone. 'I've got it saved in Maps,' he said as he handed it to Ellie.

'Oh, I think I know where that is. It's not too far away from our place. So that's handy.'

This time, when Zach smiled, Ellie thought she caught the hint of smoulder in his eyes. Again, her skin flamed. Which was crazy. She was imagining things. She hoped she would calm down soon.

'There's a beach here,' she said, jumping to her feet. 'It's called the Lido. We'll have to check it out.' It was the first thing she could think of to break the silly spell she'd been sinking under. Luckily, it seemed to work.

'Does this beach have surf?' Zach asked.

'I'm not sure.'

'So you haven't been there yet?'

'No.'

He grinned as he stood and hefted his backpack. 'We'll add it to the list then.'

'We have a list?'

'Of the places you're going to show me? Of course. Why else would I be here?'

CHAPTER THIRTY-TWO

'Marc, have you heard from Anna?'

'No, Bronte. Why? What's up?'

'The hospital's letting your mum go home. Anna's at the ward and picking Daisy up as we speak.'

'Oh, good. That's great news. Thanks for letting me know. I'll be heading back to the apartment soonish.'

'Where are you?'

'In a café, getting some work done.'

Of course he was. Bronte sighed. She was in a café, too, probably just a few calli away from Marc, but he wouldn't be keen for a chat. They'd barely spoken to each other since he'd escorted his mother to the hospital. Back at the apartment, with only his sisters as witnesses, Marc had dropped all pretence of their happy coupledom.

So, this morning Bronte had been to Murano, attending another glass-bead making class, which she'd thoroughly enjoyed. Nevertheless, she found the new stand-off with Marc almost as difficult as the pretence. They needed to sort out their future.

'Any chance I could join you now?' she asked. 'We should probably talk.'

'I'm really busy trying to catch up.' The note of impatience in Marc's voice was painfully familiar. 'What do we need to talk about?'

Bronte wanted to snap back at him, but somehow she managed to respond in calm and measured tones. 'You know damn well we've hardly spoken for days, Marc. And I'm sure you don't want to continue this cold war once your mother is home. I imagine we'll need to put our happy faces on again, at least for a bit longer.'

A grunt sounded on the other end of the phone. 'Yeah, I guess,' Marc admitted. 'I'm not sure there's much we need to discuss, though.'

Bronte supposed this was probably not the best time to mention their future, but she couldn't put it off indefinitely. Crunch time was looming. 'Well, there is some other news.'

'What's that?'

She'd been hoping to share this additional information face to face with Marc, but if he wasn't prepared to see her, she certainly wasn't going to plead for a meeting. 'Apparently Anna's tracked down Gabriele Vincini and she's bringing him to the apartment to meet the family tonight.'

The sharp hiss of Marc's indrawn breath sounded in her phone. He groaned. 'What the hell?'

With a sigh, Bronte leaned back in her chair and stretched a little, consciously trying to relax. 'I don't think it's necessarily a bad thing,' she said gently. Despite everything that had gone wrong between her and Marc, she felt total sympathy for him over the Vincini issue. She knew the pain of Gina's revelations was at the heart of his recent bad moods. 'Wouldn't it be wonderful if Gabriele could clear up the mystery for your family?'

'I doubt that's going to happen.'

'I got the impression from Anna that she's quite relaxed about the whole business.'

'Did she give you any details?'

'No, it was only a quick call.'

'Typical.'

'What do you mean?'

'Anna loves stringing us along. It's the performer in her. *Watch me, watch me.*'

'That's a bit harsh, Marc.'

'I know my sister well.'

Bronte couldn't really argue with this. As an only child, she'd never really understood sibling rivalry. She'd always thought brothers and sisters were damn lucky to have each other – for company, for sharing secrets, for good, old-fashioned fun.

As she thought about this now, her attention was caught by two figures crossing a nearby bridge.

She waved to them, but they were far too engrossed in each other.

'Speaking of your sisters —'

'What about them?' Marc snapped.

'I just saw Ellie walking past with a guy.'

'That Tyler fellow?'

'No, it definitely wasn't Tyler. But I'm pretty sure I recognised him. I think it was that Aussie friend of hers. You know, the really good mate she goes surfing with.'

'Not Zach Cassidy?'

'Yes.'

'What's he doing here?'

'Walking with Ellie. And looking very happy to be doing so.'

'That's weird.'

'Maybe, but I'd say it's nice for Ellie. She's been so down these past few days. But she looked over the moon just now.'

'Right.' Marc managed to sound distracted, as if he was itching to get back to more important things than talking about his sisters.

'I guess I'd better let you get on with your work, then,' Bronte said.

'Okay. It's piling up.'

'But you'll be there tonight for Gabriele's visit, won't you?'

'Wouldn't miss it for the world,' he said dryly.

Before the family settled themselves on sofas to wait for Gabriele Vincini, Anna had made it quite clear that she hadn't invited Gabriele Vincini to have dinner with them. This was to be a simple first meeting to 'clear the air'.

But when Ellie and Marc tried to quiz their sister about this air-clearing, Anna simply replied that she'd found Gabriele by looking up the telephone directory.

'And it's best to let Gabriele tell you his story,' Anna declared, refusing to give anything else away.

She had, however, made sure there was wine on hand, as well as cheese, olives and prosciutto, so this was clearly a social occasion.

Bronte, having resumed her expected position beside Marc, thought her husband might explode with impatience as they waited. She was inclined to agree with him now that Anna was being rather manipulative, enjoying the drama of keeping them all in suspense.

Everyone in this room had loved Leo and, with his death, their feelings had only grown stronger. No one wanted his name sullied.

Fortunately, Marc kept his cool, outwardly at least, although Bronte was acutely aware of his tightly clamped jaw and his fingers drumming a silent tattoo on the sofa cushion beside her.

Bronte had also noticed a certain coyness in Anna's manner when she spoke about Gabriele Vincini, which she found interesting and a little puzzling. Anna's demeanour wasn't unlike Ellie's blushing excitement when she announced to her family that Zach Cassidy had arrived unexpectedly in Venice, adding that Zach would be joining them later, after this 'meeting'.

Meanwhile, Daisy, seated in an armchair, still with a large plaster on her forehead and looking a little pale, seemed unusually serene about these surprising developments. Bronte wondered if the doctors at the hospital had given her drugs that were keeping her extra calm.

'So, can we open a bottle of wine now, or do we need to wait for His Excellency's arrival?' asked Marc.

'Well . . .' Anna looked uncertain.

'I think it would be polite to wait,' said Daisy.

'Unless you feel you *need* a drink,' Anna added somewhat pointedly.

Marc didn't bother to grace this with an answer, but Bronte sensed him taking deep breaths to control his mounting anger. In happier times, she would have reached for his hand, hoping to reassure him as he faced the possibility of meeting a previously unheard of, older half-brother. This evening she didn't dare touch Marc for fear he would bark at her in front of his whole family.

Luckily, Gabriele arrived promptly. Anna met him at the door, receiving his kiss on both cheeks. Not just air kisses either, Bronte noted with interest. Gabriele planted proper kisses on Anna's cheeks and she looked extremely pleased with herself as she led him into the living room.

And, *oh, man*. He was tall and fit-looking and jaw-droppingly handsome. Like an Italian movie star or a Michelangelo sculpture. The tension in Marc seemed to ramp up several degrees, and when Gabriele acknowledged him with a courteous but unsmiling nod, Bronte was sure the testosterone level in the room leapt off the scale.

'So, everyone, let me introduce Gabriele.' Anna seemed blithely unaware that two stags might be about to lock horns. 'His official title is Dr Vincini. He's a specialist paediatrician in the very same hospital where Mum's been staying.'

'Give the man a medal,' muttered Marc so that only Bronte could hear.

'In fact,' Anna continued, clearly enjoying her role as the narrator of this particular pantomime. 'Gabriele met Mum briefly in the ward this morning and now . . .' She turned and sent her guest a glowing smile. 'Come meet the rest of the Benettos, Gabriele.'

If Gabriele was aware of any tension in the room, he remained calm and charming, declaring in commendable English and with a cute Italian accent, that he was delighted to meet the family at last.

'I just bet you are,' Marc grumbled under his breath.

Bronte sent him a sharp reproving scowl, but he refused to look her way, and his jaw was so tight she half-expected to hear it crack.

Of course, Gabriele wanted to greet the Benettos individually. Ellie happily offered her cheek to be kissed, as did Daisy, so Bronte followed suit. And if Marc's handshake crushed Gabriele, as Bronte suspected it might have done, he didn't let on.

'You must sit here, Gabriele,' Anna said, directing him to the armchair opposite Daisy. 'And let me get you a drink.'

The usual small talk followed as the drinks were poured and handed around. It was easy enough to chat about Venice, the wonders of prosecco and the juiciness of the plump local olives.

'Thank you very much for inviting me.' Gabriele raised his glass, offering them all his charming, screen-idol smile. 'Salute.'

'Salute' echoed around the circle with varying degrees of enthusiasm.

Wine was sipped, cautious smiles exchanged, but it wasn't long before they ran out of pleasantries.

Bronte wondered how Anna would introduce the questions on everybody's mind. What was Gabriele's relationship to Leo? Had Gina Pesano's assumptions been correct? Was he indeed their secret half-brother?

Gabriele didn't need Anna's help, however. Looking around at the assembled group, he spoke quietly and carefully, but with unmistakable dignity. 'Anna has explained to me about the story you've been told regarding my mother and me. I understand you've drawn certain conclusions about our relationship to your father, and I'm sure this has been quite distressing.'

'You bet,' said Ellie.

Marc scowled at her. 'Let him get his story out.'

The two men locked eyes for a moment. Both watchful and cautious.

'It is true that Leo and my mother, Sofia, were very good friends when they were young,' Gabriele went on. 'They were also friends with Dante Massaroni.'

'Is he the other fellow we saw in the photo with Dad and Sofia?' asked Ellie.

'Yes, I'm pretty sure that was him,' said Anna.

Gabriele nodded. 'Dante was Leo's best friend and my mother's boyfriend.'

Ellie was frowning. 'So if Dante was Sofia's boyfriend, where does this leave our dad?'

'Apparently, Leo was also in love with Sofia.' It was Daisy who spoke now, keeping her chin high and holding a brave smile carefully in place as she shared this news.

A growl broke from Marc. 'This story is not going to end well, is it?'

'Please,' Gabriele said earnestly. 'I am explaining.'

Bronte's heart went out to Marc. This time she forgot her caution and reached for his hand. To her relief, he accepted her offering, linking his fingers with hers, and the unexpected contact with her husband's warm skin was so distracting, she almost missed the next part of Gabriele's story.

'My mother and Dante Massaroni were lovers,' he was telling them. 'But, as I've already mentioned, Leo and Dante were also very good friends. The two men set off on a holiday together, driving up into the Alps. They were planning a skiing trip.'

Everyone was listening carefully now, and Gabriele paused as he let this new information sink in. 'You've all spent some time here in Venice,' he continued, 'so I'm sure you are aware that there is little opportunity for gaining experience in driving cars.'

Marc's grip on Bronte's hand tightened and she couldn't resist rubbing her cheek against his shoulder.

Gabriele's mouth twisted in what might have been an apologetic smile. 'These men took off with the confidence of youth,' he said next. 'But the mountain roads were treacherous. It was winter and there was snow, of course, and probably ice also. Leo was driving and – unfortunately – there was an accident.'

Marc's grip on Bronte's hand was vice-like now. She looked towards Daisy, saw the silver gleam of tears in her eyes.

'Dante was killed,' Gabriele said quietly.

Marc spoke. 'And our father was driving. So he killed Dante.'

'It was an accident,' said Gabriele. 'Leo was not charged with dangerous driving, but he felt responsible, yes.'

Everyone fell silent. Bronte knew they were all thinking, as she was, of how kind and gentle and loving Leo had always been.

He would have taken his friend's death hard. So hard.

Eventually, it was Ellie who spoke up. 'So am I right in guessing that Dante was your father, Gabriele?'

'That is correct,' he said. 'At the time of the accident, my mother was pregnant, but it was still the early weeks and she was trying to keep the pregnancy secret.'

'And Sofia and Dante weren't married?' asked Bronte.

'No.'

'I imagine in those days, in Italy, having a baby out of wedlock was frowned on,' Bronte added.

Gabriele nodded. '*Certamente.*'

'Poor Dad.' Ellie looked close to tears now and Daisy was dabbing at her eyes with a tissue.

'Your father was especially upset when he learned that my mother was pregnant,' Gabriele said next.

'And he offered to marry her,' supplied Marc.

A flash of surprise flared in Gabriele's dark eyes. 'Yes, he did.'

'It makes sense,' said Marc gruffly. 'You said Dad loved Sofia, too, and it's the sort of thing he would do.'

'It was very honourable of him, wasn't it?' For the first time in ages, Anna spoke up. 'I know Dad felt guilty about the accident, but he would have been motivated by more than guilt. He would have wanted to protect Sofia from criticism, and I guess he also felt obliged to support her and her baby.'

'But they didn't get married. So what happened?' asked Ellie. 'Did Sofia turn Dad down?'

Gabriele nodded.

Bronte recalled that Sofia had never married, so the message was clear. *She had loved Dante and no one else would do.*

'Sofia must have been a strong-minded young woman to go it alone in a conservative community that frowned on single mothers,' suggested Bronte. Her refusal under these circumstances would also have been a harsh kick in the teeth for Leo.

Bronte shot another curious glance in Daisy's direction. Her mother-in-law's mouth was tilted in a lopsided, somewhat sad little smile, but all things considered, she still looked remarkably calm. No doubt she'd already heard this story earlier in the day and had come to terms with it, to some degree at least.

Again, it was Ellie who spoke up. 'So Dad left for Australia instead.'

'It seems that way,' said Anna.

Ellie frowned. 'But why didn't he tell us about this? He didn't tell you, did he, Mum?'

Daisy shook his head. 'Leo would have felt dreadfully guilty about Dante's death. I've been trying to imagine what it must have been like for him. His best friend was dead and he felt responsible. The woman he had a crush on had turned him down. I think it makes sense that he didn't want to talk about this when he came to Australia. He wanted to start a new life.'

'And a man has his pride,' added Marc.

'Yes.' A look passed between Daisy and Marc, no doubt laden with their individual memories of Leo Benetto.

'I do regret that Leo couldn't talk to me about this,' Daisy said. 'But I can understand now that he wanted to leave so much sadness behind him. And he was planning to bring me to Venice, so perhaps he was going to share his story then. It's one of those things we'll never know.'

'But even though Leo left for Australia, he vowed to look after my mother,' said Gabriele. 'She refused to marry him, but for years, he sent money to help support us.'

'Wow,' said Ellie. 'Did you know that, Mum?'

Daisy shook her head. 'I knew there was money set aside in shares, but I just thought they were some kind of retirement investment. It was only when I spoke to our accountant about planning this trip that I discovered the money was held in trust for Sofia.'

'That must have been a shock,' said Anna.

'Yes, it was puzzling, but I assumed it was being paid into some kind of charity.'

'I guess it was, more or less,' said Marc, but he no longer sounded bitter, Bronte was pleased to hear. He had also released his tight grip on her hand, but she knew he was still tense. Stealing a sideways glance, she saw the movement of his throat as he swallowed and she caught a suspicious shimmer in his eyes.

Gabriele, for his part, looked visibly concerned. 'I can assure you, my mother and I have not drawn on that money for ten years or more. And I apologise. I thought Leo knew this and had made other arrangements.'

'Perhaps there was a communication breakdown,' suggested Daisy. 'Rex Augustine, our accountant, did seem rather hazy about the details of the trust. Don't worry, Gabriele. I'll look into it when I go home.'

Gabriele nodded. 'I will most definitely see that it's followed up from our end.'

This seemed to be good news all round, Bronte realised. Gabriele wasn't a half-brother. Marc was still Leo Benetto's firstborn, and although Leo had been secretive about the sum of money he'd set aside for the Vincinis, the money had been left untouched for several years, so had probably amounted to quite a tidy sum to add to Daisy's inheritance.

If only Marc looked happier.

Unfortunately, her husband looked more upset than ever as he got to his feet. Turning to Gabriele, he held out a stiff hand. 'Thank you for setting the story straight.'

Gabriele stood quickly before shaking Marc's hand. The two men, both nudging six feet, were facing each other eye to eye. Gabriele's smile was still cautious and Marc's was grim. Why couldn't he be more generous?

'If you'll excuse me.' Marc looked around at his seated family without meeting Bronte's gaze, then promptly headed for the door.

'What's eating him?' growled Anna as her brother disappeared. No doubt she was put out that she'd gone to the trouble of tracking down Gabriele and clearing their father's name, only to receive minimal, grudging thanks from her big brother.

'Marc has a lot on his mind at the moment.' Bronte felt compelled to defend him, although she suspected that all the Benettos were well aware of their marital tensions by now.

That was another hurdle still to be tackled, when she and Marc told them about their plans. They wouldn't thank her for rocking the boat just when everything else seemed to be calming down.

'If you'll excuse me,' Bronte said. 'I'll see if I can find Marc.' She stood and held out her hand to Gabriele. 'It was lovely to meet you, Gabriele.'

She didn't wait for the cheek kissing. Waving a hand to Daisy, she hurried out into the night, in search of her husband.

CHAPTER THIRTY-THREE

'Trust Marc to spoil a perfectly lovely evening!'

Daisy had to agree with Anna, who was clearly fuming as she bounced out of her chair. After Gabriele had so kindly given up his time and taken the trouble to reassure them, it was disappointing to see Marc take off the way he had.

Hands on hips, Anna was glaring at the doorway through which Marc and Bronte had made their hasty exits. 'What about a little basic courtesy, bro?' she yelled after them before turning back to the others. 'I know Marc and Bronte are having problems, but you'd think —'

Anna didn't finish this sentence. Perhaps she'd had second thoughts and was cooling down after her initial outburst, but she'd already said enough to thoroughly alarm her mother.

Daisy had been aware of the strains in her son's relationship, of course, and she wanted to find the right moment to talk to Marc. It was a shock, though, to realise that Anna had insider knowledge of Marc and Bronte's issues.

Gabriele, meanwhile, was looking embarrassed, and Daisy didn't want to add to the poor man's discomfort by unpacking more of her family's worries in front of him.

'Gabriele,' she said now. 'I'm sure you must realise that we really do appreciate you taking the trouble to put our minds at rest about Leo.'

'Absolutely,' chimed in Ellie, who was still curled in her favourite spot at the end of the sofa.

'I think Marc's had an especially tough time over the past few days,' Daisy added in an attempt to explain her son's abrupt departure. 'My silly accident didn't help, but Gina Pesano's story about his father was such a blow. Leo was extraordinarily proud of Marc, and Marc looked up to his father. He always tried so very hard to please him. Probably tried too hard at times.'

'Please, I understand,' Gabriele told her. 'I did not know my father, but I realise that the father–son bond can be strong. There is no need to apologise.'

Daisy nodded and they shared a smile. She really liked this young man, whose father had been her husband's best friend. And she really wanted to meet his mother, Sofia, as well. After so many years of marriage, she refused to be jealous of a woman Leo had loved so long ago.

She said, 'You and your mother must come to dinner before we leave.'

Gabriele gave a polite dip of his head, but he hesitated before he answered. 'Thank you,' he said at last. 'We would like that very much. I will inform my mother of your kind invitation.'

'In the meantime,' said Anna, who seemed quite relaxed again now and had slipped her arm through Gabriele's with a surprisingly proprietary air, as if she was used to such easy intimacy with a man she'd so recently met, 'I've promised to shout Gabriele dinner tonight. It's my way of saying thank you, and I'm a woman of my word. So perhaps we'll hoof it now, too, if that's okay.'

'Yes, of course.' Daisy hoped she didn't look as surprised as she felt. Perhaps she should have guessed that something like this might happen. Anna *was* rather dolled up, in a lovely dress of coffee-toned cashmere.

Earlier in the evening, Anna had dismissed this outfit as something she'd found in a charity thrift shop in London. But now, hooking her arm through Gabriele's, she turned at the doorway to send Daisy and Ellie a cheery wave and she looked utterly glamorous.

'Wow,' said Ellie after they'd left. 'Those two are really pally all of a sudden.'

'Yes,' said Daisy. 'And doesn't Anna look lovely? I think she's hoping to impress the socks off that handsome Dr Gabriele.'

'I'd say she plans to get more than his socks off.'

'Ellie!'

'Get real, Mum. I'm sure Anna's already been sleeping with him.'

'Don't be silly.'

'Why wouldn't Anna? She's free as a bird. An actress in London. They're always jumping into bed with whoever takes their fancy.'

'Ellie!' Daisy cried again. She was quite shocked. Or at least, on one level she was shocked, although she knew there was possibly some truth in Ellie's claim. Just the same, she'd never allowed herself to think too much about Anna's love life in London, or elsewhere for that matter.

Some mothers and daughters talked easily about such things, but Anna had always been so confident and sure of herself from such an early age that Daisy had been slightly overawed by her daughter. It hadn't helped that Anna had taken off to Sydney to finish her studies and then to the other side of the world to work.

'While I was in hospital,' Daisy said now, 'did Anna sleep here at the apartment?'

'Not much.'

Right. Daisy was still absorbing this surprise when she glanced at her younger daughter and received yet another shock. Ellie had kicked off her shoes and was curled on the sofa, with her arms locked around her bent legs and her chin resting on her knees. But it wasn't the pose so much as the expression in Ellie's eyes that roused Daisy's concern – a mixture of pain and confusion, of misery, or, possibly, of longing.

The precise emotion was hard to pinpoint, but there could be no doubt that her daughter was troubled.

'Ellie, what's the matter?'

'Nothing.'

Of course. The typical teenage response.

'It can't be nothing when you look so unhappy,' Daisy suggested gently.

'I'm okay, Mum.' Abandoning her hunched pose, Ellie sat straight and fished for her ankle boots on the floor with her feet. 'Anyway, Zach's coming over.'

Zach. Of course. There'd been so many surprises in the past twenty-four hours that Zach Cassidy's arrival in Venice had almost slipped Daisy's mind.

'He should be here soon, shouldn't he?' she asked Ellie now.

Ellie nodded.

'And you'll go out with him tonight? Show him around?'

This brought a shrug from her daughter.

'Ellie? You'll have to look after Zach when he's come all this way.'

'But the others have all taken off and I'd feel bad leaving you here on your own when you're just out of hospital.'

'Oh, heavens, no.' Daisy said quickly. 'Don't worry about me. I'll be fine. I'm looking forward to a quiet night in.' She was perfectly honest when she said this. Dealing with Gabriele's revelations had quite exhausted her. 'I'll probably just have a little toast and cheese and go to bed early.'

Ellie looked doubtful.

'Honestly, darling, don't give me another thought.'

'You're sure?'

'Yes, absolutely sure. Is that what was worrying you? Abandoning me?'

'Sort of.'

'Oh, sweetheart.' Ellie really was the kindest soul. Unlike her older siblings, she'd weathered the entire storm of Daisy's heartbreak during these past twelve months more or less on her own. Daisy knew she'd probably caused her daughter more than a few nights of worry during that time.

'You have to go out with Zach,' Daisy insisted now. 'I'm fully recovered and I don't need cosseting, and Zach's come all this way. You need to hit the town with him and have a great night out.'

At least Daisy could say this without qualms. She'd known Zach since he was born and she completely trusted him with Ellie. She also knew that Venice was relatively quiet and safe at night.

'Have you invited Tyler to join you?' she asked.

Ellie couldn't have looked more appalled if her mother had asked her to amputate a limb. 'I don't have to, do I?'

'No,' Daisy quickly assured her, although Ellie's reaction was yet another surprise. 'I just thought – Tyler's another young person – and you enjoy his company.'

'Yeah, but with Zach?' Ellie grimaced. 'I can't see how that would work.'

'Okay. That's fine. It was just an idea.' Obviously, a quite ridiculous idea.

'I'll ask Tyler some other time,' Ellie said more calmly. 'Maybe tomorrow. But tonight – Zach's just got here.'

'You're right. He's probably jet-lagged and tired and wants a quiet first night. That's very thoughtful of you, actually.' Daisy supposed she should give her youngest more credit. 'I guess you'll want to change?' she suggested now.

Ellie looked down at her clothes. 'I wasn't planning to.'

She was wearing a black tunic over a long-sleeved grey T-shirt, and she'd teamed these with deliberately laddered black stockings and the black ankle boots.

Compared with Anna's lovely dress, Ellie's outfit looked rather drab to Daisy, but she supposed it was the comfortable, unpretentious look that many young people seemed to prefer. At least her hair was freshly shampooed and falling in a lovely clean and shiny tumble to her shoulders.

'I'll just stick these in the dishwasher,' Ellie said now as she got up to collect the wine glasses from the coffee table and carry them to the kitchen. 'But you stay there, Mum. Won't take me a minute.'

'Thanks, love.' As Daisy watched her daughter tipping unfinished wine into the sink and carefully placing the glasses in the dishwasher, she was conscious of a continued, puzzling tension in Ellie's face.

What's the matter now? she thought with a sigh. Was her family stumbling from one emotional crisis to another?

No doubt she'd been totally naïve to expect a holiday with her grown-up kids to be relaxing and carefree and fun. But it didn't make sense that Ellie would be worried about the arrival of such a close friend as Zach. On the other hand, it was quite amazing to think that Zach had come all this way, apparently on the strength of one phone call to his home.

Daisy had almost no time to ponder this before she heard a knock and Zach Cassidy's cheery face appeared in the apartment's open front doorway. At the same moment, the sound of breaking glass came from the kitchen.

'Ellie.' Daisy leapt to her feet. Ellie's face had turned bright red. 'Are you all right?'

'Yeah, yeah. Just dropped a glass.' Ellie was sucking her thumb as she waved to Zach, while going to collect a dustpan and broom from a kitchen cupboard.

From the doorway, Zach gave a shrugging smile. 'I have that effect on most women.'

Daisy had little doubt that Zach's sudden appearance had caused Ellie's accident, but it only increased her puzzlement. Why would Ellie be so uptight about an old friend's arrival?

Unless . . .

Daisy looked again at her daughter's blushing cheeks. Oh, dear, she was very much afraid —

'So, how are you now, Mrs B?' Zach had clearly given up waiting to be invited in and he was almost at Daisy's side when she turned back to him.

'I'm fine, Zach.' Daisy gave him a kiss and then a hug, aware of how wide his shoulders were these days, and she caught a welcome scent – of clean T-shirt or freshly showered young man, she couldn't be sure which – but somehow she was reminded of home. The Sunshine Coast, her friends, being outdoors in her garden.

'Oh, Zach,' she said, giving him another, fiercer hug. 'It's so good to see you.'

'You, too, Mrs B. You gave us all a fright. Mum sends her best, by the way.'

'Thanks. I'm sorry I caused such a fuss.'

'No worries. It's just great to know you're okay.'

Daisy touched two fingers to the plaster on her forehead. 'Such a little thing really.'

'You can't say that, Mum,' Ellie called from the kitchen where she'd found paper to wrap the broken glass. 'You didn't see yourself lying there on those cobblestones, knocked out cold, like you were dead. You really scared us.'

'Yes, well, I must admit I don't remember that part. But anyway, Zach, if my mishap brought you over here for a holiday, it can't be all bad.'

Zach acknowledged this with a nod and another grin.

'And what do you think of Venice so far?' Daisy asked him.

'It's amazing. Better than I expected.'

'I've been told there's not much surf here unless there's a big storm swell.'

'Oh, well. With streets made of water, who needs surf?'

Daisy laughed. 'That's true. Ellie hasn't been bored for a moment. How are you going there, Ellie?'

'All done,' called her daughter as she dried her hands.

'Good.' After a day that had started in hospital and had then seemed to bounce from one emotional Everest to another, Daisy felt, all at once, exhausted. 'Then don't let me hold you up.'

'Nope. I'm coming. I'll just grab my bag.'

Ellie disappeared into her room, but to her mother's relief, she returned quite quickly, although it was obvious she'd taken a moment to dash on lip gloss and a brush-stroke or two of mascara to her naturally thick lashes.

As she came back into the living room, Daisy glanced back to Zach and immediately wished that she hadn't. The blaze of heat in his eyes was unmissable.

'Bye, Mum.' Ellie sent Daisy a brief wave, slipped the strap of her bag over her shoulder and headed with Zach for the door.

Daisy opened her mouth to respond, but no sound emerged. She now knew that she'd missed an important chance for a heart-to-heart talk with Ellie. She also knew she'd been too complacent, missing vital clues about this pair.

Just last summer, Daisy and Celeste Cassidy had discussed their kids, congratulating themselves that Ellie and Zach had successfully negotiated the tricky paths of puberty unscathed, emerging with their friendship unsullied and intact. A rare but commendable phenomenon for teenagers of the opposite sex.

Now, Daisy knew that she and Celeste had been too quick to pat themselves on the back. But it was also too late to speak up without causing an extraordinarily uncomfortable scene, and, anyway, her throat was too choked.

All she could manage, as she waved Ellie and Zach goodbye, was a silent but pleading, *Take care.*

CHAPTER THIRTY-FOUR

As Ellie left the apartment with Zach, she knew she'd never been so confused or scared, or so mad with herself for feeling this way. What was wrong with her? One minute she'd been eating her heart out because she hadn't heard from Zach, but when he made the ultimate big-hearted gesture by coming all this way to actually be with her, she wanted to hide.

Seriously?

There could only be one answer. She was wrong in the head. Which probably meant she needed help. But where were her big brother and sister when she needed their advice?

'So where are we going?' Zach asked as he strolled beside her down a cobblestone calle.

'Ah . . .' Ellie swallowed, wishing she wasn't so incredibly nervous. Nervous about being alone with him, nervous about what he expected, wishing she understood exactly what it was that *she* wanted.

'How about we catch a vaporetto and find a bar to hang out?' she said.

'Sounds good.'

'Should we check with Tyler? See if he wants to join us?'

Ellie couldn't believe she'd actually asked this, and the flash of horror in Zach's eyes was probably very similar to the look she'd sent her mother when she'd been asked this same question just a few minutes earlier. But that was before Zach had appeared in their doorway and Ellie had made an unhappy discovery.

The very worst had happened. Despite every effort to resist, she'd fallen for Zach. She loved him so hard it hurt.

And now she needed to do something about these out-of-control longings that had taken hold, and she needed to act quickly, before she did something idiotic like tell Zach how she felt.

He hadn't answered her question about Tyler, though, and he looked none too pleased.

'Sorry,' Ellie said quickly. 'That was Mum's crazy idea.' Mums were handy when you needed someone to blame for your own stupidity. 'Scratch the Tyler suggestion.'

Zach's response was a silent shrug, and he remained uncommunicative as they continued to the vaporetto stop, walking with his hands sunk deep in his jeans pockets.

Poor guy. He must be wondering why the hell he'd come all this way. Ellie knew she had to get on top of this nonsense. Fast.

Things didn't get any easier, though, when they were seated side by side on the crowded ferry. Ellie should have been pointing out the sights, watching the stars come out in the indigo sky above the amazing rooftops, enjoying the music floating across the water from the café on the canal bank. But her thoughts were uselessly spinning.

How on earth had this crazy situation happened? How could she have fallen in love with Zach when they'd decided it must never happen?

She was the one who'd originally made the 'no romance rule' a condition of their friendship, and Zach had reluctantly agreed. It was back in Year 11, when Becky Hazelhurst had thrown a lavish sixteenth birthday party, and Zach had asked Ellie to go with him.

Something in Zach's manner had alerted Ellie that his invitation wasn't just the casual offer of a lift to the party, with the two of them being dropped off by his older brother Ben.

'You don't mean like a date?' she'd challenged.

Zach's normally smiling face had sobered. 'Maybe.'

Even then, she'd been aware that this was hazardous ground and she'd panicked. 'But, Zach, we can't. We're friends. We've been friends since playgroup.'

He'd shrugged. 'Doesn't mean we can't date.'

'You don't mean like girlfriend and boyfriend?'

'Wow, Ellie, you really know how to make a guy feel like a tool.'

'Sorry.' She knew she'd hurt him, but the panic had been rising through her like a swirling cyclone. In her head she'd had the logic straight. If she wanted to stay friends with Zach forever, she couldn't muck things up by having a crush on him.

Everyone knew that teenage romances never lasted. Nobody ever stayed forever in a relationship with a guy they'd started dating in high school.

Admittedly, it had been hard to keep these arguments clear in her head when her heart kept throwing up other ideas – like the possibility that she did really fancy Zach and would love to know what it was like to kiss him. And yeah, in moments of total weakness, she'd even fantasised about having sex with Zach, but then she'd forced herself to remember the dangers.

If they became boyfriend and girlfriend they would eventually split, and Ellie didn't want that. Ever. So she'd worked hard to stomp on those lusty feelings.

'We can't date,' she had told him emphatically. 'We'd muck everything up. Things would never be the same.'

'Yeah, well.' Zach had looked sad – with that kind of stubborn, tough-jawed look guys got when they were trying to hide how they really felt. 'I had this crazy idea things might be even better.'

It had taken all Ellie's strength of will to resist giving in and throwing her arms around him then.

'We can't,' she'd whispered, close to tears, and she'd wanted to explain her fears then. But although her arguments had been perfectly logical to her, putting them into words had felt way too complicated, especially when Zach was already walking away.

'You understand, don't you?' Ellie had called after him. 'It's better if we just stay friends.'

'Yeah, whatever,' he'd growled, hurling the words back over his shoulder.

He'd taken blonde and busty Megan Swift to Becky's party instead. Ellie had spent a miserable night, watching Megan's sickening eyelash batting at Zach and then watching the two of them dancing, locked in each other's arms, kissing, and later, disappearing into the dark bushes at the bottom of the Hazelhursts' backyard.

In fact, that night had almost ruined her friendship with Zach, after all. For one thing, she'd had to listen to Megan Swift raving about how hot Zach was, and in the weeks that followed, he'd been quite distracted and unavailable to just hang out with Ellie the way he'd been in the past. Year 11 had turned into a pretty awkward and crappy year all round.

It was only in the summer holidays, after Ellie and Zach hit the surfing scene with renewed enthusiasm, that their friendship had readjusted.

By then, Zach had dated several girls from their school and Ellie was kind of getting used to it. They didn't talk about his dates, of course, and slowly their friendship had settled back on track. Then, just before Easter in Year 12, Ellie's father had died and Zach had been her shelter, the steady rock in her life, and she'd discovered that what they had was bigger and better than dating.

But now . . .

The vaporetto rocked a little as it docked. Ellie's arm bumped against Zach's and the innocent contact lit flashpoints all over her body. Her gasp was an instinctive reaction, but beside her, she heard Zach suck in his breath too.

They turned towards each other and she saw in his green eyes the same burning fire that was consuming her. For the longest time, they stared at each other and when Zach reached for her hand, she let him take it.

'Do we get out here?' he asked.

'We could if you like.'

'I think we should.'

Only a few passengers were disembarking at this stop and Ellie and Zach quickly followed them onto the dock. They were still holding hands. Zach showed no sign of releasing her and she didn't mind at all.

'Know where we are?'

Ellie looked around, getting her bearings. 'Sort of.' They were on one of the many small islands, but with the Grand Canal as a central point, she figured they shouldn't get lost. 'I'm not sure there are any bars around here.'

Zach shrugged. 'Want to wander?'

'Sure.'

He was taking charge, Ellie realised, and she was perfectly happy with that. She found it weirdly liberating to surrender to a guy she totally trusted, and they set off, under an ancient stone arch and across a small campo.

A grey-haired woman, hurrying past with a basket of vegetables and fruit, nodded to them and offered a warm smile, as if she strongly approved of young couples strolling and holding hands in the moonlight.

For Ellie, another layer of worry seemed to peel away. Zach was here, no longer on the far side of the world. Her mother was well again, they didn't have to worry about shadows in their dad's past, and she was beginning to feel lighter and happier than she had in ages. At any moment now, she would feel so light she would probably start floating like a balloon, drifting higher and higher, right up to the moon.

They passed a green painted door in a crumbling stone wall.

'I guess you were wandering in streets like these when you took all those photos,' Zach said.

'I couldn't help myself,' Ellie told him. 'Everything here, even the ordinary things, are so – so photogenic. Just a doorstep can be like a work of art.'

'Did you put your photos on Instagram?'

She shook her head.

'You should. They're great. You'd have tons of followers.'

'I guess.'

'Talk to Marc. He'd be up with the very latest apps or whatever.'

Ellie wasn't sure Marc would be interested in helping her with anything in his current low mood, but she kept that thought to herself. Already, they had crossed the tiny island and had reached another canal edged by a waist-high stone wall. It was a very quiet, residential part of the city and the streets were almost deserted. Leaning over the parapet, they rested their elbows on its smooth stone and looked down at the still water and the glowing reflections from windows on the opposite bank.

'So, this Tyler guy,' Zach said, still staring down into the water. 'You really hit it off with him?'

Ellie shook her head. Zach had reached for her hand and she could feel his palm against hers, feel his fingers wrapped around hers, warm and possessive. It was suddenly important to be totally honest.

'Tyler's very nice,' she said.

'Nice?'

'Yes. There's nothing wrong with nice.'

'Jeez, Ellie, you can do better than that.'

'Well, okay. He's interesting and fun to hang out with. But I don't think you could say we really hit it off. Not – not if you mean romantically or – or anything.'

A small smile tilted one corner of Zach's mouth. 'So he's had the "let's be friends" treatment, too?'

'More or less. Yeah.'

Turning away from the canal, Zach let go of Ellie's hand and she tried not to mind. She watched a small motorboat chug upstream, breaking the reflections into glittering golden shards.

'You want to know something?' Zach said.

She was back to being nervous again. 'I guess.'

'This isn't really working for me.'

Ellie shivered. 'What isn't working?'

'This thing we agreed on. The friendship pact or whatever it's supposed to be.'

'Oh.'

Now Ellie turned, too, so she could see him properly. His eyes were extra shiny and her heart almost stopped beating. She said, 'It – it might not be working for me either.'

'Maybe we need to do something about it.'

'What kind of something?'

'Like maybe I need to kiss you, Ells.'

She wasn't sure if she should be worried or scared. She could no longer think straight. A rush of jubilation and yearning was rising inside her like bubbles in prosecco. *Yes*, was the only answer she wanted to give him. *Yes, please.*

Amazingly, she didn't need to say anything. Already, Zach had stepped closer, and now he was resting a hand on the wall on either side of her. Their faces were inches apart. She was trapped and she didn't mind one bit.

'Hey there,' he whispered, but without waiting for Ellie's response, he leaned in and touched his warm lips to hers.

So soft, that first exquisite caress. Soft yet devastating. Ellie was tingling all over. With expectation. With longing.

She let her lips fall apart and Zach kissed her again, still gently, but lingering a little this time, and an ache bloomed low inside her. When he nibbled at her lower lip, all she wanted was more. More and more and more.

Oh, help. She'd had no freaking idea that kissing Zach could be so incredibly, mind-blowingly, out-of-this-world wonderful. And perfect. And essential.

Ablaze and desperate, Ellie slipped her arms around his neck, pressed her impatient body into his and their kiss went wild.

CHAPTER THIRTY-FIVE

Anna slipped out of Gabriele's bed and crossed to a window where a faint moon glowed through clouds, casting fine threads of silver into the canal below.

For warmth, she had pulled on one of Gabriele's sweaters and now she rested her elbows on the deep stone sill, staring out into the night. She felt utterly at peace with herself and with the world. Which showed the difference a good man could make.

And Gabriele Vincini, as far as Anna was concerned, was unbelievably five-star. She adored spending time in his apartment with its quaint little nooks and its gorgeous views of domes and arches and make-you-weep beauty. Loved cooking pasta in his tiny kitchen and listening to his music. A string quartet playing Corelli was currently drifting through from the living room.

As for the man, himself, Gabriele wasn't just beautiful to look at, he was intelligent and kind. And downright ravishing in bed.

Best of all, he'd assured Anna right from the first night they'd met that he had no other romantic attachments. Meeting him had been quite magical, really.

After Gabriele had explained the story of their fathers' friendship, he and Anna had sat on his balcony for ages, talking and sharing stories. And flirting.

It was the most exciting flirting Anna had ever experienced. The whole time, their conversation had been charged with the pulsing energy of undeniable attraction, and somewhere in the conversation, Gabriele had told her about his former serious girlfriend, Cecilia.

A fellow paediatrician, Cecilia had followed a strong calling to work in Africa with Médecins Sans Frontières. Gabriele, however, still had important work here in Venice heading research into juvenile diabetes, so he hadn't joined her and they'd agreed on a parting of the ways.

For Anna, after the unsettling grubbiness of her affair with the arsehole London director, Gabriele's honesty was gloriously liberating. When they'd eventually retired indoors and ended up here in his bed, she had never felt so safe yet free.

Now, looking at the old buildings and the slice of water and sky that comprised Gabriele's view, she was conscious of a deep sense of connection to this city that had lingered within her ever since her arrival in Venice. Was it possible, she wondered, that some kind of genetic memory had passed down to her through her Italian ancestors?

'What are you thinking about?' Gabriele was still in bed, reclining against the pillows.

Man, he looked good. When Anna turned back, she was so distracted by thoughts of kissing him all over she almost forgot his question.

'I was thinking about my family,' she said, coming back to the bed. 'My Italian family, that is. Did you know Leo's mother's name was Anna?'

Gabriele smiled. 'Another Anna Benetto?'

'After she was married, yes.'

'I'm sure she was beautiful, too.'

'Oh, yes, undoubtedly.' Anna smiled cheekily as she perched on the edge of the bed. She looked about the room, at the tall narrow windows with their deep stone sills, at the marble mantelpiece that had once housed a fireplace, now replaced by a modern gas heater. 'This place must be even lovelier at Christmastime,' she said.

'Christmastime?'

'Yes. Maybe I've never really grown up, but I've always been crazy about Christmas. Do you put up decorations?'

'A few,' said Gabriele.

'I'd have lots, if I was you. A tree, of course, and gorgeous angels and candles on those windowsills. Strings of lights on the balconies.'

'You must come back here for Christmas,' he said.

Come back . . . A nervous little laugh broke from Anna.

'Have I said something wrong?'

'No, not at all.' Lifting a corner of the sheet – fine, white, high thread count, of course – Anna twisted the fabric between her thumb and two fingers.

'Anna, what is it?'

Without quite meeting Gabriele's gaze, she spoke quickly, before she lost her nerve. 'It's just – I've been wondering if I should bother going back to London. I – I love it here in Venice and my friend Renzo says he could find me work as a tour guide. I've been reading the guide books and I think I'd be quite good at it.'

Gabriele's frown had deepened. 'I'm sure you'd make a wonderful tour guide, and as everyone knows, Venice has plenty of tourists. But, Anna, what about your acting career? I'm sure you're also a wonderful actor.'

She gave a small, dismissive laugh. 'Yeah, sure. So wonderful I haven't had a gig in months.' She flinched as she told him this painful truth.

Gabriele's gaze was thoughtful as he watched her now. 'Has this anything to do with that director? What did you call him? Arse Hole?'

'That's the one,' she said with a nervous laugh. 'But I don't think I can really blame him for my empty calendar.' Even as she said this, though, Anna felt a niggle of doubt. 'Or at least, I don't think he —'

She paused, remembering the massive tantrum she'd thrown when Ethan had finally admitted the truth about his wife and kids. How she'd cursed and hurled stuff and wished him every horrible mishap she could dream up.

Might he have retaliated by somehow blackening her name? Spreading rumours through the theatre scene? Then again, if that was the case, wouldn't word of this have eventually reached her or her agent?

No, she wasn't going to buy into conspiracy theories. Her lack of success in London was her own fault. She just wasn't good enough.

Still watching her carefully, Gabriele said, 'Of course, if you really wanted to stay here in Venice, I wouldn't try to talk you out of it.'

'No, I know you wouldn't. But I haven't made my mind up yet. And don't worry, I wouldn't expect to move in here.'

Leaning forward, Gabriele looped a hand behind her neck and drew her closer. 'You'd be very welcome here,' he said, dropping a warm kiss on her lips.

'Thank you.' She was quite sure, though, that Gabriele was being polite, and even if she did stay in Venice, she had no intention of moving in with him after just a few short days. There were limits to her brazenness.

He smiled. 'On the other hand, I've also had this pleasant fantasy of going to London to watch you in a play.'

'Oh, that would be lovely.' Anna pictured herself coming back-stage, after giving the performance of her life, and finding Gabriele waiting outside her dressing room. She imagined the other actresses eyeing him off and she almost giggled with delight.

If only . . .

'Would you bring me flowers?' she asked him with a coy smile.

'Of course. What would you like? Roses? Lilies?'

'Anything except gladioli. No, actually, I take that back. Gladioli would be absolutely fine. Any flowers at all, even dandelions or thistles, would be fabulous. It would mean I had a job.'

'Is it really so hard to find work?'

Anna nodded. 'It's almost impossible. There's just so much competition. And, everyone seems to be incredibly talented.' She felt compelled to add, 'It's not that I'm hopeless. Honestly.'

'I never thought you were hopeless. Not for a moment.'

'Thanks.' She rewarded him with a kiss. 'Would you like me to perform something for you?'

Gabriele grinned. 'I would love that.'

'What would you like? Juliet? "Good night, good night! Parting is such sweet sorrow?"'

'Yes, please.' Leaning back against the pillows again, Gabriele linked his hands behind his head, as if preparing to be entertained.

'Or what about Cleopatra?' Anna hadn't moved from the bed, but she straightened her shoulders, lifted her chin to a haughty angle and gestured dramatically. '"Give me my robe, put on my crown; I have Immortal longings in me."'

At this, Gabriele gave a laughing growl and lunged forward, hauling her into his arms. 'Anna, you can't speak of your immortal longings and expect me to lie still.'

'Oh, is that so?' she asked loftily, but she didn't mind in the least as Gabriele slipped his hands under the sweater and began to trace delicious circles on her skin.

'You intoxicate me, Anna Benetto.'

Already, she was purring. 'I can assure you, Dr Vincini, the affliction is mutual.'

CHAPTER THIRTY-SIX

Bronte searched everywhere for Marc, checking every bar and osteria in their district without success. She tried to ring him several times, too, but he wasn't answering his phone.

Eventually, she realised it was pointless to keep looking. He could be anywhere and Venice offered way too many places to hide.

She tried not to worry. Marc might be a mess, but he wouldn't do anything stupid.

In between worrying, however, Bronte was angry. Had he really found it necessary to storm out like that? While Gabriele Vincini was still there as their guest? Couldn't he have held himself together for just a little longer?

And anyway, bad manners aside, what was Marc's problem? Gabriele hadn't usurped Marc's position in his family and he'd cleared Leo Benetto's name. For any normal person, this news would have been cause for celebration, surely?

Similar questions and arguments circled endlessly in Bronte's head as she walked and walked, forever on the lookout for her dark-haired, blue-eyed loner. She wasn't even sure why she was bothering, really. Marc didn't deserve her concern, and she wasn't sure what she would say when she found him. But at least she would sleep better if she could report back to the family that he was okay.

Eventually, however, Bronte had to admit defeat. She was exhausted. She had left the apartment in a hurry, wearing heels, and by now her feet were killing her, so she caught the vaporetto back to their stop.

The ferry was full, mostly with a large group of young students who'd been out on the town together, but there was a spare seat that she gratefully sank onto. In the stern of the boat, a trio of older men – in their sixties, or possibly even more senior – were giving their own rendition of The Three Tenors, belting out 'Nessun Dorma' in full force.

They didn't sound too bad, actually, and Bronte couldn't help smiling. They were having so much fun and the scene was so very Italian, with these big-chested fellows, one dark-haired, one with silver curls and the other balding, bellowing their hearts out in the middle of the canal. At least they were a cheering distraction for Bronte, and they even waved to her when she got off.

From the shore, she grinned and waved back to them, and as the vaporetto pulled away, they broke into "O Sole Mio'.

'So you've made new friends?'

Marc's voice.

Whirling around, Bronte saw him, sitting alone on a bench facing the canal.

'What are you doing here? I've been looking for you everywhere.'

'Have you?' He seemed surprised.

Cautiously, she came closer. 'We were all so shocked when you rushed off like that. Are you all right, Marc?'

'Yeah,' he said, but the single syllable was accompanied by a heavy sigh.

'I've been really worried.'

He didn't reply, but his narrow-eyed glance made his doubt about this quite obvious.

Annoyed, Bronte almost gave up and stomped away. She could tell Daisy her son was fine, but sulking, and then get to bed. Only one thing stopped her. She'd walked away from arguments with this man too many times in the past. Now, after months of miscommunication and the added turmoil of the past few days, she was determined to grab this chance, to try one more time to get Marc to talk. If it didn't work this time, stuff him.

'I'd like to understand,' she said as she lowered herself to sit beside him. 'I'd like to know what your problem is. I mean – Gabriele cleared your father's name, but that seemed to make you even angrier. I'm sorry, but it didn't make sense.'

Marc shrugged.

'Can't you give me a clue?'

At last he gave a nod. 'I'm not proud of this, okay? I know it's going to sound crazy, but when I heard that my father hadn't done anything wrong, I lost it. I found myself with a whole new problem.'

Despite her confusion, Bronte held her tongue, hoping Marc would explain.

He sighed. 'Listening to Gabriele, I couldn't help but see how honourable my father was. Dad hadn't only supported Mum and us kids, given us a fantastic lifestyle and taken great care of us, but he'd been helping out the Vincinis as well. He was a damn superhero – Father of the Year material – keeping two families happy on opposite sides of the planet.'

'And that bothered you?'

Marc looked away and blinked hard. 'It left me facing the ugly truth. I'm absolutely crap at being a husband. I can't even keep my wife happy, let alone a family.'

Oh, God. His words landed on Bronte like physical blows. Her mouth twisted out of shape as she struggled not to cry.

So here was the truth she'd feared, the truth that had sent her searching for Marc. She – not Gabriele or Leo – had been the true cause of his distress.

It was a sobering discovery, but even as Bronte sat there beside Marc, trying to rein in her galloping thoughts, the night was creating its own drama. Mist was moving in from the sea, creeping stealthily up the canal and spreading a mysterious white cloak. One by one, the buildings that lined the banks – a palace, a church, an apartment block, a hotel – were disappearing.

On a practical level, Bronte supposed they should leave this bench before they were totally enveloped by the fog. But Marc's confession felt too important. He had never before been so honest. So open. Had never sounded quite so regretful and sad, and she was sure they needed to continue this conversation. Now. Without interruption.

'I've always wanted a family,' Marc said.

Bronte had wanted one, too, but she'd longed for a relaxed and happy family life similar to the home movie Daisy had shown them, like all those scenes of Leo and his kids, so happy at Castaways Beach.

'I suppose this is stating the obvious,' she said. 'But there's really only one reason I've been unhappy and you've heard it often enough. You're always too busy with your work. You never have any time for anything else. You don't seem to want anything else.'

Hunching forward, elbows on his knees, Marc clasped his fisted hands. 'I used to blame Dad for that. He always wanted me to be the best at everything, or at least that's the way I read it.'

'But your father found time for his family.'

'Yeah, I know, I know.' This time, Marc's sigh held a desolate note.

'Mind you,' Bronte added. 'Leo didn't have to deal with the crazy competitiveness of Silicon Valley.'

'No. That certainly hasn't helped.'

Wow. Marc had never admitted this before.

'To be honest, this break's been a bit of an eye-opener,' he said next. 'I guess there's a grain or two of truth in that old saying about distance giving you a better perspective.'

The fog was inching closer. Soon they wouldn't be able to see the canal. Through the mist, the lights of the vaporetto stop glowed fuzzily, but Bronte didn't care. She was desperate to hear more from Marc. Was he actually suggesting that he might be prepared to make a few changes in his lifestyle?

'Anyway,' he said as he sat straighter again. 'That's what I've been stewing over tonight. Coming to terms with my failure and working out how I'm going to tell Mum and my sisters.'

'About?'

He frowned, as if it was obvious. 'About us and the breakup.'

'Oh, yes. I – I see.'

Until this moment, Bronte had always expected that sharing this news with Marc's family would bring a huge sense of relief. The charade was over. The weight of pretence was off her back.

But Marc's timing couldn't have been worse. A short moment earlier, he'd offered her a chink of hope that there might be a happier future for them – and now he'd slammed the door shut again.

'I guess we should tell them sooner rather than later,' Marc went on, staring grimly ahead. 'We can't leave it till the very last minute.'

'No,' Bronte agreed miserably.

The fog had crept even closer. She could feel its dampness on her skin, but neither of them moved. She wondered how, exactly, Marc planned to drop his bombshell. Would he land the blame squarely on her?

'Were you planning to talk to me about this first?' she asked.

'Well, yeah, of course. I guess you'll probably want to explain your side of things.'

Were women normally expected to explain to mothers-in-law why they were leaving their sons? 'I – I'm not sure that's necessary,' she said. 'I think, if I'm going to bare my soul to anyone, I'd rather do it with you.'

Marc frowned. 'I'm *damn* sure *that's* not necessary.'

'But we've never had a proper heart-to-heart.'

'For God's sake, Bronte, of course we have. We went to that bloody counsellor.'

'But we still didn't have a proper discussion. We just ended up arguing, like we always do. And that's probably my fault as much as yours.' She felt magnanimous admitting this.

Marc's response was a grunt. 'So, what do we need to discuss? How badly I've treated you?'

Bronte bit back an urge to snap. Not so long ago, they'd been making a measure of progress and she needed to tread carefully. 'It's not so much that you've treated me badly. Not really. But you have to admit, I've been well down your list of priorities.'

Out of the corner of her eye, she saw Marc give a slow nod.

'That's true,' he said. 'And I'm sorry.'

Bronte swallowed her gasp of surprise. This was the first time Marc had ever made such an admission and she didn't want to spoil it by overreacting.

'And I mean that,' Marc said. 'But I guess it's too late for apologies.'

They were now encircled by the eerie fog. They might have been the only two people on the planet.

'You could try, Marc.'

'To apologise?'

'Yes. Why not?'

'What can I say? What's the point? What can anyone say when they know the other person wants to leave? When they obviously don't love you any more?'

Oh, God. Bronte felt as if she'd walked into a trap. 'So this is all my fault?' Her voice cracked as she asked this.

'You're the one who wants to leave.'

'And what about you?' She was so suddenly angry, she wanted to scream. Just as well there was no one else around, just them and the fog. 'Are you claiming you're blameless? God, Marc, you knew I was unhappy in the Valley. Surely, if you loved me, you would have at least tried to consider a few options. And you certainly would have done something, or shown some kind of reaction, when I told you about the online dating and Henry.'

She jumped to her feet. It was too hard to get this out sitting down. And now she didn't care that tears were streaming down her face. 'I was at breaking point when I told you that, Marc. I made this huge confession about Henry, hoping to hurt you, or to shock you.' A sob caught in her throat. 'All I wanted was a reaction from you, but you didn't even seem to care.'

Marc frowned at her. 'I didn't care?'

'You know you didn't.'

His frown deepened. 'Is that why you left me?'

'It was the clincher. The final nail in the coffin.'

CHAPTER THIRTY-SEVEN

Marc stared at Bronte in stunned disbelief. Had he really been so thick or so sunk in despair that he hadn't even noticed when his wife had thrown him a lifeline?

At the time, when Bronte had told him she was leaving, he'd been so gutted he could barely function. Only one message had been clear to him – his wife didn't love him any more. Any feelings she'd once had for him were dead and buried. Why else would she be walking out of their marriage?

Now, he gave a dazed shake of his head. 'So that Henry bloke of yours never told you that I managed to track him down?'

'No,' Bronte replied, but she sounded less certain, and she sat down again next to him. 'You didn't track him,' she said.

'I bloody well did.'

'But how?' Straight away she answered her own question. 'Of course, you're a computer genius.' Horror now filled her lovely eyes. 'Were you spying on me, Marc? You didn't put spyware on my computer, did you?'

'No, I promise. I'd never compromise your privacy.' Just the same, a guilty grunt escaped him. He wasn't proud of his behaviour, but he'd had to know the kind of guy his wife was dating, the measure of the man he was losing her to.

'So what happened? Did you hack the online dating site?'

'Yeah,' he admitted uncomfortably. The site hadn't had great security, so it had been a relatively simple matter, using an SQL injection. 'I was kinda desperate.' But he hadn't read any of the encrypted data, or stooped so low as to read the messages. 'As I said, I didn't use spyware, but I could find out which users were talking to other users.'

Bronte still looked shocked. 'And you could see Henry talking to me,' she said coldly.

Marc nodded. He'd run a location trace on the IP address of Henry's computer. 'He was using a local internet café,' he said.

'So then you just fronted up to Henry, bold as brass? What on earth did you say to him?'

Marc shrugged. 'The truth. I know who you are and you've been dating my wife.'

Despite her understandable fury, Bronte looked intrigued. 'And how did he react to that?'

'Threw his hands up and looked panicked. Claimed he didn't know what I was talking about. He pretended to be outraged, too, but then he looked pretty damn shocked when I mentioned your name. At first, he wouldn't believe Bronte was your real name.' Marc slid her a sharp, wary glance. 'Seemed he had no idea you were married.'

Bronte looked uncomfortable at this. No doubt, she wasn't keen to admit that her husband wasn't the only one who'd been deceptive. Marc, however, could only stare at her now, remembering the feel and the taste of her soft, sweet lips. Remembering the heady rush of falling in love with her, the absurd pride that he'd felt when she'd become his wife.

This lovely, intelligent, talented woman was the gift he'd taken for granted.

How could he have been so stupid as to throw all that away?

On a fresh surge of despair, he said, 'I wanted to grab that prick by the throat and paste him all over the blasted café.'

'You didn't.'

'Of course I didn't.'

Gripping the bench on either side of her, Bronte sat very still now, staring ahead at the wall of white. 'I still can't believe you never told me this,' she said. 'I was so sure you didn't care.'

'I almost told you when I came home that day, but all you wanted to talk about was the separation. Leaving me. If you remember, you put your case very strongly.'

'Yes,' she said. 'I remember. I suppose I didn't give you much room to manoeuvre.'

'And I was too damn proud to plead.'

Lost in thoughts, in memories, it was some time before either of them spoke.

Eventually Bronte said, 'Did Henry tell you that we never . . .' She hesitated, perhaps worried about giving too much away.

'Never what?' Marc pushed.

She looked embarrassed, and her mouth turned square as if she was trying for some sort of smile but couldn't quite manage it.

'We never actually slept together,' she said. 'And I broke off all contact with him after that one and only date. He was so boring, I couldn't stand him.'

For the longest time, Marc stared at her as the true impact of this admission sank in.

'No,' he said quietly. 'He didn't tell me that.' Astonished, he let out a huff of breath. Of relief? Of joy? 'I guess the murderous look in my eyes must have put the frighteners up him. He was too busy bolting for the door.'

Bronte did smile now, almost as if she couldn't help it.

But Marc certainly wasn't in a smiling mood. It had felt good to tell her this at last, but he couldn't imagine this would make any real difference. His altercation with the Henry guy changed nothing about their lifestyle in Silicon Valley and he knew damn well that Bronte's concerns were legitimate. She hated the Valley, hated his long hours of work, the rampant competitiveness, the deals, the obsession with money and everything high tech.

And now, being here in Venice, a world away from the unreality of the tech community, her concerns made so much more sense. In this ancient, crumbling, overtly romantic city, Marc had been brought back to basics, to the importance of family and of making real, face-to-face connections with the people who mattered most. With the one person who mattered most of all.

'I'm so sorry, Bronte,' he said. 'I really am. God knows I don't deserve a second chance, but if there was any way you'd consider sticking around with me, I'd listen to what you want.'

'Wow,' Bronte said softly, and then, almost fearfully, 'even if it meant leaving the Valley?'

Marc nodded. 'Especially that.'

'Really? Coming to Venice has changed you that much?'

Too choked to speak, he gave another nod. Crazy thing was, he was supposed to be the family's clever dude, but in terms of emotional intelligence he'd been a total dunce. Now, he swallowed to ease the painful tightness in his throat and he'd never felt more terrified as he tried to explain.

'I can work anywhere really. I might not make as much money in other places, but I'd rather have you, Bronte – in Australia, in Timbuktu, here in Venice even, wherever you want.'

'Oh, Marc.' Her voice wobbled. 'You really mean that?'

'I've never been more serious about anything, Bronte. I promise you.'

***

Promises...

Bronte was remembering the time so very recently, when she'd sat in the back of the church here in Venice, watching a young couple vow to love each other forever. She remembered, too, walking out of her home in Palo Alto, determined to leave Marc and not to weaken, to never look back.

At the time, leaving Marc had made so much sense.

But now... Marc was right about distance and perspective. Coming here to Venice had changed them both and it had also reminded them what was most important.

Life was complicated, no doubt about that, and no one could ever be perfect. But it seemed to Bronte that perhaps love had a wonderful knack of clearing away the dross to make the important truths simple and clear.

'I've missed you so much,' Marc said.

'I've missed you, too.'

He turned to her, his expression an agonised mix of pain and joy.

Bronte knew there would be ongoing adjustments and negotiations to face on the journey ahead of them, but she'd walked away from this man she'd promised to love forever, and now she felt compelled to take the first step back to him. Slipping her arms around his neck, she lifted her lips to his.

Marc didn't hesitate. Gathering her closer, he kissed her and she felt herself melting, just as she always had, knowing this was where she belonged, with Marc's strong arms about her.

Their kiss was familiar, like so many kisses they'd shared in the past, but this kiss was new and different too. Deeper and more tender. A kiss to break down walls and to heal hurts. A kiss to fill her with hope.

'I love you, Bronte.'

Her response was a rueful smile. 'I love you, too. That was my problem. I never really stopped loving you.'

With a gentleness she'd almost forgotten, Marc kissed her tear-stained cheeks, her chin, the cold tip of her nose. 'So you'll stay? You'll give me a second chance?'

She was grateful she could answer this now with certainty. 'I will.' And it was so good to hug him again, to press her cheek to his chest, to feel his arms tighten possessively around her, to let the happy truth of their new decisions sink in.

'So what should we do?' she asked, eager to start planning their future. 'Where should we go?'

Marc surveyed their surroundings, as if he was seeing the fog for the first time. 'For starters, we should probably head back to the apartment.'

Bronte laughed. 'Trust you to be practical.'

'I wasn't being practical at all.'

'Oh?'

He turned to her with the confident, sexy smile she hadn't seen in ages. 'I was thinking about the bridal suite and that blasted Berlin Wall.'

'Ahh . . .' Now she was grinning, but she was heating up, too, remembering the sheer bliss of making love with Marc. The man was a genius at foreplay. She almost grabbed his hand to race off into the mist.

Somehow, she restrained herself and chose to tease him instead. 'You wouldn't be planning to knock those lovely cushions down, would you?'

'Hell, yeah. There's every chance they'll end up out the window and in the canal.'

'Simonetta wouldn't like that.'

'I'll buy her a new set.' Marc was on his feet, holding out his hand to her.

'We'll have to be careful,' she said looking ahead at the blank wall of white. 'There's no traffic to mow us down, but we don't want to fall into a canal.'

Already, Marc had pulled out his phone and flipped on the flashlight. As its beam lit up the paving in front of them, he threw his arm around Bronte's shoulders. 'Stick with me, kid.'

Bronte smiled. 'That's the plan.'

They only took two wrong turns before they finally arrived at the little courtyard attached to the apartment. Everything was in darkness, which wasn't surprising, given the lateness of the hour, but as Marc set the key in the lock and pushed the door open, a light came on inside.

Daisy appeared in her bedroom doorway, wrapped in a blue shawl. In bare feet and with the sticking plaster on her forehead, she looked older. More vulnerable.

'Oh, thank goodness it's both of you,' she said. 'I've been so worried. Isn't the fog terrible?'

'Sorry, Daisy,' said Bronte. 'I meant to ring you, but then I – I got sidetracked.'

'You found Marc.'

'Yes.'

'And I'm fine, Mum.' Marc crossed the room to give Daisy a hug and a kiss. 'Sorry if I worried you. I shouldn't have taken off like that. I'll explain in the morning. Are the girls okay?'

'Yes. Well, at least I've heard from Ellie. She was caught in the fog, too, so she's at Zach's place. She's spending the night there.' Daisy gave an eloquent roll of her eyes as she shared this news.

Bronte, remembering the young couple, so happy and so oblivious to the rest of the world, smiled.

'Well, at least you know she's safe,' said Marc.

'I suppose so.' Daisy didn't sound quite so sure.

'What about Anna?'

'The last I saw of her, she was taking Gabriele out to dinner.'

'Oh, well. I'm sure she's safe, too.'

'No doubt.' Daisy gave another eye-roll.

'At least none of us has been hit by falling masonry.'

This time his mother smiled. 'And I'm certainly grateful for that.' Hugging the shawl more tightly around her, she let her gaze linger over Bronte and Marc. An expression that might have been suspicious or even shrewd shimmered in her bright blue eyes. Cautiously, she asked, 'So everything's okay with you guys?'

'Yes, Mum,' Marc assured her again.

'Am I right in thinking that you both look – happier?'

With his arm around Bronte's shoulders, Marc hugged her close. 'You're dead right, Mother dear. But if you don't mind, we'll tell you about it in the morning.'

'Oh, that's wonderful and I don't mind at all. Goodnight.'

'Goodnight.'

Immediately, Marc was steering Bronte towards the staircase, and it took all her self-control to walk sedately and not to rush up those stairs to the honeymoon suite and the soon-to-be demolished Berlin Wall.

CHAPTER THIRTY-EIGHT

Daisy splurged on new clothes to wear to the Vivaldi concert. The decision wasn't influenced so much by a deep desire to impress Charles Davenport, but rather by necessity. On the night of the accident she'd ripped a hole in her blue wool dress and none of her other clothes seemed quite smart enough.

Anna and Bronte had accompanied her on a shopping expedition, and the three women had enjoyed themselves immensely. It was the sort of excursion Daisy had looked forward to when she'd first planned this holiday, and now she was the proud owner of a pair of glamorous black evening slacks and a divine scoop-necked silk shirt of shimmering silvery grey.

'And you must take my pashmina,' Anna had said, extracting the red and silver wrap from her wardrobe. 'You should keep it, Mum. It goes perfectly with your new outfit.'

Daisy protested. 'I'll just borrow it for tonight.'

But Anna insisted. 'No, hang on to it. I know it looks swish, but honestly, I bought it for next to nothing at a stall in Covent Garden. Go on, Mum. I do so little for you. And you've given us this gorgeous holiday. I want you to have it.'

The fact that Anna had solved the Vincini mystery was payment enough, as far as Daisy was concerned. She gratefully accepted the pashmina, however. The wrap complemented her outfit perfectly and, as the only other new clothes she'd bought in the past twelve months had been practical necessities like undies, she felt like a new woman, quite transformed. Which was, perhaps, appropriate for her first evening out with a man who was not her husband.

Daisy might have been nervous about this small adventure if Charles Davenport hadn't been so charming and diplomatic . . . and so recently widowed.

Even so, the look Charles gave her when she opened the front door to him was more appreciative than she'd expected. She was pleased she'd made a short trip back to the hospital with the result that she now had only a very thin piece of sticking plaster on her forehead, which she'd managed to disguise by arranging her curly hair just so.

The concert was to be held in the former church of San Vidal, and beforehand, Charles took Daisy to dinner at a restaurant nearby. They dined on seafood with gnocchetti in black squid ink, a new experience for her that she found surprisingly delicious, especially when it was washed down with a delicate white wine.

As they ate, Charles told her a little about Vivaldi, including the interesting snippet that he had been so sickly when he was born that the midwife had immediately christened him.

'Luckily for us, he survived,' Charles added. 'Although Vivaldi was always severely asthmatic.'

'I don't suppose the dampness of Venice would have helped,' Daisy suggested.

'I guess not.'

'I've heard some of his other music, but I really only know *The Four Seasons*,' she admitted, and she was pleased she could confess this without feeling foolish. That was one of the things she really liked about Charles. He was obviously well educated and sophisticated, but there was nothing snobbish about him. He always made her feel comfortable, even interesting, as if he genuinely enjoyed her company.

'*The Four Seasons* is certainly Vivaldi's most famous piece,' he said. 'But he wrote a massive amount of music for the church as well. He spent ten years training as a priest. The story goes that his mother promised God that if her son survived his delicate infancy, he would enter the priesthood.'

'Goodness,' said Daisy. 'I wonder how Vivaldi felt about that. I guess he wasn't given much choice. Imagine trying that with our kids these days. I can't even push Ellie into settling on a university course.'

Charles smiled.

'Speaking of Ellie,' Daisy added. 'I've been concerned that she might have hurt Tyler's feelings. She dropped him like a hot brick as soon as Zach arrived. Young people can be so rude and self-absorbed.'

'Tyler's fine,' Charles assured her. 'He might have been hurt for about five minutes. I'm sure his ego didn't enjoy being thrown over for the Aussie fellow, but he bounced back almost straight away.'

'I'm afraid Ellie and Zach have been best friends since forever.'

Charles, in the process of topping up their wine glasses, shot her a sceptical glance. 'You don't really believe that, do you? That those two are just best friends?'

'Well, I did for years, but I must admit everything changed after Leo died. Ellie and Zach became closer than ever. For a while there, I wondered if Ellie saw Zach as some kind of father substitute.'

Charles let out a noisy guffaw.

Daisy laughed too. 'Okay, I was seriously naïve. I can see that now.'

'Judging by one or two comments Tyler's made, he'd already figured that Ellie was obsessed with someone back home.'

'Really?' Not for the first time, Daisy wondered how she'd missed these clues. Of course, it was more than possible that she'd also been too self-absorbed in recent months.

She sighed. 'Ellie's rather young to be so obsessed with one fellow.'

'Is there ever a sensible age to fall in love?'

As Charles asked this question, Daisy looked up, caught a flash of vulnerability in his eyes, and a *ping*, like the arrival of a message, landed deep inside her.

For a heady moment she was quite overcome, aware of possibilities she had never considered. But she was imagining things, surely?

'At any rate,' Charles continued smoothly, as if to confirm that her imagination had run amok. 'Tyler spent most of today on the beach at Lido with Ellie and Zach, and he tells me he had a great time.'

'Oh, that's good news.' Daisy gave a quick shake of her head to clear it of foolish notions. 'I knew they were heading over there today, but Ellie hadn't come back before I left. I'm glad they enjoyed themselves.'

And then it seemed important that she keep talking. 'It's so complicated having all my grown-up children under one roof. I don't know what I expected. I wanted to gather all my chicks together, from all over the globe, so to speak, but the dynamics are so tricky.' She thought of the revealing conversation she'd had with Marc this morning, the talks she still needed to have with both Anna and Ellie. 'Life was so much easier when they were little.'

'I believe you,' said Charles. 'We only had the one child and, I must confess, I was always preoccupied with my work when he was younger. I left most of his raising to Molly.' He speared a piece of seafood with his fork. 'That's partly what this trip is about.'

'Giving you and Tyler a chance to get to know each other properly?'

Charles nodded. 'I'm working on the principle that it's better late than never.'

'Indeed. Losing someone teaches us that, doesn't it?' she said. 'And right now, having an only child sounds like very good sense to me.'

Daisy had been upset to learn, finally, during her talk with Marc, that his marriage had been in even worse shape than she'd guessed. She'd been quite shaken to know that he and Bronte had been on the very brink of divorce, and that coming on this holiday to Venice had actually saved their marriage.

Anna, on the other hand, was still playing her cards close to her chest, but Daisy couldn't help feeling that coming to Venice had been an unhelpful distraction for her daughter. Anna had dropped disturbing hints that she was seriously considering abandoning her London career and moving here to Italy.

To top things off, Ellie and Zach were dreaming of backpacking around the world. Daisy had no doubts about how Leo would have reacted to Anna's and Ellie's plans. *Nonsense*, he would have called them, and he would have had no hesitation in putting his foot down.

But Daisy wasn't so sure that ham-fisted intervention was the right approach. Even Ellie, at almost nineteen, wasn't a child any more, and Marc and Bronte had sorted themselves out without any help from Daisy. It seemed to her that parents of grown-up offspring walked a very fine line between meddling unhelpfully and giving wise, useful advice.

'Mind you,' she said now to Charles, 'they say a crisis brings out our true colours, and all of my children were wonderful when I had the accident.'

'Absolutely.' Charles raised his glass. 'From what I've observed, you've raised a family you can be proud of. Congratulations.'

'Thank you, kind sir.' She lifted her glass to touch his. 'And congrats to you, too. Tyler is as charming as his old man.'

Across the table, they shared a chuckle and perhaps the briefest hint of a flirtatious smile, then downed their drinks and left for the concert. Which proved to be truly amazing.

Like almost everyone on the planet, Daisy had heard *The Four Seasons* several times, but it had never sounded as good as it did this evening. The beautiful old church setting helped, of course, and the acoustics were fabulous, but the musicians played with such skill and passion she could feel the music reaching deep inside her.

She loved the other pieces they played too – the violin concertos and sacred music that Vivaldi had composed for the illegitimate and abandoned girls he'd taught in the orphanages here in Venice.

'Thank you so much. That was sensational,' she told Charles as they left the church and headed out into the cool late-spring night. 'So good for the soul. I feel quite rejuvenated.'

'Thank you for joining me. It wouldn't have been nearly the same, listening to that music on my own.'

'No,' she agreed, realising with a degree of surprise that she hadn't spent the evening thinking over and over about Leo. Perhaps the uplifting music had inspired her to look forward rather than back.

It felt like a step in a new direction. The right direction.

'And now, how about coffee?' Charles suggested. 'Or a nightcap?' And then, with a twinkling smile, 'Or both?'

Daisy didn't hesitate. 'Why not?' She was in no hurry for this lovely evening to end.

With the elegant pashmina wrapped around her shoulders and Charles's gentlemanly hand at her elbow to guide her, they made their way along several narrow, winding calle until they reached a charming little trattoria set on a narrow canal bank. The compact space was defined by strings of lights and the décor was simple, with small wooden tables covered with white cloths and candles set in bottles.

'This is a find,' Daisy said as she looked around at the other quietly chatting patrons, including a group of men dressed in overalls, who were almost certainly locals. 'How on earth did you discover it?'

Charles tapped his forehead. 'Research.'

'Clever you.'

She had never tasted coffee with sambuca, but when Charles suggested it, she was more than happy to give it a go.

'Oh, yes,' she said after her first sip. 'That's a very grown-up taste.'

'But you like it?' Charles asked, smiling as he watched her.

'I do.' She took another sip, savouring the coffee laced with anise. 'I might even love it.'

They laughed and Daisy, feeling happier than she had in a long, long time, let out a deep, contented sigh.

Long after the coffees with liqueur were finished, they lingered at their table. The waiters didn't seem to mind and Daisy and Charles talked for ages – about everything really – their homes, their jobs, their school days, their travels.

Eventually, their conversation circled back to the subject of Venice and the ironic contrast between the Serene City's timeless romantic beauty and the Benettos' recent melodrama.

'I think I've actually reached a point where I'm now almost grateful that we had that little hiccup,' Daisy found herself saying. 'It's been a wake-up call for the whole family.'

'By hiccup, you mean your accident?' Charles clarified.

'Yes.' She smiled, realising it must sound strange to dismiss this as something so minor. 'The accident was part of it, but I suppose I really mean the whole business of Leo and the Vincinis.' She had filled Charles in about this when he'd visited her in hospital and then again after Gabriele's visit. 'At first, I was devastated to realise that Leo had kept secrets from me. I was sure that shouldn't happen between a husband and wife. I mean – I'd always looked on marriage as two becoming one, sharing everything. No secrets.'

She paused, allowing Charles to comment, but he merely nodded, as if encouraging her to continue.

She said, 'I now realise that my husband's secrecy about the Vincinis has shown me the reality – that Leo and I were not this single unit bound together for eternity, but two individuals who were genuinely fond of each other and had chosen to live together.'

Hesitating again, Daisy took a quick breath to calm herself. 'Sorry if I'm rambling, but sometimes it helps to try to put muddled thoughts into words. What I mean to say is that by keeping his secrets, by not sharing a part of himself, Leo has helped me to let go of him a little. Does – does that sound too terrible?'

'Not terrible at all.'

'It makes sense?'

'It does. It makes very good sense,' Charles said gently. 'I think letting go is the hardest part of grief. It doesn't mean we've stopped loving, but once we've taken that difficult step, we can reach an important level of acceptance.'

'Yes,' Daisy said softly. 'Thank you. I think that's what I was trying to say.'

'I guess it was easier for me,' said Charles. 'Molly and I had quite a long goodbye and during those years, while she was sick, we had our ups and downs, including a couple of unhappy arguments, but all that time we were learning so much about love and about letting go.'

Reaching across the small table, Daisy gave Charles's hand a reassuring squeeze. She couldn't imagine how hard his journey had been.

She thought again about Leo. No question, her husband had been a take-charge kind of fellow. She wasn't sure if this was because he was an Italian male, but he'd certainly been the head of their household. And she'd been far too dependent on him during their marriage. She'd allowed him to take responsibility for just about everything.

Deep down, she'd always longed to be stronger, more courageous, to stand on her own two feet, but she'd kept herself in Leo's shade. Now that shade was gone. She was on her own. In full sun.

As a gardener, this was a situation Daisy understood. While some plants lifted their faces to welcome the sun's light, others needed assistance to adapt to their new conditions.

'I'm pleased to report that I feel stronger now about getting on with my life. On my own.' Looking up, she met Charles's intelligent and considerate gaze. 'I suppose I've finally accepted that I'm responsible for my own happiness.'

'Good for you.' Charles's gaze lingered on her for longer than was necessary, as if he wanted her to know that he really liked looking at her.

His smile was as warm as sunlight.

CHAPTER THIRTY-NINE

Woken by the smell of freshly brewing coffee, Ellie wandered into the kitchen to find her mum leaning against the counter, coffee mug in hand.

'Morning, sleepyhead,' her mum said.

'Morning.' Ellie yawned.

'What time did you get in last night?'

Ellie yawned again. 'Not sure.'

'Both you and Anna were still out when I got back and that was late enough.'

'Mmm.' Ellie hoped she wasn't in for a lecture. She found a mug, poured coffee, added sugar and milk. 'How was your concert?'

'It was amazing, actually.'

The unexpected brightness in her mother's voice caught Ellie's attention. Turning, she saw a sparkle in her mum's eyes, a glow in her cheeks that she hadn't seen in ages, almost as if the happy, cheerful mother she used to know was back. At last.

'I think the whole family would have enjoyed the Vivaldi,' her mum said. 'It wasn't at all stuffy or boring.' She glanced towards the bedroom door. 'Is Anna still in bed?'

'No, she's gone out with Renzo and Zach.'

'Oh? I didn't realise Zach had met Renzo.'

'They're meeting for the first time this morning. Anna's taking Zach on one of Renzo's tours.' Ellie perched on a stool and took a deep sip of her coffee. It was strong and sweet, just the way she liked it. 'He's taking them to the bell tower in San Giorgio Maggiore to see the views. I wasn't all that keen to go again. I'd already been there with you, so I decided to have a lie-in.'

'Those views are certainly stunning,' her mother agreed. 'But Anna's seen them, too. I'm surprised she has the energy to head off there again this morning.'

'She's beefing up her tour-guiding skills.'

'Why would she want to do that?'

Ellie winced. She'd assumed that her mum had heard about Anna's new interest in tour guiding. Seemed she'd put her foot in it.

Predictably, her mother wouldn't let the matter rest.

'Anna's not really going to give up acting to become a tour guide, is she, Ellie?'

'Um – I think I might have heard her mention something along those lines. But I probably got it wrong. You know Anna, a bright idea every five minutes.'

'Ye-es.' Her mother sounded uncertain.

It was clearly time to change the subject. 'Have you had breakfast?' Ellie asked.

'I was about to pop the last of the ciabatta in the toaster. Marc and Bronte have gone out, so there's enough for both of us. And there's still some of that lovely lavender honey.'

'I'd give anything for a bowl of muesli with yoghurt and banana, or blueberries.'

Her mum laughed. 'Yes, these Italian non-breakfasts are hard to get used to. I should have bought bacon and eggs for a fry-up.'

'Don't,' groaned Ellie. 'I'm starving.'

'Maybe you should go out then. Find yourself a proper breakfast.'

'Nah. Too lazy this morning. Toast and honey's fine.'

As her mother sliced the end of the ciabatta, she said, 'You know you wouldn't be able to have muesli and yoghurt every day if you were backpacking.'

'It wouldn't be too hard to carry a packet of muesli in a backpack.'

'Well, no, I guess not.'

A new note in her mum's voice sounded a warning gong for Ellie. Was she gearing up for a 'big talk'?

Her mother would have to be blind and deaf not to know that Ellie's life had taken a 180-degree turn since Zach had turned up in Venice. But everything with Zach was all so new and exciting – and private – Ellie didn't want to spoil the magic by talking about it. She was still trying to understand the amazing changes in herself. She couldn't quite believe how crazy she was about Zach, now that she'd allowed her true feelings to flourish. Or how totally carried away she'd been, alone with him in that little studio flat he was renting. Sleeping with Zach was beyond amazing. Ellie had discovered a whole womanly wildness in herself she'd never dreamed of.

And then there was the perfect feeling of closeness, of the two of them in total privacy, in their own little world. It didn't matter that the flat had dodgy plumbing and a precarious ground-floor position, which no doubt had to be abandoned when the acqua alta tides arrived. For Ellie, it was just amazing to spend time there with Zach, sharing dreams and laughter, discovering the special rightness of just being together.

Falling in love was a thousand times better than just being friends. Now, though, facing her mum in the kitchen, Ellie wished that Anna and Marc were around, so she might be spared a parental inquisition. But she and her mum were home alone. Yikes.

When the toast popped up, Ellie jumped to free the thick slices and, as she helped herself to the butter and honey, she wondered if she could escape with her plate and mug, back to the safety of her room.

'So, darling,' her mother said as she spread a glob of golden honey over her own slice of toast. 'I know this is an awkward question . . .'

Oh, God. Ellie stiffened and her heart took off at a gallop. She was terrified of what was coming next, but she knew she had as much chance of stopping it as she had of stopping an asteroid zooming towards Earth from outer space.

'I'd be irresponsible if I didn't ask,' her mother said. 'Is Zach taking precautions?'

Gulp. The question wasn't nearly as invasive as it might have been, but Ellie was still gripped by nervous panic. 'Yeah,' she said tightly. 'Of course.'

'Oh, that's a relief.' Her mum actually gave a little laugh. 'I've been so worried. I knew you weren't on the pill.' She looked up from the toast she'd been cutting. 'You're not on the pill, are you?'

Ellie's face was burning as she shook her head.

'I guess you'll need to see Doc Miller when we get home.'

Stunned into silence by this calm acceptance of something so momentous, Ellie could only give a shrugging nod.

'Or there's a nice young female doctor my friend Jo was telling me about,' her mum said. 'Apparently, she's joined Jim O'Brien's practice. You might feel more comfortable talking to her.'

'Yeah,' Ellie managed to say. 'Okay.'

She wondered what would come next, but her mother proceeded to munch on her toast. Ellie took a bite, too, but she was still so tense it seemed to stick in her throat. She'd been expecting a lecture – about sex, or about how young she was and the need to settle on a university course before anything else, about the stupidity of the backpacking idea.

Perhaps her mother was 'giving her space', or whatever. And perhaps it was working, for Ellie felt compelled now to talk. 'Actually, Zach was offered a job yesterday.'

Her mum gaped at her. 'Really? Here in Italy?'

'Yep. Working on a boat as a deckhand and mechanic.'

'Goodness. How did that come about?'

'We were over at the Lido with Tyler, and then we went on a bus and a ferry to Pellestrina. It's gorgeous there, Mum. You should check out Pellestrina if you still have time. There's all these cute little cottages painted in every bright colour you can think of, like a paintbox, and scads of fishing boats moored along the wharf. Zach was blown away. He just loved the place. I'm not quite sure how he managed to find anyone who spoke English, but he did, and next thing Tyler and I knew, he was being offered an actual job – as long as his visa comes through.'

'Goodness,' said her mum again. 'I guess that just shows how useful it is to have a trade.'

'Hell, yeah.' Lucky Zach had never had anyone pushing him towards university.

'So what sort of boat would he be working on?'

'A yacht, a huge glamorous one that takes tourists around the Adriatic – Croatia, Albania and Greece. Maybe even as far as Turkey.'

'Wow.' Her mum was clearly impressed. 'That would be an amazing experience.'

Encouraged by this unexpected enthusiasm, Ellie said, 'Zach reckons he could get me a job, too, as a kitchenhand and deckhand.'

'Oka-a-ay.' This response wasn't quite so warm as her mother concentrated on the simple task of cutting a corner off her toast. 'Would you like a job like that?'

'Well, obviously. It'd be awesome.'

Her mum gave a thoughtful nod. 'And if you continued to travel, I suppose Zach would be able to find a job just about anywhere.'

'Seems like he'd have to have a really good chance. He's so handy with mechanical stuff and he's already got his small boat licence and he can drive tractors, small trucks and mini buses.'

'That's quite a list.' Her mum gave a strange little smile. 'I hadn't realised.' She picked up her toast, set it down again. 'So is Zach going to take this job?'

'He hasn't decided yet.'

'But if he did, and if there was work for you too, would you want to go?'

'It would be your fault if I did decide to take off, Mum,' Ellie teased. 'You brought me to Italy and opened my eyes to a whole new world.'

'So what does that mean? You'd go?'

On the brink of declaring that of course she'd jump at the chance in a heartbeat, Ellie hesitated, unexpectedly finding herself torn between the thrill of the adventure and the look of concern on her mother's face. She was also aware of a tiny doubt lurking deep within her.

'Do you think I should?'

Her mother sat for a bit, poking at the toast and then abandoning it. 'I can certainly understand how tempting it would be,' she said carefully. 'I guess you'd need to know quite a bit more about the set-up on the boat before you agreed to something like that, though. You're still —' Her mum swallowed. 'Still so young.'

'Not really.'

'Well, no. You're not too young to travel, but you're not especially prepared, Ellie. It would help if you'd at least saved up a bit first.'

'Yeah, I know. Zach and I have talked about that.' Having finished her toast, Ellie gnawed on a thumbnail.

'What is it, darling? You look worried.'

Ellie sighed. She wasn't sure if she should bring her tiny niggle of doubt into the open where it might grow into something big and scary.

'I'm guessing that you and Zach are quite serious.' Her mother was obviously fishing.

'Yeah,' Ellie said.

'I've always liked him. The Cassidys are a good, solid family.'

'It's not that. It's just —' Ellie shook her head. 'It's nothing. Everything's fine.'

'Oh, Ellie,' her mum said in that gentle, loving voice she'd used when Ellie was little and needed a cuddle.

And now, Ellie found it impossible to hold her worries in. 'It's just – I still don't know if it's all right for good friends to become girlfriend and boyfriend.' She couldn't bring herself to say the word 'lovers'.

Her mum looked surprised, as if this wasn't what she'd expected at all. She took her time before answering, and Ellie could tell she was trying to be careful, to make sure she didn't say the wrong thing.

'Well, I know it works the other way round,' she said. 'People fall in love and then they also become best friends. I mean, when the first rush of romance wears off, you need something solid underneath. I'd say there's a mix of love and friendship in most healthy relationships.'

'But I'm scared that if we start too young it won't last.' Ellie was annoyed with herself for still fretting over this. When she'd mentioned it to Zach, he'd just laughed and kissed away her fears. It was only when they weren't together that she started to worry, almost as if their newfound love was too wonderful and precious to last.

'If it's any help,' her mother said now, 'do you remember the Crawfords?'

'Those people who used to run the little supermarket down on the beach?'

'Yes, they sold out to Aldi and made a fortune. But anyway, they were in my class at school. Rosemary Little and Bob Crawford. They went to the Year 12 formal together.'

'And they've been together ever since?'

'As far as I know, and they seem perfectly happy.'

'So I'm stupid to worry?'

'Darling, none of us can predict the future, but if you really love Zach —'

'I do, Mum. That's my problem.'

'It's not a problem if he loves you, too. And I'm sure he does. Isn't that why he jumped on a plane and came rushing over here when you were upset?'

'Yes,' Ellie whispered, still amazed by the truth of this.

Her mum came and hugged her then. 'We all follow our hearts, Ellie,' she said. 'That's how it seems to me, at any rate. We can try to be unemotional, to work everything out sensibly in our heads, but in the end, we can't ignore our hearts.'

Ellie was impressed by this new calmness and confidence in her mum. Seemed a knock on the head could be a good thing?

'So I should just hang out with Zach and stop worrying?'

'You can't help anything by worrying, but perhaps you'd feel a little more confident if you didn't rush into this travel idea. I understand why you want to travel now when you're young, and Marc says he can help you find outlets for your wonderful photographs. But perhaps, if you came home and kept working for another six months or so, you'd be able to get a good reference and save so you have a backup. I'm sure Zach's parents would prefer a little more warning before he ups and leaves them too.'

'Yeah, that actually makes good sense, Mum.' Ellie smiled. 'So you're not going to push me to go to uni?'

'It wouldn't hurt to apply for a course. You'd have it as a backup plan, but you can always defer.'

'You'd be okay with that?' Ellie asked.

'I would, yes.'

Ellie grinned now, amazed by how much better she felt. About everything.

CHAPTER FORTY

The silence of evenings in Venice was a source of wonder for Anna. In London the streets were always busy with traffic, day and night, but here, without the street vendors or tourists, the only sound she could hear was the quiet splash of a gondolier's oars.

Leaning over the railing of a quaint bridge on a backstreet canal, she drank in the view of ancient arches and walls adorned with overflowing window boxes, and she couldn't deny she'd fallen in love with this amazing city. She appreciated Venice in all its moods – bathed in silent moonlight or cloaked in a veil of mist, shimmering in the glow of a rosy dawn, or bustling at midday when tourists thronged the crowded markets. She was fascinated by Venice's sense of history, by the romance of its architecture and the drama of its tenuous relationship with the sea.

As if these Venetian attractions weren't tempting enough, Anna also had Gabriele to dream and swoon about. A girl would have to travel a very long way to find another man as perfect. And given her plummeting career prospects in London, the idea of moving here to Venice had become more enticing with every passing minute.

Now, after spending an entire morning conscientiously trailing the sights with Renzo, watching his adept handling of his party of tourists, Anna was not merely intrigued by the prospect of tour guiding, she was hooked. She'd been impressed by the way Renzo worked his crowd, winning and holding his audience with the same skills he'd developed as an actor.

She knew she'd be great at this job, too. Like Renzo, she also had the bonus of an Italian heritage and, although her interest in all things Venetian was a newly discovered love, it was a genuine one.

In a few days' time, however, her family holiday would be over. Her mum would fly back to Castaways Beach, while Bronte and Marc, who'd miraculously patched up their relationship, were excitedly making plans to relocate. They were talking about Paris, which was pretty damn amazing. Ellie and Zach were cooking up something, too, although their plans seemed to change on an hourly basis.

No doubt about it, this holiday had been a watershed for her family, and Anna was becoming more and more certain that coming to Venice had been especially meaningful for her as well. Standing alone on the bridge, watching the reflection of the slender moon in the quiet canal, she wondered if this night could actually mark a key turning point in her life. A night she would remember forever and, perhaps in the future, tell her children about. The night she'd finally decided to turn her back on acting.

Would she? Could she?

Was she brave enough? Crazy enough?

She wished the lovely, silent night could whisper the perfect answer.

To Anna's dismay, as she battled with this question, she felt her eyes fill with tears. Annoyed, she turned and left the bridge, swiping at the damp tracks on her cheeks as she stomped away. Only an outrageous prima donna with a massive super-ego would turn such a simple decision into a life-and-death choice of epic proportions.

Get a grip, girl. You either stick with acting or you don't.

Anna was almost home now and, although she had dried her tears, she wasn't ready to face the family, so the choice to head to the nearest bar and drink limoncello was an easy one.

Perched on a stool, surrounded by happily chatting locals, she stared into her glass. Okay. A little calm thinking was necessary. Maybe she should start with the bald facts?

One thing was certain – there were pros and cons on both sides of this decision, so it should not be made lightly. If she came to Venice, a wonderful new adventure awaited. If she stayed in London, she still had a chance of making it as an actor.

Small though that chance might be, it was still her best opportunity to fulfil her lifelong dream. Which led to another question – was that dream a valid one?

Anna's thoughts flashed back to her high-school days, to the school plays and the hours and hours she'd spent learning and perfecting lines of Shakespeare, of Chekhov or Oscar Wilde. She remembered how impressed her teachers had been.

Even the school's principal had taken her aside and told her how well she'd performed the role of Varya in a local production of *The Cherry Orchard*. 'You have true talent, Anna. Don't waste it.'

She'd grown up believing she was born to act.

Had she been deluding herself? Living in fantasy land? Had the encouragement from her family, her teachers and friends been fuelled by loyalty and love, rather than any sound understanding of the acting industry? Admittedly, the teachers at the Sydney drama school had been clued up and yet they'd also been full of praise for Anna.

So why hadn't she made it? Was it a simple matter of bad luck? Of not trying hard enough?

With a hopeless sigh, Anna drained her glass and thought about buying another.

'Anna.' A voice sounded behind her.

Swivelling on the stool, she was met by five feet eleven of gorgeous Italian male. 'Gabriele!' She smiled in delight. 'How did you find me here?'

'I went to your apartment. Daisy said you had gone for a walk, but she didn't think you would be far away. So . . .' He gave a smiling shrug, then pointed to Anna's reflection in the mirror behind the bar. 'You looked very serious, so deep in thought. Perhaps I am interrupting?'

'No, no, it's lovely to see you. I thought you were working late.'

'Not as late as I expected.'

'That's great. You'll join me for a drink, won't you?' Perhaps this wasn't the night for huge decision making after all.

'Grazie. I'd like that,' he said. 'What are you drinking? Can I get you another one?'

'Thanks. I'm on limoncello.'

Gabriele lifted a dark eyebrow but made no comment. 'I think I will have a beer.'

'Have you eaten?' she asked after he'd ordered their drinks.

'A quick supper at the hospital. And you?'

'A slice of pizza. That was enough. I'm not really hungry.'

'You are troubled,' Gabriele said as he settled on the stool beside her.

Anna nodded. 'I am, actually. Seems I'm not very good at making decisions, not the hard ones at any rate.'

'Let me guess. You are trying to decide about your career?'

'I am,' said Anna. 'And to be honest, I'm almost at the tipping point. I'm seriously tempted to give London away and move here.'

She shot a quick glance in Gabriele's direction, hoping to see his approval, but at the same moment the barista set their drinks in front of them. Distracted, Gabriele thanked him, then turned to Anna and raised his glass.

'Salute,' he said. 'Here's to making the right choice.'

'Salute,' she responded. 'And if you have any advice about making the best choice, I'd be very happy to hear it.'

He acknowledged this with a slight nod. 'I do have some experience.'

'Oh, yes, of course. When your girlfriend left for Africa. That must have been hard.'

'Sì. Certamente.'

'But, honestly, Gabriele, I don't think there's any real comparison between you giving up your important medical work and me giving up prancing about on a stage.'

'You are belittling yourself, Anna.'

Was she? Or was Gabriele just being kind?

'Medicine is about keeping people healthy and happy,' he said. 'And I suppose good entertainers can do that, too?'

His words hit home. At one time in her early days in London, Anna had fiercely put forward a very similar argument in defence of her art. When had she lost sight of that?

'Can you remember why you wanted to be an actor?' Gabriele asked.

Anna laughed. 'Well, of course, I've always loved showing off. Loved the applause.' Then she saw the way Gabriele was looking at her. 'Don't you believe me?'

'I think you are still – how do you say it? Not valuing yourself?'

'Putting myself down?' Anna sighed. 'Maybe you're right.' She gave the contents of her glass a swirl. 'So why did you want to become a doctor?'

Gabriele took a thoughtful draught of beer before he answered. 'When I was little, my mother was very sick,' he said. 'She had very bad influenza and pneumonia. She was so pale. She could barely move or speak. I had never seen anybody so ill and I was terrified I would lose her. I already had no father and if I lost my mother, I would have no one. For me, when the doctors saved her, it was like a miracle.'

'I can imagine,' Anna said softly.

'Later, when I studied medicine, I became fascinated by the science, and then, by the idea of helping children. I wanted to see them begin their lives with the healthiest possible start.'

'That's a wonderful ambition, Gabriele.' Anna blinked, desperate to keep her eyes dry. 'But it really does prove my point. Your motives are truly noble and I feel even more like a ditsy egomaniac.'

'Don't.' Gabriele looked almost angry.

Mollified, Anna took a sip of her drink.

'I am no saint, Anna,' he said. 'I was proud of my work here. I enjoyed a certain amount of —'

'Fame?' she supplied as he searched for the right word.

'Yes,' he agreed. 'And I wasn't prepared to give that up.'

Anna was grateful for his honesty. It was time to drop the self-deprecation. Gabriele deserved better. He was trying to help her, and it was time for her to be honest, too, with herself and with him. 'I do remember the night I realised I wanted to be a professional actor,' she said. 'I was in the bath, actually.'

'I am interested already.' Smiling, Gabriele leaned forward and dropped a lovely warm kiss on her cheek.

'Don't distract me,' she warned him. 'I'll completely forget what I was going to tell you.'

'Mi dispiace.'

'And don't talk to me in Italian. You know how it turns me on.'

He laughed at this and for a moment Anna almost forgot the seriousness of their conversation. She was swept away by blissful memories and by an exciting fantasy of how this night might end.

'Anyway, as I was saying,' she continued, adopting a more businesslike tone now that she'd collected herself. 'I was at home in the bath. The door was shut and the rest of my family were out in the living room watching TV. No, actually, Marc was probably in his bedroom studying – he was always such a nerd. Anyway, the point is, I felt very private and I was practising my lines for a school play. I was to be Eliza Doolittle in *Pygmalion*, and I was running through my part, mouthing off lines like "gin was mother's milk to her" – and – "not bloody likely". Only my teacher made me change it to "not *ruddy* likely".'

She paused for a moment, smiling at the memory. 'I was carrying on like a pork chop —'

'You were a piece of pig?'

'Sorry, that's just a silly Australian saying. But I was having a great time delivering these lines when I suddenly realised – I'd *become* Eliza. I was no longer Anna Benetto lying in the bath. I *was* Eliza Doolittle, complete with a Cockney accent – or my best attempt at a Cockney accent – in a posh London drawing room. It was almost like a transcendental experience. Somehow, I had lost myself in that act of creation. Of creating Eliza. But it also felt as if I'd found myself, too, found what I was meant to be. I know that's a contradiction. It's hard to explain, but it was a very heady moment that I've never forgotten.'

Gabriele was smiling. 'That's beautiful.'

'Mmm.' Anna still wasn't sure that a single memory from her teens justified pushing on now against overwhelming odds.

And yet, if she was truly, transparently honest, despite her failures, she still knew, deep down, that she was damn good at acting. And in London, even though the jobs had been scarce, she'd thrown herself into them every chance she had.

The need to perform had been with her since kindergarten, really, since the time she'd been a flower fairy in a little show their teacher had written for their parents. Anna had been an insignificant Fairy Petunia, not nearly as important as Fairy Sunflower or Fairy Rose, or even the Garden Gnome, played by one of the boys.

But Anna had thrown her heart into delivering her one short line and the audience had laughed and clapped, and Anna, at the age of four and a half, had never forgotten the buzz of knowing they were clapping in response to her.

It wasn't really the applause that she longed for now, though. She loved the rehearsals, the backstage excitement and sickening nerves, the spine-tingling moment when the curtain rose.

Damn it, she loved the whole process, the mysterious act of creation, of bringing a character to life. A stage performer was, after all, just another form of creative artist, like a writer or a musician.

'Sometimes,' said Gabriele, 'I think our jobs can wear us down. We encounter disappointments, unhelpful personalities and tiring hours, all kinds of restrictions. We can lose sight of the original reasons we wanted that work in the first place.'

'You're not wrong.' Anna drained her glass, loving the bold sweet and sour flavour and wishing she hadn't finished the limoncello quite so quickly. She let out another heavy sigh. 'So, you think I should go back to London and keep trying?'

'Anna, you know I'm not trying to get rid of you, don't you?'

She smiled. 'Yes, of course. You're too nice for that.'

He reached for her hand, linked his fingers with hers. 'For myself, I would love you to stay here in Venice, but I'm not convinced that it would make you happy – or perhaps, it will not keep you happy for long.'

Anna nodded sadly. 'You just want what's best for me.'

'I'm thinking of my own interests, too. I still want to see you in a play. I want to go to London and bring you those flowers.'

She pictured that moment again, returning backstage, flushed with success, with the audience's applause still ringing in her ears, and finding Gabriele waiting with a magnificent bouquet.

'I think I want that, too.' Anna spoke quietly, but as the words left her lips, she felt a thud in her chest.

Whoa. Had she really said that out loud?

She had, hadn't she? She'd just made her decision. Locked it in. Shut the gate.

She wasn't going to guide tourists in Venice after all. She wasn't going to continue to enjoy life in this beautiful city with this gorgeous guy.

She was going back to London to the dodgy flat she shared with Florrie. She was going back to wait on tables in the vain hope that she still had a minuscule chance of breathing life into her almost dead career.

Really, it wasn't a matter of choice. Anna didn't have a choice. She had always known she was meant to be an actor. Successful or not, it was the way she was wired, and yeah, even though it meant she was doomed to being penniless and disappointed most of the time, it was the right choice for her. *Damn it.*

'I'll bring you every kind of flower I can find,' Gabriele said.

'I'll hold you to that.' Suppressing the urge to sigh again, Anna managed to smile instead, but she couldn't help worrying that Gabriele's faith in her might be as unwarranted as her mother's. There was still every chance she would let them both down.

CHAPTER FORTY-ONE

Daisy was throwing a party. A farewell bash, Anna had dubbed it, which Daisy supposed was as good a name as any.

'I want to gather all the lovely people we've met here in Venice,' she had told her family. 'So it will be a thank you and a goodbye party.'

'Sounds great,' they'd agreed and so the invitations had been issued and acceptances received.

The Benettos needed to leave a day for recovery and tidying up before they had to travel, so the party was to be held in the apartment on their second-last night in Venice. Zach would be joining them, of course, and Simonetta was coming, along with Sofia and Gabriele Vincini, Gina Pesano, the Davenports and Renzo, plus Renzo's boyfriend Angelo. Too many for a sit-down dinner, so it would be a matter of finger food, or cicchetti, as the Venetians called it.

On the day of the party, the apartment buzzed with preparations. Ellie and Zach offered to vacuum, dust and mop, which was a delightful but welcome surprise for Daisy. Shopping lists were prepared and divided up among other family members who planned to head off to the different markets to gather supplies of wine, cheese and pastries, as well cold meats and salads from the *gastronomia*.

Before they left, however, Marc – using his phone, of course – cleverly found a place that delivered platters of cicchetti, which would save them a ton of fiddly preparation. So with fresh consultations, the shopping lists were trimmed and the shoppers dispersed.

Anna arrived back from her sortie with armfuls of fresh flowers, which she happily set in vases and glass jars scattered around the living area. 'We can leave them here for Simonetta or her next guests,' she said when Daisy expressed concern that they had too little time to enjoy the flowers. 'And anyway, the lilies are worth having just to make the place smell divine.'

Daisy couldn't deny that Anna's arrangements added a certain touch of class and the scents *were* heavenly.

Bronte, who was also in a decorating mood, produced strings of twinkling fairy lights that she'd found in a little backstreet shop and which she proceeded to wind around the staircase railing. 'They looked so pretty in the store, I couldn't resist them,' she confessed, and her eyes were sparkling, her cheeks glowing, as if she, too, was lit from within.

Recalling the tension that had simmered between Marc and Bronte from the first moment of their arrival in Venice, Daisy marvelled at this transformation. No longer were her son and daughter-in-law sitting stiffly and carefully apart on the sofa. No more bristling silences or sharp, angry glances. No hissed and muffled arguments coming from upstairs.

Instead, Marc and Bronte were relaxed and smiling and excitedly planning a summer in Paris where Bronte would take a series of fine art classes. After that, they planned to return to Australia, most probably to South-East Queensland.

'We're going to settle for a lower income and lower stress,' Marc had confided to Daisy. 'I'm going to start my own business, but I won't be shooting for the stars. I certainly won't be working sixteen- to eighteen-hour days like I did in California.'

'That's the best news ever,' Daisy had assured him.

Marc's mouth pulled into a rueful smile. 'I don't know that Dad would have approved.'

'Oh, Marc. Why wouldn't your father have wanted you to come home?' Daisy could think of nothing more wonderful than to have Marc and Bronte living somewhere nearby with the prospect of grandbabies in the not-too-distant future. The realisation that Marc was still trying to please his father was disturbing.

'He always wanted me to reach the top.'

Daisy shook her head. 'Not at the cost of your marriage. I'm quite sure of that, darling.'

'Thanks, Mum.' Marc slipped an arm around her shoulders. 'And I owe you a huge thank you for inviting us here on this holiday.' He'd looked as if he'd wanted to say more, but his eyes had glistened.

Daisy, who also had a huge lump in her throat now, hugged her son. 'I'm so glad you came,' she said, after a bit, when she could speak. The words seemed inadequate, but she knew Marc understood that she was glad about so much more than sharing a simple holiday.

He nodded. 'Me, too.'

It was all he could manage. It was enough.

And now, this morning, Marc had taken a *carello*, a little shopping cart on wheels, borrowed from Simonetta, and had lugged home bottles of wine, white and red and sparkling, as well as two bottles of limoncello.

'For you, Anna,' he'd joked.

'And I just might need them both,' his sister had responded.

Daisy had no idea whether this had been mere banter between brother and sister, or whether the exchange carried deeper significance. Anna had announced on the previous evening that she was definitely going back to London. The possibility of working with Renzo as a tour guide had been abandoned. Anna would stay in touch with Gabriele, but she had no plans to move in with him.

This was good news, Daisy supposed, but she would have felt happier about this announcement if Anna hadn't delivered her little speech with the air of an Antarctic explorer heading off into a blizzard, or a soldier returning to battle.

On a couple of occasions, Daisy had almost cornered her daughter, hoping to find out more about her situation in London, and she still hoped to have a chat to set her mind at ease before they left Venice. Anna, however, seemed to have a wily sixth sense about potentially awkward questions and, so far, had managed to slip away every time.

***

By evening, the kitchen bench had been turned into a bar with bottles and ice buckets at the ready and gleaming rows of glasses, including extras borrowed from the wonderfully accommodating Simonetta. The dining table and coffee table were covered with platters and bowls. Cutlery had been placed where needed, along with neat piles of paper napkins. Candles had been lit to lend atmosphere and, with everything in place, the family members had retired to their rooms to get ready.

Upstairs in the space that Bronte and Marc still jokingly referred to as the bridal suite, and which had been getting a good workout in that capacity lately, Bronte had finished in the shower. And now, with her hair carefully blow-dried, she switched on the lights above the bathroom mirror and prepared to apply her makeup.

Usually, she made do with tinted moisturiser, a quick swipe of lip gloss and perhaps a swish or two of mascara, but tonight she was going to go the whole hog, with foundation and eye shadow, eye liner and powder, blusher and lashings of look-at-me lipstick.

She wanted to look good for Marc, but mostly she wanted her appearance to match how happy and confident she was feeling now.

As she unzipped her makeup bag, however, she found a folded piece of paper lying on top of her powder compact. Strange, she had no memory of leaving it there.

Mystified, Bronte unfolded this and discovered a sheet of yellow letter paper covered in Marc's handwriting. She wasn't especially familiar with Marc's script as he nearly always typed, using emails or texting, but she'd seen enough of his signatures on documents, or the occasional Christmas card, to recognise his hand.

But what on earth?

Bronte didn't stop to wonder. She was too busy reading.

Dearest Bronte,

When we first met, on the very day we met, actually, you told me you were a pen and paper kind of girl, and that is why I'm writing this note by hand. At the time I was paying attention, you see, but when we reached the Valley, I let myself become distracted. I know that's a massive understatement – I was way, way too distracted.

I was such a fool, Bronte. When I think about how close I came to losing you, I am terrified to the depths of my being. I know I've apologised, but I also know that actions speak louder than any words. I plan to actively show you how much you mean to me, my dearest girl. From now on,

I promise to listen to you and to consult with you, to make sure our lives stay on track and in sync.

In the meantime, keep a lookout for the odd pen and paper message.

Yours till forever,
Marc xx

Oh. My. God. Bronte was too surprised to laugh or cry. For ages she could only stand there in her undies, staring at the note, thinking back to the day she'd met Marc, when she'd seen him on the front porch of the share house in Brisbane, in daggy jeans, bare feet, a holey T-shirt and with a day's growth of beard. Even then, on first sighting, she'd thought Marc was cute.

She glanced again at the words he'd written . . . *keep a lookout for the odd pen and paper message . . .*

What did that mean? Bronte went to the bathroom doorway, but Marc had already left. No doubt he was downstairs, preparing to be barman. She would have to wait till she was dressed to speak to him. But as she was turning back to the mirror, she caught a glimpse of yellow out of the corner of her eye – a small piece of paper in the middle of their huge white bed.

Of course, she had to check it out. Again, the paper was folded, but when she opened it, the message was simple.

In this room, 10 reasons why Marc loves Bronte.

He hadn't, surely?

But, yes, another piece of paper was peeping from under a pot plant and Bronte could see yet another poked between the closed window shutters. She almost resisted. She hadn't really time to go on a paper chase now. She mustn't be late for Daisy's party, but the temptation to read Marc's notes was too tempting.

With luck, they'd be easy enough to find. Perhaps if she hurried . . .

The note under the pot plant read – *You make the best Thai seafood curry ever.*

Okay, Bronte thought with a wry smile. Nothing too exciting about that. She only knew how to cook Thai meals thanks to the classes she and Marc had taken together. But hell yeah, her curries were damn good and it had been a while since she'd made one.

She crossed to the shutters, curious to read another note. It read – *You have the prettiest dimple in all history.*

Awww, that was sweet, but perhaps she shouldn't keep searching now. The rest could wait till —

Another note was tucked under a bedside lamp, so of course, she retrieved it.

You forgave me when I didn't deserve to be forgiven and I will be forever grateful.

Bronte drew a deep breath when she read this. She was beginning to suspect that she would treasure these scraps of paper, and she would also be sure to thank Marc for being so thoughtful and honest. There were renewed promises of her own that she needed to make clear to him, too.

And stuff it, if she was five minutes late for the party, no one would notice. She needed to find the rest of Marc's notes.

It didn't take long to find the next few and Bronte smiled and giggled in turn, loving the sentiments each piece of paper revealed.

You have the courage to chase your dreams.

You're the most beautiful woman in the world.

You make wise choices. You'd rather come to bed with me than watch TV.

Bronte grinned at this one, but she was pretty sure her wisest choice now would be to stop this hunting and to continue getting ready. With fresh resolve, she returned to the bathroom and began to work quickly, smoothing on foundation.

In the end, she didn't worry about eye liner. Smoky eye shadow and mascara were enough. She could hear voices below and she guessed that their first guests had arrived. It was time to get dressed and downstairs.

Tonight, Bronte was wearing a dress of smoky green silk that blended nicely with her autumn-toned hair. With the zipper in place, she took a moment to check her reflection, pleased with what she saw. In the bottom of the wardrobe, she fished for her shoes – black high-heeled pumps – and found another note tucked inside the left shoe.

I love your feet. I'm jealous of this shoe.

And yet another note was hidden in the right shoe.

I love you even when you're not naked.

She was grinning again as she opened the drawer where she kept her jewellery and yet another piece of yellow paper caught her eye.

I love your smile.

And I love yours, Marc. It was so good to see him smiling again.

Bronte carefully stashed all the notes in the jewellery drawer, but as she put them in place, she couldn't help counting. There were nine, which meant one was missing, but she really didn't have time to go searching for it now.

Anyway, she rather liked the idea of saving something for later.

***

The party was going well and Daisy was thoroughly enjoying her role as hostess. Meeting Sofia Vincini hadn't been nearly as stressful as she'd once feared. The woman was as charming as her son, although her English wasn't nearly as good as Gabriele's. In this regard, however, Leo's cousin Gina was a godsend. Once she and

Sofia got over awkward explanations about the past, they'd begun to enjoy themselves immensely, chatting nineteen to the dozen and catching up on the years they'd missed, so that was good.

Charles Davenport and Marc seemed to be enjoying a rather earnest conversation as well, Daisy noted as she flitted from group to group, making sure everyone had enough to eat and drink. In fact, the apartment was abuzz with conversations. In one corner Renzo was telling a joke that had Anna and Gabriele in stitches and, in another, Bronte and Simonetta were discussing recipes, while Ellie and Zach were checking out something of apparently monumental interest on Tyler's phone.

It was when Daisy paused in the kitchen to uncork a new bottle of prosecco that she heard a strange quacking sound. At first, she couldn't imagine what on earth it could be. Then she remembered that Anna's phone had a similar sound as its ring tone.

A glance in Anna's direction showed her daughter still doubled over in near-hysterical laughter, and Daisy was closer to the quacking, so rather than making a fuss by calling out to Anna, she hastily located the phone amidst the bottles and general disorder on the kitchen bench.

'Hello?'

'Is that Anna?'

'No, it's Daisy, Anna's mother. Sorry, it's a bit noisy here. We're in the middle of a party. I'll get Anna for you.' And because the caller was male and sounded very British and self-important, Daisy asked, in her most pleasant voice, 'Who's speaking, please?'

'George Prescott. I'm Anna's agent.'

'Oh? Right.' A frisson of excitement trembled through Daisy. 'Just a moment.' Holding the phone aloft, like some kind of trophy, she hurried across the room. 'Anna, a phone call for you.'

Her daughter, her face still lit with laughter, turned and frowned.

'It's your agent,' Daisy said as she drew near. 'George Prescott?'

At this, Anna stiffened, almost as if she'd been slapped, and all traces of laughter drained from her face. 'Oh, thanks.' She looked pale as she held out her hand for the phone. 'I'd better take it outside.'

It wasn't quite the reaction Daisy had anticipated.

CHAPTER FORTY-TWO

A phone call from her agent was the last, the very *last* thing Anna had expected this evening. Coming in the middle of a rollicking good party where she was enjoying the company of highly entertaining Venetians, a call from London felt like a cold slap of reality.

Anna hoped this wasn't George's monthly report, where he justified his own job by giving her a summary of her most recent lost chances and knock-backs.

'Hi, George,' she said shakily as she stepped outside the apartment.

'Hello, Anna. Sounds like you're having a good time.'

'Yes, I am rather.'

She didn't fancy taking a business call in the echoing staircase, so she hurried down the steps to the little courtyard below and sat on the stone doorstep next to a candle that Simonetta had set in a decorative metal holder to welcome their guests.

'I hope you can spare a moment for business?' There was no missing the note of sarcasm in George's voice.

'Of course.'

'Glad to hear it.' He paused significantly. 'Because I have some news.'

'Oh?' Anna tried not to sound too nervous. Tonight, while enjoying the party and chatting with so many lovely people, many of whom lived here in Venice and clearly loved the city's unique lifestyle, she'd already been questioning the wisdom of her decision regarding London. Now she wondered how 'good' George's news could possibly be.

'I've had a call from Owen Wetherby,' George said.

Anna cringed. Owen Wetherby was the casting director who'd witnessed her spectacular phone quacking stuff-up. George had to be mistaken. Whatever his news was, it couldn't be good.

'I see,' she said cautiously.

'Owen wants you to audition for him, Anna. He asked for you specifically as he has you in mind for a major role in a brand-new play.'

It was just as well she was sitting down or she might have stumbled at this jaw-dropping news. As it was, Anna nearly let the phone slip through her fingers. But she must have misheard, surely? Owen Wetherby couldn't have asked for her by name. He would have asked George for any actors on his books who were suitable for a particular character and who matched the required gender, age and height criteria.

She pressed a hand against the thumping in her chest. 'I'm sorry, George. Could you say that again?'

'Owen Wetherby wants you to audition, Anna. He has high hopes for this play. It was written by an Australian, actually – can't remember the name offhand – but Owen's raving about it and as I said, he's asked for you by name.'

'But he doesn't even know my name.' Anna was too dazed to think straight.

'You've auditioned for him before.'

'Yes, but along with hundreds of others.'

'You clearly stood out,' George said with some impatience. 'He remembered you and he went to the trouble of tracking you down. He seems to think you've got whatever he wants for this particular role.'

'Oh, my God,' she whispered.

'Yes, it's fan-effing-tastic, Anna. If you play this right, it could be your big break. I've seen the script and it's got legs.'

She still couldn't believe it. 'Are you quite sure? Mr Wetherby really asked for me?'

'For Chrissake.' George was losing his temper now.

'Sorry,' Anna said quickly. 'So – so when does he want to see me?'

'Are you free first thing in the morning?'

Panic shot through her. 'I'm in Italy, George. I'm in Venice with my family.'

'Oh drat, I thought you were in bloody Brighton or somewhere.'

'I'm due back the day after tomorrow, but I could try to get on an earlier plane.'

'No.' George sounded frustrated rather than angry now, frustrated but resigned. 'The day after should still be all right. I'll let Owen know.'

'Th-thanks.'

'As long as you're not too late.'

'It's a morning flight.'

'Good. I'll email you the script and audition notes.'

'Thank you.' Anna wanted to jump and scream, and her thoughts were spinning as she tried to make plans. Packing her few things would take hardly any time at all. She could help tidy the apartment in the morning, but she should be able to spend most of the day reading her part and rehearsing. Perhaps Gabriele would let her use his place, while he was at work, so she'd have space and privacy.

Oh, my God. This really was happening. Owen Wetherby wanted her. He'd singled her out. Tracked her down. Anna was almost faint with residual shock as she got to her feet.

She looked about her at the little courtyard that she'd fallen in love with on her very first night here in Venice – at the old walls and cobblestones, the flowering peach tree in the corner, the clothesline, the pots of geraniums. She'd been seduced by the charm of this city's courtyards and canals, and she'd come within a hair's breadth of giving up her acting dreams. But in spite of the allure of her father's birthplace, it was here that she'd finally discovered the important truth about herself.

Who would have thought that coming here to Venice would provide the perfect conditions to sort herself out? And now . . .

Now, Anna, having finally understood and accepted what she truly wanted, had, amazingly, been given another chance to reach for that dream. And this time she wasn't going to stuff up. No way.

Looking up to the black night sky sprinkled with stars, she whispered. 'Thank you, Dad.' And then she went back up the stairs to share her good news with Gabriele, but most importantly, she wanted to thank her mum for this amazing holiday and the unwitting part she'd played in this miracle.

***

'Can I top up your drink?' Marc's smile held special warmth as he approached Bronte.

'Thank you, kind sir.' Bronte held out her glass and smiled back at him as he filled it with bubbling wine.

The two of them had been smiling all evening, actually, sending covert, happy grins across the room while they were circulating and chatting. Bronte had also managed to murmur a quick thanks to Marc for the trail of notes he'd left for her, but there'd been no chance to really talk about them.

Now, Gina and Sofia had departed, with Daisy accompanying them downstairs for a final farewell, and Ellie, Zach and Tyler had headed out for a final session at their favourite bar. Meanwhile, Anna and Gabriele were relaxed on the sofa chatting to Charles.

More or less alone at last, Bronte stepped a little closer to Marc. 'By the way, I could only find nine of those little pieces of paper.'

'So you were counting?'

'Course. You did name a specific number, after all.' She sipped at her drink. 'I thought maybe you ran out of time for number ten.'

'Or maybe I was saving it for last?' Marc said, a fresh smile lighting his eyes.

'Or that, too.' Bronte could feel the warmth of his smile reaching deep inside her. Over the past few days, she'd become more and more confident that the worst was behind them. She and Marc were going to make it.

Standing next to him now, at the end of a lovely evening, she knew she'd been falling in love with him all over again. Impulsively, she leaned closer, brushing her lips over the dark, shadowy stubble on his jaw.

His eyes burned with a mix of amusement and heat. 'You want to read number ten now?'

'Do you have it with you?'

'I do, actually.' Reaching into his shirt pocket, he withdrew a folded piece of yellow paper and held it up between two fingers, as if to tease her.

Too impatient to wait, Bronte helped herself to the note, but she needed to set her drink down, so that she could open it.

Glancing up, she saw Marc watching her intently and she was a little nervous as she began to read.

Reason No. 10
You know this isn't a fairytale, but you're still brave enough to believe in happy endings.

'I struggled a bit with the wording,' Marc said.

'It's beautiful, Marc.' Bronte's smile trembled. 'And I get it. We've both learned the hard way that life isn't a fairytale.'

Bronte pressed the note to her lips. 'I love it.' Slipping her arms around her husband, she kissed him. 'And I have my happy ending right here.'

CHAPTER FORTY-THREE

Daisy was so excited she wasn't sure she would be able to sit still as she was shown to her seat in London's Piccadilly Theatre. Her heart was pounding, her hands sweaty, her whole body tense with expectation.

The theatre was magnificent with three tiers of red plush seats filled with an audience dressed to the nines for the opening night of a brand-new play. Diamonds sparkled and pearls gleamed while women's colourful silk and velvet gowns were complemented by the smart black and white of men's penguin suits.

Daisy had to pinch herself. All these people were here to watch an unknown Aussie actor called Anna Benetto star in a play with the dubious title *Down a Back Road,* written by a mostly unheard-of Australian playwright.

'A risky gamble,' the British papers were calling it. After all, the Piccadilly Theatre had hosted famous plays like *A Streetcar Named Desire* and *Who's Afraid of Virginia Woolf?* Henry Fonda, Judi Dench and Dame Edna had played here, so scepticism about this play's chances of success was rife.

'We're not letting those comments put us off,' Anna had told Daisy when she'd rung her just a week ago. 'I'm just warning you now in case you see any of that rubbish in the press when you arrive here in London. Everyone involved in this play is totally confident, Mum. The producer, the director, the cast. We're going to knock London's socks off.'

'Of course you are, Anna. I'm so proud of you.'

Daisy was indeed proud. This evening she'd texted Anna with the traditional 'break a leg' message that she'd sent her daughter before every performance since her first stage appearance back in primary school. Just the same, she couldn't help feeling nervous tonight.

She hadn't hesitated, though, when Anna had first rung her, just a few days after her return from Venice, with the thrilling news that she'd got this part.

It was the break her daughter had been waiting for, the chance she'd almost missed. Mind you, Daisy might not have understood the significance of this event for Anna, if she hadn't spent those precious weeks with her family in Venice.

'I'll be there with bells on,' she'd said, and she'd booked her flight to London almost straight away, before she had time for second thoughts, much to the surprised amusement of her friends Freya and Jo when she caught up with them at their favourite café.

'That holiday in Venice has done you the world of good,' Freya told her. 'You're a different woman, Daisy. So happy and confident now.'

'And impulsive,' added Jo. 'But in the best possible way. I think it's wonderful that you're racing back overseas.'

Freya and Jo had also escorted Daisy on a tour of their favourite fashion boutiques to help her choose a suitably elegant outfit for this special occasion. The gorgeous dress of cranberry lace had cost way more than Daisy had ever spent before, but now that she was here in Piccadilly in the specially reserved seating, she was glad she'd splurged.

The rest of the family were just as thrilled about Anna's big break, of course. Bronte and Marc had also jumped in and booked flights, as it was an easy matter for them to pop over from Paris.

Ellie would have loved to join them, but she was working at two waitressing jobs on the Sunshine Coast and saving madly so that she and Zach could travel.

The two youngsters were having a wonderful time researching and making their plans which, much to Daisy's amusement, involved less obvious tourist options like volunteering at an elephant sanctuary in Thailand, or sleeping in hammocks on a beach in the Caribbean. To Daisy's relief, they were also getting plenty of good advice from Zach's dad, who had enjoyed backpacking adventures when he was young and still had plenty of contacts.

Now, as Daisy looked down at the glossy program in her lap, Marc, who was sitting next to her, leaned closer.

'There's a journalist who wants to interview you after the show,' he said.

Daisy turned to him in dismay. 'Interview me?' What on earth could she tell a London journalist?

'I think he might be a reviewer,' Marc said. 'Apparently, he saw the dress rehearsal and he was blown away by Anna's performance. He told me he wants to meet her mother to find out more about her background.'

'Goodness.' Daisy wasn't sure if she was shocked or relieved, but it seemed, perhaps, that Anna and the rest of the cast and crew had been right about the play.

You'll show them, darling.

In the next moment, Daisy was hit by a slug of sadness as she thought of Leo and how bursting with pride he would have been if he'd been able to come here tonight. She still missed him desperately and thought about him all the time, but her aching sense of loss wasn't as quite as suffocating as it once had been.

At least she was now at peace with the decisions Leo had made. She knew that he wouldn't have deliberately left her with a worrying mystery. If he'd been given any kind of warning that he was about to die, he would have made sure she understood about the Vincinis. He'd always been a stickler for order and neatness and leaving no loose ends.

I'm here tonight for both of us, Leo.

She told herself that he heard her, that he was smiling and proud. And not just proud of Anna, but of Marc and Bronte and Ellie as well.

And I'm proud of you, too, Daisy girl . . .

'Here's Gabriele,' said Marc as the young Italian, looking more handsome than ever in a formal evening suit, made his way along their row to the seat they'd reserved for him.

'Good evening,' he said, bending to kiss Daisy's cheeks. 'You look beautiful.'

'Thanks, Gabriele. Anna will be so pleased you could make it.'

'I promised her I would be here. I couldn't possibly miss this night.'

Anna had told Daisy about how helpful Gabriele had been when she was struggling to make the right decision about her career. And while the phone call from her agent might have clinched Anna's decision anyhow, Daisy was glad that her daughter had already realised how much acting still meant to her, even when things were tough.

Gabriele took his seat just as the house lights dimmed. A hush fell over the audience and the huge velvet curtain began to rise. Daisy's stomach tightened and her arms prickled with goosebumps. For a moment she was suddenly so scared, she feared she might be sick. But then, the brightly lit stage was revealed and there was Anna in a blue cotton dress, leaning on a timber post-and-rail fence in a setting that could only be the Australian outback.

Instantly entranced, Daisy settled back in her seat and took a deep and hopefully calming breath . . .

Afterwards . . .

'Sensation' was the word on everybody's lips. The audience had been enthralled as they were swept through a three-act roller-coaster of emotions that took them through hilarity and despair and edge-of-the-seat suspense. There'd been a standing ovation at the end and rousing cheers as the playwright took a bow, along with the director and Anna and her leading man.

In the green room and out in the foyer, champagne corks popped and people chatted excitedly about how marvellous the play was. Cameras flashed.

Gabriele, his arms filled with enormous bouquets of every flower imaginable, had disappeared backstage and emerged sometime later with Anna, changed into a tiny dress of silver spangles, glowing and triumphant.

'Oh, Mum, there you are.' She rushed with arms outstretched. 'Thanks for coming. It meant so much to have you here.' And she hugged Daisy hard.

'You were amazing, Anna. Just —' Daisy searched for a better word. 'Just dazzling. I was so proud.'

They both wept a little, even though they were grinning madly.

Anna hugged Bronte and Marc as well. 'It was awesome that you guys could make it.'

'We wouldn't have missed this for the world,' Marc assured her.

Then Anna slipped her arm through Gabriele's, as if it was essential to have him close at her side.

'I need to catch up on all the family's news,' she told them. 'I've been living in another world for the past six weeks. But —' She was interrupted by a rather pompous, white-haired man in tails, who tapped her on the shoulder. Turning to him, Anna nodded, then swerved back to her family. 'But maybe not for the next hour or so,' she said with an apologetic smile.

'Most definitely not,' agreed Marc. 'Too many other people need to talk to you.'

'It's the price of fame,' added Bronte with a grin and, almost immediately, Anna was engulfed by a swarm of strangers.

It was around midnight when Daisy rang Ellie. 'Just had to let you know that it all went really well.'

'I know,' exclaimed Ellie. 'Zach and I have been keeping an eye on the internet and already there are a couple of rave reviews.'

'Isn't it wonderful? Such a relief.'

'Fantastic,' Ellie agreed. 'No surprise to us, of course.'

'No, we always knew Anna would make it.'

'Now she might believe it, too.'

'Yes.' Daisy couldn't help noticing, as she had several times lately, how grown up Ellie sounded these days.

Still holding the phone to her ear, she crossed to the window of her hotel room, which offered a view down a short street to the Thames, where lights from city buildings shone in golden splashes on the smooth face of the water.

The water reminded her of Venice and she smiled, reassured to know that by bringing her family together, she'd made the right decision. Such a quiet and simple holiday it had been on the surface and yet, despite the unexpected angst, all the Benettos, herself included, had emerged stronger, more certain of their way forward.

'So how are Bronte and Marc?' Ellie asked.

'They're incredibly happy, Ellie. They both love Paris and Bronte's so excited about the art courses she's been doing.'

'That's great. Are they still planning to come back to Australia?'

'Yes, in another month or two.'

'Good. I won't feel so bad about deserting you when I take off, then.'

'You don't need to worry about me, Ellie. I'm fine these days.'

'I know, Mum,' Ellie said gently. 'I'm so happy for you, and I think it's brilliant that you're coming home via New York. Say hello to Tyler and Charles for me, won't you?'

'I will.' Daisy was smiling again.

'Go you, Mum.'

Yes, she thought as she hung up. *Go me*.

ACKNOWLEDGEMENTS

A story comes together from so many different sources. I'm grateful to a writer friend who told me about a widow she knew who dipped into her husband's investments to bring her scattered family together for a gathering in Europe. Immediately my imagination was set spinning. Another friend has a brilliant son in Silicon Valley, so there was another spark. And our own daughters both took up the challenges of artistic careers – one in music and one in dance.

Added to these points of inspiration, my husband and I visited Venice some years back at the end of a nine-week holiday in the UK and Europe and, for me, even though I'd already been enchanted by everything I'd experienced, this uniquely romantic city stole my heart.

Despite the appeal of these simmering ideas, however, I might never have cobbled them into this story without an enthusiastic 'yes!' from my publisher, Ali Watts. Indeed my gratitude extends to Ali and all those at Penguin Random House Australia who have given my books such wonderful support – in particular Amanda Martin, Sofia Casanova, Caitlin Jokovic, Nerrilee Weir, Jordan Meek, Louisa Maggio and Nikki Lusk.

As always my wonderful man, Elliot, read my manuscript in bits and pieces as it emerged from my keyboard and, once again, he provided the reassurance and encouragement all writers crave. Thanks, too, to my son-in-law Carson Dron, who was ready to answer my questions about the tech world. And a big thanks to my entire fabulous family. Your love and laughter and tears sow seeds of inspiration every single day.

BOOK CLUB NOTES

1. For Daisy and her family, coming together in Venice brings unexpected challenges, including Leo's secrets about his past. Why did he hide the truth from Daisy? Do you think this was a mistake?

2. Daisy decides that parents of grown-up offspring walk 'a very fine line between meddling unhelpfully and giving wise, useful advice.' Do you agree? Have you experienced this kind of difficulty in your own life?

3. How do each of Daisy's children change and grow during their time in Venice?

4. Bronte has made sacrifices for her husband's career. Do you think this happens often for women? What about men?

5. If, like Anna, your child showed promising talent as an artist, actor, or musician, would you encourage her to follow her dreams, or would you urge her towards more 'sensible', 'safer' options?

6. Which member of the Benetto family did you relate to most? Who did you relate to the least?

7. Predict the future for Ellie and Zach. Explain why you think this will happen.

8. At the beginning of the novel, Daisy hoped that in time she would be 'one of those very capable widows she admired in books'. Do you think she grew stronger?

9. What thematic similarities did this novel share with Barbara's previous novels?

10. Have you been to Venice, or is it on your bucket list? Did this setting suit the storyline?

The Summer of Secrets

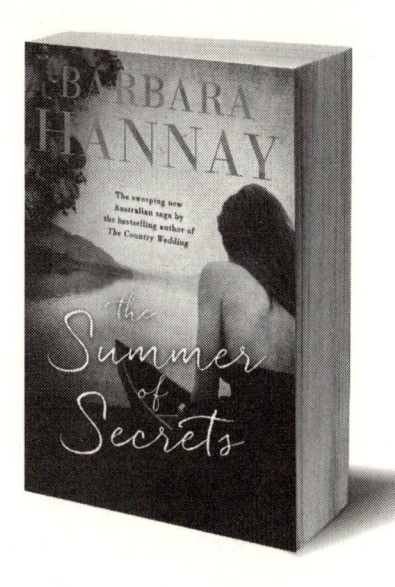

Sydney journalist Chloe Brown is painfully aware that her biological clock isn't just ticking, it's booming. When her long-term boyfriend finally admits he never wants children, Chloe is devastated. Impulsively, she moves as far from disappointment as she can – to a job on a small country newspaper in Queensland's far north.

The little town seems idyllic, a cosy nest, and Chloe plans to regroup and, possibly, to embark on single motherhood via IVF. But she soon realises that no place is free from trouble or heartache. The grouchy news editor, Finn Latimer, is a former foreign correspondent who has retreated after a family tragedy. Emily, the paper's elegant, sixty-something owner, is battling with her husband's desertion. Meanwhile, the whole town is worried when their popular young baker disappears.

As lives across generations become more deeply entwined, the lessons are clear. Secrets and silence harbour pain, while honesty and openness bring healing and hope. And love. All that's needed now is courage . . .

'It's a pleasure to follow an author who gets better with every book.'
Apple iBooks, 'Best Books of the Month'

'In beautiful, fluid prose, Hannay once again puts together all the ingredients for a real page-turner.'
The Chronicle

The Country Wedding

In the tiny Tablelands township of Burralea, Flora Drummond is preparing to play in a string quartet for the wedding of a very close friend. The trouble is, she can't quite forget the silly teenage crush she once had on the handsome groom.

All is as it should be on the big day. The little church is filled with flowers, the expectant guests are arriving, and Mitch is nervously awaiting his bride – but she's had a sudden change of heart.

Decades earlier, another wedding in the same church led to a similar story of betrayal and devastation. Hattie missed out on marrying her childhood sweetheart the first time around, but now she has returned to the scene of her greatest heartache.

As Flora is drawn into both romantic dramas, a dark threat from her own previous relationship looms. But the past and the present offer promise for the future and Flora discovers that they might all help each other to heal.

From the rolling green hills of Far North Queensland to the crowded streets of Shanghai on the eve of the Second World War, this is a beautiful romantic saga that tells of two loves lost and found and asks the questions – do we ever get over our first love, and is it ever too late to make amends?

The Grazier's Wife

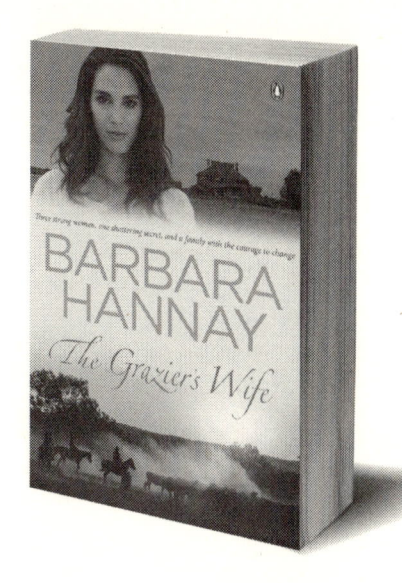

For three generations of Australian women, becoming a grazier's wife has meant very different things.

For Stella in 1946, it was a compromise in the aftermath of a terrible war.

For Jackie in the 1970s, it was a Cinderella fairytale with an outback prince.

While for Alice in 2015, it is the promise of a bright new future.

Decades earlier, Stella was desperate to right a huge injustice, but now a long-held family secret threatens to tear the Drummond family of Ruthven Downs apart. On the eve of a special birthday reunion, with half the district invited, the past and the present collide, passions are unleashed and the shocking truth comes spilling out.

From glamorous pre-war Singapore to a vast cattle property in Queensland's far north, this sweeping, emotional saga tests the beliefs and hopes of these women as they learn how to hold on to loved ones and when to let go.

Discover a new favourite

Visit **penguin.com.au/readmore**